I0632277

Elder Northfield's Home

....

Legacies of Nineteenth-Century American Women Writers

SERIES EDITOR

Theresa Strouth Gaul, *Texas Christian University*

BOARD OF EDITORS

Martha Cutter, *University of Connecticut-Storrs*
Frances Smith Foster, *Emory University*
Susan K. Harris, *University of Kansas*
Mary Kelley, *University of Michigan*
Venetria Patton, *Purdue University*
Karen Sanchez-Eppler, *Amherst College*
Elizabeth Young, *Mt. Holyoke College*

Elder Northfield's Home

....

or, Sacrificed on the Mormon Altar
A Story of the Blighting Curse of Polygamy

A. JENNIE BARTLETT

*Edited and with an introduction
by Nicole Tonkovich*

University of Nebraska Press
Lincoln and London

© 2015 by the Board of Regents
of the University of Nebraska.
All rights reserved. Manufactured
in the United States of America.

Library of Congress Cataloging-
in-Publication Data
Switzer, Jennie Bartlett, author.
Elder Northfield's Home: or,
Sacrificed on the Mormon Altar,
a story of the Blighting Curse of
Polygamy / A. Jennie Bartlett;
edited and with an introduction
by Nicole Tonkovich.
pages   cm.—(Legacies of
Nineteenth-Century American
Women Writers)
Includes bibliographical
references and index.
ISBN 978-0-8032-7184-5 (pbk.: alk. paper)
ISBN 978-0-8032-7406-8 (epub)
ISBN 978-0-8032-7407-5 (mobi)
1. Mormons—Fiction. 2. Marriage—
Fiction. 3. Polygamy—Fiction.
4. Utah—Fiction. I. Tonkovich,
Nicole, editor. II. Title.
PS2964.S838E43 2014
813'.4—dc23
2014038549

Set in Adobe Caslon Pro
by Lindsey Auten.

Contents

Acknowledgments

In preparing this edition of *Elder Northfield's Home*, I am indebted to two wonderful friends and mentors—Sharon M. Harris, whose efforts to recover the work of nineteenth-century women writers has reconfigured the academic discipline in which we work—and Theresa Strouth Gaul, with whom I have had the pleasure of working closely for the past five years, and whose commitment to locating, editing, and teaching work by early women writers has inspired my own.

I am grateful, as well, to the staff and editors of University of Nebraska Press. Despite financial pressures, the Press has retained its commitment to producing high-quality academic books. I am especially indebted to the vision of the editors who supported the Legacies of Nineteenth-Century Women Writers series, of which this book is a final publication. Working with Kristen Elias Rowley and Kyle Simonsen has been a privilege.

Rob Melton, humanities research librarian at University of California, San Diego, gave me invaluable advice and his own insight as I struggled to establish the publication history of this novel. Gary Hoffman helped me locate the little genealogical information available about A. Jennie Bartlett Switzer. I also thank the reference librarians of the Thomas Crane Public Library in Quincy, Massachusetts.

I have twice taught this novel in graduate seminars about marriage, law, and family. Each time, my appreciation of the book's importance increased through discussions with insightful graduate students who have articulated the connections between its nineteenth-century context and present-day federal regulation of family matters. I have also taught the novel in three undergraduate courses and have found students to be almost uniformly enthusiastic about its content. I am especially indebted to comments made by two students, N. M. Rosen and Joe Steinberger, which directed my attention to several points I cover in my introduction.

Under the sponsorship of University of California, San Diego's Faculty Mentor Program, N. M. Rosen and Mika Kennedy consulted with me about words, phrases, and concepts that needed to be footnoted to make the text accessible to a modern reader. Mika Kennedy researched and drafted the footnotes for this edition. I am especially grateful to her for her dependability and insight.

Editor's Introduction

Although the novel you are about to read has not been in print for more than a century, in its day it was well received. A reviewer of *Elder Northfield's Home* called it "a soul-disturbing story . . . with plenty of honest indignation and honest feeling in it and love of honest things."[1] As did nearly a hundred similar novels and nonfictional exposés that condemned polygamy, it responded to a perceived national scandal that began in 1852, when the Church of Jesus Christ of Latter-day Saints (popularly known as Mormons) publicly announced that plural marriage was a part of its doctrine.[2] Such books, according to Sarah Barringer Gordon, fueled what "may well have been the single most successful nineteenth-century political and legal reform campaign," resulting in the church's rejection of polygamy in 1904.[3]

Elder Northfield's Home follows the fate of Marion Wescott, orphaned and newly emigrated from England, who accompanies her Mormon missionary husband, Henry Northfield, to Utah Territory. Both have heard rumors that Mormons practice plural marriage, but believe that should this scandalous gossip be true, they can remain untouched by it. Henry promises Marion he will not take other wives, but becomes convinced that it is his religious duty to do so, and marries two more times. Later chapters follow the lives of Marion's two children. Her son Forest outdoes his father in his devotion to duty. As a young man, he leaves Salt Lake City to serve as a missionary in New England, where he hopes to convert many souls to Mormonism.

However, after "observ[ing] the domestic relation of Gentile life," he renounces his Mormon beliefs (291).[4] Her daughter Mayon escapes to New York, where she lives with Marion's aunt, attends school, falls in love, and marries an upright and devoted man. The Northfield siblings ultimately convince their entire family to renounce polygamy, reject Mormonism, return to the Northeast, and assume a conventional family life.

While *Elder Northfield's Home* argues that polygamy is a barbaric practice against which federal legal measures must be taken, this novel differs from many antipolygamy works of its time. First, although it relies to some extent on sensationally melodramatic devices, it is largely factually accurate. Thus, we might assume its readers gave it more credence. Second, the book demonstrates that whether federal legislation succeeds or fails, well-educated women—both inside and outside of polygamy—can successfully repudiate the doctrine and the church. Finally, it urges concerned non-Mormons to prepare to repatriate polygamy's victims upon their escape.

Elder Northfield's Home borrows heavily from other reform fictions, including the century's most efficacious protest novel, Harriet Beecher Stowe's *Uncle Tom's Cabin*.[5] In a scene echoing Eliza's escape from the Shelby plantation, Marion Northfield, shocked that her husband has taken a second wife, flees her home at midnight, toddler son in her arms, pulling her worldly goods in his toy wagon. Unlike Eliza, Marion does not escape. Bound by her marriage vows, she returns to her husband, but remains opposed to plural marriage. Henry Northfield, like Augustine St. Claire, is a tortured soul. He knowingly causes pain and suffering by supporting a corrupt system, but is too deeply attached to its benefits to resist it. Northfield is not the most deplorable of polygamists. He takes only two additional wives, takes them seriatim, and does so not to sate his sexual desires, but because he sincerely believes it is his duty.[6]

Because these fictional victims of Mormon polygamy lack control over their lives, most of the characters of *Elder Northfield's Home* do not grow and develop in complexity and insight. Long-suffering plural wives, subject to the vagaries of fate and the whims of men, are "sacrificed on the Mormon altar." Emphasizing this condition, the novel's plot is punctuated by disconnected events such as a train wreck, a boating accident, lost or stolen letters, and an abduction. The novel's characters function within a melodramatic universe: polygamous husbands and Brigham Young, who fuels their mania, are duty-driven demagogues; their wives are innocent victims; their sons become tyrants like their fathers; and their daughters can expect only to become wives and breeders. The intrusive narrator, who signals plot developments such as "[S]he was to be disappointed," or "[l]ittle thinking that this was to be their final parting," exercises a control that rivals that of Brigham Young over his minions (21, 30).

Yet originality of plot and psychological subtlety do not reliably correlate with a text's popularity, sociopolitical relevance, or what scholars term its "cultural work."[7] Readers familiar with other best-selling reform publications, such as T. S. Arthur's temperance novel *Ten Nights in a Bar-Room*, or newspapers such as the *Advocate of Moral Reform and Female Guardian* or the *Anti-Polygamy Standard*, likely found this antipolygamy novel to be interesting, inspiring, and compelling. Such readers shared similar values, read similar books, held similar Protestant religious beliefs, and lived in similarly structured heteronormative and monogamous families. These shared values are the basis upon which *Elder Northfield's Home* calls its readers to action.

Values of home and geographic stability, monogamous devotion, and familial affection emblematize the very few details that are available about the life of Abigail Jane Bartlett Switzer.[8] She was born on 27 April 1855 in the same Connecticut town in which her immediate family members were born, lived, and died.[9] She was the first child of Samuel Wells Bartlett and Electa Almira Seymour and had one younger brother, Merwin Alexander, to whom she inscribed a copy of *Elder Northfield's Home* in 1882.[10] At age twenty-four she married Elmer Franklin Switzer of Monson, Massachusetts. The couple remained childless and lived in Massachusetts for the next half century. Jennie Bartlett Switzer died on 28 April 1930.

The Church of Jesus Christ of Latter-day Saints as an Intentional Community

Mormonism emerged from the normalcy of everyday life in nineteenth-century New England, but its doctrines exaggerate those norms in startling—even sensational—ways. Joseph Smith, the church's founder, was the third son of an impoverished farmer. His large family, like thousands of other northeasterners, was swept up in a fervor of Protestant religious revivalism now known as the Second Great Awakening. In 1820, at age fourteen, Smith recounts, he received a heavenly vision telling him to join none of the current denominations; he thereafter founded a new church. In 1830 he published a new scripture, The Book of Mormon, which he claimed to have translated from golden plates buried by aboriginal inhabitants of North America. Similarly grandiose claims had been advanced by his contemporaries: William Miller, for example, predicted that the Second Coming of Jesus Christ would occur in 1843. "Mother" Ann Lee, founder of the Shakers, claimed to have seen a vision of Adam and Eve's transgressive carnal relations.

Members of Smith's new religion formed an intentional community, one of "nearly seventy" such groups founded in the mid-nineteenth century, most of which, according to Nancy

F. Cott, "sprang from a critique of the conventional arrangement of work and marriage."[11] The Shakers advocated celibacy. John Humphrey Noyes's Oneida Perfectionists practiced what he called "complex marriage": with Noyes's approval, any member of the community could enjoy a sexual relationship with any other. The self-styled "Prophet Matthias" regulated intimate relations within the Kingdom of Matthias, a community in which Sojourner Truth briefly resided. The Mormons, the longest lasting and most visibly successful of these groups, embraced polygamy.

Applying religious precepts fervently to one's life, often despite painful sacrifice, was not unusual in the nineteenth century. Religion led Mormon converts to emigrate to unpromising and dangerous frontier locations far from their natal families and to embrace unconventional family structures. In the mid-1830s Mormon missionaries attracted converts in the English industrial centers of Liverpool and Birmingham. These new believers, like other immigrants of the period, fled economic recession and sought new opportunities in the United States. Joining converts from the Northeast, they moved westward with Smith and his followers, who hoped to find a place in which to build a "theodemocratic" latter-day Zion.[12] Here the churchly citizens could be governed by God's laws delivered directly to the ear of his prophet. Thus the allegiances of early church members tied them not to the United States government, but to the church, whose leaders ordered not only worship but also economic structure and sexual and family arrangements.

Like other intentional communities, Mormons pursued economic reform based on commonly held property and equal distribution of resources. Their clannish behavior and their propensity to vote in a bloc provoked their neighbors, and thus the group relocated relatively quickly from New York, where

Smith had received his revelation, to Kirtland, Ohio, in 1831, and thence to Independence, Missouri, in 1838. Here, because most church members were non-slaveholders, their presence provoked proslavery Missourians to guerilla violence. Again they removed, first to Quincy, Illinois, and then to a swampy locale on the banks of the Mississippi River where they built a city they called Nauvoo. For this new settlement, according to Lawrence Foster, they "secured a city charter that, if freely interpreted, made Nauvoo virtually independent of the state."[13] Within a city they had planned and built, the group's insularity increased and Joseph Smith became mayor; head of a private militia; "king of Israel," as his followers denominated him; and, in 1844, candidate for the presidency of the United States.[14]

At a very early point in this period of growth, mobility, and social experimentation (likely in 1831), Joseph Smith began secretly to take additional wives, guided, as he claimed, by a revelation from God that stipulated "if any man espouse a virgin, and desire to espouse another, and the first give her consent, . . . then is he justified."[15] Gradually he introduced the idea to his closest associates. Some embraced the concept; others, appalled, left the church. Although about 150 plural marriages were performed in Nauvoo, the majority of church members heard no official acknowledgment of the practice, although they, like the fictional Marion Northfield, surely were aware of gossip about Smith's sexual experiments.[16] Smith finally made the matter more or less public in 1843. By then he had taken thirty-two additional wives.[17] Rumors of his multiple wives coupled with speculation that he planned to build a "Mormon empire," repeated and exaggerated by disaffected Mormons, infuriated neighboring settlers.[18] Smith was arrested on charges of treason, and, in June of 1844, imprisoned and awaiting trial, he was assassinated.

The church split over the question of succession, but the

majority of members endorsed Brigham Young as their next leader. Meanwhile, the settlers at Nauvoo had become subject to sporadic episodes of vigilantism. They abandoned the city and emigrated once more, this time to the valley of the Great Salt Lake. Even in exile Mormons were more mainstream than unique, joining thousands of other emigrants streaming west, most of whom hoped to claim land in Oregon Territory. While those bound for Oregon maintained their ties to the nation, Mormons fled national and state jurisdictions. Rejecting outside interference in their economy and their marriage practices, they intended to establish their theocracy outside the reach of federal and state law.[19] Thus it might be said that the history of the polygamy era is the history of delineating the relation of church to state.

In 1847 when the first groups of Mormon emigrants arrived in the valley of the Great Salt Lake they settled in territory belonging to Mexico. In this relatively isolated location, Brigham Young intended to build a nation-state he called Deseret. Almost immediately he began to colonize large portions of the Southwest. He also began to re-establish the practices of communal economy and plural marriage. In 1848, under the terms of the Treaty of Guadalupe Hidalgo, the lands comprising Deseret were among those ceded to the United States by Mexico and the Saints became once again subject to federal policies, which included the power to regulate marriages in the territories. Young promptly petitioned for statehood for Deseret. As he told an interviewer some years later, "all the states have laws on [marriage], and [Deseret], when a State, will have an equal right to make laws protecting polygamy."[20] Congress rejected the plan, and, as a part of the Compromise of 1850, greatly diminished the boundaries of Young's empire, created the Territory of Utah, and named Young as territorial governor. With territorial status came federal oversight: non-Mormon judges were appointed and sworn to uphold federal, not theological law. Commonly held lands were measured, mapped, and assigned to individual owners. Unsurprisingly, polygamy came under close scrutiny.

Despite federal involvement, local governance continued to overlap with theological administration. Within the new territory Mormon leaders encouraged practices that emphasized insularity. They advocated a communal economy, known as the United Order, but met with mixed success. The church printed currency and chartered a bank; it controlled education, and established the University of Deseret (now the University of Utah), whose faculty designed and promoted the Deseret alphabet, an alternative phonetically based system of orthography and spelling. In 1868, Young wrote that he planned to have the Book of Mormon printed in the Deseret alphabet "to take the place of readers generally used in our schools."[21] Church interests dominated the flow of information within the territory since church members owned the newspapers. Most notably, plural marriage became an official church doctrine.

In 1852, the year in which Stowe published *Uncle Tom's Cabin* in book form, Brigham Young assigned a close confidante, Orson Pratt, to deliver a public address in which he declared, "the Latter-day Saints have embraced the doctrine of a plurality of wives, as part of their religious faith."[22] As *Elder Northfield's Home* makes clear, polygamy was a patriarchal practice that strengthened the religious and political authority of the men who embraced it. Men of means who held important church offices were the most frequent practitioners. Brigham Young, for example, married fifty-five wives; his friend and counselor Heber C. Kimball espoused forty-three.[23] Most polygamous men, however, resembled the fictional Henry Northfield and took many fewer wives—between two and five. The church closely regulated plural marriages and at times counseled or commanded men to take additional wives, as is the case in this novel.

Almost all the women in Utah married in their early twenties; just over 35 percent of them entered polygamy.[24] The fictional Marion Wescott typifies many women who "married within a year" of emigrating, about half of whom joined polygamous families.[25] Bowman observes, "Women without a father in Utah were far more likely than other single women to enter plural marriage.[26] The details of Henry Northfield's plural marriages are also typical. Subsequent wives were often friends of the family or "sisters-in-law, cousins, or nieces of earlier wives. . . . Some of these marriages were never consummated, nor would the new husband and wife live as such."[27] A polygamous family might share a single home, occupy separate houses in the same town or city, or even live in different towns or states.

In portraying Mormondom as a closed society from which exit was nearly impossible and whose members, should they escape, would need extensive repatriation, *Elder Northfield's Home* largely ignores the extent to which, regardless of Young's efforts at separatism, the Saints did not—and could not—remain isolated from the surrounding nation. Once gold was discovered in California in 1849, floods of emigrants passed through Salt Lake City. Some remained; others returned after failing in the gold fields.[28] Transcontinental telegraph lines joined the nation in Salt Lake City in 1861. The east- and west-bound sections of the railroad met in northern Utah in 1869, bringing both immigrant Saints and Gentile merchants, miners, and farmers to the area. Significantly, the railroad also enabled disaffected Mormons to take "flight *from* the Territory," as does Mayon Northfield, whose escape to her maternal aunt reverses Huckleberry Finn's fantasy of escape from his aunt Sally's plans to adopt him (2, emphasis added).

Polygamy and Nineteenth-Century Social Reform

In 1869, as territorial Utah became less geographically isolated and its population diversified, a coalition of non-Mormons and disaffected Saints who opposed plural marriage and the church's political dominance established the Liberal Party, presenting what Peggy Pascoe characterizes as "the first serious challenge to Mormon civic leadership."[29] While ongoing federal efforts to curb polygamy proved ineffectual, organized opposition strengthened in Utah. In 1880, antipolygamy activists founded the Ladies' Anti-Polygamy Society of Salt Lake City; it quickly achieved national status. The group organized demonstrations of protest in major American cities. As Nancy Bentley observes, "[O]ne rally in Chicago drew 12,000 participants. According to one estimation, at the height of the opposition over 10,000 antipolygamy meetings were held within a six-month period."[30] The Society published a monthly newspaper, the *Anti-Polygamy Standard*, edited by Jennie Anderson Froiseth, wife of a non-Mormon federal employee.[31] The most visible, if unsuccessful, symbol of local opposition to plural marriage was the Industrial Christian Home, built with federal funds solicited by antipolygamy women who had "argued that the home would serve as a refuge for 'escaped' plural wives, who could then be trained as domestic servants. The home, which never attracted more than a few dozen residents, was closed in the early 1890s, and the building was eventually torn down."[32]

Orson Pratt's 1852 proclamation solidified local and national opposition to polygamy, as church leaders had anticipated, for the speech had emphasized that plural marriage, now "actually embraced" by church members "as part and portion of their religion . . . is constitutional."[33] The announcement drew the church into an intensifying adversarial relationship with the rest of the nation over issues of slavery, state's rights, race, and women's rights. Incendiary terms—barbarism, tyranny, despotism, and democratic consent—were common to these debates, signaling their interwoven nature.

Antipolygamy discourse became part and parcel of mid-nineteenth-century debates over the degree to which the federal government could or should intervene in regulating "domestic institutions," be they marriage in Utah Territory or slavery in the South. As Cott puts it, "When Mormon polygamy was discussed, slavery was never far from politicians' minds, and the reverse was also true."[34] To some, the authority of polygamous patriarchs over their wives mirrored the paternal rights of slaveholders over the human chattel they owned and provided for. Northern partisans rejected Young's apparent intent to make Utah into "an intolerable *'imperium in imperio,'''* that would pit "Federal Authority against Polygamic Theocracy."[35] Such a possibility led the Republican Party in 1880 to advocate that Congress "suppress the system of polygamy within our territory and divorce the political from the ecclesiastical power of the so-called Mormon church. . . . [T]he law so enacted should be rigidly enforced by the civil authorities, if possible, and by the military if need be."[36] Although *Elder Northfield's Home* does not overtly address these issues, they are nevertheless apparent in small details. For example, Forest, warning his sister Mayon that she must resign herself to be a plural wife, pontificates, "I do wish . . . that you and mother could agree with the rest of us on these points. 'A house divided against itself cannot stand,' you know" (180). His reference is not, of course, to the Union, but to the theodemocratic polity of Mormon Utah, for the children of plural marriages were citizens whose first loyalty was to a church that claimed doctrinal as well as civil jurisdiction over its members.

Debates over states' rights involved overt racialist logic, link-ing Mormons to enslaved African Americans and other racialized groups, especially those associated with orientalist stereotypes. Based on information they had gleaned from scientific anthropology, popular travel narratives, and missionary discourse, legal theorists of the day declared monogamy to be "one of the pre-existing conditions of our existence as civilized white men," a logic that linked polygamy to "savage and slavish places" and nonwhite peoples.[37] So intertwined were the issues of slavery, race, and polygamy in the public mind that the 1856 Republican platform had declared it to be "both the right and the imperative duty of Congress to prohibit in the Territories those twin relics of barbarism, polygamy and slavery."[38] Bartlett echoes this logic in the preface to her novel, asking, "Is not this slavery of the West a much more despicable one than that of the South, in that it is a slavery of defenceless women? . . . Where in all the enlightened countries of the globe, can be found so foul a stain, as that which *blackens* the otherwise fair fame of our nation?" (4, emphasis added). These ideas took vicious and exaggerated visual form, as Bentley notes. She describes a "political cartoon" that shows "a bearded white elder in bed" with several women of color, drawn in grotesque caricature. "Another shows an Elder standing hand in hand with a multi-racial chorus line" of Chinese, African, Native American children.[39] In an era when Protestant missionaries had crossed the globe and reported their experiences to those at home, Christian monogamists could not be unaware that polygamy was the world's dominant pattern of marriage. Even Orson Pratt had used the argument, claiming, "I think there is only about one-fifth of the population of the globe, that believe in the one-wife system; the other four-fifths believe in the doctrine of a plurality of wives. They have had it handed down from time immemorial, and are not half so narrow and contracted in their minds as some of the nations of Europe and

America, who have . . . deprived themselves of the blessings of Abraham, Isaac, and Jacob."[40]

Others, however, may have seen Pratt's statistics as evidence of the widespread tyranny of polygamy as opposed to Christian monogamy and consent-based democracy. As Frances E. Willard wrote in her introduction to Froiseth's *Women of Mormonism*, "[I]t is written in God's Book of Fate, which man calls 'Natural Law,' that the mother's relation to the Home, Society, and the State, shall determine their degree of elevation or ignominy. Modern Mohammedanism has its Mecca at Salt Lake. . . . When we consider that the country which permits this abomination of desolation to continue, is the 'bright consummate flower' of Christian civilization; when we remember what o'clock it is in the Nineteenth Century . . . we are tempted to change Sojourner Truth's famous words, 'Is God dead?' from a question into a heart-sick affirmation."[41] In this passage Willard signals the importance of heteronormative monogamy to American democratic ideals deriving from the English common law concepts of consent and coverture. Under the reciprocal relations of coverture a married man "[represents] himself and his dependents in the civic world." Heading a family gives a man his civic identity; his wife consents to cede her rights and possessions to him, and she and the couple's children exchange their "obedience and service" for his financial support and his political advocacy of their interests.[42] Such a system regulates the inheritance of property by stabilizing sexual relations, (re)produces citizens for the state, and undergirds democratic ideals. Consent in marriage figuratively echoes the basic principles of representative democracy. As Judith Sargent Murray wrote in 1790, the "family is a well regulated Commonwealth," embodying in small the governing principles of the state.[43]

Elder Northfield's Home shocked its readers with a funhouse-mirror exaggeration of family stability and mutual devotion in

Utah Territory, where polygamous families were headed by a father who embodied the civic and theocratic identity of the family. This patriarch presided over not just one wife and her children, but several spouses and their children. His wives had knowingly and apparently willingly consented to the perverse arrangement. The family may have included so many offspring that a father could not recognize his own children on the street, much less advocate for their interests, meet their daily needs, or ensure their rightful inheritances.

When the structure of the putatively normal monogamous family is altered, other perversions inevitably follow. By making the story of plural marriage a multigenerational tale, Bartlett invokes the possibility of incest, as did the sensation fictions of the period. Mayon, having escaped Salt Lake City, falls in love with Will Saxon, whose name signals his racial worthiness. Saxon fortuitously learns, however, that he is Mayon's half-brother, the son of Henry Northfield's secret first marriage to an Englishwoman who is now dead. He dissolves the engagement with the words, "My darling Mayon is my sister, if never my wife" (287). Then, just ten pages later, Saxon marries his father's now-divorced third wife. "Think," he muses, "of the strangeness of the fact that I am to marry my father's wife!" (299). Thus, polygamy may taint even the relationships of those who have never practiced it.

If monogamy guaranteed stability, polygamy epitomized disruption. Every additional wife changed the family's internal dynamics. Moreover, Utah's territorial legislature had enacted the nation's most liberal divorce law. As Bowman observes, "Brigham Young . . . staunchly defended the right of plural wives to seek divorce for lack of affection, desertion, or economic neglect."[44] This embrace of divorce elicited contradictory responses among women's rights activists. Some feared that the ease of obtaining a divorce in Utah undermined the stability of monogamous marriages nationwide. Others cautiously applauded the intent of such laws, but balked at the fact that women who divorced retained no right to custody of their children. As Susan B. Anthony had put it in her 1848 "Declaration of Sentiments," "[Man] has so framed the laws of divorce, . . . in case of separation, to whom the guardianship of the children shall be given; as to be wholly regardless of the happiness of women—the law, in all cases, going upon a false supposition of the supremacy of man, and giving all power into his hands." In Utah, as in the Gentile world, the children of a divorced wife remained the property of her husband. In *Elder Northfield's Home*, although Marion Northfield's husband has broken his promise to take no other wives, she does not seek a divorce. Rather, the couple compromise, "agree[ing] that the teachings of one [spouse] must not contradict the statements of the other. . . . [T]o Marion should be given the religious training of their daughter, while the son should be instructed by his father" (149). Thus Bartlett inscribes a conservative path for Marion, one that affirms her identity as a virtuous woman who understands the deep importance of her marital vows. As well, this outcome affirms the principle of mutual consent under which the couple had originally married, for it honors each partner's interests.

When Northfield embraces polygamy, however, he perverts the consensual partnership of benevolent patriarch and supportive wife. A first wife presumably consents to each subsequent marriage and signals that consent by attending the wedding(s) of subsequent spouse(s) to her husband, placing the hand of each new wife in that of her husband. Yet although permission of prior wives was recommended as a public demonstration of faith in the principle of plural marriage, it was not required. The objections of a wife who withheld her consent meant little if a church authority had counseled a man to take an additional wife. Thus, although Marion argues and objects, Northfield eventually embraces polygamy. His additional wives, who knowingly and willingly consent to a nonexclusive sexual relationship, are vastly inferior to Marion. Helen Crosby is selfish and unsympathetic. Edith Parker, an orphan and a family friend, is young enough to be his daughter. Within their platonic marriage Edith assumes "her place as assistant to her friend and sister-wife in the domestic cares, and in the care of the children" and "wish[es] to live more as a helper in the family and companion to Marion, than as a wife" (170).

Antipolygamy novels sought to "make a woman's consent to polygamy almost literally unthinkable," according to Bentley, by including wedding scenes in which "first wives regularly faint after speaking their consent, the first sign of an illness that usually kills or drives them mad after this injury to their womanhood."[45] In *Elder Northfield's Home*, however, Marion does not faint after giving Helen to Henry. Nevertheless "[s]he could not remain in [her] house after it had been polluted by the entrance of her husband's new wife" (124). She flees with her young son, intending to "go into the Gentile world," but is convinced to return by a friend who warns her, "In your condition you will perish before you can complete such a journey" (124, 127). Her "condition" is a second pregnancy, a detail that compounds the horror she has recently undergone, for Helen and Marion both soon give birth to daughters. Aware of the damage he has caused, Northfield does not take more wives, trusting that his having two families will fulfill his duty to the church. Helen dies, however, and Northfield again disregards Marion's objections and takes another wife, Edith. This time, after "[giving] him another wife, seal[ing] unto herself a new doom of misery, . . . she became faint, and fell to the floor" (159). In presenting such scenes, Bentley posits, "antipolygamy novels pronounced a kind of paralegal judgment that women never did and never could freely consent to plural marriage."[46]

Yet many Mormon women, in fact, publicly and vociferously supported polygamy. In 1870, for example, women in Salt Lake City staged public demonstrations protesting a federal bill that would give them the vote on the presumption they would then "vote polygamy out of existence."[47] The *Woman's Exponent*, a paper founded by Mormon women in 1872, "often carried editorials defending the practice."[48] Women who supported plural marriage mentioned the pleasure they found in the company of other wives, with whom they devised ingenious systems of cooperative housekeeping and childcare. Ellis Reynolds Shipp, for example, earned a medical degree and became a practicing obstetrician, leaving her children to be cared for by sister wives while she pursued her education.

Belinda Marden Pratt, who had become a plural wife to church official Parley P. Pratt in Nauvoo in 1844, defended polygamy in a letter to her sister who remained in New Hampshire (a situation that parallels that of the fictional Marion and Elsie Wescott).[49] Because her letter exemplifies the logic frequently used to defend plural marriage, I quote from it at length. She wrote:

[A] nation organized under the law . . . of Abraham, and the patriarchs, would have no institutions tending to licentiousness; no adulteries, fornications, etc. . . . . No houses, or institutions would exist for traffic in shame, or in the life blood of our fair daughters. Wealthy men would have no inducement to keep a mistress in secret, or unlawfully. Females would have no grounds for temptation in any such lawless life.

Neither money nor pleasure could tempt them, nor poverty drive them to any such excess; because the door would be open for every virtuous female to form the honorable and endearing relationships of wife and mother, in some virtuous family, where love, and peace, and plenty, would crown her days.[50]

Pratt's argument that polygamy offered the support of a husband to women who might have no other offer of marriage was a common one, although no convincing statistics support such a claim. She raises concerns that would have been shared by those who had established the Industrial Christian Home in Salt Lake City.[51] Later in the letter, Pratt claims that because a couple must abstain from intercourse during pregnancy to ensure the health of the unborn child, the husband who has other wives can legally satisfy his sexual urges, concluding "Polygamy then, as practiced under the Patriarchal law of God, leads directly to the chastity of women, and to sound health and morals in the constitutions of their offspring."[52] Harriet Beecher Stowe, who controlled the number of children she bore by strategically absenting herself from her husband—frequenting water cures, visiting relatives—might have seen in Pratt's letter an intriguing point of shared concern.

Testimonials like Pratt's sought to counter "[a]lmost 100 novels, . . . many hundreds of magazine and newspaper stories," and a large number of public lectures produced by antipolygamists.[53] Disaffected plural wives whose stories were collected by Froiseth in *The Women of Mormonism* decried the jealousy, infighting, favoritism, and inequities of support that were common to polygamous arrangements. Other plural wives publicly supported the doctrine but privately decried and resisted it. Often they were married to men who "were expected to serve honorably in the church, to be community leaders, and . . . to support their large families economically."[54] Although they derived status from their husbands' positions, such women might be abandoned emotionally and economically if their husbands became unable or unwilling to meet the demands of wives, children, work, and ecclesiastical obligation. These women suffered the consequences of their devotion while remaining faithful to their beliefs. For example, Annie Clark Tanner, daughter of an early polygamist who had known Joseph Smith and who became the second wife of a prominent Mormon leader, wrote *A Mormon Mother*, an honest, balanced, and complex account of the challenges of living in polygamy and maintaining the faith after being abandoned by a husband who held important public and church positions. Tanner's memoir, written in 1941, traces her life beginning with her marriage to Joseph Marion Tanner in 1883, after the Edmunds-Tucker Act had outlawed polygamy. During the next twenty years, he took several more wives and gradually withdrew his attention from Annie and her six children. In 1912 he informed her "that he intended to contribute no more" to their support.[55] The concluding chapters of the book chronicle her success in raising her family and making a new life for herself.

Thinking beyond the ending

Although *A Mormon Mother* was composed and published in the twentieth century and did not join the chorus of fictional and nonfictional discussions of plural marriage, it does forcibly illustrate a problem overlooked by many reformers who had not thought beyond the ending of polygamy.[56] Although federal legislation eventually prohibited plural marriage in the mainstream Mormon church, it left ambiguous the status of those already living the principle. Should a polygamous man divorce or disown all but one of his wives, who would support them? What would then be the legal status of their children? *Elder Northfield's Home* suggests an answer to those issues. Like *Uncle Tom's Cabin*, the novel concludes by considering the aftereffects of the reform it advocates. Stowe, who anticipated the challenge of educating, employing, enfranchising, and integrating hundreds of thousands of freed people into the social fabric, advocated "receiv[ing] them to the educating advantages of Christian republican society and schools, until they have attained to somewhat of a moral and intellectual maturity" and then promptly repatriating them to Liberia.[57] Stowe's Liberia solution is not organically related to the plot of her novel, but is part of a chapter titled "Concluding Remarks." In *Elder Northfield's Home*, however, the transition of polygamous family members back into monogamy and a normal home life is integral to the novel. Beginning with Mayon Northfield's first escape from Salt Lake City in chapter 12, the novel explores how those who had been caught in polygamy's web might be welcomed back into the national family.

Bartlett makes a three-part argument about how polygamy might be expunged. First, as her preface makes clear, the federal government must make the practice illegal. She asks, "Will our government weakly allow its laws to be trampled under foot and ignore the defiance of a body of men, fast increasing in numbers and influence? Let it attack this great evil with the energy which characterized the putting down of the rebellion and the blotting out of slavery, or even with the same relentless persistence with which the poor Indian is driven from place to place on his native soil, and polygamy will be a thing of the past" (4). Second, recognizing that federal legal sanctions had thus far been unsuccessful, Bartlett demonstrates that strong women can contribute to the practical erasure of polygamy. Women who are logical thinkers and confident debaters can resist the blandishments of seductive missionaries. Without consenting women, polygamy cannot succeed. Self-reliant educated women who can "make [their] own way in the world" need not rely on the economic protection of a husband (175). Marion is such a woman, confident in the rectitude of her beliefs. Although she remains with Henry Northfield because she is committed to her marriage vows, she is not cowed by Brigham Young's threats. Rather, she saves her household money and sells her jewelry to purchase the railroad ticket that will carry her daughter to freedom; she teachers Mayon to read and write and appreciate outside culture so she will easily adapt to life in the Northeast. Her plan is, of course, an act of treason against her husband, but it is a just treason, for Henry has betrayed her consent by taking additional wives. Marion tells him, "I was obliged to do it. . . . I have in a certain sense acted the part of a traitor to you, but better that than a lifetime of misery for Mayon" (208). Mayon, in turn, becomes the means by which her brother Forest—and eventually her entire family—escapes Utah. Third, *Elder Northfield's Home* anticipates how those who have been confined in insular Salt Lake City might be repatriated. If polygamous and repressive marriages are dissolved, wives and children freed from their thrall will lack economic support. If these women have no education, no marketable skills, and are not adept at normal interpersonal relations, how will they provide for themselves and their children? this book implicitly asks. Moreover, and notably, the novel foresees that men, freed from the oppression of Young's theocratic dominance, will recognize their dependents' rights to consent and represent their concerns in the political world. They will need to learn to be productive members of society, earning their wealth and civic status not as the reward of blind obedience to religious authority, but by honest work.

Bartlett's emphasis on repatriation explains one of the oddities of *Elder Northfield's Home*. In early parts of the novel she follows the usual Mormon practice of using the word "Gentile" to refer to non-Mormons. For example, one of the Mrs. Smiths explains to Marion, "We should remember that [amicable relations among plural wives] is something the Gentiles are quite unused to" (48). Bartlett later modifies her use of the word, signaling her vision of a pan-sectarian coalition of New England Protestants. Consequently, Marion expresses a hope that her husband will "be converted back to the Gentile belief" (163) and her daughter Mayon, newly escaped to the East, finds "attendance at church [to be] always a great delight. Never had she heard the preaching of the Gentile religion, and . . . she drank in every word that fell from the minister's lips" (219). Bartlett carefully avoids naming any specific Gentile denomination, for if repatriation is to succeed, the various Protestant churches must look beyond their factional and doctrinal divisions and unite to care for the freed victims of a practice they have agreed to deplore.

In its emphasis on what would happen after polygamy's defeat, *Elder Northfield's Home* differs from a number of other antipolygamy fictions with which it was contemporary.[58] Still other differences mark its dominant stance of modest, earnest, and rational appeal. As Gordon observes, in many antipolygamy novels, women who are "[f]aced with polygamy . . . met with one of two fates: the virtuous suffered, even died, the weak descended into viciousness and vulgarity."[59] The virtuous Marion and Mayon Northfield and the weak Edith Parker do not meet these fates. Rather, each woman exercises resolve and courage at key junctures. In the most successful of the bestselling antipolygamy thrillers, sentimental appeals alternate with sensational episodes of abduction, rape, sexual torture, and graphic physical abuse. While *Elder Northfield's Home* contains its share of sentimental, implausible passages and even dabbles halfheartedly with an abduction plot, overall it is surely less given to sexual sensationalism.

Even purportedly factual memoirs and documentary accounts of life in polygamy relied on lurid details and profited from the scandalized response they elicited while also touting their respectability. For example, in 1872 Fanny Stenhouse published *Exposé of Polygamy: A Lady's Life Among the Mormons*, a memoir based on the contents of the public lectures she had given the preceding year. Two years later, she produced an expanded and revised version of the book, *"Tell It All": The Story of a Life's Experience in Mormonism*, adding to it a preface written by Harriet Beecher Stowe, who emphasized, "It is no sensational story, but a plain, unvarnished tale of truth, stranger and sadder than fiction."[60] Stenhouse's book saw multiple reprintings in the nineteenth century.[61] Similarly, in *The Women of Mormonism* Jennie Anderson Froiseth repurposed the stories she had first published in the *Anti-Polygamy Standard*. Frances E. Willard, then head of the Women's Christian Temperance Union, wrote an introduction to the collection, declaring, "I have read its pages with thoughts too deep for tears. Some sulphur-shrouded planet may have a vocabulary fiendish enough to fitly characterize what they reveal, but mere English is only the vocabulary of a prating parrot in presence of such pathos and such woe."[62] These endorsements by women with stellar public reputations added a tincture of respectability to books that, although putatively factual, contained salacious details that threatened to stain the reputation of the author who dared to write of such things.

In 1875, Ann Eliza Young published her memoir, *Wife No. 19: The Story of a Life in Bondage*. Young, who had first been married to and then divorced a Mormon man, had knowingly consented to marry the already much-wedded Brigham Young.[63] She then divorced him, wrote her memoir, and, like Stenhouse and others, gave public lectures denouncing polygamy's abuses and promoting her book. By all accounts a charismatic and compelling public speaker, Young spoke in dozens of major cities over the next ten years.[64] In the 1870s, for a woman to appear in public, speaking to "promiscuous" audiences (that is, both men and women) about a topic that necessarily implied sex—and nonnormative sex, at that—was still considered to be scandalous. As a twice-divorced woman and a former actress, Young herself fell short of respectability. Thus she took care to appear in the company of upstanding public figures—Protestant ministers, for example—who "[lent] their moral support to the lady" and "spoke a few words in regard to the good work Mrs. Young was doing."[65] As had Froiseth and Stenhouse, Young capitalized on her notoriety and published a follow-up book, *Life in Mormon Bondage* (1908), updating the content of *Wife No. 19* and answering questions that book and her lecture had raised.

Unlike these women who were her near contemporaries, A. Jennie Bartlett Switzer apparently avoided notoriety, writing a novel that, as a reviewer noted, "differ[ed] from several works of fiction in the same field by avoiding the extreme of sensationalism." The review continues, "Certainly no other novel has explained so rationally the methods of the Mormon apostles in securing the intelligent members of their flock. . . . 'Elder Northfield's Home' is by no means a clever performance. On the other hand, it does not belong to the catch-penny, morbid class of books. Its lack of literary art makes it more impressive; a girlish book by a girl, but no bad tract to put in the hands of the kind of person who finds the Mormon apostle attractive."[66] Anonymity seems to be part of Bartlett's rhetorical strategy. She did not protest polygamy as a celebrity advocate, nor appear under the endorsement of a well-known reformer. She did not identify herself as a former victim of polygamy, although many of the details of her book mark her intimate familiarity with Mormon church doctrines and vocabulary. She assumes an authorial stance as an everyday woman, devoted to her husband and her Gentile faith, whose intense concern for other everyday women—like her, but who are subject to such abuse—has driven her to write this fiction. From this position of relative anonymity, Bartlett published *Elder Northfield's Home* in three different editions, each coinciding with a public legal milestone marking polygamy's abolition.

Polygamy's demise

First published in 1882, *Elder Northfield's Home* begins in the mid-1850s, thus emphasizing the failure of early federal attempts to ban polygamy. Ten years after the church publicly endorsed polygamy, the Morrill Anti-Bigamy Act invalidated all Utah laws that condoned or enabled plural marriage. But because the law allowed Congress to intervene in "domestic institutions" in federal territories, it threatened the rights of slaveholders and went largely unenforced. It was roundly ignored by the church.

Following the Civil War, federal attention once again focused on Utah. In a test case before the Supreme Court, Brigham Young's secretary, George Reynolds, was charged with bigamy. The church argued that his acts were a constitutional expression of his First Amendment rights. In 1879, *Reynolds v. United States* (98 U.S. 145) upheld the Morrill Act. The court ruled that the First Amendment did not protect polygamy as an expression of freedom of religion, a landmark decision that established the legal basis for the subsequent separation of church and state. Three years later the Edmunds Act once again attempted to make the Morrill Act enforceable, but with limited success. In that same year, the twenty-seven-year-old A. Jennie Bartlett published *Elder Northfield's Home*, opening the book by asserting that plural wives "look towards the government with hope for themselves, as each law is passed for the suppressing of polygamy. But their hope is turned to despair as they witness the inability of Congress to enforce the laws it passes, and the successful defiance of the law-breaking citizens of Utah" (3).

Over the next decade, various legal measures intensified the consequences for the Mormon Church's defiance of federal law. According to Ray Jay Davis, "About 1,300 LDS men who had practiced plural marriage were jailed by federal officers pursuant to the Edmunds Act."[67] The 1887 Edmunds-Tucker Act dissolved the corporation of the Mormon Church and sold church properties. Men who actively practiced polygamy were disfranchised, and their plural wives were required to testify in court against their husbands, although "many . . . were found 'in contempt of court' and jailed for refusing" to do so.[68] Finally, the mounting legal pressures, combined with Utah's ongoing but unsuccessful efforts to gain statehood, led church president Wilford Woodruff to announce "that my advice to the Latter-day Saints is to refrain from contracting any marriage forbidden by the law of the land."[69] Just one year later, publisher J. Howard Brown brought out a second edition of *Elder Northfield's Home.*

Woodruff's "Official Declaration" did not end polygamy. Neither the stroke of a legislative pen nor the word of a church prophet addressed the complex problems of how or whether to dissolve existing polygamous families. According to Peggy Pascoe, "Mormon women . . . point[ed] out that the legislation would result in moral stigma for them and illegitimacy for their children."[70] Hence, not only did most polygamous families continue to exist, but the church also continued to solemnize plural marriages in Canada and Mexico.

Polygamy's more effectual terminus came more than a decade later, the result of political rather than moral imperatives. As Utah Territory continued to petition for statehood, the appeal became conditional on the abolition of polygamy. Following Woodruff's 1890 declaration, Presidents William Henry Harrison and Grover Cleveland issued federal pardons and restored the civil rights of those who had been disenfranchised by antipolygamy legislation.[71] Yet the federal government remained wary that the church was not fully compliant and continued to intensify legal penalties while denying statehood. In 1892 a new statute prohibited bigamists from immigrating into the United States, a law that remains in force today.[72] The Enabling Act of 1894 "forever prohibited polygamous marriages, not just cohabitation."[73] Finally, in 1896, Utah was admitted to the Union.

As the debate raged about whether and under what conditions the forty-fifth state would join the Union, the J. Howard Brown company apparently sold the lithographic plates for Bartlett's novel to a Boston-based publisher, B. B. Russell, who brought out editions of *Elder Northfield's Home* in 1894 and 1895. Essentially unchanged from the earlier printings, these two versions altered the book's subtitle to signal its continuing relevance. In 1894 the title page included a new subtitle, *A Story of Territorial Days in Utah*. In 1895 the subtitle became *A Story of Utah*.

Even after Utah joined the family of states, its most distinctive social institution persisted among those who believed polygamy to be a divine mandate. Plural marriages continued, particularly among high church leaders, albeit without public church recognition. As late as 1901, for example, Owen Woodruff, son of church president Wilford Woodruff, took a second wife, Eliza Avery Clark. Finally, in 1904, a renewed national scandal over the seating of Utah senator-elect Reed Smoot, a polygamist, impelled church president Joseph F. Smith to issue another "official statement" on the matter. In it he denied that any "such marriages have been solemnized with the sanction, consent, or knowledge of the Church of Jesus Christ of Latter-day Saints" and declared, "I hereby announce that all such marriages are prohibited, and if any officer or member of the Church shall assume to solemnize or enter into any such marriage he will be deemed in transgression against the Church and will be liable to be dealt with, according to the rules and regulations thereof, and excommunicated therefrom."[74]

Yet well into the twentieth century, many Mormon men continued to cohabit with multiple wives, some within the boundaries of the United States, and others in Mexico and Canada. Only their deaths finally dissolved the complex families they had formed decades earlier. The practice of plural marriage continues today, although not as an official doctrine of the mainstream church. Breakaway denominations, often structured around large and extended polygamous networks, continue to follow a practice they deem to have been revealed by God to Joseph Smith and abandoned by a weak-willed church leadership in exchange for political and social respectability. Polygamous relationships continue to be the subject of popular, if sensationalized, attention and of serious debate. Since 2006, two successful television series, HBO's *Big Love* and TLC's reality show, *Sister Wives*, have fed a continuing fascination with this practice. In the presidential election of 2012, Mormon beliefs were central to the campaign of the Republican nominee, Mitt Romney, whose family once practiced polygamy. Even more recently, Supreme Court decisions related to the 1996 Defense of Marriage Act and to California's Proposition 8, which prohibited same-sex marriage, have once again opened the question of how extensively federal law may regulate interpersonal relations. Apparently the cultural work of *Elder Northfield's Home* retains its contemporary relevance.

Notes

1. Review of *Elder Northfield's Home*, 11.
2. The term *polygamy* includes both polygyny (one man's taking multiple wives) and polyandry (one woman's taking multiple

husbands). It is commonly used to describe polygyny, especially as practiced by believing Mormons in the nineteenth century.

3. Gordon, "'Our National Hearthstone,'" 339.

4. All quotations from the novel are taken from the present edition and will be cited parenthetically in the text. In this novel, as in the nineteenth century generally, Mormons refer to non-Mormons as Gentiles.

5. A *New York Times* ad for *Elder Northfield's Home* emphasizes its similarity to Stowe's novel, declaring, "It will open the eyes of the nation to the evils of Mormonism, just as 'Uncle Tom's Cabin' did to the evils of slavery" ("New Publications," 5).

6. Bartlett insistently repeats the word *duty* in *Elder Northfield's Home*. For example, in chapter 5, as Marion discovers how deeply polygamy has hurt Elder Parker's wife, the word appears nineteen times. In chapter 7, as Northfield tells Marion he intends to marry again, *duty* is used twenty-one times.

7. Several decades ago in *Sensational Designs* Tompkins argued that attending only to the aesthetic dimension of a text obscures fiction's significant effects on politics, behavior, and social policy. More recently, Alémán and Streeby have demonstrated the connection between the "melodramatic" forms of sentiment and sensationalism and nineteenth-century debates over slavery and freedom, imperialist expansion, and wars of aggression (*Empire*, xvii).

8. Throughout this essay I refer to the author by her family name, under which she published the 1882 edition of *Elder Northfield's Home*, although she owned the copyright as A. J. Switzer. Not until 1891 did the author's name on the book's title page change to Jennie Bartlett Switzer.

9. The little biographical information available about Bartlett comes from censuses and city directories. I have collected these references in "Elder Northfield's Tree," posted on Ancestry.com.

10. His copy is owned by the Barrett Collection of the University of Virginia.

11. Cott, *Public Vows*, 71, 70.

12. Bowman, *The Mormon People*, 87.

13. Foster, *Religion and Sexuality*, 140.
14. Bowman, *The Mormon People*, 87.
15. Doctrine and Covenants 132:16.
16. Bowman, *The Mormon People*, 124.
17. Bushman, *Joseph Smith*, 437.
18. Bowman, *The Mormon People*, 86.
19. Even in this intent, Mormons were not unique. Other states— Texas, which had first been the Lone Star Republic, and California, which first incorporated as the Bear Flag Republic—had existed first as polities separate from the United States.
20. "The 'Twin Relics,'" 4.
21. Qtd. in Neff, *History of Utah*, 853.
22. Orson Pratt, "Celestial Marriage," 54.
23. Bowman, *The Mormon People*, 129.
24. Bowman, *The Mormon People*, 130.
25. Bowman, *The Mormon People*, 130.
26. Bowman, *The Mormon People*, 131.
27. Bowman, *The Mormon People*, 131.
28. Young responded to these intrusions by making Salt Lake City a refueling and reprovisioning stop, filling the Saints' coffers with larger profits than they likely would have made mining gold. According to Hyde, Mormons "controlled trade and travel in the [Great Basin] region using kinship connections, price controls, and fear" (*Empires, Nations, and Families*, 358).
29. Pascoe, *Relations of Rescue*, 22.
30. Bentley, "Marriage as Treason," 344.
31. Bennion, *Equal to the Occasion*, 44.
32. Gordon, *The Mormon Question*, 170.
33. Orson Pratt, "Celestial Marriage," 54.
34. Cott, *Public Vows*, 73.
35. Chief Justice of the Utah Supreme Court James McKean, qtd. in Cott, *Public Vows*, 111.
36. Frederick, *National Party Platforms*, 57.
37. Cott, *Public Vows*, 115, 117–18. On racialized images in antipolygamy novels, see Bentley, "Marriage as Treason," 356–61.
38. Frederick, *National Party Platforms*, 28.
39. Bentley, "Marriage as Treason," 357.

40. Orson Pratt, "Celestial Marriage," 60–61.

41. Willard, Introduction, *Women of Mormonism*, xv–xvi. In *Elder Northfield's Home*, Bartlett also engages this rhetoric. Northfield tells his wife that plural marriage requires sacrifice as a way of pleasing God. She retorts, "Is God pleased to see the Hindoo mother throw her innocent babe into the Ganges as a sacrifice to appease His wrath? . . . . [N]ow you propose to make a living sacrifice of me." Northfield, scandalized, exclaims, "Marion, it is simply blasphemous for you to associate the religion of the Latter-Day Saints with heathenism, in the way you do" (112).

42. Cott, *Public Vows*, 7. For an extended discussion of the concept of marital consent, see chapter 6, "Consent, the American Way."

43. Murray, "On the Domestic Education."

44. Bowman, *The Mormon People*, 135.

45. Bentley, "Marriage as Treason," 348, 349.

46. Bentley, "Marriage as Treason," 349.

47. Cott, *Public Vows*, 112. Because *Elder Northfield's Home* does not consider the issue of suffrage, I do not discuss it here. For an extended examination of how suffrage became a bargaining point in antipolygamy legislation, see Gordon, *The Mormon Question*, 164–72.

48. Thomas, "Woman's Exponent," 1571.

49. Parley P. Pratt was first married in 1827. By the time of his death in 1847, he had married eleven additional women. He was the brother of Orson Pratt, who delivered the announcement of polygamy in 1852, and the great-great-grandfather of 2012 presidential candidate Mitt Romney (Dobner and Johnson, "Polygamy was Prominent").

50. Belinda Marden Pratt, "Defence of Polygamy."

51. In a public address, "On Marriage and Divorce," Elizabeth Cady Stanton enumerated "three kinds of polygamy in our midst": Mormon polygamy, fraudulent bigamy, and "the form well known to society, . . . where a man lives with one wife . . . but who has many mistresses. This is everywhere practiced in the United States" (70).

52. Belinda Marden Pratt, "Defence of Polygamy."

53. Gordon, *The Mormon Question*, 29.

54. Bowman, *The Mormon People*, 130.

55. Tanner, *A Mormon Mother*, 236.

56. Here I echo the title of *Writing Beyond the Ending*, DuPlessis' influential study of narrative strategies of twentieth-century women writers.

57. Stowe, *Uncle Tom's Cabin*, 386.

58. Here I focus specifically on antipolygamy texts, but it should be noted that polygamy figured prominently in works by well-known writers such as Arthur Conan Doyle's *A Study in Scarlet*, Edward L. Wheeler's dime novel *Bullion Bret*, Zane Grey's *Riders of the Purple Sage*, and Mark Twain's *Roughing It*. For extensive lists of such texts see Pingree, "'The Biggest Whorehouse,'" 229n14 and the entirety of Arrington and Haupt, "Intolerable Zion."

59. Gordon, *The Mormon Question*, 42.

60. Stowe, Preface, vi. Predictably, Stowe linked polygamy with "a cruel slavery . . . which debases and degrades womanhood, motherhood, and the family."

61. See DeSimone's edition of Stenhouse's *Exposé of Polygamy*, 172–78 for a list of the book's editions.

62. Willard, Introduction, xvii.

63. According to Derounian-Stodola, Young was "Brigham Young's fifty-second wife and, apparently, his nineteenth *living* wife (the total number of his wives is believed to be fifty-five, but may be as high as seventy)" ("*Legacy* Profile," 150–51).

64. The 20-year-old Jennie Bartlett may have heard Young speak in Sudbury, Massachusetts in 1875.

65. "Mrs. Young," 3.

66. "New Books," 3.

67. Davis, "Antipolygamy Legislation," 53.

68. Davis, "Antipolygamy Legislation," 53.

69. Woodruff, "Official Declaration 1." This declaration is also known as the Manifesto of 1890.

70. Pascoe, *Relations of Rescue*, 68.

71. Magrath, "Chief Justice Waite," 540.

72. Davis, "Antipolygamy Legislation," 53.

73. Snyder and Snyder, Introduction, 7.

74. Smith, "Official Statement," 75. This declaration is sometimes termed the Second Manifesto.

Works Cited

Alémn, Jesse, and Shelley Streeby. Introduction to *Empire and the Literature of Sensation: An Anthology of Nineteenth-Century Popular Fiction*, xiii–xxix. New Brunswick NJ: Rutgers University Press, 2007.

Anthony, Susan B. "Declaration of Sentiments and Resolutions." *The Elizabeth Cady Stanton and Susan B. Anthony Papers Project*. Rutgers, 2012. Web. 29 July 2013.

Arrington, Leonard J., and Jon Haupt. "Intolerable Zion: The Image of Mormonism in Nineteenth Century American Literature." *Western Humanities Review* 22 (1968): 243–60. Print.

Bennion, Sherilyn Cox. *Equal to the Occasion: Women Editors of the Nineteenth-Century West*. Reno: University of Nevada Press, 1990. Print.

Bentley, Nancy. "Marriage as Treason: Polygamy, Nation, and the Novel." *The Futures of American Studies*. Ed. Donald E. Pease and Robyn Wiegman. Durham NC: Duke University Press, 2002. 341–70. Print.

Bowman, Matthew. *The Mormon People: The Making of an American Faith*. New York: Random House, 2012. Print.

Bushman, Richard Lyman. *Joseph Smith: Rough Stone Rolling*. New York: Knopf, 2005. Print.

Cott, Nancy F. *Public Vows: A History of Marriage and the Nation*. Cambridge: Harvard University Press, 2000. Print.

Davis, Ray Jay. "Antipolygamy Legislation." Ludlow, 52–53.

Derounian-Stodola, Kathryn Zabelle. "*Legacy* Profile: Ann Eliza Webb Young (Denning)." *Legacy* 26.1 (2009): 150–59. Print.

Dobner, Jennifer, and Glen Johnson. "Polygamy Was Prominent in Romney's Family Tree." *Deseret News*. Church of Jesus Christ of Latter-day Saints, 25 Feb. 2007. Web. 29 July 2013.

Doctrine and Covenants. *The Church of Jesus Christ of Latter-day Saints*. Intellectual Reserve, Inc., 2011. Web. 29 July 2013.

DuPlessis, Rachel Blau. *Writing Beyond the Ending: Narrative Strategies of Twentieth-Century Women Writers*. Bloomington: Indiana University Press, 1985. Print.

"Elder Northfield's Tree." *Ancestry.com*. Web. 25 May 2014.

Rev. of *Elder Northfield's Home; or, Sacrificed on the Mormon Altar*, by A. Jennie Bartlett. *Independent* 31 Jan. 1884: 11. *American Periodicals Online*. Web. 29 July 2013.

Foster, Lawrence. *Religion and Sexuality: The Shakers, the Mormons, and the Oneida Community*. Urbana: University of Illinois Press, 1984. Print.

Frederick, J. M. H., comp. *National Party Platforms of the United States*. Akron OH: N. p., 1896. Google Books. Web. 29 July 2013.

Gordon, Sarah Barringer. *The Mormon Question: Polygamy and Constitutional Conflict in Nineteenth-Century America*. Chapel Hill: University of North Carolina Press, 2002. Print.

——. "'Our National Hearthstone': Anti-Polygamy Fiction and the Sentimental Campaign Against Moral Diversity in Antebellum America." *Yale Journal of Law and the Humanities* 8.295 (1996): 295–350. Print.

Hyde, Anne F. *Empires, Nations, and Families: A History of the North American West, 1800–1860*. Lincoln: University of Nebraska Press, 2011. Print.

Ludlow, Daniel H., ed. *Encyclopedia of Mormonism: The History, Scripture, Doctrine, and Procedure of The Church of Jesus Christ of Latter-day Saints*. New York: Macmillan, 1992. Print.

Magrath, C. Peter. "Chief Justice Waite and the 'Twin Relic.'" *Vanderbilt Law Review* 18 (1965): 507–43.

"Mrs. Young in the Pulpit." *San Francisco Chronicle*, 12 Oct. 1874: 3. *ProQuest Historical Newspapers*. Web. 29 July 2013.

Murray, Judith Sargent. "On the Domestic Education of Children." 1790. *Judith Sargent Murray Society*. Hurd Smith Communications, 2014. Web. 29 July 2013.

Neff, Andrew Love. *History of Utah, 1847 to 1869*. Salt Lake City UT: Deseret News Press, 1940.

"New Books." Rev. of *Elder Northfield's Home; or, Sacrificed on the Mormon Altar*, by A. Jennie Bartlett. *New York Times* 24 Mar. 1884: 3. *ProQuest Historical Newspapers*. Web. 29 July 2013.

"New Publications." *New York Times*, 2 Feb. 1884: 5. *Pro Quest Historical Newspapers*. Web. 29 July 2013.

Pascoe, Peggy. *Relations of Rescue: The Search for Female Moral Authority in the American West, 1874–1939*. New York: Oxford University Press, 1990. Print.

Pingree, Gregory. "'The Biggest Whorehouse in the World': Representations of Plural Marriage in Nineteenth-Century America." *Western Humanities Review* 50 (1996): 213–32. Print.

Pratt, Belinda Marden. "Defence of Polygamy, By a Lady of Utah, in a Letter to Her Sister in New Hampshire." 12 Jan. 1854. *Internet Archive*. Web. 23 May 2014.

Pratt, Orson. "Celestial Marriage." *Journal of Discourses*. Vol. 1., 53–66. Liverpool: Latter-day Saints' Book Depot, 1853. BYU *Harold B. Lee Library Digital Collections*. Web. 30 April 2014.

Smith, Joseph F. "Official Statement." *Seventy-Fourth Annual Conference of the Church of Jesus Christ of Latter-day Saints*, 75–76. Salt Lake City UT: Deseret News Press, 1904. LDS *Scripture Citation Index*, Brigham Young University. Web. 29 July 2013.

Snyder, Lu Ann Taylor, and Phillip A. Snyder. Introduction to *Post-Manifesto Polygamy: The 1899–1904 Correspondence of Helen, Owen, and Avery Woodruff*, 1–42. Ed. Snyder and Snyder. Logan: Utah State University Press, 2009.

Stanton, Elizabeth Cady. "Mrs. Elizabeth Cady Stanton's Address at the Decade Meeting, on Marriage and Divorce." *A History of the National Woman's Rights Movement*. Comp. Paulina W. Davis. New York: Journeymen Printers' Co-operative, 1871. 59–83. Print.

Stenhouse, T. B. H. [Fanny]. *Exposé of Polygamy: A Lady's Life among the Mormons*. 1872. Ed. Linda Wilcox DeSimone. Logan: Utah State University Press, 2008. Print.

Stowe, Harriet Beecher. Preface. *"Tell It All": The Story of a Life's Experience in Mormonism. An Autobiography* By T. B. H. [Fanny] Stenhouse. Hartford: Worthington, 1875. vi. Print.

———. *Uncle Tom's Cabin: Authoritative Text, Backgrounds and Contexts, Criticism*. Ed. Elizabeth Ammons. New York: Norton, 1994. Print.

Tanner, Annie Clark. *A Mormon Mother: An Autobiography by Annie Clark Tanner*. Salt Lake City UT: Tanner Trust Fund, 1991. Print.

Thomas, Shirley W. "*Woman's Exponent*." Ludlow, 1571–72.

Tompkins, Jane. *Sensational Designs: The Cultural Work of American Fiction, 1790–1860.* New York: Oxford University Press, 1985. Print.

"The 'Twin Relics of Barbarism.'" *New York Times,* 18 Jul. 1869: 4. *ProQuest Historical Newspapers.* Web. 29 July 2013.

Willard, Frances E. Introduction. *The Women of Mormonism; or, the Story of Polygamy As Told by the Victims Themselves.* Ed. Jennie Anderson Froiseth. Detroit: C. G. G. Paine, 1887. xv–xviii. Print.

Woodruff, "Official Declaration 1," 1890. Doctrine and Covenants. *The Church of Jesus Christ of Latter-day Saints.* Intellectual Reserve, Inc., 2011. Web. 29 July 2013.

Young, Ann Eliza. *Wife No. 19; or, the Story of a Life in Bondage.* Hartford: Dustin, Gilman, 1875. Print.

A Note on the Text

A. Jennie Bartlett's book, *Elder Northfield's Home; or, Sacrificed on the Mormon Altar. A Story of the Blighting Curse of Polygamy*, was first published in 1882 by J. Howard Brown in New York. (Although the author used her family name on the title page, she held the copyright to it under her married name, Switzer). Brown issued a second printing of this book in 1891. Shortly thereafter the press must have sold the lithographic plates for the book to Boston's B. B. Russell, which printed a second edition of the book in 1894. This edition differs from the first in three details: the book's sub-subtitle has been altered to *A Story of Territorial Days in Utah*, and the author's preface has been omitted; both details reflect the changed status of antipolygamy statutes and the cessation of the practice of polygamy by the LDS Church. Finally, in the second edition, the author's name, as well as the copyright, are given as Jennie Bartlett Switzer. Russell issued one more printing of the book in 1895, changing the sub-subtitle once again, to *A Story of Utah*, recognizing that Utah was to be admitted to the Union in 1896.

A number of facsimile electronic editions of this text are widely available, but most have serious errors, either omitting pages entirely or including pages from entirely different books in the place of pages from this text.

I have used the text of the 1882 edition to prepare this work, for the intent of that publication was to garner support of antipolygamy activism. It included Bartlett's impassioned preface pleading for federal officials to enforce antipolygamy legislation already in place and links what Bartlett saw as the plight of wives in plural marriage to that of enslaved women in the South in decades past.

To preserve the sense of this book as a nineteenth-century text, I have retained nineteenth-century conventions of spelling and punctuation, including hyphenated compound nouns. I have, however, silently corrected several obvious printer's errors.

Elder Northfield's Home

Preface

Sad as the scenes depicted by the succeeding pages may seem, revolting though they appear to a right-minded community, savoring as they do of barbarism and superstition, and displaying tyranny and oppression which our so-called free America should blush to tolerate, yet not one representation of the workings of Mormonism and Polygamy has here been given which has not its parallel in actual life in Utah at the present day.

The pollution of the marriage relation, the wife literally giving away (being forced to do so) other so-called wives to her husband, the invasion of her home-happiness by those fiendish attributes—hate and jealousy—the neglect and often cruelty woman must suffer from him who should love, cherish and honor her, by the forcing of young and innocent girls into repulsive matrimonial alliances—these are not vagaries of fancy, portrayed to excite the emotion of sensation-loving minds, but facts, which exist in defiance of our laws to the contrary in our otherwise glorious republic.

This horrible system is said to have had its origin with Joseph Smith, the great founder of Mormonism, and was introduced by him as a religious institution, to screen his own wrong-doing from public censure. It was claimed by him to be the direct revelation from God, and as founders of new religions are often believed in by their followers as almost supernatural or infallible, so the followers of this man received his teachings with the unreasoning faith that fanaticism and religious excitement will sometimes produce in even the most well-balanced minds. So polygamy was established as an important doctrine in the religion of the Latter-day Saints.[1] The women are taught that only by patiently bearing their cross, submitting to and obeying their husbands, and advancing his interests, can they hope for happiness in the future life. If the question arises, why are they so simple-minded as to receive, and submit to such teachings? the answer is apparent. They know no other life; they receive no other instruction than that which instills the Mormon religion into their minds. All the influences by which they are surrounded from very infancy, tend toward deceiving them into a belief in their religion. They have been kept ignorant by the authorities lest a cultivation of the intellect stir up rebellion against their oppressors. For a successful reign of tyranny and oppression, ignorance in the subjects is a necessity. All despotic rulers know this, and as the recent slave-holder of the South allowed the poor African no opportunity to obtain an education, lest he rise up and defy him, as the Roman priesthood discourage any education in the church save a strictly Romish one, lest it loose its power over its vast dominion, so the Mormons look upon education in their subjects as destructive to their institutions.[2]

There have always been men and women in the Mormon Church who did not believe in the religion they professed to accept. But though broken-hearted, though stung to madness, though plunged into the deepest despair by their wrongs, yet the possibility of liberating themselves from their bondage scarcely occurred to the women, and indeed has not existed many years. If a desperate soul sought relief from her troubles in flight from the Territory, she was pursued, not by the blood-hound that scented the African refugee, but by the blood-hound in human form, who sought to capture her and return her to the miseries of Mormon life. And this was done in the name of religion!

The hearts of these women cry out in anguish for deliverance. Their prayers to a merciful Father ascend day and night, that his hand will relieve them from the sorrows of their life. They look towards the government with hope for themselves, as each law is passed for the suppressing of polygamy. But their hope is turned to despair as they witness the inability of Congress to enforce the laws it passes, and the successful defiance of the law-breaking citizens of Utah. But they can only suffer in silence. They dare not raise their voice to plead their own cause. More helpless are they than the negro slave, for they are of the weaker sex, and must submit to the power of physical might. Will our nation suffer this wrong to go on, to perpetuate itself, to increase and spread as it is rapidly doing now? Will it at a fearful sacrifice of money and life, by one of the mightiest, grandest movements a nation ever made, abolish one terrible curse to our country, and ignore the existence of its equal, when a comparatively insignificant struggle would suffice to exterminate it? Is the freedom of the black man and his redemption from ignorance to be considered more imperative, more desirable than the freedom of women from the most degrading life a woman can lead? Were the cries of the slave under the lash more pitiable than are the heart miseries of these women? Were the separation of husband and wife by the stern decrees of the auction block more to be deplored and abolished than the constant misery of a polygamic life? Is not this slavery of the West a much more despicable one than that of the South, in that it is a slavery of defenceless women, a doubly debasing institution, and in that the sorrows of the victims are brought upon them by their own husbands? Again, the slavery of the South, though justified by its participants, was not adopted as a religious ordinance. In Mormondom hearts are wantonly crushed, homes polluted, the basest of wickedness perpetrated, and all in the name of religion. What blasphemy against a just and pure God! Where in all the enlightened countries of the globe, can be found so foul a stain, as that which blackens the otherwise fair fame of our nation?

Will our government weakly allow its laws to be trampled under foot and ignore the defiance of a body of men, fast increasing in numbers and influence? Let it attack this great evil with the energy which characterized the putting down of the rebellion and the blotting out of slavery, or even with the same relentless persistence with which the poor Indian is driven from place to place on his native soil, and polygamy will be a thing of the past. Then will the United States stand proudly forth, the grandest, noblest nation on the globe.

Chapter 1

"Well, Marion, here we are!—trunks packed; farewell calls made; passages engaged; tears all shed;—wish I were sure of the last. O how hard I find it to leave my dear home and country, much as I always wished to go to America, and to have a home with aunt Wells! But you, Marion, seem so very happy. I wonder if I should be in such a delightful frame of mind if I were on the eve of marrying a Mormon elder,[3] and emigrating with him to Zion,[4] as you call it, where the people are all of one faith, the women dress so simply, and think and care for nothing but their religion. I am afraid I should make a poor saint, Marion. I couldn't give away all my fine dresses, jewelry and ornaments, as you have done; I should keep them, and at least dress in them once in a while, if but to admire myself and not forget how I used to look when I belonged to the world, and I should not want to attend meetings so constantly. This emigrating to Zion seems to me altogether uncalled for. The new people seem to be a very good, religious people, with many good precepts in their doctrine. But there is much in their belief that calls for an amount of faith which I am incapable of exercising. I do not see why these other denominations are not quite as likely to tide us safely into heaven as Mormonism, and certainly their ways are much pleasanter."

"Ah, Elsie," responded Marion, "you seek to get into heaven by an easy way. 'Straight is the road, narrow is the way, and few there be that find it.' Doesn't Christ say 'follow me,' and was his life here on earth an easy one? Did he not say, 'Thy will, not mine, be done?' Did he not cast in his lot with the despised and lowly, and should the disciple be above his Master? Are we to expect to wear the crown, if we do not bear the cross, in this life? I am filled with peace and joy, the more so the more sacrifice I make for the kingdom. I never knew such happiness before, and I feel like being just as holy and obedient to God as possible. The greatest pleasure I have now is in attending these meetings. The Spirit of God is powerfully manifested, and as you know, many who come to scoff go away converted, or thoughtful at least, and you, Elsie, I think, cannot deny that the power of God is with them, as though they were his chosen people."

"Yes, Marion, I must admit the meetings have an influence over me when I am present, and the elders seem to prove all they say from the Bible, and I can't for my life reason their arguments away. But when I am alone I begin to think for myself, and somehow I can't have faith in these divine revelations to Joseph Smith and Brigham Young. I know, as they say, the Bible says 'your young men shall dream dreams, and your old men shall see visions.' I know they say, 'If men were inspired in olden times, why not now?' Perhaps Mormonism is the true religion; but I can't believe that our own dear mother, that dear old aunt Eunice, that Agnes Ainsworth, who died so sweetly, after living such a good life, and that our minister, and all the good people we know, must be shut out of heaven because they were not gathered into the Church of Latter-day Saints. Their idea of a new dispensation[5] is not clear to me. But I have not received so many private lectures on the subject as you have, Marion. After so much conversation as you have enjoyed with Elder Northfield, you ought to understand the mysteries of the doctrine perfectly. O, do not try to hide your blushes! They are very becoming—or would be if you were not so plainly dressed, and if the effect were heightened by some of the vanities you have discarded and packed in my trunk. It would be but a poor reward for all his devotion, his earnest love-making and missionary zeal, if you did not sympathize with him in his religion, which seems to be a part of himself. But I can't help thinking that he has rather neglected me, and that if some of these hours devoted to you had been spent in preaching to me, he might have been rewarded for the sacrifice by adding another convert to his list."

"I wish he had, Elsie; indeed I do."

"Well, but you did not seem to wish so then, Marion."

"I will not be so selfish any more, and I will ask him on the voyage to teach you, and explain all these things, for somehow I am not good at explaining them myself, though they are so clear to me as Henry expounds to me the doctrine."

"God grant, dear sister, that you may always be as happy in your religion as you are now! I never thought we should be separated, but I cannot go with you to Utah, for I am not a Mormon—unless Henry converts me on the way, and I fancy his bride will have most of his attention, as she has heretofore."

"O, I pray you may yet see the light and go with me! The separation from you is the only cloud in my sky. With you and Henry, I should be happy anywhere!"

"Marion, forgive me if I say anything to grieve you, but to-morrow I give you to Henry; and this is our last confidential talk while you are mine, and perhaps for a great while, for we shall scarcely be alone hereafter, and something tells me our old confidence will not be the same after you are married, so I want to tell you all my thoughts tonight. Are you sure that your happiness, peace, and joy come from this heavenly love entirely? I observe that when Henry is the speaker in the meetings you are aroused to much more enthusiasm for your religion than at other times. Now might you not mistake your happiness, and love for him, and your interest in everything that interests him, your sympathy with him in all he thinks and believes, for religious devotion? Are you sure you know your own heart, Marion?"

"O, sister, how can you ask me?"

"I did not mean to pain you, but I feared your religion alone might not always give you such peace. I hope, with all my soul, it will. It is very beautiful to think so."

"I know it will, Elsie! I love Henry, O, so much! You cannot think how much. I love him even more than I love you, Elsie! but I truly believe I love God and my religion more. Henry himself has taught me that 'whosoever leaveth not father and mother, sister and brother, husband and wife, for God and the gospel, is not worthy to be reckoned a saint.' I think—yes, I *think*—I would leave them all if God required the sacrifice."

"Then, Marion, dear, I did you injustice in my thoughts, and with all my heart I hope, in your new life, you will be, as you seem now, perfectly happy."

"Except for the thought of leaving you behind; and one other thing which of course it is very silly to mention, or to be troubled with. But I will open my heart to you, as you have to me, on this last night we may be alone together. Of course it cannot be true—it must be a scandal—the report we heard of some of the saints in Utah having more than one wife. But once in a while—only once in a great while—my heart suddenly sinks, so that it seems as if I should faint, and the thought of that report flashes into my mind, and I dismiss it as suddenly. Then I am all right again. I have talked with Henry about it, and he says it is a foul slander against the church of God. That always God's chosen people have suffered persecution for righteousness sake, and he quoted the words, 'Blessed are ye when men shall revile you, and shall say all manner of evil against you falsely for my name's sake.' Henry does not in the least believe that, or any other wickedness is sanctioned there. You know the saints are not popular, and many are poor, and public opinion is against them. But in the Celestial Kingdom,[6] they will have honor enough to compensate for all their trials here. Henry says if he for a moment supposed that this rumor was true, he never could believe in Mormonism. When we were in London, at the conference, we went together and asked an elder from Utah, and he was astonished and indignant, and denied it positively. So of course there can be no truth in the rumor, and I feel that it is wicked to even think of such an unholy thing. I resolve never to think of it again, but still the thought comes like a black shadow across my path. Now, Elsie, can it be possible, do you think, that such a thing is practised there?"

"Of course it cannot be, Marion! I do not for one moment doubt the elder's word. I wonder you even think of it at all—though the possibility of such a thing would be terrible to you, of course, as you are to be a Mormon elder's wife. These men are good, moral men, I do not doubt in the least, however mistaken they may be in their belief, and as they study the Bible, and take everything so literally, they would be the last to disregard its plain teachings on that subject. Why! only the vilest of men could be guilty of such a crime, and certainly these Mormons we have seen are intelligent, noble-minded men. Your own promised husband is a man of whom a woman might well be proud, Marion. I respect him as I respect few men, and admire his kind-heartedness, his intellect, his untiring zeal for 'the truth,' as he calls it, and think it is very noble of him to sacrifice his position and fine prospects as he did, for what he deemed his duty, and cast in his lot with this people. If I *must* lose my sister, I could not have chosen better for her. But O, if he were not a Mormon, and would not take you away from me to that wild and far away place! Marion, darling! when shall I ever see you again after you leave me in New York!"

"Come with me, Elsie! O, that you might be persuaded to

give up all for religion! You would be so much happier! See how I am changed—naturally not light-hearted like you, rather inclined to sad, morbid feelings; but they are all gone, and now I am much the happier of the two. Cast away your doubts and go with me to Utah, and you will then see and know for yourself the beauties of religion, I do believe. O, my dear sister, won't you—won't you come with us?"

"I can't, Marion, I can't! I shiver at the thought, though why I don't know!"

Then these twin sisters mingled their tears in silence, and their hearts were knit together in the purest and strongest of sisterly love.

Made orphans two years before, by the death of a kind and loving father, they became more dear to each other in their common sorrow, and were one, in heart and soul, as sisters seldom are. Reared in comfort in a happy home in England, and with no care or thought of poverty, it was a great change to find with their father's death, they were nearly penniless.

Charles Wescott fully lived up to his income, and indulged himself and daughters to many luxuries and extravagances which were usually confined to people in a higher grade of social life. He literally took "no thought for the morrow," and his young and sorrowful daughters found that they were dependent on their own exertions for their daily bread. Elsie obtained a situation as teacher in the public schools, and Marion was kindly employed by her friends to teach music to their children. Recently a sister of their mother (who died during their infancy) had written to them from her home in New York, begging them to come to her, as she had just lost by death her only daughter, and her elegant home was desolate and lonely. They resolved to go, as soon as they could properly conclude their engagements. Meanwhile a crisis came in one life at least.

They had heard of the Mormons, or Latter-day Saints, and

their curiosity was excited. One day as they returned from their labors to their boarding-place, and entered the parlor, they found there a gentleman, plainly dressed in black, bending over a large Bible lying open on the table. As he rose and apologized for his presence, and begged them to remain, he displayed a fine form, and handsome, thoughtful face. His eyes, large, dark, and full of a pleasant light, seemed to look beyond the surface, into the inner life. His forehead, high and intellectual, was shaded by soft wavy black hair, and as his lips parted in a smile, they disclosed the whitest and firmest of teeth. Soon he was on pleasant terms with his new friends, talking with them familiarly. As Elsie saw Marion's eyes light up, and her cheeks glow with enthusiasm, she did not fail to notice the glances of admiration the gentleman bestowed on her. At his request Marion seated herself at the piano. Her golden hair would stray from its fastenings, and peep out in little rings about her neck and forehead. Her color came and went and constantly changed her face from the paleness of marble to the loveliest pink. Her sky-blue eyes glanced shyly up as she spoke. Elsie came near, with her auburn hair and fair, piquant face, her large brown eyes beaming with love and pride in Marion's accomplishment. Their new acquaintance joined them in their songs and displayed much musical talent. Thus the hour before tea rapidly passed, and then Mrs. Newton, the lady of the house, appeared and introduced the new-comer as Elder Northfield. Great was the surprise of Marion and Elsie to learn that their new acquaintance was a Mormon elder, and that he was to hold a meeting that evening in a small hall. They resolved to attend. Mrs. Newton accompanied them. There were assembled only a few people, for the pastors of the churches were universally opposed to the new movement and had warned their flocks against it. The young elder, after an earnest prayer, in a clear and attractive way proclaimed the doctrines of his belief, and, with Bible in hand, proved every assertion from its pages. Verse after verse, chapter after chapter, he readily turned to or repeated, until it seemed that they were listening, not to *his* words, but to the words of the Bible brought forth in a new light, and by one filled with inspiration from on high. His eloquence and earnestness increased as he proceeded, till his face was transformed and his eyes were filled with what seemed a heavenly light. His words carried more or less of conviction to every heart. The deepest silence reigned. All eyes were riveted on the speaker, and breathlessly they listened to his closing appeal to cast away their sins, enter the true Church of God, and enjoy that wonderful abiding peace—the fullness of joy. He offered a short prayer, appointed another meeting, and gave out a closing hymn, which was sung by the whole congregation. As Marion listened to *his* voice among the others, its sweetness thrilled her through and through, and she felt that to cast her life in with such a people, to be filled with the same holy joy with which this man was blessed was then her greatest desire.

The meetings continued and increased in size and interest, in spite of the efforts to oppose them. Marion became a convert to the new faith. Mrs. Newton also cast her lot with the saints, and Elsie attended the meetings faithfully with her sister, but she did not come into the faith. The elder, Marion, and Mrs. Newton, who, with Elsie, then comprised the family, labored with her, to bring her into the church, a saved and happy member. All to no purpose, however. She resisted all their arguments and earnest appeals, and failed to have faith in the divine revelations. This was a cause of grief to Marion, and also to her sister, who had heretofore never essentially disagreed with Marion.

Soon the admiring glances, and slight attentions of the elder, to the golden-haired Marion, gave place to long conversations and quiet walks, and often Elsie would miss her sister, who would return and blushingly confess that the elder had been explaining to her more fully some points in the doctrine; or that the elder had asked her to walk with him, and she had just returned. At length Marion confided to her sister that Elder Northfield had asked her to be his wife, and that she had promised him, and they were to be married and emigrate to Zion as soon as he should be permitted to leave the missionary work in other hands. She earnestly pleaded with her sister to accompany her, but Elsie sorrowfully refused, and said she would go with them to New York, and there remain with her aunt.

There were a number of Mormons—elders and converts—on board the sailing-vessel, besides Elder Northfield and his bride, who, with Elsie, had left the shores of their native England, and were sailing across the ocean to America. Elsie's predictions were fulfilled as to the elder's devotion to Marion on the voyage, to the exclusion of everything else, save always his religion. He evidently had given up all attempts to convert her to the new faith, and she was glad, for she was secretly wearied with it, and regarded it as very annoying to herself, and as being the cause of her separation from her sister, who would leave her soon among perfect strangers with not one face near her on which she had ever looked before. Elsie's heart was very heavy at times, and all Marion's cheerfulness and joy could not dispel the gloom. She watched her sister and her husband, in their relations with each other, with an anxious mother interest, to assure herself that Marion's fond anticipations were realized. She was satisfied. Elder Northfield was by his wife's side almost constantly, except when engaged in conversation with the elders, some of whom were from Salt Lake City, and now returning, after having converted many to the new faith who were about to emigrate in great numbers to Utah. Elsie soon conceived a great dislike for one elder on account of a foolish infatuation he did not attempt to conceal, for a pretty girl who was young enough to have been his daughter. Marion had not noticed this, for her own love affairs had so engrossed her attention, and she had the most unbounded faith in all the elders, and in Elder Parker especially, as he was directly from Zion and had lived on intimate terms with Brigham Young himself. She was one day talking of the elders to Elsie and casually spoke of Elder Parker's wife.

"Elder Parker's wife, Marion! Has Elder Parker a wife?"

"Certainly, and five children. Why do you seem so astonished? I see. You think strange of his leaving her to come to England and preach the gospel. Think of the sacrifice it must have been for him to leave her and his little ones, of whom they say he is very fond. I am told that his wife, who is very devoted to him, even urged him to accept the mission, and accounted herself happy and honored in giving him up for the church. O, Elsie! Could I ever be willing to part with my Henry if it were my duty! I fear I am not submissive enough, but hope I shall become willing to do, or be anything in God's hands, when I am fairly within the fold in Zion. But speaking of Elder Parker, now how happy his family will be made by his arrival. I quite like to think of it, and imagine the meeting between him and his wife."

Elsie thought she would not like to imagine or witness a meeting between him and his wife at that moment, for on deck the lovers were standing, hand in hand, and at the elder's whispered words the color came into the girl's face and then left her quite composed. She did not directly answer Marion, but from that time she began to lose faith in the goodness of the Utah Mormons, though she still believed her countrymen and women were honest and sincere, though they might have been deceived. Marion's husband she believed was a good man. He had become converted and joined the saints in England,

and on account of his talents and zeal, had been ordained[7] elder, and had acted efficiently in that capacity. He believed in his religion as devoutly as he did in his Marion. He loved it as he did Marion. He endeavored to conscientiously obey every word of counsel, from those above him in the church. He devoutly believed all they taught, and accepted their teachings as being the revealed will of God to man.

Elsie began to notice a cloud on his brow, and a sorrowful glance occasionally at Marion, when the latter did not observe him. She saw him holding a great deal of very earnest conversation with the elders, and by his appearance he was antagonistic to all the others. They appeared to change the subject as Marion approached her husband, and he lovingly took her arm in his. Jealously watching everything likely to affect Marion, it made her uneasy. Marion at last seemed to notice a change in her husband, or in his ways, and said to Elsie, "I wish Henry would not talk with the elders *quite* so much, though I fear it is wrong for me to wish that. I am so selfish that I want him with me all the time. Of course it is right that he should learn all he can from them and talk with them a great deal. I am glad he is so devoted to his religion."

A day or two later she said to Elsie: "Elsie, do you know what the word polygamy means? I went up to the group of elders to speak to Henry, and I heard the word polygamy uttered two or three times, and then something about Abraham and the olden time, and that was all I heard, for they noticed me then and stopped talking. Henry did not leave them and join me as he often does; but they asked me to be seated with them, and although I would like to have stayed with my husband, I saw that I was interrupting their conversation, so I came away. I will ask Henry when he comes what they were talking about. Have you any idea, Elsie, what the word polygamy means?"

"I am sure I cannot tell you, Marion, its meaning. Probably

it is one of the terms peculiar to the Mormon faith, like many others that are not common among the 'world's people.'"

Elsie's heart was filled with terrible forebodings, as what she saw and heard recalled the old scandal concerning the saints in Utah. She had some idea of the meaning of the word, but would not needlessly alarm Marion by telling her fears. O why had she been so sure there was no truth in the report! Why had she quieted Marion's fears, which might have been fostered and prevented her marriage and emigration! Why had she—so faithless as regarded their doctrines—trusted implicitly in their goodness and morality! Why had she not remained away from their meetings and kept Marion away! No, that would have been impossible. Marion would have followed Elder North-field anywhere. His influence was stronger than hers. Since he looked at her with those fascinating eyes, Marion had become another person. Elsie mourned that her sister was lost to her, and looked with dread upon Marion's future. Then she tried to reason away her fears and believe all was well. She told herself no religious society could be so degraded in this enlightened age as to adopt such a practice. The United States Government would not allow it, of course. And Elsie nearly persuaded herself that her fears were groundless.

When Marion was alone with her husband, she asked him what the elders meant by the word polygamy, and of what they were speaking, and why they so suddenly stopped at her approach. A look of annoyance and sadness came upon Elder Northfield's face, and his only answer was to caress his young wife. She repeated her question. "Ask me tomorrow, Marion," he said.

"But, Henry, cannot you tell me now?" and the blue eyes were filled with the tears that had been gathering all day.

"No, dearest, I can't tell you now. You love me enough to wait for my answer, I know."

"Yes, Henry, but it is strange you cannot tell me now. Is it something dreadful? You look so strange. Is it—is it—"

"Come, Marion, let us join Elsie now and think of something else."

The next day Marion came to Elsie, with weary step and faltering lips. Her face had lost all its happiness—her eye all its brightness. Pale and sad, she laid her head on Elsie's shoulder, and after a deep sigh she said: "I came to tell you, Elsie, that I have found out what the word polygamy means."

"Have you?" said Elsie. "I have found out, too, my poor child! And what are you going to do about it?"

"Do? What can I do, Elsie? There is nothing that I can do; but O! thank heaven! *I* shall never know by experience what it means. My dear, dear Henry! *He* will be true to me, and me alone."

"How can you be sure of that?"

"I have his word, and he never broke it, and I trust him but I will tell you all about it. O, I am so miserable, to think that the religion I have loved so well has proved to have such a terrible curse attached to it! Just think of it! Henry tells me that the saints (are they saints or are they sinners?) have as many wives as they please and can support, and the more they have, the more honor to them in the Celestial Kingdom. Even Elder Parker, whom I have esteemed so highly, has three wives at home, and on arriving at Salt Lake City will take another, the pretty young English girl you and I have seen with him on deck. Elsie, I think this is terrible! My faith in everything about Mormonism is shaken now—and I did so love my religion. I thought they were all so good, and Henry did, too. He never believed in polygamy being a doctrine of the saints. They always denied it to him, and since we have been on board this vessel, the elders have faithfully labored with him, to convince him that it is right. At first he was shocked. But O! Elsie! Here

comes the worst trial of all! I can see that gradually they are
influencing him and weakening his scruples. He places such
implicit trust in all the higher authorities, and in their divine
inspirations, that he has hitherto accepted anything that they
have taught him. They are now working hard to prove to him
that plural marriages are ordained of heaven. They are very skilful, and talk about Abraham and all the men in the old Bible
times having more than one wife and being blessed of God.
They say this new dispensation is to resemble the old one, and
Henry is going to get a copy of the revelation,[8] and we are to
peruse it together. He believes all the other doctrines just as
firmly as ever, while I begin to feel doubtful of everything, just
as you always have. He does not yet believe in polygamy, but
says they make it look so plausible that he cannot answer their
arguments. He dreaded to tell me, because he knew of my
horror at the thought, before we left England, but he assured
me with the strongest of promises that never would he enter
into polygamy, and I should be his only wife. He cared not for
so high a place in the kingdom, if I only were at his side. The
plural wife system is as utterly repugnant to his feelings as it
is to mine, and although others may be justified in it, he never
could. He thinks they are in error, and will see their wrong; but
they tell him when he has read the revelation, he will be fully
convinced. Now, it looks to me like wickedness, instead of error. I can look at it in no other way, and the whole of this belief that did look so bright to me now looks dark. I thought he
would leave the Mormons if this were true, but I see he has no
thought of it. He believes they are in the main right at least. O!
now I dread to enter Zion as much as I did desire to do so! To
live in the midst of polygamy, though I know I never shall enter it! I have perfect faith that Henry will always be mine alone,
or my heart would surely break. Those poor women! Though
they say it is part of their religion, and they are contented and

happy, as they consider it the will of heaven, and they submit, and God blesses them. O! I never could submit—never! if I knew I should not enter heaven! O! Elsie! Elsie! How little I thought when I left my home, such a happy bride, that I should so soon be so miserable!"

And Marion laid her head in Elsie's lap, and sobbed, while Elsie stroked her golden head, and called her by the many endearing names she had been wont in their girlhood days. "Marion," said Elsie, when the storm of grief was over, and the tearful eyes and bowed head were at last raised, "Marion, you must not go to Salt Lake City! You must never live in the midst of such wickedness and misery. There can be no happiness for my darling sister there."

"Elsie, you forget that I am married, and that where my husband goes, I must go. Where he goes, I want to go, and in his hands lies our future," Marion answered with some spirit.

"Your husband must not go to Utah. He must not take you away from me, to a place where you will be unhappy. I could give you up if I felt sure your own life would be the peaceful one you have thought it would. But to go now, Marion—no, Elder Northfield must not take his bride to any but a happy home. Persuade him to remain in New York. He can easily find employment there. Plead with him not to go to Utah. Use all your influence—and it is great, Marion—to persuade him to give up his project of emigrating to Zion. He loves you too much, I do believe, to refuse your earnest entreaties."

"No, Elsie," sadly answered Marion, "you are wrong. I did not think I would tell you, but I will. I did ask him not to go to Utah, but to remain in New York, and though he did not positively refuse me, I can see that he considers it our duty to go on, and duty to him is law. Much as he loves me, I believe he loves his religion better, and it grieves him to see me so sad, especially after his repeated promises not to bring sorrow to my heart. So I will not trouble him more than need be, for this has been a trial to him, too. I mean to go with him cheerfully, and after a little, I dare say I shall become quite contented again, and perhaps when I know more of Mormon life, it will appear less repugnant to me. Certainly my own home may always be a happy one, and if other women are not made miserable by polygamy, why should I make myself miserable by my sympathy for them?"

"O," thought Elsie, "that I could have Marion's confidence in her husband. Oh, that I could feel sure as she does, that *her* husband never will bring sorrow to her heart. He means all he says, no doubt, now, but in the coming years, in the midst of Mormon influence, and with all his faith in Mormon teachings, will he still be true to my darling? O, why did I not see all this and prevent it?"

It was this dark foreboding, this unspoken dread, that caused Elsie to resolve to prevent her sister from ever arriving at her intended destination.

With this resolution she sought an opportunity to convince her brother-in-law of the unhappiness he was bringing to his wife. Believing that Marion had not allowed him to know the intensity of her disappointment and sorrow, she felt sure his heart would be easily touched by a plea for her, and he might be persuaded for *her* sake to abandon his purpose of spending his life in Utah. But Elsie was the one person with whom Elder Northfield did not care to be left *tête-à-tête*. He avoided her clear, penetrating eyes, and shrunk from the scorn with which he knew she would treat the new doctrine. Uneasy and dissatisfied himself, and uncomfortable at the thought of his young wife's sadness, he did not wish to be made more so by Elsie's sharp arguments or appeals, so he took good care not to be alone with her during the few remaining days of the voyage. This she observed, but consoled herself by thinking that when they arrived at New York, where all the Mormons on board were to remain for a few days, until the arrival of the next emigrant vessel, and then journey together to Utah—there at her aunt's he could not so easily avoid her. In this, also, she was to be disappointed.

Chapter 2

The voyage had been a tiresome one, as all voyages were in the days of slow sailing vessels, and now as they were nearing land, a general cheerfulness pervaded the whole ship. Anticipations of meeting friends, excitement of life in a new country, and last visits with acquaintances formed on the voyage, caused a lively, pleasant excitement, quite in contrast with the former monotony on board. Elder Parker and his infatuated English girl were rapturously happy, and were thinking of celebrating their marriage immediately after their arrival in New York. All the Mormon elders were very jovial now (save, perhaps, Elder Northfield), and even Elsie and Marion had regained some of their former good spirits, and were anticipating much pleasure in spending some days together with their aunt and seeing the attractions of the great American metropolis. But one day Elder Northfield came to his wife, saying, "Marion, I have made excellent arrangements for our accommodations on our arrival in New York, close by the Mormon boarding-house and publishing rooms. There is no room for us at the boarding-house, but Elder Crosby promises to secure us board in a private Mormon family, near where he is to board, and where Elder Parker will take Carrie when she becomes his wife."

"O, Henry, I never for a moment supposed we would go anywhere except to my aunt's. She expects us and will be very much disappointed if we do not go to her home. And Elsie will be there—and—and—I thought—" Marion's voice failed her, and her eyes filled with tears. This new trial was too much for her composure.

"Why, Marion, I thought you would be pleased with the arrangement, and supposed you expected to give up all Gentile[9] associations. You know, dear, we are to give up the world. You have sacrificed all for religion, haven't you, Marion, and cast in your lot with mine? And the elders all very much disapprove of associating with the world's people, and we cannot directly disobey counsel. Besides, I think in your state of mind, you are much better off entirely away from all Gentile influence. I am sure you will be quite contented there. The elders say it is a very pleasant boarding-place. We will look over the city together, and cannot my darling be happy with me? Marion, I am quite jealous of Elsie. I did think you loved me more than any one else, but if Elsie is necessary to your happiness, what can I infer from that?"

"O nothing, Henry, only that I am to go so far away from her, and perhaps never see her again, and you know she is so very dear to me, and we never have been separated. I *do* love you best. O, please do not doubt that, and I will willingly go wherever you think best. But it is a disappointment to me, for we should have such a pleasant visit altogether at my aunt's; but as you say I am perhaps better away from such influence, for I am so in doubt about the doctrines that it would require but little to take away all my faith. As I am to be a Mormon, I shall be happier in believing in Mormonism than in rebellion against its teachings. Henry, believe that I do love you with my whole heart, and where you go I will go."

For reply her husband tenderly drew her to him and pressed a kiss upon her lips.

"But, Henry," Marion resumed, "I wish Elder Parker and Carrie were not going to be near us. Somehow I feel such a disgust for that man. And that pretty girl who seems so happy and so perfectly trustful in the future—how I pity her—to be a man's fourth wife! All living wives, too. She cannot know what she is doing. She must be a weak-minded person, it seems to me, to ever become resigned, and even happy in contemplation of the future."

"Perhaps, Marion, she is wiser than you in accepting the doctrine so implicitly. It may be no other Mormon woman looks at polygamy with the horror you have of it. They tell me the women of Utah are happy and contented in their life and religion, and I hope my wife will become again the trustful, happy believer in the faith that she was before this revelation was made known to us."

"My faith may come back to me as I once believed, but *never! never!* can I believe in polygamy or accept it as from God. But it is not necessary for me to believe in *that*, Henry, because we are never to know personally what it is."

"No, darling; no other shall ever enter my home or my heart. You are the only one I shall ever call 'wife.'"

It was on one of the sunniest mornings of early spring that an elegant private carriage was driven up to one of the New York hotels and a sad-faced lady, clad in the deepest of mourning, alighted and entered the house. After searching the register, with a dissatisfied look, she requested to be shown to the room of Miss Elsie Wescott. Just as she reached the door, it opened, and standing just within stood Marion. She had regained much of her former sprightliness in the excitement of her arrival, and some remark of Elsie's had caused a smile to light her whole face; her hair was allowed to fall in wavy masses down her shoulders, and a ray of sunlight made it sparkle and shine like burnished gold. Each stood gazing at the other for a few seconds, when the elder lady exclaimed:

"I know this is Marion!"

"And I know this is aunt Wells! Elsie! Elsie! Aunt has found us before we have had time to find her." And the sad-faced lady, after lavishing kisses and caresses on the two, took one face between her hands and said:

"You, Marion, are like your mother, my dear sister Marion, as I last saw her, and you, Elsie," as she gently caressed Elsie's auburn hair, "are like my own dear Lillian, who has left my heart so desolate, and who now lies by her father's side. How I shall love you both, and how I thank God for sending you to me in my loneliness. I should not have waited till to-day had I known of the arrival of your vessel yesterday. I was very fortunate in finding out your hotel—but we will not talk any more here, for I shall have you in my own home presently, and *your* own home, too, it must be. And O! my darlings! I do hope you may be so happy there that you will not leave it for many years. Now, how soon can you be ready to go with me? You are mine now. Tell me that it is so, Elsie—Marion."

"I will be yours, O! so gladly, aunt," said Elsie; "but Marion belongs to another. She is spending this morning with me in this my room; but her husband is coming to take her away in a few hours, and my twin sister is soon to be separated from me, perhaps forever."

"O! Marion! Is this true? And you are so young to be a wife! Why did you not tell me and spare me this disappointment?"

"I did not know it myself for a certainty the last time I wrote you, and then afterwards I thought I would rather tell you than write it. I scarcely realize all that has passed myself."

And Marion spoke truly. It seemed to her that all things had so changed since the day she first met Elder Northfield that years, instead of a few short months, must have passed.

"But tell me of your husband and what this separation means. What is your new name?"

"I am Marion Northfield now, aunt Wells, and my husband is—is—"

O how Elsie pitied her sister, as she saw how she dreaded to utter the word Mormon. Marion seemed to choke, and her eyes sank beneath the gaze of her aunt. Elsie longed to help her, but was silent.

"My husband is a Mormon elder, and we are on our way to Salt Lake City," Marion answered.

"Marion! You the wife of a Mormon elder! Elsie, tell me, can that be true! My sister's child a victim of that greatest curse and blight of our country, not even excepting slavery!"

"Yes, aunt, it is too true," said Elsie, "and Marion is soon to be in the midst of it."

"No, never, if I can save her! Child, you must never go to Salt Lake City! You must never leave me! You poor deluded girl! Would you ruin your life? Would you be forever miserable in polygamy?"

"No, aunt Wells, polygamy will never make me miserable, except as I may sympathize with others if I see them suffering from it. My husband will never enter into it. He dislikes it as much as I do, and only on our voyage from England did we learn that it was one of the doctrines of the saints. I have his most solemn assurance that *never* will he take another wife while I live, and I know he will be true to me and his word. I shall go on with him to Salt Lake City, aunt Wells. He considers it his duty to go there, and it is my duty to go with him and also my desire."

Mrs. Wells was astonished at the change so suddenly come over Marion, as she answered her with so much wounded dignity. Her blue eyes, so mild and timid a moment before, now flashed with resentment at her aunt's implied scorn for her husband and his religion. Her slight figure was drawn up to its utmost height as she tried to control her anger.

"Forgive me, Marion, for having offended you; but, my dear, let me tell you what I know. I know other young, trusting wives, who were as sure of their husband's fidelity as you are of yours, and I know how cruelly they have been deceived. One of my dearest friends—my little Lillian's governess—married a Mormon elder, who promised with all a lover's warmth and enthusiasm as your husband has promised. That man has broken his vow and his young wife's heart by marrying two more wives since he arrived at Salt Lake City. She lives utterly neglected, I have heard, with her two little ones, a few miles from the city, striving by every means to keep herself and babes from starving, and yet she was as young and, perhaps, as fair as you are. That man is Elder Parker. Do you wonder at the horror I have of seeing my sister's child—her own image—exposed to such sorrow? Do you wonder that I have no confidence in the promises of a Mormon?"

Marion had sank into a chair and looked so miserable and frightened that her aunt's heart ached for her.

"My dear, I would not torture you with my fears—I grieve to do it—but you know less of Mormonism, probably, than I do, although you are a Mormon yourself. You know little of the influence that will be brought to bear upon your husband when directly under Brigham Young's control. You know not how almost impossible it is for a man to withstand the constant commands and counsels to marry again. No doubt, Marion, your husband is sincere now, but in the years to come, when the roses have faded from your cheeks, and the sparkle gone from your eye, when lines of care and sorrow have come into your face, will he be more true than every other man just as honorable and sincere as he now is?"

"Yes, I believe he will, and I cannot bear that you should speak so of him. Please do not any more. I see no reason for your trying to destroy my faith in my husband. I think it is wrong—unkind of you."

"It would be, Marion, the most cruel wrong I could do you were it not to save you from greater trouble. It is not your faith in your husband as a man, as a husband, that I would weaken; but your faith in him as a Mormon."

"And if you succeed, aunt Wells, what will you have gained, except to have made me miserable, and needlessly so?"

"I will have gained everything, child—everything for you. I will have saved you from a miserable existence—from a life of grief and despair. I will have secured to you the happiness and confidence you heretofore have enjoyed in your husband. For with the influence you must have over him, the horror you will have of a life in polygamy, you will, through some means, persuasion, or stratagem, or rebellion, even, keep him away from that city where my poor friend's life and so many others have been wrecked."

"Aunt Wells, you do not know my husband. He does love me—Elsie will tell you so—with his whole heart, but he loves God most, I believe, and what he thinks it his duty to do, that he will do. I have grieved him enough by rebelling against his wishes and his religion, and I cannot believe, as you would have me, that his vow to me will be broken. I do not believe in this religion as I did before we learned of polygamy. I hate that; but before I was so happy in the new faith, and was so glad at the thought of gathering with all the saints, prophets and apostles, under the direct guidance of the great leader of the Mormon Church, that I cannot throw away all my hopes of happiness yet. If I could believe as you do, aunt Wells, that my husband would ever take another wife, all would be changed. No! I believe I should not change! I should love him still!"

"But, Marion, you will at least try to persuade him. There is room and a welcome for you all at my home; there is employment or business enough in New York for Elder Northfield. I want you near me; Elsie wants you. Do not leave us without at least trying to prevent it."

Marion threw her arms around her aunt's neck, and said: "Dearest aunt! How I should love you! How I wish it might be as you say! How I suffer at thought of parting with Elsie! I know you say all this for what you think is my own good. But I believe you are mistaken: you do not know my husband. Elsie knows him, and she does not think this of him, I am sure. I have willingly consented to go with him to Utah, and in return he has promised to devote his life to me and my happiness. How can I thwart the most cherished desire of his heart? How can I ask him to make such a sacrifice for me, and be unwilling to make any for him? It will seem like disputing his faithfulness to me to ask him to remain. I know it would break my heart to lose his confidence, and I will not deprive him of mine. Please, dear aunt, do not look at it in such a terrible light. I feel sure my life will not be ruined, but I look forward to a happy home of our own, whatever our surroundings may be."

At her aunt's recital of a passage in Elder Parker's history, Marion's faith had failed her in spite of herself, and she was sick at heart with terrible fear and apprehensions for her own future. Only for a moment, however, for her love for her husband conquered every doubt, and she was again the confiding, hopeful wife. Her aunt felt how utterly useless it was to entreat her further. Elsie had listened eagerly to the conversation, hoping her aunt's arguments would be effective. Marion's answer was so decided, and so evidently final, that her aunt and sister felt that there was no more to be said. They sat in silence for a few moments; then Mrs. Wells said: "Why are we wasting our time here? I came to bring you home with me, and you will go, will you not, Marion, if only for a few hours?"

Marion readily assented, and soon with Elsie was enjoying

the beauties and comforts of their aunt's elegant home. It was to be Elsie's home, but Marion did not covet it, for no place, however beautiful, could be home to her without the one who was to henceforth share her joys and sorrows. Her aunt exerted herself to give her niece all the pleasure her house, with its books, its music, its flowers, and its beautiful grounds, could afford, in this her first visit in the new world. But the hours soon fled, and Mrs. Wells sent her carriage back to the hotel with Elsie and Marion, saying, "During your stay in the city, Marion, you must come and see us every day, and your husband also shall be welcome."

At the hotel Elder Northfield had just arrived, and was searching for Marion, when she returned and explained the cause of her absence. Elsie noticed the fond smile as he greeted his wife, and the tenderness with which he wrapped her in her cloak and arranged the cushions and blankets of the carriage with the utmost care for her comfort, and his devotion inspired her with hope that after all, Marion's life might be an exception to that of most Mormon women. Marion, too, now seemed to have forgotten the unpleasantness of her aunt's first conversation, and in her pleasure at being again united with her husband after a few hours' separation she did not notice the sadness that would come into Elsie's voice as she said, "Good-bye, darling; come and see me to-morrow."

"Yes, Elsie, if I can," she replied, and she left her sister, who returned to her aunt, little thinking this was their final parting.

But Marion grew very thoughtful as the events of the day came back to her, as she thought of all her aunt's words, and she could not repress her sadness at the thought of that wronged wife suffering in Utah. She thought of the bride Carrie, who was to be taken by that heartless husband as a fresh insult to the miserable woman he had promised to love and cherish till death did part. She remembered the reverence with which she had looked up to him, and now her soul was filled with contempt. An involuntary sigh escaped her.

"Marion," said her husband, "you seem thoughtful and sad. You should have been made happy by a visit to your aunt. Has anything unpleasant occurred? What have they been saying to you to make you look so gloomy?"

"Aunt Wells has been telling me a sad story of a friend of hers who, when a bride, went to Utah."

"Is that the way in which she entertained you? Really, I think she might have shown more tact and chosen some subject more pleasant and quite as appropriate to your circumstances. No wonder you look sad. I see. She is one of the many persecutors our faith has, and has chosen to show her love for her niece by attacking her religion. I do not—"

"O! Henry! She would never persecute any one. She is so good and kind I cannot help loving her. I wish you had seen her. But she was very much astonished—yes, and evenshocked—to learn that I had married a Mormon. Of course, it made me very angry at first to listen to her attacks on the Mormon elders, and I could not answer her pleasantly; but when she told me what she knew of them, and especially of her friend who was so cruelly treated—and, Henry, let me tell you, this friend was the first wife of Elder Parker, and now he cruelly neglects her and leaves her to suffer alone and support her two children—when she told me this I could not be angry with her, and did not wonder at her prejudice against all Mormons. And, indeed, Henry, I fear there are many bad men in the Church. Aunt Wells has the advantage of living in this country and knowing more of the native Mormons than you and I do."

"There are some bad men in every church. Even among the twelve apostles there was a traitor; but, Marion, you have only heard one side of Elder Parker's story. I have been told that his first wife has caused him a great deal of trouble, and has been so rebellious and wicked that it was impossible for him to live with her. His other two wives live together most harmoniously and are quite willing he should take a fourth. I see no motive but a bad one in your aunt talking to you in the way she has. To say nothing of the insult of inviting you to her house and making your visit unpleasant, the inference from her words was not what was due to your husband."

"O, she meant no disrespect to you, Henry, and wishes you to come with me to her house any time."

"Marion, tell me, did she try to destroy your faith in me? Did she intimate that your husband would ruin his wife's happiness as others have? Did she tell you I would break my vow to my wife?"

"She said I never could be happy in Utah, and showed me how much misery there was, and begged me to persuade you to remain here. She told me there was room in her home and a welcome for us all, and you could easily find employment or business in the city, and she wanted me near her and Elsie."

"Marion, you have not answered me! Did your aunt try to make you believe I would ever take another wife?"

Marion was frightened at the anger she saw in those deep, dark eyes, and she answered:

"She said no doubt you were sincere and honorable now, but she feared you would not love me so much when I am older and less attractive, and that it would be almost impossible for you to withstand the commands and counsel to marry."

"And you allowed her to talk to you thus!"

"O, please do not look so angry. No! I did not allow her, but told her I thought she did very wrong to talk to me so, and that it was to no purpose, for I would not even ask you to give up going to Zion when I knew how your heart was set on going, and I assured her that nothing could ever make me doubt my husband's fidelity to me alone. She asked my forgiveness for having offended me, and I could not refuse to go with her, as she seemed so disappointed in losing me. She said no more on the subject, and made my visit a very agreeable one—asking me to come every day to see her and Elsie."

The anger had all died out of Elder Northfield's eye as Marion told him of her assurances to her aunt of faith in her husband, and given place to a look of great tenderness as he said:

"God bless my darling wife. She shall never regret her trust in me."

They were silent a few moments; then Elder Northfield said:

"Marion, do you wish to go to your aunt's every day while we are in New York?"

"I—I—think I should like to, but perhaps I had better not."

"I thought when you were telling me what she said to you we would neither of us go there, but you shall do as you please. I think, however, judging from this first visit, that her society will not conduce to your happiness, and the less you are with her the better. Intercourse with Gentiles is very effective to destroy the saints' peace of mind, for they are so prejudiced and opposed to the Mormons that they will use every means in their power against them. The elders will condemn us if we do not withdraw from the world. Elsie, I think, is a hindrance to you in the exercise of your faith, and I hope when we are safely in Zion, away from all these influences, to see you again the happy enthusiast you once were."

"Henry, do you wish me to keep away from Elsie and aunt Wells?"

"Not altogether, Marion. It would be cruel to deprive you of your sister's society entirely. I will not ask that sacrifice; but you know my views in regard to the matter, and I believe it is for your good to avoid them as much as you can, but let your own heart dictate to you, my dear. I want you to be happy. It is for you to decide what will most conduce to your happiness in the end."

But Marion was spared the trial of holding herself aloof from her aunt and sister or disregarding her husband's wishes. Her course was decided for her, and she had no choice but to acquiesce in the decision.

Henry Northfield, though not a man of abundant means, was not as poor as many of the emigrants were. He had given liberally, according to his means, for the benefit of the Church and assistance of the poorer emigrants, but had not, like many in his circumstances, given his all. In this he had been slightly censured by the higher authorities of the Church, and accused of a lack of faith, but still he prudently withheld something for the future wants of himself and wife. Thus he had been able to emigrate with the other elders and a few of their converts at his own expense, independent of the emigration fund,[10] and with much less discomfort and privation than usually fell to the lot of Mormon emigrants. Their journey from New York to Utah, however, was to be postponed till the arrival of the next emigrant vessel, and made in company with the poorer emigrants. But the dispensations and revelations of the Mormon Church are subject to many sudden changes, which would seem very human were they not so positively divine. A message was received that night from Brigham Young directing the Mormons who might be in the city on their way to Zion not to tarry, but to gather immediately to Zion without any delay.

Marion had not accompanied her husband to the meeting that evening, but had remained at her room, arranging for her temporary stay in the city. It was late before he returned, and she would have been lonely, but she had that day made the acquaintance of Carrie, Elder Parker's bride, and now was being entertained by the latter, who had also remained at her boarding-place while Elder Parker attended the meeting. She

had come into Marion's room to chat with her. Marion grew
quite interested in Carrie, who was gratifying her curiosity and
interest by being very communicative in regard to her circumstances and expectations. Carrie seemed quite resigned to being
the fourth wife, for she said she was not fourth in her husband's affections, but was, he had told her, the first and only
one he had ever really loved. She was not aware that each of
his previous wives had received the same assurance and been
made to believe it. As for his other wives, she should not have
the least jealousy for them—poor things—but should be very
kind and indulgent to them, though she should take care that
they understood her position with relation to them, as Elder
Parker had decided that she was to be mistress of the house.
There were three children belonging to the two wives, but she
did not care for that, as she liked children, and presumed they
were very attractive. She knew she should love them, for they
were her dear husband's children. She expected to take life easy,
for, of course, the other wives would not expect much of her in
the domestic line, as she was so young, and her time would he
so entirely devoted to her husband. She had sacrificed all for
Mormonism and Elder Parker, including father, mother, brother and sisters, much against their wishes, but these separations
were as nothing when weighed in the balance of duty and religion. In short, Carrie was quite as contented and self-satisfied
a person as one might wish to meet with. Marion wondered
at her tranquil frame of mind, but could not but admit that, as
her husband had intimated, she was the wiser of the two, and
that it was well to believe that what must be, was what one desired should be.

Elder Northfield returned to a very cheerful wife late in the
evening, and was quite prepared to sympathize with her mood,
as he joyfully told her of the word of command from the head
of the Church, and that they were to resume their journey to-

wards Zion by daybreak the next morning. It had not occurred to Elder Northfield in his preoccupation that to Marion this would be the most unwelcome news—that it meant final separation from her loved sister and a closer contact with a system from which, in its best phase, she shrunk. He did not realize how utterly bereft of enthusiasm Marion was in the religion which had once been so dear to her. He could not know the repugnance which a woman felt towards coming in close contact with what she felt to be a great wrong to her sex. His devotion to his religion and desire to gather to Zion were so great that all obstacles in the way were completely lost sight of, and he could not sympathize with her in her grief, as it seemed that so suddenly cutting all the ties that bound her to her former life was like the cutting of her heart-strings. And worst of all, it was impossible for her to see Elsie again. Had she only known sooner she might have spent that evening in a last visit with her sister. O, how could she part with Elsie with no farewell word! How could she leave her so soon, perhaps forever! Why must they be constantly controlled in every movement by the Mormon authorities! Rebellion was working in Marion's heart, and all her husband's sympathy and kindness could not lift her load of sorrow. Her hope in the future forsook her for the time, and all looked dark. But she bravely tried to cast her sorrow from her for her husband's sake, and set about undoing the work of the evening and preparing for her journey.

The next morning Elsie, leisurely sipping her coffee in her aunt's pleasant breakfast room, received the following letter:

MY DEAR SISTER:

I pity you for the sorrow and grief you will feel when you read this letter, and realize that Marion is gone—when I tell you that as you read I shall be journeying fast on my way to Salt Lake City. O, Elsie! Elsie! Would that this

night, instead of writing to you, I might have your arms
twined lovingly once more about me, that I might lay my
cheek against yours, and be comforted in my trouble as I
have so often been. To leave you without a word, without
one farewell kiss, seems cruel to us both. I had hoped for
so much pleasure with you and aunt Wells before I left
you! I thought that not quite yet must the saddest side of
Mormonism be thrust upon me—a little while longer I
might be in the world if not of it, and enjoy something of
its pleasures. For I must admit, Elsie, that the world gives
me more pleasure now than my religion does. You
remember that on the evening before we left England, you
expressed your fear that my religion alone would not
always give me the peace I then enjoyed. Little did I then
think how soon your fear would become a reality. Now
there is little in it that seems attractive. O, that I might
have the unwavering faith that I once had, and this trial of
leaving you would not seem so great. Still I have no doubt
that I shall recover my usual spirits soon. I have been
trying to hide my feelings from Henry, as he seems so
troubled and sorry for me, though before he realized how I
would take it, he was very much delighted that we could
so soon proceed to Zion. He only learned of the change in
the plan to-night at the meeting, and returned very late—
too late for me to go to you; and besides there was no time,
for we had immediately to repack all our goods
preparatory to an early start. I can only write you a
farewell, Elsie, in the small hours of the morning, and it
must be brief, for Henry insists that I shall try to get some
sleep before I start. Dear aunt Wells! Tell her how I regret
that I can see no more of her. Ask her to forget and forgive
the resentment I showed in return for her kind interest in
me. Assure her of my thankfulness that my sister has

found so good a friend and protector in her, and do not either of you let your hearts be troubled for my future. Sad though I am at leaving you, and dreading to come face to face with polygamy, yet I have no apprehensions of evil coming across my own pathway, and I leave you, Elsie, with confidence that when the present trial is over, and we are finally established in a home of our own, I shall be again the cheerful Marion who left dear old England with you. And now I must stop writing. How can I say farewell! I leave you, Elsie, now, not as I once thought I should, for my religion's sake, but for my husband's. And with him I cannot be unhappy, I feel sure. I know in the future you will not forget me, and sometimes perhaps we may be permitted to write to each other. God bless you, and grant that we may meet again, if not in this world, in the eternal world never to part.

MARION.

Elsie read this letter; then without a word, but with a face showing the intensity of her emotions, she placed it in her aunt's hands, and repaired to her own room, there to calm her sorrow, and struggle with her hatred of a religion which had bereft her of her dearest friend.

Chapter 3

Emigration to the West in those days was not the easy matter it is to-day, for only a part of the journey could then be performed by rail. Instead of crossing the plains with the rapidity and comfort that the introduction of the great Pacific Railway gives, the emigrants slowly travelled with ox-teams, advancing as far as might be by day, and pitching their tents and camping out for the night. There was much of hardship, privation and weariness in even the most well provided of companies, of which the little band of Mormons now gathering to Zion was one. But of the sufferings from cold, hunger and overpowering fatigue, of the deaths from exposure, from sickness, and from the wolves which attacked the larger and poorer emigrant parties, they knew comparatively nothing. There was much in the novel method of travelling that exhilarated and interested Marion at first, and all were so cheerful and jovial and seemed so happy in the thought that they were "a day's march nearer home," as they sung in their meetings by the way, that she caught the infection, and much to the joy of her husband began to look upon her new life with much less of her late discontent, and something of her old belief in the faith was revived as she earnestly desired and sought that it might be. What one wishes to believe one will more readily believe, and Marion wished to believe in Mormonism. Elder Northfield congratulated himself that complete isolation from Gentile companionship, and a strong Mormon influence were doing their work as he had predicted. And he looked forward to a time when Marion would be filled with the same zeal and love for her religion that characterized her in the days of her conversion to Mormonism. That time never came.

Day after day and week after week passed, and the monotony of the journey increased. The women and children grew very weary, and the longing to arrive at their destination grew intense. The men strove to make them as comfortable as might be, and tried to cheer them by songs and prayers, and assurances of the happiness in store for them just a little ahead in Zion. The heat of summer had now arrived, and in the burning sun they slowly advanced across the prairies. At last the end of the journey came, and as the sun was slowly sinking in the west, the travellers came in sight of the Great Salt Lake valley. Here before them in all its verdure lay the haven they had sought. In the distance, like a silvery sheet, lay the beautiful Salt Lake. And down in the valley, now shrouded in gloom from the everlasting hills surrounding it, lay the Zion of their hopes. Marion did not wonder that with their belief the Mormons called this place the "chamber of the Lord in the mountains," for it did seem like a chamber or room, so shut in was it from the rest of the world. As she stood by her husband's side, gazing with him at the promised land, now just before them, she felt that, after all, her reluctance and dread of entering this city had perhaps been entirely unreasonable. Certainly there was nothing in the sight before them to inspire one with dread. On the contrary, everything had a very peaceful look, as the elders had always represented. As for her husband, he took Marion's hand tightly in his and gazed with all the delight and satisfaction that the full realization of his long cherished hope could give him.

"Marion," said he, reverently, "thank God that at last we behold this beautiful place, and may we go no more out of it forever."

Suddenly a change came over Marion. She withdrew her hand from his.

"No!" she exclaimed, excitedly, "do not say so!" as at that moment they saw Elder Parker advancing towards them.

"Marion, tell me," said her husband, "what do you mean?"

"Five minutes ago this place looked to me like the abode of peace. Now, as I look down there, it seems to me I see sorrow and misery on the faces in those homes. I do not wish to stay here forever, Henry, and the sight of Elder Parker often fills me with the strangest of gloomy feelings."

"Then we will not see him. We will walk directly on to the wagons."

And they did so; for as it was impossible to find homes for themselves that night, the party had decided to camp where they were, and early in the morning descend into the city.

In those days the city was not composed of well-built houses, but principally of small low buildings of wood or even logs. It was, however, beautifully laid out, with wide streets and walks, and streams of water from the mountains were running through the streets. Small trees were extending their branches, and giving promise of beautiful shade in future years. Every spot of land seemed to be in the highest state of cultivation.

As Marion descended into the valley and entered the city the next morning with her husband, she noticed all these things. Nothing escaped her. This was to be her home—probably for life. She was now in the Zion for which she had so joyfully left her native country. She thought of the day she bid farewell to all that had been dear to her in England (save her sister), and was impressed with the change that had come over her since that time. She felt the contrast between the joyful anticipations of that time, and the gloominess of their realization. She thought of the system the knowledge of which had taken away all the pleasure of her religion, all the brightness there had once seemed to be in it, and destroyed her faith in everything pertaining to the doctrines of the Latter-Day Saints. She shrank from a more familiar knowledge of its workings, and weary and worn-out with her journey though she was, the prospect of rest did not dispel the sadness from her heart. But work for the mind and body are excellent remedies for mental depression, and Marion found plenty of work awaiting her. A house had to be secured, which was very difficult, for each man built his own, and seldom had any one a house to let. Toward nightfall, however, Elder Northfield succeeded in obtaining the use of a small log house towards the outskirts of the city. It was not a very attractive place in itself, but the wearied emigrants approached and entered it with thankfulness that even such a shelter might be theirs. They gathered to the spot all they had been able to bring with them, and what they could there obtain with the now failing resources of their pocket book, for the furnishing of their home. And although used to better surroundings, Marion experienced the same pleasure all young housekeepers feel in arranging their first home. She cheerfully made the best of everything, and exerted her feminine ingenuity in supplying many a deficiency and concealing the roughness of both house and furniture. When all was done, she was pleased with her success, and looked to her husband for the approving smile, which he did not fail to give, saying, "Marion, humble though this all is, we can be happy here." And Marion in her heart could at that moment echo the words.

Early the next morning Elder Northfield set out to look about the city for employment, and Marion busied herself pleasantly about her domestic duties. It was nearly noon when she heard a knock at the half-open door, and approaching her visitor she found him to be a small boy who had evidently made an attempt to array himself in a proper visiting toilet. His straw hat, which was minus the rear portion of the brim, had been carefully cut around the edge, thereby alleviating in a degree its ragged appearance. His hair, too, had evidently undergone the clipping process recently, and that, too, by unskilled hands, judging from the lack of uniformity in its length. The eyes were gray, and the face, which had been made to shine with soap and water, was rather a prepossessing one. A respectable jacket, evidently a borrowed one, from its size and the length of the sleeves, was buttoned around the boy. Of the pantaloons not much could be said, for there was but little of them visible, but beneath their ragged extremities were feet which, though bare, were comparatively clean. The hands were also clean, and Mrs. Northfield considered him quite an interesting person, especially after he politely removed his hat and proved that his conversational powers were equal to the occasion, without requiring much assistance from her. He was familiar with the place and its former occupants, with her neighbors, and much that was transpiring about town, and entertained his hostess with his information till she began to weary of him. He had told her his name was Johnnie Mordaunt. At last Marion said:

"Well, Johnnie, don't you think your mother will want you at home by this time?"

"O, no; she will not miss me, there's so many others."

"How many are there?"

"Well, only sixteen now, since Juba got married and Willie and Tommie died of scarlet fever; but you see there's four or five of us fellows all just about of a size, and it makes it mighty handy when one of us wants a vacation, as I did this mornin'."

"Sixteen children! Do they all belong to one mother?"

"Why, bless you, no! There's four of 'em. There's Sarah—I belongs to her, and six others are hern. Martha she's got four; Jemima three—darn 'em, we fellers can't have a thing that they won't smash—and Mary Ann has two little squalling things. We fellers, you see, aint big enough to work, so the women set us to tendin' their babies. There's five of 'em have to be run after, kept out of the molasses-jug and the pig-pen, and rocked to sleep by us boys; and I'm havin' the worst of it, 'cause, somehow or other—I don't know how—the young ones all take to me lately, and act afraid of t'other boys. I dispect 'em of doin' somethin' on the sly to make 'em 'fraid of 'em. I remember I did once, but I never would ag'in, if I was goin' back thar. It's too mean."

"What do you mean by saying 'If you were going back there?'"

"Now you's hit it, and I'll tell you. This morning I dressed the twins—they're Martha's—pulled Sammy—he's ours—out of the swill-pail and cleaned him up; heard Mollie crying and found her with her finger shut under the window and a pan of milk spilt over her; got dad's watch away from Jerry (Jerry he's Jemima's boy) and then started on a run after Willie and Pete down to the brook. My ma and the others' mas came out and scolded me for letting the children go, and they say I sassed 'em. I told 'em I wouldn't take care of children any more, and they said if I wouldn't I'd have to get another home. So I thought maybe I'd find some of these emigrant folks that would like a boy like me and that is what I's been up to this mornin'."

"Have you called on any of the other emigrants?"

"La! yes. One man told me I was a naughty boy and I must run home to my mother. At another place the woman said, 'What a horrible looking child,' and I didn't stop to talk with her. At another, the woman took quite a fancy to me, for I told her all my troubles, and I was a goin' to stay with her, but first I knew in come two or three children; then their noise set a baby to screaming somewhere in the house and I thought I'd better get out of there. Then I come here, and I've been here long enough to see your children, if you had any, and I seem to like here pretty well, so if you'd like to have me I'll stay and be your boy. My folks can spare me out of sixteen, when you haint got any, and I'll be a fust-rate boy. I can do any kind of work, and like all kinds, but minding children."

Here the boy paused, more from lack of breath to proceed than from any other cause. Marion really pitied him in his struggle for freedom. He seemed confident that he would be appreciated, and apparently thought this childless home would be benefited by his adoption. Marion quite disliked to undeceive him. She explained to him that, although she should no doubt like him very much, their circumstances were such that they could not do more than support themselves at present, and that she really did not need help, as her labors were not hard.

Johnnie looked very much disappointed and surprised, but was comforted by an invitation to remain to dinner, which he accepted, and soon proved that his troubles had not destroyed his appetite. He left Elder Northfield's house after dinner rather discouraged in his attempts at finding a new home and somewhat inclined to follow the advice he there received to return to his home and family cares.

In the afternoon another caller made an appearance. This time it was a little girl, plainly but neatly clad, with a very sober, pinched face, which would have been pretty had not sorrow, so painful to see in the young, been written there. She modestly explained that her name was Ella Atwood, and that she lived in the next cottage. Her mother had sent her to ask if she could be of any service to her new neighbors, and would have come herself, but Nettie was very poorly that day and she could not leave her. She would be glad if Mrs. Northfield would call upon her soon. Mrs. Northfield promised to call, and inquired who Nettie was.

"Oh," said Ella, "she is my sister, and she is going to die. She was married two years ago—and I remember how much William loved her, and how good he was to her; but now he has taken another wife and has treated Nettie very cruelly. The elders called her a rebellious wife and counselled William to leave her. The doctor says she has the consumption, but mother says Nettie is dying of a broken heart. Mother has tried to have William come and see her, and he has promised to come, but Nettie says he will not come till too late."

"Has your father more than one wife?" Marion could not help asking.

"Yes; father has two wives; but he is kind to us all, though mother has not been the same since his other wife came. She never sings now, and so often says to me, 'My poor little Ella.' I wonder at that, for father's other wife never troubles me any, only as I see mother is more unhappy when she is near. Mother never goes to walk now with father, because she does not like to go with his other wife. They do not seem to like each other, but now she has been very kind to Nettie, and I think mother likes her better."

"Have you a brother or sister besides Nettie?"

"No, ma'am; no real brother or sister since Neddie died. He was my baby brother; but now the other wife has a baby, and I play with him a great deal. He is very fond of me, but mother does not seem to love him at all. I thought she would after Neddie died, but she never pets him. She is willing I should, though, and I'll bring him some time to see you if you would like me to."

Marion assured the child that she would like to see the baby—"father's other wife's baby"—and Ella soon departed.

That night Marion and her husband had much to say to each other of the events of their first day of life in their new home. Elder Northfield had found it more difficult to obtain employment, with comfortable wages, than in England, and had been obliged to accept an engagement which promised hard work and but a small income. Marion, however, felt thankful for even that, and told her husband that if their income was small their expenses were also in the same proportion.

He was not in the best of spirits, for in his intercourse with the native brethren he had missed the warm, brotherly feeling that characterized the saints in England. Religion, too, which he had expected to find engrossing almost the entire thoughts of the people in the city—the great centre of Mormonism, and the place chosen by God for the revelation of his will towards men—was certainly not the subject first in the minds of the people. Marion, too, was not at all reassured by what she had learned in one day of the effects of polygamy. Little Ella's call had left a gloomy impression on her mind, which she could not shake off.

One day soon after this, as Marion seated herself by the only window which looked toward the centre of the city, she saw a small procession coming down the walk, consisting of—first, a woman, drawing a clumsily-made little cart, containing a baby; next, two other women, very similarly dressed, and last, a woman, leading a very small boy. They proved to be on their way to her house to call upon the newly-arrived elder's wife. Among the Mormon women the emigrants from time to time arriving in the city were objects of much interest. Friendly calls upon them were immediately in order by these fortunate females, whose domestic cares did not make this impossible, or whose hearts were not too full of their own sorrows and troubles to seek out others. Marion's callers belonged to this class, and as they approached, cheerfully chatting together, she thought "surely these are not women whose lives have been associated with polygamy." But to her surprise, as they entered and the leading one introduced herself as "Mrs. Smith," she turned and said: "This is the second Mrs. Smith, Ellen we call her, this is the third, Josephine, and this is Mrs. Ruth Smith, the fourth wife of our husband."

Whatever embarrassment Marion would otherwise have felt in confronting together the four wives of one man, the perfect composure of the speaker put and kept her at her ease. The other wives joined the first in conversation, and all were very sociable. The baby and small boy came in for their share of attention, the baby's mother, Mrs. Josephine, dwelling particularly on its attractions. At length one of her visitors asked Marion where the other wives were, or was she the only one yet? Marion could scarcely conceal her repugnance at the thought, as she replied, "Yes, I am the only wife, and expect I always shall be. My husband, though a Mormon, is not a polygamist, and never will be."

"Indeed! Indeed! But I think you are mistaken, Sister Northfield. If he is a Mormon, he is, or will be, a polygamist." "You surprise me," said another; "how can you know what your husband will be?" "I fear you are not rooted and grounded in the faith," said a third, and the fourth approached her, and sitting down by her said: "My dear sister, I once thought, as you do, that my husband would never marry another, and I did not wish him to, but here we are, four living testimonies to my mistake, and I have learned better than to wish it otherwise."

"But how can women live together as the wives of one man with anything but hatred for him and each other? Excuse me for asking, but you all seem to be very friendly, and I confess it is a puzzle to me."

"Yes, I see it is, and that is not strange. We should remember that it is something the Gentiles are quite unused to. And I have heard that you were brought up a Gentile."

"Yes; I have been a Mormon only a few months."

"O, well, you will soon understand why we are so contented in this way of living. It is part of our religion. We know it is right, and the more we advance our husband's interests and kingdom the higher place we shall have in heaven. Women should be perfectly submissive to their husbands and to the commands of their elders. Not that any of us have always been as resigned as we are now—and, to tell the truth, we never have lived entirely harmonious until lately. Indeed, Ellen and I used to almost hate each other; didn't we, Ellen?"

"Yes," replied Ellen, "but we have overcome that and are now very friendly. We both were very much opposed to Josephine, and Ruth, too, and altogether we four made each other and our husband a great deal of trouble, and I don't mind telling you that we were censured by Brother Brigham as rebellious wives."

"What has caused the change?" asked Marion, "and how long have you lived so peaceably together?"

"Only a year," the quartette replied, and then Josephine took up the thread of the narrative.

"The change was caused by a little black-eyed minx of sixteen, who coaxed and flirted around our husband until his head was turned, and although he had declared that he never would have but four wives,—and he can scarcely support them and all the children,—yet a few weeks ago he married this girl, and then I was thankful, as I was when Ruth was married to him, that I was not the first wife."

"Why were you thankful for that?"

"O, don't you understand? Well, I should remember that you are probably ignorant of a great many of our customs, but we will try to teach you. The first wife always gives her husband all his other wives. And Caroline has had to place the hand of each of us in our husband's, at the ceremony in the endowment house.[11] I did not think, by her appearance when she gave me to him, that she would ever be so good a friend to me."

"Well, about this last wife?" Marion inquired, for her curiosity was getting the better of her disgust.

"Yes, about her I was speaking. We were all perfectly agreed that no such person should come into our house to deprive us of our rights and domineer over us. In short, we perfectly hated her!"

"But you were saying that women should be submissive to their husbands, and that religion should make you live peaceably with the other wives. Why should you hate her any more than each other?"

"She is such a chit of a thing, not much older than his oldest daughter."

"Four wives are enough!"

"He robs us of what we and our children need to make her presents."

"There is no room for her in the house, besides, we hate to have our husband make such a fool of himself," the four wives chimed in chorus.

Mrs. Caroline proceeded to explain. "If she had been the proper person, it would have been different. But a little young thing, with no bringing up for work, and nothing but her red cheeks and black eyes, which some say are so handsome, but which look only bold and impudent to me. If he had even asked our consent, we should not disapprove so strongly of the marriage. If we had consented, and had been allowed to select his fifth wife, and needed her help in the house, and she were a plain, sensible woman, instead of the useless doll she is, and if our husband's circumstances had been different, it might have been very well. But we are unanimously of the opinion that it was decidedly wrong, and we pledge ourselves to show our disapprobation under all circumstances."

"But did you not feel the same with regard to your husband's taking his other wives, Mrs. Caroline and Mrs. Ellen?"

"Well, yes; that is,—I suppose we did to some extent, but we have no ill feelings now about it. But this is so entirely different. Such an outrage upon us all; and we are resolved not to endure it."

"Yes," said another, "and the new wife is finding her quarters not quite so agreeable as she expected. Not that we treat her badly, O, no! We never would do that! But we try to make her about as uncomfortable as we can, and as there are four of us, we have met with some success. Of course we do not do this when our husband is by to see it, but she brings her complaints to him, and then when he remonstrates with us, we tell him of her disrespectful treatment of us, until, really, if I did not feel it my duty to harden my heart, I should quite pity the man."

"But," here interrupted another, "we told him how it would be, and I guess he does not enjoy himself quite as well as he expected."

"Well, but what is your object in such a course? Why not make the best of it, now that it cannot be helped, and try to make yourselves and the new wife more happy, and live on good terms with her as you do with each other? Do you not think it wrong to treat her so?"

"It would be very wrong if it had been right for him to marry her. But he was not counselled to marry her, and there is another man who wanted her, and had been counselled by Brother Brigham to marry, and that man has only one wife. So you see that it is all wrong, and we are going to do what we can to right the wrong. First, we mean to make it desirable for her to live in some other house. If we get her out of the house, that will be one important step. Then we count on the help of the man who should have been her husband, and if we finally get her divorced, we shall then be all right again, and shall take good care not to get into another such mess."

"We very seldom," said Mrs. Caroline, "speak of our domestic life to others, and especially to strangers, and we never would have confided all this to you, but felt it our duty, as you appeared to oppose polygamy, and I, for one, wished to convince you of your mistake. Now you can see for yourself how agreeably we four wives live together, and what a happy family we should be if only we were rid of this fifth wife. There is such a thing as carrying things to excess—even polygamy."

"But we have spent a long time in convincing you that polygamy is right, and almost forgotten our errand," said Ruth, who was less talkative than her sister wives, and more personally interested in their errand.

"Yes," said wife number three, "and I hope you will not think we are asking too much, but will you be kind enough to let us see your best bonnet and most stylish dress, and if you have any late fashion books, will you lend them to us? As you come directly from the Gentiles, of course you know what are the latest styles, and here we do not get them till they are old. Our husband has bought his new wife a very fine suit, bonnet and all. The bonnet was made by our best milliner, and the money should have been used for the benefit of us and our children. The brazen-faced thing looks so fine and proud, as she goes with our husband to church, that we are resolved to take her down. Now with a little of your assistance in the matter of taste and style, we can get up a suit for Ruth that will be finer than hers. We will buy the goods on credit, and order the bills sent in to Mr. Smith. Ruth will look far finer than she looks, dressed equally as well. She was always called handsome, and I like to imagine that girl's mortification and rage at seeing Ruth outshine her, and perhaps the bills will help bring our husband to his senses. Now, Mrs. Northfield, don't you think this is a good plan, and can you give us any assistance?"

Marion was now thoroughly disgusted with her visitors, and replied that she did not think it was a good plan, and that she could not assist them, for she had not followed the fashion herself since she became a Mormon, and supposed that giving up the world meant giving up its fashions, also. In England, that was what the elders preached.

"They preach it here, too, but they do not practice it," answered one of the four. "They all dress their last wife as fashionably as they can till they are tired of her. But if you do not mean to help us, after all we have confided in you, we had better be going. We should like to have you return our call with your husband and his other wives, when he gets them." And with this malicious remark, the four women, with their little ones, who had been alternately crying and laughing, during the visit, took their departure.

Marion breathed a sigh of relief, and mentally exclaimed, "If all Mormon women are like these, I never wish to see another."

But all were not like these, as she afterwards found, and many and strong became the ties which bound her to some of the women of Utah.

It had formerly been an earnest wish of Marion's to meet with the Mormon brethren and sisters in public meeting for worship in their stronghold Zion. She wished to hear the word directly from Brigham Young and the Apostles[12] themselves. Of late her desire to attend such a meeting was not caused by religious zeal and enthusiasm, but rather by a hope that in the meetings there might be something to counteract the feeling of dissatisfaction of which she was possessed with regard to her experiences of Mormonism, so far. She hoped that her faith might yet be renewed, and something of her old peace of mind return to her.

Elder Northfield, too, was eager to hear the words of wisdom from their inspired leader and the other favored servants of God. So they made their way on the first Sabbath after their arrival in the city to the tabernacle,[13] each anticipating a blessing from attendance there.

In the tabernacle was gathered the great body of Saints, with their wives, their children, and their whole households. Marion watched them as they entered, two or three, or often more, wives, with their children, following the head of the household up the aisle. Involuntarily she noticed the lack of courtesy in the bearing of the men towards the women. Those delicate little attentions and preferences in regard to seats usually accorded to women in Gentile society were wanting here, and they were left with the children to look out for themselves as best they might, except it might be some one wife who was apparently the reigning favorite for the time. She noticed the striking effect of the great variety of costumes of the worshippers, especially of the women. Some were clad in the plainest and poorest of clothes, with an utter disregard for taste or comeliness; others were well dressed in a quiet way, while a third class were conspicuous for their evident desire to outshine their sister worshippers in the display of gaudy clothing and a plentiful supply of jewelry, which was of necessity of the cheaper kind. This latter class showed that even the Mormon women were not free from that trait so commonly considered a feminine attribute. Brigham Young was the speaker, and every emigrant eye was riveted upon him as he arose. There was their inspired leader, their guide, their counsellor, their ruler. In him they now beheld the man whom God had chosen to receive his divine revelations and to present them to his people. Henceforth his word was to be law to them, and under his direction they were to devote all their energies to the up-building of the Latter-Day Saints. It must not be supposed that all were possessed of this fanatical state of mind. There were many exceptions, and Marion was one of them. But she was not entirely free from the awe with which her fellow emigrants listened for the thrilling words of exhortation or the inspired interpretation of the scriptures, as they expected to witness a display of the power of God surpassing that they had enjoyed in the meetings in England. But they were disappointed. Brother Brigham was very matter of fact in his discourse. It began with a request for money to be brought in to him with a lavish hand for some public works, and an exhortation to the brethren to greater diligence in laboring to support the church, and ended with remarks to the women of the church regarding obedience to its teachings, and to their husbands as set forth in the New Testament by the Apostle Peter, and instructions with regard to spending their husband's substance for the outer adornment of their persons and homes, instead of devoting it to the upbuilding of Zion. The sermon contained an exhortation to the newly-arrived emigrant to faithfulness, and was interspersed with bigoted remarks to the praise of the Mormon Church, and eulogies in bad grammar were attempted for the deceased leader of Mormonism, Joseph Smith, and his associates. Strong denunciations against the Gentile world were in order, and the whole discourse though from the lips of the great head of the church was far from meeting the expectations of those who now heard him for the first time. Marion was surprised and disappointed. She thought of the eloquent sermons delivered by her own husband in England, carrying conviction to every heart. She thought of the earnestness and Christian kindness towards all men, which was noticeable in them, of the intelligence and force with which his arguments were presented, and felt that her husband and many another elder might have edified and strengthened the Saints to a much greater degree than Brother Brigham had. She had come hoping to be strengthened in the faith, but went away more unbelieving, if that were possible. Marion could not confide her every thought to her husband with the freedom of a few weeks ago, for with his faith in Mormonism—the Mormonism as he knew it in England without the doctrine of polygamy—still unshaken, he could not sympathize with her in her disbelief and dislike of what she here saw and heard. It troubled him that she could not shake off her depression of spirits and again rejoice in her faith in their religion. And Marion, as she noticed this, gradually became in one respect like most of the Mormon women, keeping her thoughts and many of her troubles locked in her own heart. Her husband was ever kind and indulgent towards her, and his devotion was unflagging. In their own home together they spent many happy hours, and Marion wrote a very reassuring letter to Elsie, which gave the latter much comfort, as she looked with fewer apprehensions toward the future years of Marion's life.

Marion's domestic duties had kept her at home quite closely for the first few days after her arrival in the city, and she really had little desire to go out of it, for there peace and domestic happiness reigned whatever might exist beyond. She had learned enough of polygamy so soon to cause her to shrink from a further encounter of its effects; but she knew she must become accustomed to its sights and sounds, and so one morning she set out for a walk in the city. On one street, where the poorer classes of Mormons lived, she passed a miserable cottage, or hut, where—as was common among that class—the family, large or small, lived in two rooms. Several children were engaged in an excited quarrel over what appeared to be a small kitten. Two or three were crying most vigorously with grief and rage, and struggling with each other for the possession of the kitten, and all were indulging in excited and angry exclamations.

At this crisis the door of the hut opened, and there appeared upon the scene a woman, clad in a dirty and ragged dress, and with features sharpened by poverty and trouble. She advanced to the scene of warfare and proceeded to settle the difficulty by separating the combatants and distributing blows right and left; then took the much-enduring kitten and gave it to a small girl who had stood one side and taken no active part in the proceeding. By this time two other women had emerged from the house and joined the group, and Marion had come near enough to see that the eyes of one were swollen with weeping. Altogether the three females presented anything but an attractive appearance. The hard lines about the mouth, the look of misery and defiance in the eye, and sullen, hopeless expression of the whole countenance, impressed Marion vividly. They sided each with those children who seemed to belong to them respectively, and the quarrel was continued by the three mothers principally, the children ragged, dirty, and open-mouthed, watching and listening to the angry exclamations and fierce denunciations which fell from the lips of those mothers who should have rebuked their children by example as well as precept. Marion could hardly refrain from putting her hands to her ears to shut out the disgusting sounds, and hurrying past, she breathed more freely as she came into a street where a better class of people resided. She had not proceeded far when a boy came running after her, saying, "Marm! marm! I guess you've lost your pocket-book," and turning she reached out her hand to receive the lost article, which, however, she had not missed, and another boy of about the same size came up and snatched it away from boy number one. This one was much better dressed than the first, and had a look and air of importance as he clung to the pocket-book and said: "I was the one that found your money, ma'am. I see it drop, and was picking it up, when this boy that I never see afore run and snatched it away from me to give it to you."

"No, he warn't pickin' it up, neither; he was pickin' it open to git some money out fust, and I grabbed it then and run to you, and it's all right, ma'am, if you'll just look and see."

But the difficulty seemed to be in getting an opportunity to "look and see," for boy number two held on to the money in his anger with the grasp of a miser. After a word of persuasion, however, he gave it to Marion, then turned again to his newly-made enemy, who had dared him to fight, and said: "I guess you don't know who I am! I am Brigham Young's son." "And I guess you don't know who I am," returned the boy with ragged trousers and torn hat, and he drew himself proudly up with all the dignity and importance of a king's son as he added, "I am Brigham Young's son." The brothers stood abashed, and for a moment speechless in their astonishment, and Marion shared their sensations to such a degree that she stood with her eyes riveted on them. At that moment she recognized an elder whom she had known in England approaching on the walk. With him was a portly man with strong features and a pleasant expression. The former kindly greeted Marion, and stood speaking with her, while his companion turned to the well-dressed boy, who was somewhat cowed now, and exclaimed, "Jack, what does this mean? What are you and this ragamuffin doing here?"

"Why, father, he says he is your son!"

Brigham Young's face crimsoned, and the ragamuffin stepped timidly up to him and said, "Yes, sir, and please, sir, mother sent me—"

"Well, well, I hardly knew you, you have grown so fast of late; but don't come into the city again in such a rig as that. Why didn't you put on your best clothes, my boy?"

"I did, sir; please, sir, these are my best clothes, and mother sent me to tell you we've got a—"

"Well, well, I can't be hindered now; I'm in a hurry. Tell your mother I'll come and see her in a few days. Now run home. Come, Jack."

And here the prophet, priest, and king, the inspired man of God, joined his companion, who bid good-day to Marion, and walked on with Brigham Young and his favored son. The other son winked and blinked to keep the tears back, as he walked by Marion's side, at her request, and told her his story.

"Your mother had sent you, hadn't she, to ask Brigham Young to give you a new suit of clothes?"

"No, ma'am, she sent me to ask him to come and see the baby, and give her some things she needs."

"The baby! And how old is the baby?"

"Two weeks, ma'am, and father hasn't seen it yet; but when he does, I know he'll give mother the things it needs, for if it ain't crying, it'll look so cunning and pretty he can't help liking it, I know. Why, ma'am, you never saw so pretty a baby—such cunning faces as it makes up, and such pretty little hands, and such curly hair."

"How far from here do you live?"

"O, just out of town a mile or two."

"Has your father many wives scattered out in the country?"

"No, I guess not. Most of 'em live in the big house up yonder; but my ma says she ruther live alone with me and baby."

"But are you very poor? Is your mother suffering from want?"

"O, no! Not now, for the neighbors have given us things, and we have molasses on our bread, now, too. But mother thought father ought to know about baby, and I should had to a gone up to the big house if I hadn't a seen him. But, O, dear! ma can't have the things now, and most likely he'll forget to come and see about it at all."

The boy heaved a deep sigh, and Marion placed in his hand a piece of money, which she bade him give his mother, and tell her it was a reward for her son's honesty. The boy thankfully accepted it, and bidding her good-bye, turned in the direction of his home.

This was Marion's first personal encounter with Brigham Young. It did not give her a very elevated opinion of his character or of the results of polygamy. But all efforts on her part to regard Mormonism with favor, or to believe in its teachings, had ceased, and now all she could hope was in "getting used to it," as the elders said, and in freedom from it in her own home.

That same evening the elder she had met called upon them. Naturally they referred to the occurrence which the elder and Marion had witnessed in company that day, and Marion expressed her disgust with the system which left one wife and her children in the extreme of poverty while others enjoyed the luxuries of life; which caused a father to forget almost his children's very existence.

The elder replied, "Ah, Brother Brigham knows what he is about, and what is right, and no doubt this woman gets all she deserves."

This slightly angered Marion, and she said, "In the Gentile world no such barbarity could exist, save in heathen lands, and much less be spoken of in the contented way in which you speak of this poor woman."

"Hoity! toity! My dear sister, you take a good deal upon yourself to speak in that way. The sisters here never indulge in such remarks against their leaders, but learn submission and obedience, and I would strongly advise you to do the same, Sister Northfield."

"I will obey and submit to my husband, most gladly, and once I was ready to blindly obey any direction or counsel of any Mormon elder, but I confess those days are past. The knowledge you and the others imparted to my husband concerning polygamy, while on shipboard, has destroyed my faith in Mormonism and taken away my happiness, and were it not for my husband, I never should have been here. I am only happy now when in my own home, away from all sight or sound of polygamy."

"You will soon get over that. Indeed, I did not know you were so weak in the faith, or, rather, destitute of it, and I am very sorry, indeed, for Brother Northfield's sake, and your own, that such is the case. I advise you, as a friend, however, never to express such thoughts again, for I fear you will get into trouble. You show your ignorance of social life here, in speaking so boldly. You will call down the attention of the Apostles, and Brigham Young himself, and they have it in their power to make you bitterly repent of your rebellion against your religion. That is not all, nor the worst. You will lose all hope of eternity in the Celestial Kingdom, and be separated forever from your husband, who deserves and will have a place on the right hand of God."

"It may all be as you say, and I have not said much on the subject before, but in the few days I have been here I have had so many glimpses of the, to me, terrors of polygamy, of the sorrow of woman's life, that my heart is full, and in my indignation at your want of sympathy, I very foolishly, no doubt, expressed my feelings."

"If you have only seen the dark side of polygamy, it is time you saw the bright side, and I will show it to you."

"Is there a bright side to polygamy?"

"Come to my house and judge for yourself. I have four wives, sweet submissive women, happy and kind to each other, sharing the labors of our home, caring for their children and each other's children, in the kindness of their hearts. There are seven children, and as there are so many mothers, they can be cared for with ease, and all their little troubles and wants attended to. In the evening we all meet, and the children, always neat and clean, indulge in a merry play of some kind, the mothers fondly watching them, and the father sometimes joining them in their play. My family is my pride, and if you could have seen the welcome I received from them all on my return from England, you would say surely there is a bright side to polygamy. I love all my wives devotedly, and they return my affection, without any jealousy, believing that the more wives a man has the higher he, and they through him, will be exalted in the Celestial Kingdom. If you doubt this, I and my wives will be pleased to have you call upon us, with your husband, and see with your own eyes that what I have been saying is the truth."

"I most certainly shall call, Elder Atkins, for it will be a great pleasure to me to see such a picture as you represent. I have not yet seen one woman who seemed to be happy in polygamy, and I should be very much gratified to meet one."

"The reality, as you will probably find, sometime, will not be near so disagreeable as you imagine. I have known women quite as much opposed to polygamy as you are, to ultimately become quite contented in it. You should strive to conquer your prejudices, and believe that the authorities of the church are better judges of what is right and best for you, than you can yourself be, and allow me to say here, Brother Northfield," and the speaker turned to Elder Northfield, who had listened very uneasily to the turn the conversation had taken, "allow me to say that in my opinion the sooner you and your wife enter into this matrimonial state, the better for you both. I would respectfully advise—"

Here Elder Northfield interrupted him. He saw the flush of unwonted enthusiasm die on Marion's face, and in its place came the paleness of marble. Her quick breathing and expression of pain did not escape him, and he could hear no more.

He said, hurriedly, "Let us change the subject, if you please, Brother Atkins. It does not concern my wife and me, and never will, personally."

"As you wish. Brother Northfield; but ten years from now— yes, or even five—you will not tell me so."

Here the subject was dropped, and a decided coolness was felt by the three, until the guest departed.

"Marion," said Elder Northfield, as he seated himself by her side, and lovingly drew her to him, "I little dreamed you were feeling so bitterly about this thing. You surprised me tonight, but I hope you will be more guarded in future, my dear wife, for such sentiments expressed may bring us into trouble."

"Henry, is there any danger of our being forced into polygamy, as my aunt in New York intimated?"

"No, there is no danger of my ever being forced into polygamy. Cost what it may to me, I will never take another wife. Does that comfort you any, my wife?"

Marion wished to accept Elder Atkins' invitation, and accordingly she and her husband called one evening upon him and his family. The elder's account was, in the main, a truthful one, though Marion felt sure the faces of those wives were not those of happy women. In repose they had a sad, worn expression, which contrasted widely with their cheerful and almost gay manner in conversation. Truly they were kind and ladylike, cultivated and intelligent, and made a very agreeable impression upon their visitors. Marion enjoyed her call exceedingly, the more so as the children seemed so bright and attractive; but as the ladies invited her to repeat her call, she resolved to do so, and that too when neither of their husbands were present, to learn whether they were really as happy as represented or not, for from the expression of their faces she could not help thinking they were acting a part. At parting, Elder Atkins said to her in an undertone, "Have you seen the bright side or not?" Marion answered him evasively, and they wished their host and hostesses good-night and returned to their home.

Chapter 4

Marion embraced her first opportunity to call again on these ladies, whom she liked very much. She found only one of them at home, but did not regret this, for she felt much more free to converse with one alone; besides, this one was particularly attractive to her, as she was the youngest of the four—about her own age—and the last wife. She was kindly caring for three little ones whose mother had gone out, besides her own, a lovely boy of a few months old. The young mother was very fair and beautiful; but to-day there was no effort at gayety, or even cheerfulness. She seemed quite sad. Marion, rather cautiously, expressed her doubts and dissatisfaction with polygamy, and related part of the conversation which had occurred between her and Elder Atkins. She referred to the pleasure which her call that evening had given her.

"And did you think we were happy?" asked Elder Atkins' wife.

"You seemed so, and I thought if you really were I might look at things in a different light."

"Listen to me. When I married, I loved my husband so much that I thought I could be happy with him, even if his attentions were divided between me and three others. But I am not happy. I grieve to confess it but I do not bear the cross that all our women should bear cheerfully. I know it is wrong, and I pray God to forgive me; but I do so often wish I were the only wife, and these other wives—who I will say are the kindest and best of women—were only friends of ours. Then I know I should love them. I think they feel the same towards me, and I pity rather than blame them for it. I think every attention our husband pays to one wife or more causes a pang in the hearts of the others, and yet not one of us would be so selfish as to wish to monopolize all his attentions. He is very just and kind in his treatment of us, and shows no preference, and if we cannot be happy or affectionate, we can be kind, and we try to do every duty faithfully, hoping for our reward in heaven. We mean to be cheerful and hopeful before our husband and keep our sadness from him. I think he believes we are happy. He is very proud of his family. We sometimes confess our feelings to each other and kneel together in prayer, asking God to help us to submit, and patiently, even joyfully if possible, bear our cross together. We hope for forgiveness for all wrong thoughts and wishes, but in spite of all, I am wicked enough sometimes to wish the Gentile religion[14] were the true religion, for their family relations, as I have heard of them, seem to beautiful to me. But this, I suppose, is all selfishness. Brother Brigham tells us such wishes are selfish. As to our being happy, however, in this life, we each have a great deal of happiness in our little ones, and what is this life compared to life in the Celestial kingdom, where, if faithful here, we shall be eternally happy."

And the youthful face was quite radiant with hope and faith in the future, and the speaker seemed for the moment quite carried out of herself with enthusiasm, which was the first Marion had witnessed in the native women. She carefully avoided saying anything to disturb her friend's mood, and heartily wished that since she must be a Mormon, she, too, might be a Mormon in heart as well as in name. She felt, however, that if this woman's experience was the bright side, the dark side must be even darker than she had thought it. Undoubtedly Elder Atkins had chosen wisely in the taking of his wives, and it was his boast that he never knew them to disagree or exhibit any jealousy of each other. He knew nothing of their heartaches, their sorrows, and womanly longings for as much affection from their husband as they gave to him. He knew nothing of their constant sacrifice that he might not be annoyed, and in his heart he believed his wives were content. Marion never entered another polygamic home which seemed as happy even as this, and her impression gradually deepened that there was no bright side to polygamy.

Marion was quite surprised to learn that any such worldly amusement as dancing and theatricals were allowed and practiced by the saints. In England, although a lover of dancing, she had given up the ball-room and its associations for her religion, and was greatly surprised to learn that it was approved of and patronized by Brigham Young, and that he regularly attended the balls with his wives. She was not sorry, however; for her religious scruples never troubled her now, and heartily accepted her husband's proposal that they should attend the first ball after their arrival. She thought as she was dressing for this ball of the many merry times she had had in England, when, with Elsie, she, with a girl's love of making herself beautiful, had arrayed herself in her prettiest costume and passed many an hour in the pleasures of dancing. She had supposed all such earthly pleasures were past; but here she was preparing again for a ball, but under what different circumstances! She thought of Elsie as they used to assist each other in dressing, but who was now so far away. She thought of whom her probable partners in the dancing would consist, and her anticipations were clouded. Finally, Elder Northfield entered the room, and instead of finding her dressed, he found her with her face on her pillow sobbing like a child. She had given way to her feelings of homesickness that night, and though vainly trying to repress her tears, searched for something of her former finery, without, however, much hope of finding anything, for she had given everything of that description to Elsie. But there at the bottom of a large box lay a small one, enclosed in a wrapping of paper. Marion opened it mechanically, and what was her surprise to see a beautiful necklace, with jewelry to match! It was one which had been given her by a dear friend in England, and she supposed it was in Elsie's possession now. With the jewelry was a folded paper, containing an old-fashioned gold ring and these words: "I cannot take these, Marion, for some time I believe you will want them. Who knows but you may find them at just the right time to adorn your fair beauty for some festive gathering of the saints? Wear them, dearest sister, and be happy if you can."

Marion threw herself on to her pillow then and sobbed, though not entirely from grief. But at her husband's approach, she wiped away her tears and put on the ornaments, which she had once given up forever, as she had thought, and in her youthful beauty, brightened by her ornaments, and with all traces of her tears vanished, Elder Northfield looked at her with all a lover's enthusiasm as he said: "You are beautiful, my Marion! Take care that you make no conquests to-night."

"Never fear, there is no one here for me to conquer," she laughingly replied.

"Nevertheless, I predict that you will be the belle of the evening."

"Well, at any rate you shall not be neglected."

Elder Northfield's prediction was fulfilled in a certain sense. Marion fully intended at first thought of that ball to spend much of her time in cultivating an acquaintance with the ladies, for she was not prepossessed in favor of the Mormon men, and intended to dance but very little. She, however, found herself dancing in nearly every set with much more pleasure than she thought possible for her in dancing with Mormons. Her partners, however, she was able to select, and she accepted few but very young men, for she determined not to dance with any man who was liable to be neglecting his wife or wives by dancing with her. Her husband, whom she had "not neglected," watched her and the admiration she excited, and was truly proud of her beauty and grace. He had scarcely seen her so gay in spirits since they left England, and he fondly rejoiced in her apparent happiness. The women watched her, too, as she gracefully moved about, and some were envious of her. In justice to them, however, it should be said that many saw with gladness that one woman among them had not lost her youthful spirits or her fresh young beauty by sorrow. Brigham Young was there with several of his wives, and after dancing once with each of them, he considered himself at liberty to dance with whom he would. He sought the reigning beauty of the evening, whom he recognized as a witness of the quarrel between his two little sons, and honored her by asking her to dance with him. She refused him, as she had the other older men who had asked her. Her husband was shocked at her refusal to dance with their leader, who seemed very much astonished and not a little piqued. No native Mormon woman would have dared refuse a dance to the prophet, even if the great honor did not make it undesirable to do so, and Marion was slightly censured by a few ladies with whom she was on speaking terms, and later, by her husband, all of whom tried to convince her of her rashness. She told her husband privately that she did not wish to dance with polygamists, and certainly not with the greatest of them. The last hour before they left the hall Marion would not dance. She wished to watch the people, who were a study to her in their variety of costumes, moods, and manners. She did not fail to see that not all, and indeed few, were as happy as she, if their faces were an index of their hearts. The "wall flowers" were very numerous, and as Marion realized it, she felt guilty at having danced all the evening, while so many had scarcely danced at all. Many of them looked much more as if they had come to a place of mourning than to a place of amusement. Marion watched the long rows of women as they sat by the wall talking sadly together in twos and threes. There was no life, no animation, no cheerfulness, and, Marion thought, no hope on their faces. They could sit there and see their husbands, once so devotedly dancing attendance upon them, but now apparently unconscious of their existence, all absorbed in the charms of a later wife, or some maiden who had captivated the truant husband's fancy, and who would eventually possess a place in his home as well as his heart. What wonder they looked with sadness upon the scene and upon their own future? What wonder that every spark of hope and joy had died in their hearts? Why should they not solace themselves with the only comfort the ball-room gave them—the opportunity to tell each other their sorrows and comfort each other? Among this class at last Marion espied her callers, the Mrs. Smiths, or at least three of them, Caroline, Ellen, and Josephine; but where was Ruth? The former three were eagerly watching some of the dancers, and at last Marion, with difficulty, recognized Mrs. Ruth dancing with a man whom, on inquiry, she learned was her husband. Evidently the suit which was to eclipse the bride's had been manufactured, and Ruth was resplendent in it, and apparently had regained something of her former favor with her husband. Now, where was the black-eyed destroyer of the family peace? Marion inquired, and she was pointed out to her, dancing very contentedly with a much younger man than Mr. Smith. This was the man who "should have been her husband," and the four first wives were a little chagrined to see how little taken down the fifth was at Ruth's fine appearance. She manifested no resentment, no sense of neglect by her husband, or, indeed, any other emotion concerning the matter, and apparently was enjoying the evening very much. The sequel to this story may as well be given here. The plan of the four wives worked well, too well for the happiness of three of them, for Ruth became again the reigning favorite, something very singular in Mormon life, but resulting partly from a quarrel between the last wife and the husband, and partly from Ruth's great effort to attract and please. The man upon whose help the wives counted did not fail them, and the result was, as they hoped, a divorce,[15] which could always be obtained by paying Brigham Young ten dollars. But now a new trouble arose, for Ruth received all her husband's attentions to the entire neglect of the others. These attentions, however, were abundantly offset by the persecutions of the jealous sister wives, who had placed her in that position.

But to return to the ball-room. Marion had not seen her friend Carrie since their arrival in the city, and she was quite curious to know how she succeeded in carrying out her domestic plans. Carrie was here to-night dancing nearly every figure. At last Marion found an opportunity to speak with her, and the young wives were soon interchanging accounts of life in Zion. It seemed from Carrie's tale that the proverb was verified, which says, "The course of true love never did run smooth." "I never was so surprised in my life," she said, "as I was at the way Elder Parker's other wives received me. They would hardly speak to me, and when I attempted to assert my right as mistress of the house, they laughed at me and called me a child, and as such they have treated me ever since. They send me on errands, and somehow or other they make me go. I have nothing to say about how things shall go in the house, for when I gave any directions about anything they would proceed to work in just an opposite way. For instance, if I said we would have certain dishes for dinner, they immediately cooked something else. If I try to cook anything myself, they send me away, telling me they will do the cooking, and I may wash dishes, sweep, etc., for that is little girls' work. If I attempt to speak when we have callers, they immediately commence talking and drown my voice. In short, they treat me in such an insulting way that I am miserable, and why should they do it? I have never done the least thing in the world to injure them."

"Only to win their husband's affections," said Marion.

Carrie opened her eyes in astonishment at this, but did not reply. Marion inquired, "But why do you not go to your husband with your troubles and have them righted by his interference?"

"I have been to him and he tried to set things right, but they made him believe that I mistook even their kindness to me for ill-treatment, and now he says if I get into trouble with the other wives I must fight it out. He does not believe in interfering in such matters. But there is one way that I hope will bring me out of my troubles. I have half persuaded him to give me a house to myself, and even if I don't see so much of him, I shall not be tormented by his wives. I think he will do this for me, for he is very fond of me, you know."

"Well, Carrie, I hope he will do so for your sake, and for the sake of the other wives, for I really pity you and every other woman who is not the only wife."

Elder Parker soon came up to them, and after a few moments general conversation, they separated and returned to their homes. And thus had passed Marion's first evening in public society of Salt Lake City. After all, as she laid aside her ornaments and thought of Elsie, she felt that she would give all the pleasure of a hundred such evenings for one quiet hour with her sister. But she never could have Elsie again, and she must not think of her so much. She had given up all for her husband, and did not regret the sacrifice.

Chapter 5

Since her aunt had told her something of the early history of her friend, Elder Parker's first wife, Marion wished to visit her for her aunt's sake, and, if possible, be of some service or comfort to her in her trouble.

She had been in the city several weeks, however, before an opportunity was presented. But one day some acquaintances were going out into the country, and as their way was directly through the little village where she had learned that the forsaken wife lived, she accompanied them as far as the village, which was but a few miles out of the city.

She inquired of the villagers for the cottage of Mrs. Parker, and following the directions received, she made her way to the poorest dwelling place the village contained. Her own humble home seemed elegant by comparison. This one seemed scarcely more than a hut, with its low roof and two small windows. The yard was the redeeming feature of the place, for it was swept free from litter, and the grass was growing with all the thrift and verdure of the Salt Lake Valley. There were white cotton curtains at the windows, which, if ragged, were very clean, and pressed against the window panes were two small, pinched faces, with pale cheeks and large black eyes, which, with the locks of raven black hair that hung in a long curly mass down the shoulders of the girl, and the gaunt wistfulness of the boy, gave them a look of weirdness. Marion's summons was answered by the mother, a counterpart of the girl, except that the black eyes were sunken, the jetty locks abundantly streaked with grey, although the woman not yet passed her youth; the thin face had lines of misery and sorrow on it, and, altogether she had the appearance of more wretchedness than Marion had ever seen on the face of woman. Her eyes had a hunted look, and had a gleam of wildness in them that made Marion feel almost afraid of her. She very coldly but courteously invited her visitor to enter and be seated, offering her the only whole chair in the room. Marion felt that she was considered an intruder, and hastened to apologize for her visit by referring to her aunt in New York, and saying she had come hoping to cheer and comfort her, as she knew her aunt would gladly do, if it were in her power. She spoke of the love and pity with which her aunt had referred to the friend of her earlier days, and then it was that the cold stony look on the woman's face gave place to a softer expression, and pressing her handkerchief to her eyes, she wept without restraint. The little ones looked astonished and frightened, as though tears were strangers to their mother's eyes.

Marion gently stroked the bowed head, with its wealth of jetty and silvery hair, and said, "Forgive me, if I have made you sad. O, what have I done! I sought to comfort you, and I have only added to your grief."

"You have comforted me, do not think you have not. These tears are the first I have shed for many a month, but somehow they relieve my aching heart. Some of my misery seems to have gone with them. To know that one of my former friends, one of the friends of my happier days, even one whose counsel I heeded not, whose kind, loving entreaties I resisted, and thus ruined my life, both in this world and in the next—that she remembers me is a comfort, indeed. But tell me of little Lillian, the child I loved so, and whose nurse I was for three years. Let me think—how many years have passed since then? Sometimes I am confused and can't remember; but isn't she nearly grown, almost a young lady?"

"She was quite grown, and a beautiful girl, my dear friend; but a few months ago she was laid in the grave."

An expression of sadness came over the poor woman's face, but it was only momentary, and she remarked:

"There is nothing for which to mourn in that. I envy her the assurance that her child can never suffer a wretched womanhood. Perhaps I am wicked, but I often think as I look at my Edith, I would thank God to take her away from all misery and wickedness. And I have had times of terrible temptation, when I think I have hardly been myself, and have prayed God to keep me from doing anything dreadful. But what am I saying," she cried, excitedly, "and whom am I saying it to? Are you a Mormon woman or are you a Gentile? Gentiles seldom come here; but you do not look like the Mormon women. You look young, fair, and happy, except as I see your pity for me in your face."

"I am a Mormon woman, and yet I am not a Mormon, for I do not believe in their religion now, although I did believe it once, before I knew polygamy was a part of it. I have lately come from England with my husband and twin sister, whom I wish you might see."

Marion sought to interest her in other topics than her own troubles.

"Elsie is almost the image of the lost Lillian, aunt Wells says, and she has come to make her home with her. Aunt wanted me to remain with her, too, but—"

"And why didn't you? Why have you come to this infernal place—this hell upon earth? Why have you come to a place where women are little better than slaves; yes, even worse than slaves; where not their bodies, perhaps, but their very souls, their hearts, are crushed? Why were you deluded by their fanatical teachings and their falsehoods? Where and what is your husband?"

"He is in the city, and he is a Mormon. He still believes in the religion."

"Then God pity you! for he will break your heart some day, as mine has been broken."

"No, my friend," said Marion, though at the thought her heart sank, "my husband will never forsake me. A kinder, truer, nobler man never lived, and he has repeatedly promised me, by all that is sacred, never to take another wife."

"And you believe him!" exclaimed the woman.

"Yes, I believe him. I know others have been deceived, and many a man has made such a vow only to break it, but my husband is not like other men. He will be true to me, I know. He does not believe in polygamy himself, although a devoted Mormon in other respects."

"My poor child, poor child. I wish I had the same faith for you that you have for yourself. Now I see the secret of your happy face. You have hope. Other Mormon women have no hope. God grant you years of just such security as you feel now. I would not destroy your faith in your husband and make you unhappy, but I have known men just as noble and good, as you say your husband is, when they came here, but I never knew one to remain many years noble and good. When I married Elder Parker, I believe no nobler, more honorable man, than he, ever lived. He was deceived and deluded into believing in Mormonism, but he promised me never to enter into polygamy, and I believed him, and sacrificed everything for him. Look at me now, friendless and alone; look at my children, look at our home, and tell me if you wonder that I have no faith in the promise of a Mormon."

"Have you no friends in the village?" Marion asked.

"Not an open friend. No one dares to have much to do with me, for fear of getting into trouble, and I dare not speak un-guardedly, for the same reason. But still I am not entirely for-

saken, for the people show me great kindnesses, secretly. I have
for years kept my sorrows locked in my own heart, and now it
seems such a comfort to have one to sympathize with me, that
I can hardly refrain from intruding my sorrows upon you, and
asking you to help me about a matter that gives me some hope
for my children. I need a friend, and if you will be that friend
to me, God will reward you."

"I will be your friend, and will do anything in my power for
you, and in return I hope you will have perfect confidence in
me, and tell me anything that it will comfort you to confide in
me. Tell me of your life and troubles here, if you will."

"First, let me send my little ones away, for God knows they
are sad enough, at best, without hearing their mother's troubles."

She sent her children to play in the garden, and then resumed:

"I was alone in the world, my father and mother being dead,
and my only brother, who, though very fond of me, was in
California, and is there still. Your aunt gave me a home and
employment in her family, caring for and teaching her little
girl. She made me very happy, treating me more like an elder
daughter than like a governess. She cultivated my taste for music and books, and with her I went into the society in which
she moved. There I met a man with whom I might have been
this day living a happy wife. I know now that my heart was
not wholly my own, though I would not, at the time, have admitted it, even to myself. But Mormonism was then agitated
in New York, and, contrary to Mrs. Wells' advice, I went with
some young friends to their meetings, at first purely from curiosity concerning them.

"But there was something about their religion and their earnestness, that fascinated me, I do not know what. It seems to
me now that I could not have been in my right mind.

"I soon became acquainted with Elder Parker, a handsome young preacher, and my acquaintance with him grew into an engagement to marry him, not, however, without his most solemn promise never to enter into polygamy.

"When Mrs. Wells knew this, she tried by every means in her power to dissuade me from my purpose. She told me then that the young man of whom I spoke had asked her permission to pay his addresses to me. But it was all too late. I was completely infatuated with my new religion and my new friend. I left my old friend and benefactor with tears, and it seemed to me I could hardly part with darling little Lillian; but I came to Salt Lake City and married Elder Parker. He was very devoted to me, and I felt sure, as you do now, that though other homes were polluted by polygamy, mine never would be. But by and by he began to be out evenings a great deal, and when I asked him where he had been, he evaded replying. He seemed to grow so cold, too, in his manner towards me, and, after a while, he never played with our baby, or noticed him at all. If he cried, instead of taking him up and amusing him, as he had done, he would take his hat and leave the house. O! the sadness of my heart then, as I feared I was losing my husband's love. How I tried with all my power to win him back to me! How I exerted myself to perform a thousand little offices of love for him, as only the most devoted of wives will do! But he never knew it. He appreciated none of my kindness and devotion to him. Still, I did not dream that he had so soon forgotten his vow as to be seeking another wife. The truth was thrust upon me rudely enough. One of those creatures, who, being miserable herself, wished to see all other women miserable, said to me one day, 'How soon is your husband's other wife coming to live with you? He has been courting her quite long enough, I should think.'

"I told her she was altogether mistaken, my husband was not

thinking of taking another wife. We both became somewhat excited, and almost quarrelled, and she left me.

"After she had gone, I began to think of what had passed, and O! the misery of that hour, dreading to hear my husband's footsteps, yet longing for him to come and tell me my fears were groundless. Hundreds of little actions and circumstances, before unnoticed, recurred to me, all tending to awaken my fears that my visitor had spoken truly.

"Why had I been so blinded before! And ere the sun had set I felt almost sure, as it went down and its brightness faded, that all the brightness of my life had faded with it. But not quite sure: hope was not quite dead. At first I thought I would demand of my husband where he spent his evenings; then I resolved to wait and watch; but I did not have to wait long, for that very evening he coldly and cruelly told me that he had decided to take another wife. Then my heart turned to stone. I felt as though it were another woman asking him how he could break his vow so solemnly made. He answered 'that that was not now binding upon him, as the elders, apostles, and even Brigham Young, had plainly assured him that it was his duty to take another wife and live up to his privilege, as his circumstances were good, and that by so doing he would exalt both himself and me in the Celestial Kingdom. An earthly promise was inconsiderable compared to the duty of obeying heavenly laws. He was only performing a duty which was painful to him, as well as to me, and the less said about it the better.' Then my anger rose, and never was a woman more enraged than I. For the moment I was in a perfect frenzy of madness. I asked him why, if it was only a painful duty to take a second wife, he did not take her at once without neglecting his other wife week after week, and giving her only cold and often unkind words and devoting his entire time to the new wife. I told him that the alacrity with which he dressed himself with the utmost care, the pleasure noticeable in his preparation to visit his betrothed, and his constant attendance upon her, showed that he was performing this painful duty with commendable cheerfulness. Indeed, I said I never knew him to perform a painful duty so cheerfully, and I thought God would reward him, though not in the way he expected. I told him he was a base hypocrite to pretend that it was his duty. I told him that I regretted the day I ever met him; I regretted the day I was born; he had ruined my happiness forever. My anger then gave way to grief, and I burst into tears, and kneeling at his feet, begged and pleaded with him by the memory of our former happy life and home, by the love which I knew he had borne me and our boy, by all that was sacred in family associations, not to blight my life. I asked him to forgive my angry words and love me again and me alone. I promised him that no earthly means should be unused by me to make his life and home happy. It seems as though no man could have been cruel enough to refuse such pleading. But this man was. He coldly told me to get up and not behave in that manner; such tragic scenes would have no effect on him. I then rose from my knees and cursed him. I told him that I hated him more than I ever loved him. I said I would rejoice to see him suffer as he had caused me to suffer. But I told him I would thwart his plans. He never should have a second wife while I lived, for I never would place the hand of another woman in his in marriage ceremony, and I knew that was an essential part of the service. My reason was not jealousy then, for my love had all turned to hate, and it was my very hatred towards him that prompted my wish to give him all the trouble in my power. That was very little, however, as it proved. He then, pale with wrath, ordered me to my room, and threatened that I should find myself in greater trouble if I behaved in that way. I replied that there could be no greater trouble, that death itself would be happiness compared with it, but that I was glad that

he had suggested my leaving the room, as I had polluted myself and innocent babe long enough by remaining in the room
with such a devil as he—yes, I used the word; no word could
be bad enough to express my hatred of him—and catching my
babe in my arms I darted from the room. As I passed him, he
raised his arm, I think, to strike me, but he did not. I wished
he would—I wished he would strike me dead. I went to my
room, and there remained the most of the time for a week. I
prepared my husband's meals as usual, but never joined him at
the table. He did not see me or my boy during the week. He
probably never missed us, so engrossed was he in the attentions to his new duty. I was sure, however, that he could never
marry without first divorcing me, for I would never give him
a wife, and I knew he would dread the publicity and talk a divorce would occasion. None but a Mormon woman could know
what I suffered. I cannot tell it. No human tongue can tell. I
felt forsaken by man and by God. I hated everybody. I hated
God, and at times, even my little boy. I think there was never a
woman whose heart was more full of misery and fiendishness
than mine was then. I was a Mary Magdalene, but never have
I, and never can I, by the casting out of the wickedness within me, become the gentle woman she became. My heart was
hardened never to soften. I might say I have no heart. Well, in
about a week my husband called me to come down from my
room. I went. He had just come in apparently, and was dressed
in a new suit of fine broadcloth. He presented a very elegant
appearance. Beside him was a young woman, also well dressed,
and very good-looking. She, however, appeared nervous and
timid. He presented me, then, to his second wife, and delivered
a little speech regarding kindness in the family and the courtesy
due from one wife to another, and ended by saying he hoped I
would do my duty as a faithful wife should under the circumstances. It seems that he dreaded the publicity that he feared

might be given to our affairs, and the reproach of having a rebellious wife, and had flown to Brother Brigham for counsel.
He was then in good favor with Brigham, and it was arranged
the ceremony should be performed without my assistance, on
the plea that as I had so wantonly disgraced my religion and
marriage covenant, I was no longer worthy to be considered
Elder Parker's wife, and that he should then for the time being be considered a single man and be married as one. But if I
afterwards came to terms and submission, as no doubt I would
when I found resistance useless, then I was to be reinstated in
my position as first wife, and thus all disagreeable remarks and
notoriety would be avoided. Brigham was very accommodating
towards my husband, and were it generally known, no doubt
he would have gotten himself into trouble, for many women
would willingly be temporarily divorced to avoid the terrible
ordeal of giving her husband another wife.

"'Yes,' I said, 'I will do my duty towards her and towards you,
too. I will send you where you belong and will prevent her from
ever feeling the misery I feel now. If I had seen you die when I
loved you and you loved me, that would have been no trouble.
O, yes, I will be good to her,' and I shudder to tell it, but while
speaking I had seized a loaded revolver, which my husband kept
in a corner of an old secretary near me, and was raising it to aim
at his head, when I seemed to realize what I was doing and I
threw it on the floor, and was darting from the room, when he
seized me and dragged me to my room, hurting and bruising
me severely. He locked me in with my child. Days passed, and
I scarcely touched food or drink. A scanty allowance of bread
and water was doled out to us daily, but my babe ate most of
it, for I could not eat. God only knows why or how I was again
kept from a terrible crime. I could not bear, as my beautiful boy
played around me in his childish innocence, or slept in my arms
so pure and sweet, to think that he would grow up to break

some woman's heart—to change, perhaps, from a kind, honorable man to a man like what his father now was.

"I wanted always to think of him as pure and innocent as he was then; I could not if he grew up. Now, if he died, God would take him, and he would eternally be pure and free from sin and misery.

"I had a bottle of laudanum[16] in my room, and was almost irresistibly filled with an impulse to give him one last, long, eternal sleep. But God, if he had forsaken me, had not forsaken my boy, and something stayed my hand. And lest I should yield to temptation, I threw the bottle from my window, and saw it shivered to atoms on the stones below."

Here the speaker paused and pressed her hands to her burning brow. Then she pressed one hand to her heart, and Marion feared she would faint.

"My poor friend," she said, "don't tell me any more. It is hurting you."

"O, don't stop me! don't stop me!" she cried. "You don't know what you do. I must tell all. I must tell it all for their sakes," as she pointed towards the garden, where her children had gone. "Have you seen a large brick house on the side of one of the mountains, just out of the city?"

Marion replied affirmatively.

"Do you know what that building is?"

"No," said Marion, "I do not."

"Then I will tell you, for I know. It is where they carry the women when their miseries, and sorrows, and unutterable agony of mind robs them of their reason. When Brigham Young, by inculcating a system and religion that he says comes from God into the minds of his dupes, has ruined the lives, the hopes, the reasons of his subjects, one by one, he kindly provides a place where they can be cared for, away from the rest of mankind, where they will cease to annoy their unfortunate friends.

"His generosity is so great that the insane asylum is free to all, and its annual expenses are met by tithing the people to an amount far greater than its expenses. Any surplus, however, goes to the Church, and as Brigham is the Church, you see he is very generous.

"Well, after I saw the laudanum bottle in a thousand pieces, I remember nothing more till I found myself inside that building. When you come there I will take you into my room, for I shall go there again, I think, before long. You will come, too, though not for many years; but you are a Mormon's wife, you know."

Marion was now thoroughly frightened at the woman's words and manner, and tried to quiet her, asking her to finish her story at some other time, but she would not be interrupted, and went on.

"They were kind to me there, and after a while I realized that my baby was not with me. I asked for him, and they promised that next day he should be brought to me. And he was, but where he had been meantime I did not know, and do not to this day, nor how long I had been there. I think, however, not many weeks. The keepers are very careless there about keeping doors and gates locked, and one evening I wandered out unnoticed, and walked on and on with my boy, till I came to this place. A kind man, now moved away from here, befriended me and took me into his house, and his wife cared for me and nursed me through a sickness, during which I came near to death's door. When my strength began to come back to me, they came and laid in my arms my little babe—my Edith. From that time I have lived for my children's sake, and I have hope for them. When I recovered I took this cottage, or hut, as it is, in comparison to my former home, and the people of the village have very kindly given me employment enough to barely support myself and children. They can do no more, for they are poor themselves; besides they fear the wrath of Brigham Young.

Many of these women are kind and pitiful to me in secret, but their husbands warn them against me, as I am regarded a rebellious woman. I do not, or, rather, have not cared what I did or said to influence any one, Mormon or Gentile, against Mormonism, and they fear my influence somewhat, poor as I am. But I must say that I have opened my door in the morning and there found a pile of wood which I know no woman brought. I have found my house repaired, and by no woman's hands, on returning from a day's work out. I have found food and warm garments for my children on my doorsteps, and tracks of large feet in the snow near the door. I have been overpaid repeatedly for work by the Mormon men. Yes, thank God, there are some whose natural humanity and kindness of heart even Mormonism has not destroyed. I hate to think of the time when these men will have lost all the better part of their natures.

"But I must hasten with my story. The authorities at the asylum supposed I had returned to my home, but did not trouble themselves to ascertain positively. So Elder Parker did not know I had left the asylum till my babe was several weeks old and I was established in my new home, and then he did not trouble himself to inflict his presence upon me, for he was no doubt devoting all his time and attention to his new wife, as he had formerly been devoted and kind to me.

"At length, however, he came and informed me that I was practically divorced from him, which I very well knew. My own course had caused this result, as my conduct was beyond forgiveness. He soon left me, and I have scarcely seen him since; but I was told that he soon took still another wife, and then I wondered how much that pale-faced, frightened girl suffered. Not as I did, I feel sure, for she was not the first wife.

"I have of late lived in constant fear and apprehension of being robbed of my children.[17] While Elder Parker was in England, I breathed more freely; I have not been so guarded as I otherwise should have been, and I did not know that he had returned until one day, a few weeks ago, he came here, and I nearly fainted as I saw him look at my Edith, and stroke and caress her curly hair. He then threatened that unless I ceased to say such wicked things against the Mormon Church, he would punish me by taking away my children. He had Brigham Young's advice for so doing. I was terribly frightened, but I have since the day I first took my little girl in my arms, resolved that they should not grow up Mormons. My girl must never suffer as I have, my boy must never cause the anguish his father has caused. The friends who took me in, in my trouble, are still my friends, though many miles from here. They have apostatized[18] and are Gentiles now, and live in the southern part of the State. They have promised to take my children and keep them till some emigrant parties shall pass through their place, and they can send them to my brother in California. I have heard from him through them, and he requests me to send them to him, and he will rear and educate them with his own children. He also earnestly requests me to come, too, but that cannot be. All that I seek now is my children's safety from this hot-bed of iniquity and misery. Some day they will carry me back again to that house on the mountain-side, and then my children will come to you; they know the way into the city; and you will in some way see that they are conveyed to my friend, whose address I will give you. Will you—will you do this for me?"

And the woman paused, and her eager eyes searched Marion's face for an answer.

"I will with all my heart," said Marion.

"And you must do it as secretly as possible, lest their father learn of it and prevent it."

Marion assured her she would fulfil her trust to the best of her ability.

"I do not think," said the mother, "that Elder Parker cares

enough for the children to wish for them, as his family is already so large. I only fear that he will take them to prevent their ever going to the Gentile world. Mormons hate apostates with a dreadful hatred, and there has been a time when to apostatize was to risk one's life. There is too much to be told of Mormon life by an apostate Mormon to allow him to enter the Gentile world, and only Elder Parker's almost perfect indifference to me and my children gives me hope that they will escape without his knowledge. I have trained them up to hate Mormonism, and have tried to give them all the knowledge of the ways of the Gentile world that I could, but that is of no avail if they remain here. Edith will be forced to marry, and Francis will grow up a Mormon."

"But," said Marion, "since your brother has so kindly offered you a home with him, why do you not go with your children and live the rest of your life peacefully? Why stay here and be so miserable? Or, if you can find a way to go to New York, I know my aunt will receive you and yours with joy. She would only be too happy to save you from this life, and have you with her again. Won't you let me write to her about you?"

"No! no! I will not! You must not think of escape for me. I do not want to enter the Gentile world again. It would only make me more miserable. There is no happiness for me anywhere in this world or in the next. Why I am a murderer, did you know it? I wanted to take two lives, and nearly did. I am a murderer at heart. *He* has made me one. I was good once. I was kind once. I never spoke an unkind word to him till—till—I told you when. No, such a woman as I must stay where misery is at home. My brother must never see the wreck his sister is, and I would not go back such as I am now to burden your aunt after leaving her as I did. Besides, I *could not* escape and my children, too. He would find it out if I attempted so much, and we should all be brought back. But if anything should happen to me, he very likely would not know it; and if he did and were told that friends had taken the children, I think he would not interfere or burden himself with their support. I shall not be here long. I may be in the asylum; I may be in a narrower asylum. But wherever I am, if you know, don't let him know. I don't like the way he looked at Edith. I am troubled with fear that if the children remain here long he may get them away from me and then they will be lost. I had rather see them dead. Yes, dead!" she cried wildly, and Marion was again frightened at the gleam in her eye and the wild tones of her voice. At last her mind seemed to be relieved, as she had told her story, and as Marion assured her that she would fulfil her request, she seemed satisfied and sank back into her chair exhausted by her excitement. Marion then told her of Elder Parker's last wife, of whom she was ignorant, and gradually led the conversation to other subjects, telling her of all that had happened in the city recently that she thought would interest her. Marion secretly resolved to write to her aunt, informing her of her friend's circumstances and state of mind, that she might persuade her to leave Utah.

She did not wonder now at her aunt's horror of the Mormons. She felt alarmed at the wildness of the woman's manner during her story; and then how she longed for the means to make her and her children more comfortable, but her husband's income would scarcely supply their own wants. She could only give her kind words and sympathy, and amusement to her children by telling them story after story, till their wan faces glowed with interest and amusement. But these attentions were worth more than money, and the mother received that for which she hungered—as she had never hungered for bodily food—heartfelt sympathy and promise of help in the fulfilment of the greatest wish of her heart. The few hours still left before her departure passed rapidly, Marion striving by every means in her power to interest and please her hostess. The children showed her their little gardens, and were delighted with the interest she took in them, and altogether, that day was remembered by mother and children as an oasis in the desert of their lives.

When Marion and her husband sat down that evening for their usual chat, she rehearsed the events of the day and repeated the story she had heard, and reminded him of what he had said in New York about there being two sides to the woman's story. But he could not believe that Elder Parker would ever treat a wife so cruelly, and thought her mind was in such a disordered state that she did not know what she said. Marion was grieved to find that he disapproved of the part she had promised to take in getting the children away from Mormonism. But as the scheme was probably but a fancy of a disordered mind, and Marion was so anxious about it, he kindly promised at least not to interfere if the opportunity ever presented itself, which he did not expect.

Chapter 6

Marion saw so many children of all sizes playing about the streets at all hours of the day that she at last inquired why they were not at school and where the school buildings were. She had not seen one there. She was told that there were no schools; that Brother Brigham did not approve of educating their children. They were to be unlike the world's people—not seeking worldly wisdom, but wisdom from on high. It was sufficient for the girls to be taught reading, writing, housework, and needlework, and the boys should go so far as to learn a little arithmetic. The parents were expected to teach them, but especially to instruct them in the religion of the Church. Schools had been attempted, but had been broken up or given up, because the parents were counselled to keep their children at home. Education was a stepping-stone to apostasy. The leaders knew this, and did not mean that this stepping-stone should be furnished the people. The theatre, however, which was a much-patronized institution, was a source of education in itself to the people. For there scarcely any but Gentile plays were acted, and on the stage was depicted Gentile life, domestic, social, and public, which had its charms to those who knew personally nothing but Mormon life, and doubly so to those who had come from homes pure and sacred to one wife and mother to homes where polygamy reigned. The theatre, if a pleasure to the Gentile world, was to the Mormon world like a glimpse into some far-off land, which to many seemed like a paradise, to others like the home of their earlier days, and to still others it had no meaning, save the amusement of the hour.

The theatre fostered a taste for reading on the part of the young, but that taste could not be gratified, for there were no books to be had, save a few concerning the doctrines, rules, etc., of the church. If books were brought in by Gentiles, the authorities suppressed their reading, and in some cases even destroyed the books. Any one seeking an education was sneered at and ridiculed; in fact, education was very unpopular.

But in spite of all this, Marion conceived the idea of gathering as many children together as she could for the purpose of a school. She meant to be very wary about it, and began by having them come to her two or three hours each day for the purpose of learning to sing. She was actuated by a desire to benefit the children, whom she felt should not be left to spend their time in the streets learning mischief and viciousness, by the hope of increasing their income, if ever so little, and by her love of teaching.

She readily obtained Elder Northfield's consent to her project, and easily found twenty-five children who were glad to come and whose parents were glad to send them to her. Little Johnnie Mordaunt was one of the number, and her young neighbor, Ella Atwood, another. Ella by this time had become a frequent visitor and often came with "father's other wife's baby." If Marion found her young flock composed of a great variety in respect to size, disposition, culture, and natural refinement. Some were almost unmanageable in the exuberance of their delight; but through the influence of story-telling and singing, she was able to quiet them all and send them home the first day very much interested in the new institution and ready to sound the praises of their friend and teacher.

The school grew and progressed, until her little home was full to overflowing, and she worked with all her might to teach them what she could. No children were ever more eager to learn than they. She felt that she was rewarded for her work by the pleasure of hearing them sing, although rude and inharmonious voices were mingled with the clear and sweet tones of others. They were also slowly learning to read, and she gave them as much general information as she could and dared. Marion took a great deal of pleasure in her new enterprise, and soon loved many of her pupils very much. She had begun to feel quite secure in being unmolested by the authorities, when one day her husband returned and told her that he had been visited that day by Brigham Young and counselled to put an end to the school that was in progress at his house. Said Elder Northfield, "He told me that he had heard my wife was very weak in the faith, and asked me if it were so. I could only reply that it was. Then he said, 'I am very sorry for your sake, and for hers, too; but she must stop that school. We want no woman with Gentile faith or inclinations teaching our children. They take naturally enough to the ways of the world without help in that direction.' He seemed a good deal vexed with me for allowing you to teach the children, knowing as I did that you were not a good Mormon. I am very sorry, my dear, for I see that you have taken so much pleasure in it, and I really think it a good thing for the children; but Brother Brigham does not know what you may be teaching them, and there is nothing to do but to send your children home when they come to-morrow, and really, Marion, I think it is for your good to do so, for I fear you have overtaxed yourself. You have worked very hard—too hard for your strength, I fear."

Marion was very indignant and very much disappointed, but, as her husband had said, there was nothing for her to do but to submit. So very sadly she parted with her little flock the next day and some of the little ones cried bitterly because they could not come to school any more. But she had made warm friends for herself among the little folks, and they never forgot her or ceased to love her.

Soon after the closing of the school Ella Atwood came running into Marion's house, exclaiming, "O, Mrs. Northfield! Please do come home with me; Nettie is dying!" Mrs. Northfield had become acquainted by this time with Mrs. Atwood and her daughter Nettie, who had been wasting away with consumption. Both mother and daughter were women of refinement, and their companionship had become a pleasure to Marion. She made haste to return with Ella to the sorrowing home. There the second wife by every means in her power was kindly assisting the first in her efforts for the dying sufferer's comfort, and the first wife's child was caring for the second wife's baby. Kindness and good-will reigned there; but it was not a result of Mormonism—it was in spite of it. There are noble instincts and pure emotions whose brightness cannot be obscured by even that dark cloud—polygamy.

Marion pressed her lips to the marble forehead of the dying girl, and the eyes opened with an eager, expectant look. They feared she would not speak again, but she said, "I thought he had come. He will come. I will wait for him." She closed her eyes again. Her breathing became more labored. There was a sound of wheels at the door and a strong young man, with a look of remorse and grief on his face, entered, and kneeling by the bedside, took one emaciated hand in his, pressed it gently to his lips, and exclaimed: "O God! I have killed her!" She opened her eyes and smiled. She beamed on him a look of unutterable love and murmured: "I knew you would come; I waited for you."

"O, Nettie, my darling, my own dear wife! Would to God I dared ask you to forgive me! I did not mean to be cruel to you. I did not know what I was doing. I love you and you alone. I was only infatuated for a time with the other"—; (he did not say wife). "Nettie, my sweet wife, can you forgive me?"

She reached up her frail arms, and, clasping them around his neck, drew his face down to hers. Then her arms dropped—and Nettie was dead. But that her last moments had been happy ones there could be no doubt, for on her face was a look of perfect peace, and her lips were almost wreathed with a smile.

There came a time when Marion could no longer go to the homes of sorrow and mourning, carrying pity and comfort with her—a time when her little friends, who came often to see her, were sent quietly away—when the rooms of her cottage were darkened, and the footsteps about the house were light and voices soft and low. There came to that humble, but happy home, a new light, a new care, a new and strong tie, to bind yet firmer the hearts of husband and wife. And as the young mother beheld her baby boy, a new tenderness came into her heart, a new joy into her life, and to the father his home became more sacred, more dear for the new treasure it contained.

Marion's life in Salt Lake City had not been the happy one she had pictured for herself, for her surroundings had been such as to cause great sadness through her sympathy for the sorrows of others. That such an evil should exist under the name of religion; that the Government would permit a system so wicked to enslave the minds of men and blight the happiness of women, and more personally that her husband should still be blinded by a belief in a religion which had proved itself so utterly devoid of morality and humanity—these things had given Marion many a bitter thought, many a heartache. She longed that the scales might fall from her husband's eyes, and that he might see as she did the utter depravity of the religion she had once loved so dearly; then together they might leave this people and once more live in the Gentile world. Her former ties of friendship might be renewed, and the society of her sister again become a pleasure to her. But of all this she had no hope. Thoughts and longings for it were all she indulged herself.

But now her mind and heart were filled by her care for her little son Forest. Her home, with its priceless treasure, was the centre of her ambition. There she forgot the outside world, with its sorrows and disturbances, and lived in a little world of her own. She became much happier than before her babe was born, and their comfort and happiness was increased still more by an improvement in their pecuniary circumstances. Elder Northfield went into business for himself in the city and succeeded even beyond his hopes. In later times Marion often accused herself of selfishness at that time in driving every unpleasant thought from her and giving herself up so entirely to the enjoyment of her own blessings to the exclusion of everything else.

But one unselfish mission was not entirely excluded—that was, the fulfilment of her promise, if ever it became necessary, to the forsaken Mrs. Parker, with regard to her children. It was far from her thoughts, however, one day, when she found at her door Francis and Edith Parker, more thin and haggard than ever, and with a somewhat ragged, neglected appearance, which had not been noticeable when she saw them before. She was shocked and frightened at sight of them, but gave them a warm welcome, and proceeded to open one of two letters, which the boy handed her, and read the following:

MY DEAR KIND FRIEND:

I cannot live any longer. I am not going to the house on the mountain side. It is too large. I want rest. I want my children safe. I have tried to think and plan what you shall do with them, and how you will save them. I know you will save them from Mormonism somehow, for you have promised me, but I have forgotten how. My memory is gone. But it will not be in the way I save myself, I know. I have been sick, but I am going to take some medicine that will cure me. I shall not be a Mormon woman then. I shall not be here, but! don't let him know I am gone. I don't know where I shall go, or I would tell you; but God bless you and the children, and some time, when Edith is a happy woman and Francis a noble man, I will go and see them and know what you have done for them and me. I wanted to write something else, but I can't think what it was. My memory is poor. Perhaps I will write again. The children will bring it to you. Now good-bye.

There was no name signed, but Marion well knew who the writer was, and realized the awfulness of its import. She knew the woman's reason had quite departed, and that she would, if not prevented, put an end to her life. She trembled, but controlled herself enough to question the children. She asked what their mother had said to them as they came away.

They answered that she had told them to carry her letter to Mrs. Northfield, in the city; that she bid them good-bye over and over again, and kissed them and cried over them, and even called them back once to put her arms tight around them both, so that they could hardly breathe, and then she had said, "God bless and keep my darlings," and they came away frightened. They thought their mother was sick, and had sent for Mrs. Northfield to come to her.

She then asked them about the other letter, which she now opened.

The boy said a few weeks ago she had told him if ever he went into the city he must take that letter to Mrs. Northfield, for she wanted it, and as he knew where she kept it, he took it, put it in his pocket, and brought it with him. He did not know what it was.

It proved to be a letter from the apostate friend in Southern Utah, urging her to come to him, with her children, as secretly as possible, that he might send them all to her brother in California. It was expected that in a few weeks an emigrant party would pass through the place, travelling towards the West, and he wished her to join that party. He spoke of her brother's kindness and love for her, and of his probable disappointment if she did not avail herself of this means of escape. Enclosed in this was a letter from the brother to his sister, which proved the sincerity of all that the former had written.

Marion felt that something must be done immediately. She told the children to remain in the house, and she would see about caring for their mother. She bade them on no account to leave the house or to be seen at the windows. She provided them with food and drink, and bade them not to be frightened if she did not return to them that night.

Wonderingly, they promised obedience, and Marion left them, taking her babe with her. She proceeded immediately to her husband's place of business, told him what had occurred, and placed in his hands the letters the children had brought. He was forced now to admit that the story—at least a part of it—that the unfortunate woman had told his wife was not the fancy of a disordered brain, and that the Gentile friend and brother in California were realities. But the children at his house—children of a Mormon elder! his wife about to conceal their whereabouts from their father, about to send them privately to the Gentile world! His wife instead of building up the Church performing an act directly to militate against it! The situation was appalling. Elder Parker's first wife insane and perhaps destroying herself, and he ignorant of it and of the whereabouts of his children! His duty seemed plainly to be to inform Elder Parker of the circumstances, deliver his children up to him, and advise him to see that the poor woman was cared for, and this he tried to persuade Marion was the right way for them to act in the matter.

But she was almost frantic with grief and horror at the thought, and reminded him of his promise at least not to interfere with the fulfilment of her word to Mrs. Parker. At last, at her earnest entreaty, he left his business, and procuring a carriage drove with Marion rapidly to the humble home of the suffering woman.

Two or three women and a physician emerged from the house as they approached. They stopped to speak with the physician and make inquiries.

"Are you this woman's husband, sir?" said he.

Elder Northfield was thankful that he could reply negatively, but said that they were friends.

"If you were, I was about to suggest that you immediately retrace your steps, as her greatest trouble is the fear of his presence and his possession of her children, who she says are safe with friends in the city. At least she should be allowed to die in peace."

"She has taken poison," he continued, "and cannot live but a few hours. She is conscious at intervals, and evidently perfectly sane, which has not been the case with her of late."

He would recommend that her most earnest request be complied with, namely, that Elder Parker should not be informed of her death, and that every means be taken to prevent the fact from coming to his ears. The villagers would aid her in that, and kindly and quietly give her a burial there. The physician passed on, and tremblingly Marion entered with her husband.

Two women made way for her, and she kneeled by the dying woman's bedside, but she was unconscious. She soon, however, opened her eyes, and now the wild gleam of a few months past was not in them, and a smile of recognition lighted them, but she was too weak to speak, save in short, faint whispers.

Marion beckoned her husband to approach. He did so, and she turned to the woman and said, "Here is my husband, and we have come to try and help you. Your children are at my house, and are safe."

"Will *he* help me?" And she bent her searching eyes on Elder Northfield as she gasped the words.

"Yes, my poor woman, I will help you. What can I do for you?" said he, so touched by the sight that he could not refuse her.

"Keep them away from him," she said, with great effort.

"I will, if possible, and will see them safe with your Gentile friend, though my conscience tells me I am interfering with what I should not, and doing wrong, but for your sake I promise that your children shall leave the Mormons if I can accomplish it."

"God will bless you," she said, and she never spoke again. She sank into a stupor from which she did not rouse, and soon her sorrowful life was at an end.

But who shall say that this woman was a self-murderer? Who shall say that she was not a victim of polygamy rather than of her own hand? Who shall say that the sin of her death lay not rather at the door of a false religion than to her charge? May it not be that a pitying God, a loving Father, saw her infirmities, had compassion on her weakness, and tenderly gave her rest and peace where sorrow is unknown, where "the wicked cease from troubling and the weary are at rest?"

Elder Northfield and his wife left the dead to be cared for by the kind women of the village, and hastened home to care for the living and fulfil their duty to them. Elder Northfield was terribly harassed in mind. His conscience reproached him for having promised to perform an act which would be treason to the Church and to one of its elders. He considered it a sin to aid in sending any one from the Church into the world, thereby ruining the salvation of the soul. He was as ever a very devout Mormon, and duty had always been law to him. Conscientious in the extreme, yet with those dying eyes looking at him so pleadingly, those ice-cold lips making one last earthly request, humanity conquered his fanaticism, and he could not refuse. Little did he think when he left the city with Marion that he should return to take the responsibility into his own hands, which he had been so shocked to learn she had undertaken.

But by the memory of that dying mother he could not betray his trust, and accordingly next day arranged his affairs to leave in other hands during his absence, and prepared to start in the evening with his young charges, to place them himself in the possession of their Gentile protector.

But he was saved the commission of this sin against the Church and his conscience kept free from guilt, and Marion was called to meet one of the greatest disappointments she had ever known. Elder Parker, in spite of the precautions taken to the contrary, learned of the death of his wife, through some means, and soon proved that his indifference to her children was not so complete as she thought. He learned that the villagers were about to bury her, and did not consider himself under any obligation to interest himself further, but sought to learn where the children were. The people of the vicinity could only tell him they were with friends in the city, that a man and woman named Northfield had been there, and might know where they were. He repaired to Elder Northfield's house, arriving in the evening while he was out making arrangements for an immediate departure. Marion was wrapping up the little ones warmly for their journey, when on answering the summons at the door she was confronted by Elder Parker. He made his object known, and Marion's hope was gone. She thought of the poor mother's anguish through fear of this event, and wondered if in the other world she now looked down and beheld what was transpiring.

She boldly pleaded for the children, depicting that mother's sorrow and misery, and hoped to touch the heart of her listener. She begged that the dying request might be granted. She argued that he had children enough and to spare, and begged that these two might be allowed to go to the home so amply provided for them. Her arguments were of no avail, though she was glad to notice his evident uneasiness at hearing of his wife's sufferings. He manifested much anger towards her for the part she had taken in the proceeding, and she generously and skilfully contrived to make it appear that she was the principal offender in the case, that no blame might fall on her husband. Elder Parker left her, saying that he would send Carrie next day for the children. Soon after his departure, Elder Northfield entered. He was surprised to learn how matters stood, but Marion could hardly feel kindly towards him when she observed that he appeared to feel relieved, as the responsibility that had so troubled him was taken from him. Marion passed a sleepless night. Not so her husband; he could now rest, for he had a clear conscience, and although he remembered with pity the dying woman, he was glad to be honorably exempted from fulfilling his promise to her.

The next day Carrie came for the children. She was now in a house of her own, and was willing and glad to undertake their care. She was a kind-hearted woman, and rather lonely as her husband's devotion was beginning to flag, and at best was to be divided among three. Sorrowfully Marion parted with her little charges, though she felt sure that Carrie would be kind to them. But one thought sadly impressed her. They were after all to grow up Mormons, and the mother's fears for them would undoubtedly be realized. Not even her last wish while upon earth could be granted.

Elder Northfield was now in trouble, and called down upon himself the indignation of Brigham Young and the Church. Notwithstanding Marion's attempt to prevent any blame from falling upon him, the truth came out, and he was called to meet in conference with the Church authorities. He was accused of treason to the Church, and of being next door to apostasy. He positively denied the latter charge, declaring that he was never more determined to devote himself to his religion than then. He expressed his sorrow and humility at having allowed a dying woman to persuade him to undertake an act for which his conscience condemned him even at the time. He asked forgiveness of the Church for the offence, as he had done of God, and promised in future to be influenced only by his duty towards God and the Church. The duty of obedience was then urged upon him, in living up to all the requirements of the religion. Reference was made to his wife, who had been the means of leading him to sin, and the strong language used against her nearly destroyed all the humility and penitence he had experienced. Although she had been the cause of his humiliation, yet he could not bear that one word should be said against her. He was reminded of his lack of dignity in allowing a woman to govern his actions, and urged to act upon the principle that the man is the ruler of his wife or wives, and that his word should be the law to be unquestionably obeyed. A woman's salvation depended upon her obedience to her husband, and he who did not secure this failed in his duty towards her. His spiritual advisers went still farther and recommended him to take a step in advance in atonement for his sin and enter into polygamy. This was recommended for the benefit of his wife, also, "for," said they, "the sooner such women as she are forced into it the better. Nothing cures them of their opposition to the system sooner than being forced to submit to it." Besides, he was abundantly able to provide for an increased family, and while so many men were nobly struggling in poverty to support from two to eight or ten wives, it was a reproach to one of his income to remain longer with only one. He should see to it that he was building up his kingdom. Elder Northfield could hardly refrain then from declaring his intention of never entering into polygamy, and telling them of his promise to that effect. Their exhortations were at war with his better nature, and he felt antagonistic to them. He tried to conquer this feeling, believing it was wicked to indulge in resentment against God's chosen servants. He tried to receive their counsel in a proper spirit. He replied that he would think of the matter. He hoped thus to satisfy them without open opposition. He now felt that he and his wife were placed in a very uncomfortable position. He felt obliged to tell her what had been said to him, to warn her against any remark which might attract attention to her views. They agreed that they could not be too careful, and Marion was very much troubled, though she comforted herself by calling to mind her husband's words, "Cost what it may, I will never take another wife."

The excitement and interest in their case gradually diminished, although frequently persecuted by suggestions of polygamy. These were a source of perplexity and torment to Elder Northfield, who wished to be regarded, and wished to be, a devout Mormon. But he could not think of breaking his vow to Marion, and thus blasting her young life. He did not either feel that God called him to take that step, though he dared not condemn it in others.

And thus time passed on and another little one came to them—a second Elsie—frail and tender—a delicate flower which bloomed only for a time. She learned to lisp the names of papa and mamma, to wind her little arms lovingly around their necks, to play in her baby glee with little Forest, and then their hearts were called to mourn, for baby was no more. This was their first real sorrow. That strong man sobbed and shook with grief as his pet was laid away, and the young mother felt that henceforth her home was desolate without its cradle, the little dresses, and the prints of baby fingers.

Owing to the non-existence of regular mails, Marion had heard from and written to her sister but seldom; and even had it been possible, her husband would have discouraged a frequent correspondence, for he noticed Elsie's letters always seemed to make Marion more sad and discontented with her present life. Elsie was still living with her aunt, and expressed her perfect content with everything, save her separation from her sister.

Elder Northfield had long ago given up all hope of Marion ever again believing in the faith, but hoped that she would eventually become at least resigned and contented. He was still prospering in business, and the manner in which they were now able to live formed a strong contrast to their humble beginning. Forest was now a beautiful lad of four years, with golden hair and blue eyes like his mother's. He was the joy and pride of that home. But deep down in the hearts of father and mother was written the memory of the little girl that died, and her place could never be filled by another.

Chapter 7

Peacefully, almost happily, at times, were the days of Marion's life passing now, but her clear sky was darkening, a cloud was gathering, a storm was about to burst over her head and well-nigh overwhelm her. For a time, after the indignation brought upon them by the unsuccessful attempt to send Elder Parker's children into the Gentile world, Marion was troubled and annoyed by visits from professed friends, both male and female, who labored with a true missionary zeal to convince her of her remissness in duty and her sinful selfishness in insisting on being the only wife. Some of the brethren told her she was a curse instead of a blessing to her husband, and that but for her influence over him he would undoubtedly go on to the performance of his duty. Marion felt to thank God for this influence. She gradually withdrew herself from all society, as much as was possible, save that of her friend, Mrs. Atwood, and the young wife of Elder Atkins, with whom she had formed a strong friendship. She remained exclusively at home, finding her pleasure there in the home cares and society of her husband and little boy. Francis and Edith Parker came often to see her, and sometimes Carrie came with them.

At length and by degrees a change seemed to come over Elder Northfield. His natural cheerfulness was departing, and he had an appearance of mental depression which aroused Marion's anxiety for him. She could not interest him in conversation, and if she talked to him he seemed preoccupied in other matters. He often forgot to take his little boy in his arms for a frolic, on returning home at night, as he always had done, and the little fellow's loud demonstrations of joy at papa's return fell unnoticed on his car. Often did the child go to him with some request, and after trying in vain to attract his attention, he went discouraged to his mother with his wants. Elder Northfield sat reading now a great deal, but Marion had asked him on one or two occasions what he had been reading, and he could not tell her. He was kind as ever, and at times caressed her in the tenderest manner; again, almost extravagantly expressing his love for her and calling her by many endearing names. Notwithstanding this, at other times he seemed to have forgotten her very existence, so preoccupied was he.

At first Marion did not appear to notice the change, striving by every means to make him more cheerful, but as she failed in this, she asked him why he seemed so troubled. She inquired if his business affairs were perplexing him.

He answered that he had met with some losses and was a little embarrassed, but hoped to get through all right.

She tried to encourage him to think all would be well, and even if the worst came, they would only be obliged to go back to their old humble way of living, and that would not he so very dreadful, for had not some of their happiest days been spent in that humble cottage, where they first made a home for themselves?

But he did not seem much comforted, although he fondly kissed his wife and called her his comforter. As the weeks passed he became more depressed, and his nights were restless, his sleep troubled.

One evening Marion approached the chamber where he had repaired, and opened the door unnoticed by him. He was kneeling at the bedside. Marion caught these words:

"My God, if it is possible, let this cup pass from me and my poor Marion. Nevertheless, not our will, but thine, be done.

Teach me my duty, God, and give me strength to do it. But let me not bring sorrow on that loving heart. Stay my hand, if thou wilt, but, God—"

Marion heard no more: she turned and fled, her heart filled with the most terrible forebodings. She caught up her boy and wildly kissed and caressed him. She could not think; she felt stunned. She tried to still the beatings of her heart. At last she had discovered the cause of her husband's strange mood. She divined the truth. As continued washing wears the hardest rock away, so the perpetual influence of the Mormon leaders had their effect at last on their victim. Constant and unceasing, for nearly four years, had been their efforts to convert him to a practical belief in the one doctrine he had never embraced. Skilful had been their arguments and apt their presentations of Bible examples, and an important point was gained when they had convinced him that any man was justified in taking more than one wife. It was long, however, before he could be made to believe it was *his duty* to enter personally into polygamy. They, however, accomplished that in time; but with his intelligence and the natural nobility of his character, it never could have been accomplished, except through the fervor of his religion and his implicit faith in the higher authorities. His sacred vow and promise to his wife was of no account compared with his duty to his religion, and as it was made with a belief in its righteousness at the time, he was completely absolved from its fulfilment by the appearance of new light.

Without obeying the commands of God, neither he nor his wife could ever enter the Celestial Kingdom; therefore it was manifestly his duty, for her sake as well as his own, to obey. He had once been guilty of treason against the Church, and bitterly repented it, vowing thenceforth to perform every duty faithfully, as it was made known to him. Except his unfaithfulness in this affair, he had been a most conscientious member of the Mormon Church, and now he believed it his duty to obey counsel, but it involved the breaking of his vow to Marion, and perhaps the breaking of her heart. Within his soul raged a terrible contest between love and duty.

At last a crisis came. The patience of the Apostles was exhausted with the obstinacy of their intended convert, and he was voted a disgrace to the Church. His soft-heartedness and regard for his wife, and his fidelity to his promise to her, were ridiculed, and he was accused of submitting to woman's government.

Then Brigham Young interested himself personally in the matter, and commanded Elder Northfield to take another wife, under penalty of expulsion from the Church.

Said he, "If he will not obey, he is no Mormon, but a vile hypocrite, and will end in apostatizing. We will have no men in the Church who set themselves up above their leaders, or who will be governed by a wife instead of the church. Let him go to the d——l, where he belongs, if he will not obey counsel."

Now he could only choose between obedience to the commands laid upon him and the giving up of his religion. The former involved the striking of a death-blow to his domestic happiness, the latter a giving up of all hope of happiness in the Celestial Kingdom for himself and her, too, for he believed that outside the Mormon Church there was no salvation.

One course excluded, perhaps, all happiness in this world, and the other all happiness in the eternal world. Which should he choose? Abraham was willing to sacrifice his best beloved for his religion, and he would be doing no more in obeying Brigham Young's command. Should he wish to do less? Was not hesitating a proof of more love for an earthly idol than for God? Might it not be that if God saw his submission and his willingness to go forward in the performance of his duty, his hand, like Abraham's, would be stayed, and as Isaac was saved from being offered up a sacrifice, so might his best beloved escape?

So far had Elder Northfield's fanaticism carried him. This was the power a despotic religion exercised over the mind of man, blinding him to all sense of right, all instincts of reason, and investing the basest of crimes with the virtue of sacrifice and religious devotion. This was the religion which made men morally and mentally strong, to become weak tools in the hands of their leaders,—that worked upon the minds of men of the more emotional and religious nature, with the greatest success, making of them the most fanatical converts.

Elder Northfield was now in that frame of mind which determined him to let nothing stand in the way of duty, and he resolved to obey at the expense of everything. He went to God in prayer for help and strength. To him there was no blasphemy in praying for strength to strike a death-blow to a loving, trustful heart, no mockery in asking God's blessing on his course, no inconsistency in imploring that if need be his heart might be hardened, lest it fail him in the performance of his duty.

His mind was made up, and as Marion had once said, "Duty was law to him." He now felt a sense of relief in at last being able to decide, and decide aright, even at the expense of his feelings. He felt that God would approve of his course, and even if he did not interpose, as in the case of Abraham and Isaac, yet his blessing would rest upon them, and in the end all would be well.

Marion now knew that her husband had been persuaded or compelled to contemplate entering into polygamy. Her trust in him had been misplaced; her faith had proved a vain one. Notwithstanding his oft-repeated promise, notwithstanding his indignation that her aunt should think him capable of such faithlessness, now he was about to prove the truth of her conviction.

The words of her aunt came back to her: "You know not how almost impossible it is for a man to withstand the constant counsels and commands to marry again. Will he be more true than every other man just as honorable and sincere as he now is?"

She thought of the many expressions of confidence in her future happiness that she had uttered, and of the never-wavering faith and trust she had given her husband, of his love and affection for her, and she could not believe that he would consummate the project he now undoubtedly entertained. Such wretchedness she never knew before. She felt that her heart would be crushed with its load of misery, but yet she hoped. Seldom comes a time, a situation, where there is no hope—no single gleam to keep the pulses of life throbbing, the beatings of the heart stirring. Dark indeed, even with Egyptian darkness,[19] the hour which is cheered by not one ray of light to magnify and catch at, as a drowning man catches at a straw. Such utter darkness had not yet come to Marion's heart. She knew her influence over her husband, she knew his tenderness towards all mankind, and especially towards herself. She knew his natural humanity, which he could not crush out, had once, when weighed in the balance with duty and fidelity to the Church, turned the scale in favor of humanity, and that sympathy for misery had overbalanced all other considerations, and she hoped it might again. She knew his sorrow for that act, his strong faith, and his conscientiousness, yet she could not believe he would ruin her happiness forever.

He had been besieged and persuaded, until he could resist no longer, but she had never pleaded with him. He had never listened to her entreaties, her side of the question had not been presented to him. First, she would try the surest way to accomplish her purpose. She would still her beating heart and calmly reason with him. She would ask God to help her, and taking her Bible, try, as she never had done before, to show him his error from God's word. If she could only persuade him that Mormonism was a delusion, or even that it would be right for him to renounce his intention, she knew he would do so. She must stifle every emotion, keep her mind clear in spite of anything he might say to excite and terrify her, and with all her skill make one desperate effort to save herself. Failing in this, she would appeal to his sympathy, and at her pleadings, her loving entreaties, her sorrow, his heart would relent, and surely he could not deny her. Then they would forever leave that place where she had seen so much sorrow, and again be happy in the Gentile world.

Elder Northfield now entered the room, with a troubled but determined look.

"Marion," said he, with a husky voice, "I have something to tell you—something you will not like to hear. You have asked me what has been troubling me of late, and expressed such a brave spirit at the prospect of trouble in business, that I have hope that you will bear this trouble bravely, although of a different nature. The thought of it has made me wretched night and day for months. My own dear wife, God knows I would save you from it if I could!"

"You can, Henry! O, you can, if you will! I know what your trouble is. I know that you are deluded into believing that you must take another wife. I heard you asking God to give you strength to ruin my life, if need be. I heard you ask God to stay your hand. He will not stay it if you deliberately decide to let it fall and crush me. I heard you pray God not to let you bring sorrow on that loving heart. He will let you do it, if you will. It is not God that is doing this; it is you. You are breaking your vow to me. You are forever blighting my happiness, and, I believe, your own, too. Is it a kind and just God who bids you do this thing? Is it a merciful Father who commands you to cause such misery to fall on one whom you should cherish and shield from trouble? Is it a pure religion which leads you into such gross immorality? O, my dear husband, you are deceived! How can you believe that such miserable teachings are divine! Why will you not use the reason God has given you, and from it decide what is right? Why ignore one of God's best gifts, and trample it under foot? If He gives revelations to the heads of the Church, He also gave you a mind and heart. Were they allowed to exercise their natural functions, you never could come to this. But your mind has become warped, you cannot see things in their right light. You are stifling all the good instincts of your heart, and think, in doing so, you are doing God's will."

"Marion! Marion! You do not know what you are saying. The heart is deceitful above all things, and desperately wicked. We should not follow our inclinations, but our convictions of duty. Although my heart aches for you, yet my conscience tells me I am right. If I could bear all your part of this trouble, as well as my own, I would gladly do it. Do you suppose I could ever have come to this decision if I had not believed it to be my duty? We must crucify our own wills and inclinations, and be willing to obey God, no matter what the sacrifice may be, and in the eternal world our reward will be sure."

"Does God delight in seeing his children inflict trouble on themselves and their dear ones?" asked Marion.

"Whom He loveth, He chasteneth," answered her husband.

"Then let Him chasten. Do not take the chastening rod from His hands."

"But He works through His children, and commands them, and they must obey."

"Is God pleased to see the Hindoo mother throw her innocent babe into the Ganges as a sacrifice to appease His wrath? Does He delight in seeing the men and women of heathen lands throw themselves down for the wheels of Juggernaut[20] to crush them? Is He honored and pleased at the lifelong tortures men inflict on themselves in the hope of thereby gaining greater happiness in Heaven? Or does He look upon the cruel wickedness in the Mormon church with any degree of pleasure because the participants fancy they are doing His will?"

"Marion, it is simply blasphemous for you to associate the religion of the Latter-day Saints with heathenism, in the way you do. You never did so before, and would not thus denounce Mormonism now were it not that you so shrink from bearing the cross."

"I never felt the necessity of it so strongly before, although my convictions have been the same since we first arrived in this city. But I have forebore to trouble you with my opinions, believing it to be useless to try to persuade you to renounce your religion, until now you propose to make a living sacrifice of me. I can't submit without an effort to show you that you are wrong, without a struggle to save myself and you, too, from future trouble, for I do believe that there will come a day before you die when you will bitterly repent it if you take this step."

"I would give every dollar I possess, or ever hope to possess, Marion, to see you again rooted and grounded in the faith as you once were. It is the lack of faith that gives rise to such opinions as yours. If you could believe in Mormonism as I do, you would cheerfully submit to everything that was for your highest good and glory. You would bear this cross for Christ's sake. You would look beyond this short life; and even if the consciousness of having done right failed to give you peace and joy here, you would be sure of happiness hereafter."

"But, Henry, what does the Bible say? Does it not say 'A man shall be the husband of one wife?' Does it not everywhere teach that plural marriages are wrong?"

"My dear, was not Jacob a tried and faithful servant of God, blessed with visions from Heaven? Did he not take first Leah, then Rachel, to wife? And we have no intimation that God disapproved of his course. Abraham, too, the most favored of all God's servants, lived up to this doctrine. And what is more, Sarah, his first wife, gave unto him Hagar, another wife. No doubt she did it cheerfully, and God blessed her abundantly and in a wonderful manner."

"But that was in the old dispensation before Christ came and taught differently. You know before His coming it was said 'an eye for an eye and a tooth for a tooth,' and God's servants were allowed to indulge in revenge against their enemies, and He even led them in battle to destroy them; but Christ says, 'but I say unto you that you shall love your enemies, and do good to those that despitefully use you and persecute you.' All things were changed by his coming, and nowhere in the New Testament can be found any authority for this doctrine."

"But, Marion, your own admission of a change, caused by a new dispensation, confounds your argument. We are living in a still newer dispensation—the last one—and it is changed from Christ's dispensation somewhat, though resembling both that and the first. If we are to follow the last, then we are to follow the teachings and commands given in the new revelations. These last revelations of God to man are more binding upon us than the Bible by your own arguments. The Book of Mormon[21] and the divine revelations to Joseph Smith on celestial marriages are later authority than the Bible."

"I was not thinking of man's dispensations, but of God's. I cannot believe that God gives revelations in these days; but if so, he would have selected men more pure and holy than Joseph Smith or Brigham Young to receive them. We both know that in all the years we have spent here, we have seen many actions of Brigham Young's and the Apostles which were very questionable for saints."

"Certainly; even God's chosen servants sometimes sin. They

are human and liable to err; but that does not prove that they are not, in the main, right. We are not to judge those God has set over us. And as to the revelations, there is no reason why God should not give them in these days as well as in former times. But why argue the question further, Marion? It only distresses us both. I see my duty, and hard though it is, I must do it. I must do it for your sake, as well as mine; for though you do not believe it, if we go into the Gentile world our souls are lost; but if I live up to the light given me, God will bless me and my house and thus bring us all into his kingdom. How can I hesitate between happiness here for my darling and eternal happiness for her? O that you might look far enough ahead and see as I do what will be for our happiness in the end!"

During this argument Marion had gradually become more and more hopeless, until at last she quite despaired of success. She was utterly wretched now, and very weak from her excitement and great effort to hide her emotion. Elder Northfield had been surprised at her calmness, and greatly relieved. He expected the wildest storm of grief, and dreaded exceedingly the effect the knowledge might have upon her. He had beforehand steeled his heart against her pleadings, lest his strength should fail him. But she had been so calm and composed, giving way to no emotion, that he now felt that he had been unnecessarily rigid. He thought the worst was now over and she would gradually look at the situation in a more favorable light. He little knew of the hope that was the secret of her calmness, nor realized that her self-control was like a desperate effort for dear life. She tried to rise from her chair, but fell back into it. She attempted to speak, but could not. Her husband sprang to save her from falling, and taking her in his arms, he gently laid her on a sofa, saying, "My poor wife! I pity you! God knows I do!"

He procured a stimulant for her and she was soon able to

speak. She wound her arms about his neck and pleaded with all the eloquence of her soul. Her appeal to his reason had been in vain; now she appealed to his heart. As those blue eyes, so full of terror and anguish, looked into his, and those quivering lips begged and pleaded that he would keep his promise to her, his composure gave way, and he saw that all her former calmness was caused by her agony. She reminded him of his promise, of her never-failing devotion to him, of all she had given up for love of him, when all hope in her religion had failed her. She entreated him, by the memory of all their past happiness, their little boy, their happy home, to relent and go into the Gentile world with her and their boy.

Then it was that he hesitated. How could he dash the cup of happiness from her lips? How could he reward all her faithfulness to him by breaking her heart? His determination was weakening, and at the risk of their eternal salvation, he was almost persuaded to grant her request. He looked into her agonized face and felt that he could not refuse her; but as fate would have it, at that instant a leaf from a worn-out book of Mormon doctrines and revelations fluttered to his feet. His eye was arrested by a sentence in the latter part of the revelation on celestial marriages. He read these words:

"And again, verily, verily, I say unto you, if a man have a wife, who holds the keys of this power, and he teaches unto her the laws of my priesthood, as pertaining to these things, then shall she believe and administer unto him, or she shall be destroyed, saith the Lord your God. For I will destroy her, for I will magnify my name upon all those who receive and abide in my law."[22]

Elder Northfield read these words and he was himself again. He had almost yielded to the temptation of his wife's entreaties, but was saved as by a miracle from falling again a victim to the nobleness of his own heart. Still he was pitiful and tender,

but determined. "My darling," said he, "your pleadings correspond with my own inclinations, and I had almost yielded to
the temptation, and thus ruined our hope for eternity, but this
piece of paper has saved me. Believe me, I never loved you more
than I do now, and if I did not love you thus, I might relent,
for, dearest, you cannot know how hard it is for me to refuse
you. I would willingly sacrifice everything in this life for myself to save you this pain; but how can I sacrifice everything in
the next life for us both to grant your request? My poor Marion! Try to not think hard of me; try to love me just the same;
try to believe that it is not my wish to bring this trouble upon
you, and I will make it as light as I can. My love shall always
be yours and yours alone. I only think of this as a painful duty
which must be fulfilled."

He took Marion's cold hand closely in his, but there was no
answering pressure, and her lips could not form the answer he
craved. Her affection had received almost its death-blow, and
days passed during which she scarcely spoke or had strength to
walk about the house. She sat in an easy-chair or reclined on
her sofa, and seemed not to realize what was going on around
her. For the first time in her life her boy had no power to interest her, and his loving prattle fell unheeded on her ear. If her
husband approached her she gave no sign of pleasure; when
he left her she showed no regret. Her senses were stunned,
and she was capable of but little emotion. But as her strength
gradually returned, her realization of the situation came back
to her. Hearts may break, all human hopes may die, all interest
in life depart, and yet the body will live on; and one may wish
for death, and wish in vain.

Marion's friend, Mrs. Atwood, heard of her illness, and di-
vining the cause hastened to her to offer comfort and sympathy.
It was what Marion needed. She had her husband's sympathy
and pity, but she did not care for that. It was no comfort to her.

How could he know what she suffered? But this woman had been through the same trial, and could offer genuine sympathy from the sadness of her own heart. How she wept for Marion's grief, and Marion wept, too. These were the first tears she had shed since that evening, which now seemed so long ago. But they did her good, and soon she was able to be again about the house, but was the very ghost of her former self, with no interest, no animation, no pleasure in anything.

It made Elder Northfield's heart ache to see how she suffered, but yet he did not reproach himself at all as being the cause. And he expected that soon she would be more resigned and cheerful. There had passed no word between them on the subject during the time, but he had been goaded on by the authorities to the immediate consummation of his intention, and now felt obliged to speak again to her on the subject. He said he had no one in view for a wife, and asked her if she had any choice in the matter; if so, he would endeavor to gratify her wishes. He told her then how matters had stood with him for years, and how he had fought against it, both with his advisers and himself; how at last he was obliged by Brigham Young's command to marry, and that without delay.

"I have no choice," said Marion, "and only one request, that you say no more to me about it, but do as you will, only give her a house of her own. You can afford it, so please do not bring her here."

"It shall be as you say, Marion," and the subject was dropped.

The duty of finding a woman who was willing to enter into matrimony on short notice now occupied Elder Northfield's attention; but he had little difficulty, for Brother Brigham was always an efficient helper in such matters, and he had a blooming young woman, by the name of Helen Crosby, already for him, and all counselled to marry. As Elder Northfield was an attractive person, and his worldly prospects all that could be desired, the candidate for his affections made no opposition to his suit, and the pathway began to grow smooth to his feet.

Certainly it was pleasanter to sit and converse with the gay and sprightly Miss Crosby than to spend his evenings with his sad-faced wife, who scarcely ever spoke, except to her boy or in answer to some question. Her apparent wretchedness was a continual reproach, and the hours spent in her society were anything but a pleasure to him. Still he kindly tried, by every means in his power, to soften her grief, till he saw that it was useless, and no effort of his could lift the veil of sadness from her heart. He became discouraged, and decided that all he could do was to leave it to time to bring about a change.

He now devoted himself quite zealously to his betrothed. He must not marry in ignorance of his intended bride's qualities, disposition, etc., and as time was short, it must be improved. So evening, after evening found him in Helen's parlor, and it must be confessed that the time slipped rapidly away, until a late hour, very often. There was no love bestowed upon her, of course, for his love was always to be Marion's, and Marion's alone. This duty, that had caused him so many sleepless nights, so much grief, that had been undertaken at last almost by compulsion, was becoming less painful, and was performed with commendable alacrity and diligence.

In a word, Elder Northfield became quite infatuated with his betrothed. He never had believed any other woman but Marion could ever have his love, but without his realizing it this woman had gained an influence over him which he would never have thought possible. Her slightest wish was law to him. She could make him happy by a word or extremely uncomfortable by a look. She enjoyed exercising her power over him, and was in no haste to enter the matrimonial state, lest the present agreeable state of things become changed.

And during this time Marion saw all. She knew all that

was transpiring, though no word was spoken. She knew her husband had lost the look of trouble and perplexity he had worn so long, and that his sorrow for her grief was forgotten. Although never actually unkind to her, yet he was very unmindful of her, and she knew her place in his affections had been usurped by another. She avoided seeing him leave the house, evening after evening, in such a pleasant preoccupied way, that told so much. A thousand little actions of his were like fresh stabs to her already bleeding heart. No little loving attentions, like those of former days, were attempted now, and Marion could not have received them, if they had been offered her. Her husband was her own no longer. She felt as though she were divorced from him. It was not enough that he should take another wife, as a matter of duty, but he had also transferred his affections to her, and Marion was no longer loved by her husband. An unloved wife was she now, and she drank the cup of bitterness to the dregs. As long as her husband loved her the darkness was not quite complete, although she had thought it could not be greater, but now all she could hope and wish for was death. She prayed that God in his mercy would take her and her boy from the bitterness of this life and give them rest and peace. She never complained, and her husband, when he thought of her at all, thought she was getting resigned, and would in time "get used to it," as other wives did.

And when he told her that on the following day he was to be married to Helen Crosby, he was gratified to observe no indication of pain at the information. He did not know that she had come to that point where she could suffer no more; that her heart had become seared with its burning and pain. He asked her if she felt able to go with him to the Endowment House and perform her part in the ceremony,[23] and she answered that she would go. He kissed her and called her his brave wife, but his words and caress seemed but mockery to her, and she shrank from them.

On the following day she gave her husband a second wife. She placed the hand of Helen Crosby in his, and he was married to her for time and eternity. There was no essential difference between the bridegroom of that occasion and the bridegroom of Gentile life. There was no reason to think the young pair were not in the same blissful state of mind commonly supposed to belong to their existing circumstances. Very happy the bride seemed to be, and what was it to them that a woman, once far lovelier and fairer than she, and of a much nobler nature, stood by their side a crushed, a wretched being? They did not know it. Their fascination for each other completely blinded them to everything else. Had it not been so, neither could have been so heartless.

In the days that followed, Marion saw very little of her husband. For this she did not care, now that he was hers no longer; but those who frequented the ball-room, the theatre, and the social entertainments, saw him with his bride among the gayest of the gay. He had obeyed divine commands and was now happy. His conscience was at rest, and life was now a pleasure to him.

About this time Marion received a letter from her sister. It was written on the anniversary of Marion's wedding-day, and much was said in it about the lives of both since their separation. Elsie tenderly referred to the loss of her little namesake, but congratulated Marion that her life had been free from the trouble that she and their aunt had so strongly apprehended. She acknowledged the injustice done Marion's husband in believing he would be untrue to her, and spoke in glowing terms of the force of character he proved to possess to enable him to stand firm for the right in the midst of such overwhelming influence. She said: "Now, Marion, after all these years have passed and still you are the first and only one in your husband's affections, I can lay aside my fears for you and believe that you were right in trusting so implicitly in his word. I feel like begging his pardon for misjudging him in the way I did." Then she confided to her sister the events of her own life—the emotions of her own heart. Happily had passed the years with her at her aunt's home, and now a new joy had come into her life—a new gift was bestowed upon her. It was the love and devotion of one of God's noblemen, and Elsie was soon to unite her destiny with his in marriage. The wedding-day was appointed, "and," wrote Elsie, "the only impediment to my perfect happiness on that day will be the absence of my sister Marion. But I know her thoughts will be with me, and with all her heart and soul she will wish me joy, although I cannot hear her lips express her sentiments. Think of me that day, darling sister, and pray that I may be as faithful a wife as you have been, and that my husband's devotion may continue through the coming years as Elder Northfield's devotion has endured for you."

At the reading of this letter Marion was taken out of herself, and her sister's interests were hers for the time. But O! the bitterness of her heart as she read the undeserved praises of her husband and realized that her aunt's predictions were fulfilled, and that haunting spectre of her life, which, however, she never believed would take its abode in her home, had at last blighted her life as it had so many before her. By accident, as she was leaving the room, and unnoticed by her, the letter dropped from her hands, which were filled with letters and papers. Elder Northfield entered, and observing the postmark, opened and read the letter. He could not tell why he did so, for he usually avoided Elsie's letters, but this one he read from beginning to end. He heartily wished he had not, however, for it made him very uncomfortable. He could not get it out of his mind, and although he sought the companionship of his bride to dispel his uneasiness, yet the effects of that letter lasted many a day.

Marion's callers had become very infrequent, in consequence of her seclusion from all society; but now, since the great change in their lives, she had often to go through the ordeal of entertaining company. Some came to offer sympathy and comfort. Among this class were Mrs. Atwood, the wives of Elder Atkins, and Carrie Parker. Carrie could now sympathize with her, for she had tasted of the cup of sorrow, and her once fond husband had added another wife to his list, another jewel to his crown, another subject to his kingdom, and Carrie was ruthlessly thrust aside. She now devoted herself to the children she had taken to her heart, and in them she found much comfort. There were other callers who came or were sent to labor with Marion to reconcile her to her lot and exhort her to submission and religious devotion. And still another class, who came out of curiosity to see how the rebellious wife appeared, and "whether she would now hold up her head and boast that her husband would never be a polygamist." Among this class came two of the Mrs. Smiths, Ellen and Josephine, and they were hardened enough to taunt her of her faith in her husband. Marion's heart had been too dead to be stirred by anger, but this insult awakened her indignation and resentment. A new life seemed to be given her. Her blood boiled and surged through her veins till it seemed that it was turned to fire. Her eyes kindled, her pale cheeks crimsoned, and Marion was changed. Her visitors departed, astonished and not a little taken aback. The change in her was too great for even her husband not to observe it. He had meant to tell her of his intention of bringing Helen there on the following day that his wives might become acquainted, but something in her voice and looks deterred him from proposing that she make some friendly advances towards the new wife as he had intended. But in a few days he told her of his wish to bring Helen there for a call, and requested that she would receive her graciously. He took close observation of his wife now, and gave her more thought and attention than he had before since Helen had first occupied his mind. He was shocked to see how changed she was. Her eyes had lost their pleasant light, and her lips were drawn as with great suffering. Her cheeks were thin and hollow, and were either deadly pale or glowing with the excitement of inward pain. He thought of his beautiful and happy bride of five years before, and to his credit it may be said that he was touched by feelings of remorse.

Marion said, "Bring her if you wish," but she did not care to make any attempt towards cultivating an acquaintance. Her husband thought she was trying to be reconciled and would overcome her sadness in time. He pitied her now that he thought of her, and sought to make their conversation cheerful. It was his first heartfelt attention for a long time, but it only made Marion more miserable, for it softened the hardness of her heart and rendered her more sensitive to grief. She could have borne insult better, for anger would have stifled more torturing emotions.

Chapter 8

Marion had consented to the bringing of the second wife into her home, but she felt that she could not endure the painful ordeal that was expected of her. She grew almost frantic as she paced her chamber till the small hours of the night. She longed for escape. She could not remain in that house after it had been polluted by the entrance of her husband's new wife. She resolved to take her child and steal away in the darkness, make her way out of the city in the direction of Southern Utah, and journey cautiously and secretly to the house of the man who befriended one wretched woman in her trouble. He would help her out of the Territory, she felt sure, and she would go into the Gentile world—not among her friends— no, Elsie should never know her situation, no matter what she suffered. She and aunt Wells must never know of her humiliation and trouble, if they never heard from her again. Elsie was very happy now, and her happiness should not be clouded by her sister's trouble. In the Gentile world, among strangers, she would find employment, and there rear her little son away from all Mormon influences. Her husband would not care. He did not love her, and she did not love him now. She woke her slumbering boy with difficulty. He thrust his fists into his big blue eyes and rubbed them till the tears came. His mother told him wonderful stories to keep him awake, while she combed his long curly locks and washed his chubby face. She dressed him with all a mother's care, and then made up a bundle of a few necessary articles of clothing.

"Forest," said she, "do you want to go with mamma to see Mrs. Atwood?"

"O yes, mamma! and Ella and Robbie, too. But why don't you wait till morning? I'm so sleepy."

"It is morning, dear, but very early; and I do not want to disturb the rest, so my boy must be very still."

"I'll be very still," said he, "and I'll take my new cart in the carriage and show it to Robbie, and we'll play with it."

But in spite of Forest's promises, two or three peals of laughter escaped him, as he thought and talked of the fun he was to have with Robbie.

Marion was alarmed lest he had awakened the house, but her fears were groundless, and with what money she had in her possession, her jewelry, and her bundle, they quietly descended the stairs, and carefully undoing the fastenings of one of the outer doors, they stood free, with only the blue sky above them.

"Why, mamma, where is the carriage and where is papa?" asked Forest.

"Hush, my child, we are going to walk, and papa is not going with us."

"Then I can't carry my little cart."

"O, yes, you can; we will draw it," said Marion, willing to do anything to hush the child.

She procured the cart in great fear of being discovered, and carried it with one arm, in spite of its weight, lest the sound of its wheels should be heard, and with the other hand almost dragged her child along. When they had proceeded some distance, she put it on the ground and they drew it, and soon as Forest grew tired and sleepy, she persuaded him to leave it by the roadside, and then they hastened on.

She felt that she must see her friend, Mrs. Atwood, again, and thither she was going to bid her farewell. She had some difficulty in arousing the inmates of the house, but finally succeeded. Mr. Atwood was not at home, Marion knew. He with his second wife had gone on a visit to her friends, and Forest was much disappointed to learn that Robbie had gone with his mother. Had they been at home, Marion would not have dared approach their cottage.

Mrs. Atwood was astonished and alarmed to receive a visit from her friend at that unseasonable hour, but she gave her a kind welcome.

Marion was so exhausted with her excitement and long, hurried walk, that she could hardly speak.

Mrs. Atwood kindly bade her not to try to talk, but rest a few moments, and then tell what had brought her there.

She obeyed, and as her glance wandered around the room it rested on more than one reminder of her happier life in the cottage she had just passed. There were the books she had given Ella from which to learn to read. These reminded her of her little school, that was such a pleasure to her. Here was a picture, sketched by her one leisure afternoon; and now her eyes rested on a picture of herself and husband, taken long ago, when they were happy and true to each other.

She reached out her hand and asked for it. Her friend gave it to her. Her eyes were riveted on that face, beaming with tenderness and love. His expression had changed since the days there portrayed. Marion could not take her eyes from that face.

"He loved me then," she murmured.

"Yes, and he will love you again," said her friend.

"Do you believe that?" asked Marion.

"I do, and think he will come to his senses sooner or later, and realize that his infatuation for Helen is only an infatuation, and that it is only Marion whom he really loves."

Into Marion's heart there came a gleam of hope at the thought.

"If I could have believed that," said she, "I should not have been here now. I would wait patiently for years, and endure almost anything, if I knew he would come back to me at last, and be mine alone again—if we could have the same happy life we lived in that little cottage yonder. But it never can be!"

Then she told Mrs. Atwood of her project, and that she had come to bid her a final farewell.

"My poor, dear friend," said Mrs. Atwood, "you must not think of anything so rash. In your condition you will perish before you can complete such a journey, and with that little boy you will surely fail in your attempt. Wait till you are better able to undertake it, and if you are not less unhappy, I will help you all I can to get away from Mormon life. But, Marion, I believe brighter days are coming for you. It is always darkest just before the day, you know. Nettie's husband repented of his neglect to her, you know, even though at the eleventh hour. But his repentance is sincere, I have no reason to doubt, and another man may repent at an earlier hour. Your husband may be that man, Marion. I have hope for you yet."

And Marion began to have hope for herself.

"Yes," she said, "he may repent at my dying bed; that would be worth a great deal. Would it be worth waiting a lifetime for, or will my life be a short one, as I sometimes think and hope? If he should repent in time to give me a little happiness before I die, it would be worth living for."

Marion had thought all love for her husband had died in her heart, but at sight of his picture, old memories were revived, and her old love with them. She felt now that she could not leave her husband. She loved him still, and would patiently wait and hope to win him back to herself.

When day dawned Mrs. Atwood procured a carriage and went with Marion and Forest to their home. But Marion's exhaustion proved too much for her endurance, and she was laid upon a sick-bed, which she did not leave for many weeks. But in spite of her pain, her weakness, and bodily suffering, the load of misery was lifted, in a great degree, from her heart.

It seemed strange, as she recovered her consciousness, to find her husband by her side. It seemed like the times of long ago; O, so long ago! She wondered if the past had not been a terrible dream. In her weakness she could not comprehend the situation. But one thing she knew, he was by her side and was tenderly caring for her, almost constantly. She tried to realize that and forget everything else. But she could not help wondering, if the past was a reality, why he remained away from Helen so much. Had he repented, as Nettie's husband did? Was he ready now to grant her request, and leave Helen and all the Mormons and go to the Gentile world? the joy of the moment when Marion allowed herself to believe such was the case!

"Henry," she faintly whispered.

"Marion, my darling! Thank God you can speak to me again," said he.

Marion closed her eyes and repeated his words over and over again to herself. The words "my darling" had never sounded so sweet to her before. It had been long since she had heard them and seen in the speaker's face the old look of fondness, but it was there now and his tones were full of tenderness. He had given her back the love he had taken from her. Mrs. Atwood's predictions were fulfilled, and sooner than either thought possible. He was hers now, she knew; was he hers alone? O, could it be that another shared his heart? She had never asked him a question about Helen, and could not now. But she felt unable to bear the suspense, and hoping to end it, said:

"Have you come back to me?"

He understood her, and lest she should hope for too much, said:

"Yes, my dear Marion, my love is all yours now. God forgive me for my past neglect, and you shall be the first and only one in my heart, as you are now. I must not wrong others, but duty alone will prompt any attentions to another."

Then Marion knew her husband had not given up his other wife, had not given up his religion, and they were not to leave Utah after all. She was bitterly disappointed, for she had hoped so much a few moments before.

Elder Northfield saw it all, and said, gently:

"When you are stronger, dear, we will talk more of this; but now do you not wish to see Forest and our little baby girl?"

"Yes, my baby! I must see my baby. Bring her to me."

The mother-love had for a time overcome her disappointment, and as a little soft cheek was laid against hers, and she felt the pressure of baby hands, life yet had its charms for her, and she was far from wishing now that she and Forest might die. She saw that her little one had the deep dark eyes and black curly hair of its father, and was glad it was so.

"We have called her Marion. Shall that be her name—shall we have a little Marion?"

Marion was pleased at this token of affection, and said:

"If you wish it."

"I do, for Marion is the sweetest name to me. Now, shall I take baby away and bring Forest to see you?"

"Yes; let me see my little boy. Where has he been all this time?"

But he was in the room before they could call him.

"Mamma! mamma!" said he, "they wouldn't let me come to see you. They said I would make a noise—and see how still I am! Papa stays here now all the time, don't he, mamma? and he says next time we go to Mrs. Atwood's he will go with us, and we will ride. And he tried to find my cart, and it was all gone, and I couldn't 'member where we put it. Can't you find it, mamma?"

Her little son's words revived all that had passed during that wretched night that she had attempted to run away from her husband. She felt to thank God now that she had been prevented. Had she accomplished her object, she would never have known the blessedness of this restoration. Her life would always have been dark; but now there was hope for her. She was exhausted now, and several days passed before the subject of their estrangement was again brought up. Then Marion was stronger and better able to bear it, and her husband spoke freely to her about Helen and his relation to her.

"How I ever became so taken up with her I cannot tell. At first I went there from a sense of duty alone, but somehow or other she gained a great power and influence over me. I was fairly intoxicated with my infatuation for her and knew nothing else. I do not think I really loved her. It seems to me I could not have been in my right mind; but after a time the scales began to fall from my eyes, and I saw that she had never appreciated my devotion to her and delighted only in the power and position she had obtained. I came home and found my Marion too sick to know me and too weak to raise her hand. The sight of my poor brokenhearted wife brought me back to my senses. God only knows the anguish of remorse and penitence that I suffered, as I realized what I had done. From that time, Marion, I have tried to atone for my cruelty to you, by watching and caring for you, hoping to bring you back to life and health, for, darling, I feared I had killed you. I feared you would never speak to me again, and you cannot know how glad I am to see you growing stronger every day. Now, Marion, can you forgive me and be happy again?"

"I can forgive you with all my heart, and I think I can be happy. I thought once that it would be sufficient to make me miserable for life to have you take another wife, even if it was only as a duty; but since I lost your love, and was utterly forsaken for her, I know that I could bear a part of the load, if only the heaviest need not be laid upon me. O, Henry! You know not my wretchedness, as I felt forsaken and alone with only my boy to love me. You know not how I longed and prayed that I might die and rest from my misery. I felt that I could not bear the ordeal of meeting Helen, and so I stole away. But I am glad, so glad, that I am back again, and to prove how freely I forgive you, I will try to make friends with Helen if you wish."

"Not at present, Marion. Some time when you are well and strong I would be glad to have you become acquainted, for she, too, is my wife, you know" (Marion could not hear these words without shrinking and disputing them to herself), "and I have a duty to perform towards her as well as towards you. I have neglected her almost entirely since you have been ill, and she is quite angry with me, and not without some cause. I do not think my neglect could ever grieve her as it has you, yet I have no doubt she has been very lonely, and I am sorry for her; but still my Marion has needed me most, and needs me most now; and henceforth, though I have two wives and must do justice to both, my attentions to Helen shall be limited by my convictions of duty. Beyond that I will never go; but you will see yourself that it would be cruel to her to neglect her entirely, and I am sure you would not wish me to do that."

"No. Now that you have made her your wife you must try to do right. But how can a man do his duty to one wife without neglecting the other? I think it impossible, and if you try to do justice we shall each have a cross to bear; but I will try to bear mine patiently, for it is now so much lighter. It does not crush me now. The heaviest part of the burden is removed, and I can bear the rest. But shall I tell you what I thought when I first realized that you were with me again? I thought you had repented of it all—that you had at last seen your error, and had forsaken Helen and Mormonism and were ready to leave everything here and go with me to the Gentile world. O how happy the thought made me!"

"I almost wish it were right, Marion, for your sake—you are so unhappy here—and I would gladly do so. But I cannot believe that there is any true religion, except this one. It is God's last revelation, and though the majority of the world does not accept it, God's chosen people were always a little flock, and if I desert the cause I have espoused and refuse to walk in the light given me I know what my reward will be. I know in taking Helen I did my duty, and sinned only in allowing the matter to be anything but a duty."

The roses were not coming back into Marion's life without the thorns, and with the comfort her husband's words gave her was mingled a good deal of bitterness, as she realized that polygamy was to cloud her domestic happiness, though she believed not to altogether destroy it. And she would hope that some time he might see the fallacy of his whole belief and shake off the fetters that bound him captive to a false religion.

As the weeks passed on, Marion was tormented in spite of herself with feelings of jealousy and fear of Helen again becoming a rival in her husband's regard. He was a lover of society, and would have been glad if he could have taken both wives with him to places of amusement as other men did. But that was out of the question. Marion sometimes accompanied him, but she was anything but happy, and preferred the quiet of her own home and the society of her little ones. Fear of Helen, however, always ensured a willing assent to any request of her husband for her company.

But Helen was seen with him oftenest, and she was supposed to be his favorite wife; but she knew that she was not—her power over him had gone. He no longer lingered lover-like, loth to go, but hastened home to Marion. If Marion was jealous of the second wife, doubly so now was the second wife jealous of her. This celestial order of marriage was poorly calculated to inspire heavenly attributes in its victims.

Marion resolved at last to conquer her feelings and call upon Helen. She felt that she could not meet her first in the presence of her husband, and therefore said nothing about her intentions to him. With a beating heart she rang the bell at Helen's door, but Helen was not at home, and Marion could not avoid a sigh of relief at being spared an interview with her. She retraced her steps, and passing one of the shops saw through the window her husband and his wife, Helen, apparently making purchases together. This was the first time she had ever seen them together since their marriage, and the first time she had seen Helen at all, except on that day she had given her to their husband, and now the sight of her filled her heart with pangs of jealousy and hatred. Was she deceived in her husband and were the hours she supposed he devoted to business spent in attending Helen in her shopping expeditions? And Marion returned to her home, almost ready to give herself up to her old wretchedness. Her husband had seen her as she passed the windows and inquired at night where she had been.

This led to an explanation, which quieted her fears, and again her mind was at rest. But her life in those days was like a turbulent, fitful stream—now quiet and comparatively peaceful, now agitated by fears and apprehensions and darkened by the many heartaches that polygamy in even its most unobjectionable form must cause.

An interesting event now occurred in the other branch of Elder Northfield's family. He was presented with a daughter by Helen. His family was increasing, and his kingdom building up now in a manner approved by the Saints. Three additions had been made to it within a year, and he began to be looked upon with favor by the Church authorities. He was in good standing now with the Church and considered a good Mormon.

There was now a new attraction in Helen's home for him, and she saw with pleasure that her babe was bringing her more of the society of her husband. But Marion could only look upon the little stranger as an intruder, and upon its arrival her heart was filled with feelings of hatred. She considered it a usurper of the affection that belonged to her and her children. It seemed like a new outrage upon her domestic life, and she was very unhappy struggling with her feeling of hatred towards Helen and her child. She knew that she was wrong and despised herself for her unjust sentiments towards an innocent babe. She tried to put herself in Helen's place and to possess the spirit of kindness toward her and hers. She resolved to do as she would be done by in Helen's circumstances and conquer her jealousy. She determined to crush out her enmity and call upon the other wife and child, hoping that might lead the way to a better feeling among them.

She found Helen with her babe in her arms. She received her sister-wife in a cool, suspicious manner. Each tried to speak calmly and regard the other with ease, but both knew from this, their first interview, that there could never exist any feeling of love, or even friendship, between them. Marion tried to regard the little one with at least the same tenderness any ordinary babe would have awakened, for she was extremely fond of children, but it was all she could do to pay it the amount of attention she felt necessary. She took it in her arms, and its touch sent a chill through her. She felt her heart harden towards the innocent little one, and its mother also. She almost dropped it into the arms of the latter, who, being on the alert, did not fail to notice her visitor's repugnance. Instead of conquering her animosity, Marion had increased it by coming in contact with its objects.

Helen also resented the dislike Marion's face expressed for her little Nell, and from that time they were further than ever from becoming friendly. No further effort was made on either side to that effect, each knowing that any such attempt would but augment the unpleasantness of their mutual relations.

But Marion went home sad and self-reproachful for her wicked sensations as she held in her arms a babe just as dear and sweet to its mother as her own little Marion was to her, and for aught she knew, just as dear to her husband as was his other babe. In this last thought lay much of the sting, and she became very jealous of little Nell for baby Marion's sake.

As the little ones grew older, and were able to lisp a few words, walk about, and frolic and play, Nell became her father's favorite, for she was always pleased to see him, always ready to meet him with outstretched arms and a laughing happy face, while little Marion shrank timidly from him, and only the greatest coaxing could bring her to his side. If she was having a merry romp with her mother, suddenly the sound of her father's footsteps would change the bright dark beauty of her face to a look of fear, as she watched him and clung fast to her mother's neck.

Elder Northfield had often stood an unobserved spectator, watching her beauty and grace, her sprightliness and sweet winning ways, as she played with Forest, of whom she was very fond, and wished that he might, for just one hour, have the love and confidence of his little daughter. He envied little Forest. When he spoke to her, hoping to coax her to him, she instantly grew sober and ran away to her mother. This was a constant source of annoyance to Elder Northfield, but more so to the mother, for she most ardently wished her husband to love their little daughter, and she tried to create an affection in Marion for him, fearing baby Nell, with her winsomeness, would supplant Marion in his heart. But little Marion could not be made to love and trust in her father to any great extent, and as time passed on Nell became more and more the favorite.

Elder Northfield now spent more of his time at Helen's home, but she never regained her old power over him. It was his child that brought him there, if he came more than duty compelled him. His first wife continued to be first in his thoughts and heart, although she was often racked with jealous fears to the contrary. Helen's baby she knew had supplanted her Marion, and Helen might yet supplant her, as she had once done. She could not rest, as she had once, secure in her confidence in her husband.

Thus matters went on until the little ones were about three years old. Then Helen's health began to fail; she grew rapidly worse, and her husband felt that it was his duty to attend her as much as possible. Marion compelled herself to willingly forego her claim to his society, and was now much alone. She tried to school herself to believe that it was her husband's duty to remain by Helen's bedside, as he had remained by hers, and now into her heart came sympathy for the sufferer, and her ill feeling was changed to pity. She went with him and tried to administer to the wants of Helen, and show her that she had banished her unkind feelings towards her and little Nell. Marion really felt regretful now for her past jealousy, and wished to make amends. She did not shrink now from Nell's touch, but gently cared for her as she did for her own darling.

Helen's eyes, as she lay on her pillow, followed Marion about, as though she wondered at her kindness, but could not understand that she had forgiven her for becoming her husband's wife.

At last one day Elder Northfield entered Helen's room, and taking her hand said:

"My poor Helen, can you bear to be told what your physician says?"

"What does he say? Tell me, is there no hope for me? Must I die?"

"We fear you must, and I did not think it right not to tell you. Dear Helen, I am sorry, but I can give you no hope."

"Are you sorry? I did not think you would care. You have not loved me much since the first few months I knew you."

"Forgive me, if I have not loved you as I ought. I have tried to do right, but it was hard sometimes to know what was my duty. I have not meant to wrong any one."

"O my poor little Nell!" moaned Helen.

"Have you any wish or request to make about Nell's future? Marion, I think, is getting very fond of her, and you may rest assured she will be well cared for."

"Not by *her!* I don't want *her* to have my child. She does not love her. She hated her the first time she saw her; I saw it in her eye. I saw her shiver, almost, as she put her out of her arms. Why she came then, I do not know. Why she comes now, and seems kind to me, I do not know."

"She comes now, Helen, because she pities you, and wishes to show her kind feeling towards you."

"But she has always hated me, and my baby, too; and do you think I would now put my little one in her care? My sister will take her, and you must promise me to send her to my sister."

"But, Helen, you know how I love her, and how hard it will be for me to part with her."

"Yes, I know you love her, and perhaps I should have had more pity for you if you had had more for me. But I know that your love for her is all that has brought you here. Had it not been for her, I should have been utterly neglected. You were all devotion to me till we were married, and led me to expect you would continue to be, but how soon you forsook me! You gave one wife years of devotion, but could only give the other a few short months. It was only fair that I should have been first in your regard now, but you went back to her again, and she even grudged me what slight attentions you did pay me.

She grudged me even my baby, my only treasure and joy, and she shall not have her now. At least you will not refuse this request, now that I am going to die. I suppose she will be glad when I am dead, and no one will mourn for me but poor little Nell and my sister."

"Helen, I shall mourn for you; and if you only might live, I think we should all be more happy in our relations to each other than we have been. Try to feel forgiving towards Marion and me. Marion feels perfectly friendly now towards you."

"I never can feel forgiving towards her, even though I am dying. She has wanted all and was willing I should have nothing. She has been very selfish, I think, and cannot atone for it now I am dying. But you will grant my request?"

"Yes, Helen, it shall be as you wish. God knows I am sorry enough I have not made you any happier. I have made two women miserable, but I tried to do my duty. Our religion leads to these results sometimes, I think, and we must try to think it is all right, for it cannot always be helped, and although our wives have a cross to bear in this life, in the Celestial Kingdom they will be happy. There is hope for you, Helen. You will have a place there to reward you for all you have had to bear here, and there we know all these human weaknesses will not trouble us, and we will meet there and be happy."

"I do not think much about these things. I suppose it is so, but nothing of that kind seems real to me. I think if *she* were there with her children, I should not be any happier than I am here. I do not want to die; I want to live for my baby's sake. O, I can't die!" and Helen went into a perfect paroxysm of grief.

Marion, although the greatest sufferer, was not the only one in this case of polygamy, Helen's sorrows, or cross, as the Mormons spoke of it, had been hard to bear. Her short experience of the system had proved a sad one, and was bringing bitterness into her dying hours. She felt that she had been robbed of her share of happiness, and in the beyond there was nothing brighter to hope for. Nothing more in this life for her—her only pleasure she must leave. She lay upon her dying bed while the one who smoothed her pillow and watched over her, though bearing the nearest and what should be the dearest relationship to her, performed these offices from a sense of duty, rather than from the promptings of love. Polygamy had hung a pall over this young life, and robbed her death of all rays of light and hope. The husband, too, had suffered. Perplexed beyond measure had he been to decide how to deal justly and fairly with both wives—how to avoid giving pain to either, or neglecting one for the other. If his wives could have lived together, gone out together, accompanied him together, his task would have been easier; but he never would try to bring that affliction on Marion, and it would have been equally impossible to persuade Helen to that mode of life. Elder Northfield was not like most Mormon men, who would have "forced them into it," and who frequently advised him to that course. He knew their cross must be heavy enough at best, and humanely endeavored to make it as light as was in his power. There was constantly something too noticeable in the appearance of each wife that seemed like a reproach to him. He was able to make neither happy, and this consciousness weighed like a millstone about his neck. His domestic happiness had gone in a great measure. He did not possess the affection of one of his little daughters, and now his wife was dying with reproaches for him on her lips. He had done his duty, lived up to the light he had received, obeyed divine commands, and this was all the reward he had thus far received.

Helen failed rapidly now, and at last it was with real sorrow that her husband closed her eyes in death. Constant attendance upon her and a demand upon his sympathies had awakened something of his former tenderness for her, and could she but have realized it, the pathway to her grave might have been smoothed a little, but she could only believe that his kindness and sympathy were forced.

Marion knew how matters stood, but she could not and would not be jealous of a dying woman, and encouraged her husband to make every effort for the alleviation of her pain, both bodily and mental. And now came a trial to Marion. She had never been seen with Helen while living—had never been with her except on two or three occasions till her sickness; but now that Helen was dead, she must publicly sit with her husband as a mourner for her. A mourner for her husband's other wife! She was expected to mourn because the cause of her suffering almost unto death was removed—to mourn because the one who had robbed her of her husband's affection was beyond the power to wound her further. Her husband, she knew, really grieved for Helen in a measure; but as she thought of the time when his very soul seemed rent by the loss of their little Elsie, she could not but feel to thank God that he did not mourn for Helen as he had for their babe. Little Marion and her sister Nell had never met before, but now, with one clinging tearfully to her father's hand, and the other wonderingly walking by her mother's side, they together went through with the scenes which in their future lives, as they looked back to childhood's days, were the first they could remember. The father lifted Nell to look at her mother lying so cold and still.

"Mamma, mamma! Do wake up! Do take Nell!" she cried, but no human power could wake Helen now. Little Marion, on seeing her father lift Nell, turned to her mother and said: "Mamma, lift me, too, please. Mayon wants to see." But the mother did not grant her little one's request; she could not bear to impress upon the child's mind a sight of the cold dead face of her father's other wife. Her early impressions she would not cloud with the horrors of polygamy, and she felt thankful that her little son was prevented from being there by a slight sickness. As she stood looking for the last time at Helen, all feelings of resentment had died in her heart. She could not hate the dead; she could only pity and forgive. She mourned that she had cherished such feelings towards one who, though the occasion of her misery, was yet not to blame that she had been the one selected to supplant her in her husband's affections. It was not *her* fault that hatred had existed between them. Poor Helen! And now Marion asked God's forgiveness for the sin of hating her husband's wife. But other feelings of a conflicting nature entered her heart now. As she saw how tenderly and affectionately her husband led or carried little Nell; how sweetly trustful she was in him, as her arms were wound about his neck and her cheek lay against his, how she mourned for the estrangement that forbade any such familiarity between him and her little one! She felt again the old jealousy for Helen's baby, and rejoiced that Nell was not to become one of her family. And as she passed on and realized that she and her husband had beheld his second wife for the last time on earth, in spite of herself a sense of relief came over her. A load seemed lifted from her heart. She felt free. Her husband was again hers, and hers alone. Helen could never come between them now, and Marion was surprised and shocked as she found that her heart was being lifted up towards the lightness of other days. Was it mockery for her to be there, and was it a sin for her to rejoice in her freedom? Marion felt that it was, and conscientiously and self-reproachfully tried to crush such unworthy sentiments. But she could not. She was human. God never gave pure womanly instincts to his creatures—filled their very souls with a sense of right and wrong, and then required them to crush these God-given instincts. And Marion's struggle to that effect was in vain, and only filled her heart with a tumult of conflicting emotions, till she was almost unconscious of what was going on about her.

Chapter 9

Little Nell was sent to her mother's sister, in a distant part of the Territory, and Elder Northfield's second home was broken up. Now he had one home, one wife, one family to care for, and as time passed on he realized much more comfort than he had done in the divided state of matrimony. He missed his favorite daughter, but little Marion, or Mayon, as they now called her since she had given herself that name, was becoming less shy of her father, and by degrees lost her fear of him. But she did not love him as she did her mother and brother, and he knew it; but still he became more and more fond of her as she grew older and more beautiful every year. Her large dark eyes were full of light and beauty at times, and again, if anything saddened her, they were filled with the most mournful and often reproachful expression. Her complexion was like a ripe peach, and glowed with the beauty of health, and her hair hung down her shoulders in a shower of dark curls, and clustered about her forehead in little rings which all the combing and wetting in the world could not straighten. But her beauty was not all external. She was full of the graces of a beautiful childhood, winning the love of whoever knew her, first by her personal attractions, then by the loveliness of her disposition. Mayon had one peculiar characteristic, that of changing suddenly from the gayest of moods, the liveliest frolic, to a strange sadness unaccountable to her parents. At such times she would always seek her mother, lay her head in her lap, and sometimes would even sob and cry without being able to give any reason for it. Then as suddenly her mood would change again, and instantly her tears would be dashed away, and, with face radiant as though refreshed by a summer shower, she would dart away to her play. She had the sweetest of childish voices, and her mother delighted in training it to sing the songs she learned in her younger days.

Forest was now a manly little fellow, long ago having been relieved of his golden ringlets, which were lovingly and tearfully laid aside as a tribute to his baby days. The dresses and little half-worn shoes had been put away for "clothes like papa's" and boots. He was very fond of his mother and Mayon, but his father was chief among ten thousand to him, and his greatest pleasure was to be with him—his greatest ambition to be like him. His father had more influence over him than his mother or sister, and for his sake more than for Mayon's, Mrs. Northfield longed and prayed that he might see his error and free himself from his fanatical belief in Mormonism. She had faith that she could mould Mayon's mind as she wished, and, like another mother, so this one determined that her little girl should never be a Mormon's wife. Her future life was decided upon by her mother. If her own life must be spent in Mormonism, then in the future there was in store for her a separation from this dearest treasure, for cost what it might to her, Mayon must never suffer as she had suffered. She must go into the Gentile world when her childhood days were over, and somewhere there would be a place for her and a happy home which no counsel or command of man could blight.

She had tried unsuccessfully to save Francis and Edith Parker from Mormonism; she would succeed in her plan with her own child. With this end, this separation in view, did this mother bravely rear her little one. She taught her all she could (and Mayon proved an apt scholar), cultivated her every gift, and especially her talent for music, and tried by every means in her power to render her treasure more valuable, her gem more bright, only to part with it at last. This project of Marion's was kept a secret from every human being. She sometimes felt that she was acting as a traitor to her husband in secretly planning the escape of their daughter from Mormonism, but she was sure a knowledge of her scheme by him would be fatal to its fulfilment. His sense of duty in the matter would outweigh every other consideration, and Mayon would be forced to remain in Mormonism, and in all probability would suffer the horrors of polygamy. Anything was better than that; even death would she have preferred for her little one. And Mayon was growing up, all unconscious of the fate her mother was preparing for her, for she tried by every means in her power to render her strong in body and mind and self-reliant, and to give her all the knowledge of the Gentile world that it was in her power to do, that when the dreaded time came, when she must send her forth from her protecting arm, she might be competent if need be to make her own way in the world. She would have been glad to have sought the society of what few Gentiles there were in the city, but that would have been to attract the attention of the authorities, and after her attempt at making apostates of the little Parkers, would have excited their suspicions of her intentions with regard to her own children. She now had a little school in her own family and taught Forest and Mayon much more than Mormon children usually learned of books. In one branch, however, they were sadly deficient—that was of the doctrines and teachings of their religion. She entirely neglected this branch of instruction, the one considered the most important; but Elder Northfield tried to be faithful in this matter, and imparted much moral and doctrinal instruction to his young son. Forest accepted as eagerly all his father said, as his father had accepted the teachings of Mormonism in his younger days, and he was as devoted a little Mormon as his father might wish, and inherited his missionary zeal to such an extent as to exercise it upon his sister upon all possible occasions. When quite small he would mount a chair and with Mayon for his audience, would proceed to proclaim to her the mysteries of the revelations and doctrines of the Latter-day Saints. His gestures amused her, his earnestness inspired her with awe, and her admiration for him kept her such an attentive audience that Forest thought he had made a deep impression upon her. He longed for the time to come when he should be a man and stand in the pulpit and preach to an attentive throng as Brigham Young now did. He delighted in reciting poems or speeches to as great an audience as he could command, or even to an imaginary audience. Mayon, with her dolls, her kitten, and her bird, always formed a part of these audiences, and sometimes the whole. There was no doubt that Forest had a talent for public speaking, and his father took great pride in his son's proclivities, but to his mother they were a source of trouble. She believed he was destined to exercise a great influence over others, and the indications now were that he would wield that influence to perpetuate Mormonism in all its frauds. As he grew older he began to take Mayon aside and teach her the doctrines he had learned from his father's lips, until her mind would be full of wonder at the remarkable visions and revelations God had sent to men, and her large eyes would dilate with fear, as Forest portrayed the great battle which was coming on the earth between the Saints of the Most High and the wicked Gentiles. Forest enjoyed the impression he made upon his sister's mind exceedingly, but he was not aware how deep was the effect of his words. Much of the time she seemed to have a half-frightened appearance, and developed a timidity altogether new to her. Her mother watched this new trait with anxiety and wonder. At last, however, she discovered the cause.

One morning Mayon awoke screaming with terror. As soon

as she could be calmed enough to say anything she exclaimed: "O, mamma! I've had a vision!"

"A vision, my child!"

"Yes, mamma, a vision. I saw God coming down from heaven with a great sword in his hand, and he went into the Gentile world, and all the little Gentile children were running away from him and begging him not to kill them. Then I ran after him to plead for the poor little children, and he raised his sword to strike me, and then I screamed and you came then, mamma. O, will God destroy all the little Gentile children, mamma?"

"Certainly not, Mayon. Why do you think so, and why do you call your bad dream a vision?"

"O, it is a vision, mamma. Forest told me all about visions, and he says they are always true."

"Did Forest tell you this, my little girl?"

"Yes, mamma, and a great deal more that makes me afraid."

"Tell me what it is."

"He says if we don't obey the elders God will destroy us, and that by-and-by all the Mormons will go against all the Gentiles, and they will try to kill each other; but the Mormons will not be killed—the Gentiles will, though, and then there won't be any Gentiles, and there won't be any aunt Elsie, will there, mamma, for you to tell me about?"

"My poor frightened Mayon, Forest has told you wrong. There will be no such attempt to kill each other as he has told you, and there is no such thing as a vision in these days."

"But, mamma, papa told Forest so himself; but I did not think I should have a vision; I was afraid of it though. O, mamma, I think visions is dreadful!"

What could the mother say now to her child? These frightful assertions had their origin from her father's lips, although they had become somewhat distorted in coming to Mayon.

How could that mother tell her child that her father's teachings were false, and thus destroy the little faith and trust she had worked so hard to establish in her little one? How could she bear that the Mormon doctrines and hideous beliefs should be instilled into Mayon's mind to terrify her young heart? It was hard enough to see that her loved son was growing up a willing victim to the delusions of his father's faith—that he would no doubt be the cause of misery to some woman or women—without sacrificing her little girl too.

"Mayon," she said, "Forest did not quite understand papa. He did not mean exactly as Forest told you; and what you saw was a bad, naughty dream, and no vision at all."

"And won't God kill the little Gentile children?"

"No, my dear; God loves little children, no matter whether they are Mormon or Gentile, and He will take them in his arms and bless them."

"O, mamma, don't let Him take me in His arms! I am afraid of Him."

"No, darling, mamma will keep you from all harm."

"But didn't papa say that God would destroy all the little Gentile children? Forest said he did."

What could Marion say now? Her husband had told her son what she was now denying to their daughter. The father was making assertions which the mother contradicted. How was family government, parental confidence, and domestic harmony to prevail, with matters in such a state? Marion saw that the situation was indeed deplorable. She did not answer Mayon's question; and Mayon, after waiting in vain for an answer, said:

"I'll ask papa, and he will tell me."

Mrs. Northfield hoped, however, that she would forget about it by the time her father returned, for he had gone on a visit to his little daughter Nell. But Mayon did not forget, and almost the first thing she said to him was:

"Papa, did you tell Forest that God would destroy all the little Gentile children?"

"Yes, my dear; why do you ask?"

"Mamma said Forest didn't understand you, and that God loved all little children, and would not kill any of them. O, papa! don't let God kill those poor little children."

And Mayon's quivering lips and pent-up tears could be controlled no longer. She sobbed and cried, and her father took her in his arms and endeavored to soothe her.

"My little girl," said he, "God knows what is best, and my Mayon will be safe in his fold, and the little Gentile children will be saved, too, if they come into His Church."

"But, papa, who told you so? and why did mamma say it wasn't so?"

"The men God sent told me so, and mamma denied it because she doesn't believe it."

"O! well then, I guess, papa, I don't b'leeve, too. I think those men that said so are naughty men, 'cause mamma said God loves little children; and papa, do you love little children?"

"Yes, Mayon, I do."

"And you wouldn't want to kill the little children, would you?"

"No, Mayon."

"Then God wouldn't, would He? I guess, papa, those men told you wrong, 'cause mamma knows, and she said it wasn't a vision—only a bad, naughty dream."

"Why, Mayon, what did you see in your dream?" Mayon then told her dream, and her father wisely led the conversation to other matters, and soon she slipped away from him, saying:

"Please, papa, don't tell us or any little children what those naughty men said, it makes me so afraid."

And well she might be afraid of a belief, called a religion, which had brought, was bringing, and would in the future bring untold misery to her sex.

Mrs. Northfield now felt that something must be done to prevent the recurrence of such scenes. She talked with her husband on the subject. Elder Northfield wished to bring up his children in his own religion, and his wife dared not allow him to suspect her determination with regard to Mayon's future. But they agreed that the teachings of one must not contradict the statements of the other. If husband and wife could not agree in this point, each must make some concession in favor of the other.

So they at last agreed that to Marion should be given the religious training of their daughter, while the son should be instructed by his father. Thus Marion was bound, to save Mayon from false teachings, to allow her son to grow up deceiving and being deceived; to allow him to be blinded by Mormon absurdities and make no effort to remove the scales from his eyes. How she wished that he was again the little innocent child that fled with her on that terrible night from their home, that she might have kept him ignorant as he then was of all the superstitions and depravity of Mormonism, and that she might have always moulded his mind as she could then. She was very sad as she realized the situation; but even if she could have been allowed to teach her son, in all probability her influence would have been unavailing against his father's.

He was a beautiful boy, full of noble qualities, and he did not realize that his preaching and teaching were having such a painful effect on his sister, or he would have spared her sensitive feelings. Now, however, he was forbidden to speak to Mayon on the subject of Mormon religion, and it was never broached in her presence by any member of the family. If introduced by herself, no encouragement was given her to ask questions, and after a time her interest died away, although she did not entirely forget her "vision."

Mrs. Northfield had come to realize that there could be no real happiness for her in the Mormon world. As long as her husband remained a believer in Mormonism, so long would her life be clouded by its effects. There was reason to believe he would be a Mormon till he died, and therefore she could see no great brightness in the world for her. But she had much to comfort and give her peace now in her domestic relations. Her husband was again devoted to her, and her children were a source of pride and pleasure. She might escape any great sorrow, her heart might never again be wrung by its former anguish, but yet there was always the fear in her soul that polygamy would again send its crushing influence to plunge her into her former darkness. The effects of her past misery were lasting, and never, under any circumstances, could she have gained her old lightness of heart. The wound might heal, but the scar disappear, never.

Another source of sorrow, unknown, unsuspected by any one, was the separation that she had decreed, in her own mind, should take place between herself and daughter. As long as she could keep her with her, she would, but when the time came, as it would, alas, too soon, that others should seek to link Mayon's destiny irrevocably with Mormonism, then she must send her darling forth alone, and her home would be desolate.

Marion had not seen little Nell since she was sent to her mother's sister, at the age of three years. She knew nothing of her beyond what her husband told her of his occasional visits, but after the lapse of several years she was to renew her acquaintance with the child in a way she had not expected. Helen's sister died suddenly, and her friends sent word to Elder Northfield to that effect; also, that Nell was unprovided for, and he was requested to immediately assume the responsibility of her care or instruct them how to proceed with reference to her.

The way seemed now to open to bring his little daughter home, and the father was glad that it was so, for his affection for Nell was still strong; but how would his wife receive her? Would she be willing to take Helen's child into her home? He stated the facts to Marion; nobly she answered, "Bring the motherless child home with you, and I will try to be a good mother to her."

She feared she never could love Nell very much, but she could at least be kind and fulfil a mother's duty towards her.

So Nell came to them, and Mayon had a playfellow and her mother a new care. Mayon received Nell warmly, for she had few playmates of her own age, as her mother wished to keep her secluded as much as was possible from their Mormon surroundings. Nell proved to be a bright, winsome child, when all her moods and whims were indulged, but her temper was almost ungovernable if she was thwarted or crossed in her desires. She was very selfish, and of an envious, jealous disposition. To offset these defects, however, she was extremely affectionate and kind at intervals, and became much attached to Mayon. But in spite of Nell's fondness for her, Mayon suffered much from her unevenness of disposition, and her little heart was often grieved by Nell's unkindness. The latter would sometimes seek to make up for her wrong to her half-sister by a spasm of generosity, which would make all right again.

Nell was a pretty child, with light-brown hair and keen gray eyes. Her face had a bright, piquant look, which attracted people, and although the beauty and regularity of Mayon's features were missing in her, yet she had a certain beauty of her own. She had been brought up so far in true Mormon ignorance, and could scarcely read at all, while Mayon could read well, and had advanced beyond most children of her age, even in Gentile society, in her knowledge of arithmetic and geography. In geography she was especially interested and well informed, as her mother pointed out to her on the maps her native country, the course she took in sailing from it. New York, her aunt Elsie's home, and the entire Gentile world, and told her of its people, its manners and customs.

Mayon was also beginning to be an apt music scholar. Her father had procured her an organ—a luxury enjoyed by few Mormon children—and he was gratified to see that she was making good use of her opportunities. She was very ambitious, and her love for books was only equalled by her love for music. As his two little daughters were brought together. Elder Northfield did not fail to note a wide difference between them in every respect. The culture that Mayon's mind had received from her mother gave an acuteness of intelligence to her that was lacking in Nell. Their dispositions, too, were so totally unlike that often by comparison Nell became positively disagreeable. Nell did not bring as much happiness to her father's home as he had expected, and not being opposed to education, as most Mormons were, he could see that Mayon's superiority lay to a degree in the cultivation she had received from her mother in both mind and heart. He desired the same advantages for Nell, and as they could not be obtained outside of his own home, Marion granted his request and undertook first to teach Nell to read. She proved a dull scholar, and was a great trial to her foster-mother. The latter felt that she was robbing her own child of time that would otherwise be devoted to her, and as only a few years more could be hers to care for and teach Mayon, she could not willingly devote her time to Nell with no apparent good result. Nell was very capricious and could not be made to study hard by any means whatever. She often was very rebellious and caused Mrs. Northfield a great deal of trouble. The latter was discouraged, and her husband became discouraged also. Nell was a perverse, wilful child, who wanted her own way entirely, but given that, she could make herself very winsome and sweet. Thus it came about that she was left very much to her own sweet will and therefore appeared to much better advantage.

Marion had given up all society as far as was possible to do without neglecting her duty to her husband, but one institution, namely, the theatre, she assiduously attended with Mayon, young as she was. Her husband nearly always accompanied her, and now Nell went with them whenever she wished. Elder Northfield often wondered at his wife's fondness for the theatre to the exclusion of every other amusement, and also at her habit of taking Mayon always, when on all other occasions she insisted on the child's early retiring. He did not know that she was educating her for a Gentile life, and desired to make her familiar with the Gentile scenes which were portrayed on the stage. Her means were so limited for teaching her Gentile beliefs, manners and customs that none must be slighted, and many pleasant thoughts were awakened in Mayon's mind, many agreeable impressions formed concerning the Gentile world. This was as her mother intended. Although it would not do for her to openly speak to her against Mormonism and in favor of Gentile life, yet she could and did constantly throw around her little unseen influences which were doing their work. As long as was possible she had kept her daughter ignorant of the existence of polygamy, but now she had arrived at the age when, with it all around her, she could not fail to notice the plurality of wives and contrast it with the Gentile custom in that respect as it was portrayed by the theatre, by the few books Marion had been able to put in her hands, and by her mother's description of life in the Gentile world. Of the misery of polygamy she knew nothing, and was too young to realize its existence.

Chapter 10

Between Elder Northfield and his wife there seldom passed any words with reference to polygamy. Each felt that it was a painful subject to be avoided by them, as they could never agree upon it. Marion had no means of knowing whether her husband ever contemplated again entering into the patriarchal order of marriage. She was constantly in fear of it, however, but never for one moment did she think of interceding to prevent such a calamity again coming upon her, or of obtaining his promise to the contrary. She knew he would never bind himself again to a course that might conflict with his sense of duty, and even if he would, she had learned from past experience that such promises would avail nothing. So she could only wait, and fear, and hope, and accept her fate, whatever it might be. She would not have been surprised at any time had he told her he was thinking of taking another wife, but she was not prepared for the announcement that he one day made to her that on the morrow he was to be married. Marion heard her husband, but she did not comprehend him. The blow fell so suddenly, so heavily, that it shattered her reason for the time.

"Married—married, did you say? Who is to be married?"

"I am to be married, my dear wife; don't you understand me?"

"Yes, I do. I know you were married. I remember it well. I gave her to you, but I thought she was dead."

"Helen is dead, Marlon, but I am going to take another wife to-morrow. Marion! Marion! why do you look at me so? My poor, dear wife! Believe me, I pity you. I have put this off as

long as I could for your sake." And now he threw his strong
arms around her, and pressed her lips with kisses. But she heeded them not. "I have not told you," he continued, "because I
would not pain you sooner than need be. I *could* not bear that
you should know what was coming and suffer in anticipation.
So I let you be happy as long as I could, Marion, and as it could
not be helped, why should I tell you before? It is not my wish
to do this, but my duty; and my love is all your own. I will not
forsake you as I did once for another. Marion! Marion! speak
to me!"

But Marion could not speak. She did not hear his sad tones
as he tried to soften the effects of the blow he had dealt her.
He looked into her face, white and immovable as death, and
exclaimed:

"My God! have I killed her?"

But she had only fainted, and though it was long before she
could be brought back to consciousness, yet at last she opened
her eyes and at sight of her husband bending over her, anxiously watching for a token of returning life, she turned her
face aside and groaned.

"Marion," said he.

"Don't speak to me!" she cried. "Don't look at me! I can't bear
it! I expected it, but not like this—not thus suddenly. Henry
Northfield, you either *do not* love your wife, or you are crazy!
Yes, crazy with Mormonism! I could not comprehend what
you said at first. Now, I do. I have dreaded it these years, and
expected to be able to bear it, but now to think of living over
the old misery worse than death. I find I cannot bear it, and I
will not. If I must be wretched, I will be wretched somewhere
else. Henry, I'll go to-morrow to the Endowment House and
give you another wife, and then you may bring her here, devote
yourself to her, and make her happy, till duty compels you to
take another, and I will go. One wife is enough at a time. Yes, I

will take Mayon, and we will go somewhere among the Gentiles. We will separate. We can never be happy together again—we will not try. But my boy! My Forest! How can I part with him! O, why was I ever created to be so wretched!"

"Marion, is Forest the only tie that would bind you here? Have you no love for your husband? Pity me, my wife, and believe that my heart aches for you, and that I feel my load is hard to bear, but God does not willingly afflict. Marion, do you wish to leave me?"

Marion could not answer. At last she said: " I *must* leave you. I feel that I shall go mad if I stay. Would to God I had never loved you!"

This thrust cut into her husband's very soul. He felt that he did not deserve it. He would not willingly have given the slightest pain to his wife and sought by every means to make her happy, only he had placed his duty to God and religion first, and when that duty conflicted with his happiness he had sacrificed the latter. He was very wretched now, and disappointed at the violence of her grief. He had thought that a second trial of this kind would not seem so hard as the first. He believed something in the Mormon theory of "getting used to it," but he did not know a woman's heart. He did not know that a second crushing blow was more terrible in its effects than the first.

"Marion," said he, "let me tell you about the one I have chosen, and I think you will feel better about it."

"No need of telling me; I care for only one thing. Tell me that, please, and no more. Will she be kind to Forest?"

"I am sure she will."

"And if not, you will be; and he is not a little child now, or I could not leave him. Perhaps I shall come back again, some time. But tell me one thing more: Henry, will you be happy with her when I am gone? I do not want you to be miserable," and a shade of tenderness came into Marion's voice as she asked this question.

"Happy! Happy without you, Marion? Never! Do you realize that you are the only one on earth that I love? I never have spoken to this young woman but four or five times in my life. I never have whispered one word of love to her. I asked her to be my wife, for I was obliged to ask some one, and after much thought she has consented. Happy with her alone! Marion, do not think of leaving me; I cannot let you go! You must not leave me."

And tightly her husband clasped her hand in his. Marion struggled to free herself, and exclaimed:

"Stop! Do not dare to keep me! I must go! I must go!"

"Marion, we will put off the marriage till you feel better."

"I never shall feel better, here. You shall not put the day off; the sooner it is over the better! Do not fear that I shall make a scene, Henry; I shall be very calm then, and she will never know what I suffer."

In vain did Elder Northfield strive to persuade his wife to relinquish the idea she had conceived, or to allow him to postpone his marriage. He would have insisted on the latter, however, if he had believed that she would adhere to her determination. But he relied on her calmer consideration of the matter, and her affection for him, to change her determination, and preparations for the marriage went on accordingly.

Mrs. Northfield scarcely realized her situation. She was not quite herself. One thing impressed itself upon her mind to the exclusion of everything else: she was to save Mayon from Mormonism, much sooner than she had expected. She was to go with her herself to the Gentile world. After all, the much dreaded separation was never to take place. Mayon should be hers always. Her beautiful, darling child was not to be sent into the wide world alone, but she was going with her, and together they would escape from this hateful place. One idea filled her mind, and that was their departure from Mormonism. She spent what little time remained in preparing for her departure. She sent to Mrs. Atwood's, asking the gift of the picture of herself and husband, and then clipping a tress from among her golden locks, which were still beautiful, though of a paler hue now, and one long, shining curl from Mayon's head, she placed them, with the picture, where he would find them on first entering the house after his marriage, saying to herself:

"He shall not think I went away hating him. If he should grieve for us these little tokens will comfort him."

The next day Mayon came to her father with a tearful face.

"Papa," said she, "are you going to get another wife, to-day?"

"Yes, Mayon, and she will come home with me to-night. How did you know? Has mamma told you?"

"No, Forest told me. I go to mamma and she hardly speaks to me, and looks so sad and miserable, and I saw her wipe away some tears this morning, and she shuts herself into her room and into my room, and doesn't let me come in when I ask her. I sat down and cried a little while ago, and Forest came and asked me what I was crying for, and I told him, and asked him what ailed mamma, and he said you were going to get another wife to-day, and that was what she was crying about. Papa, please don't get another wife; it makes mamma feel so bad. We don't want another mother, and you can't be mamma's husband and hers, too. Isn't mamma a good enough wife, papa?"

"Yes, child, too good for me to have."

"Is that why you are getting another, then, papa? Do you want the new one to do the work and teaching mamma does, so that mamma can go out with you, and always be dressed nice, and have time to play with us all she wishes? That wouldn't be so bad, but mamma doesn't want her at all, so please—please, papa, don't get her."

Elder Northfield had listened till he could hear no more, and untwining her arms from his neck, he put her away from him and hastily left the house.

At the appointed hour Marion accompanied her husband to the Endowment House, not, however, without first throwing her arms around his neck and sobbing like a child, with her head on his shoulder.

She that day gave him another wife, sealed unto herself a new doom of misery, and hardly knew what she did. She had no interest in the bride, and scarcely saw her or anything else. She felt bewildered. Only one thing was clear to her: her carriage was to be ready at her door for an immediate start towards some Gentile settlement she knew the location of, and she and Mayon were to leave Mormonism forever. But suddenly, as she comprehended some words of the closing part of the ceremony, she became faint, and fell to the floor.

Her husband, *their* husband he was then, left his bride's side and lifted her with all the tenderness he would have felt had she fainted on her own wedding-day.

And now came a blank in Mrs. Northfield's life; a long blank to which in the future she looked back with the feeling that a part of her life had been lost to her.

Her first rational impression, after the ordeal passed in the Endowment House, was of a small, dimly-lighted room, plainly furnished, but so pure and neat, with its white muslin curtains, its little round table, with its vase of flowers, two or three chairs—one an easy-chair—and the bed of spotless purity, on which she lay. She had one glimpse of the outer world through a half-closed shutter. Instead of looking through an open window at summer skies and verdant foliage, as she last saw the face of nature, the window was now closed, a fire was burning in an open grate, and the trees that swayed in the wind were leafless. She comprehended that time had passed unconsciously to her. She looked about on her surroundings, felt the sweet soothing influences around her, and dropped into a light slumber.

Again she awoke, and then all the past came back to her. She was doubtless somewhere in the Gentile world, escaped at last from Mormonism. But where was she? and how did she come there? who was so kindly caring for her? and where was Mayon? Then she thought of her home in Salt Lake City, and of her husband living in their old home with his new wife. She wondered if he missed her and Mayon—if he found the keepsakes she left for him, and cherished them for love of his dear ones.

Again she slept, and on again awaking, a new charm had been added to her room. Drawn up before the fire was the easy-chair, and in it the familiar form of Edith Parker. Edith had become a woman now, and all through her childhood and youth had been one of Marion's few friends. The calm purity that pervaded the room was now increased by the sweet pale face of Edith, which had never outgrown the look of sadness it had worn in her childhood.

"Edith," said Mrs. Northfield, "I am glad you came too; but where is Mayon?"

Edith's face lit up with glad surprise, as she turned toward the bed and said:

"Dear Mrs. Northfield, I am so glad you are better. Mayon is in the next room, and you shall see her if you will promise not to talk any more now." Marion felt like a willing and obedient child under the influence of sweet Edith Parker, and she gave the desired promise. Edith left the room and soon returned with Mayon, who, fearful of disturbing her mother, came in noiselessly, but with a face radiant with happiness.

"Mamma, darling," said she, as she laid her face beside her mother's, "you know your Mayon now, don't you? I have mourned so because you did not know your little girl, and would not have her with you, but they let me come in when you were asleep, and watch you, and I did love to do even that, mamma."

But the mother forgot her promise not to talk, and Edith saw she was tiring herself with Mayon, so she gently persuaded her to send her away, and so weak was the sufferer that she was now exhausted by her excitement.

Days passed, and she remained so weak that she could scarcely talk at all. She was unconscious much of the time, but at intervals her mind was clear, though it partook of the feebleness of the whole body. As she lay there watching Edith glide in and out, felt her soft touch on her throbbing brow, listened to her sweet voice, as she spoke in low tones words of cheer and affection, she seemed to Marion like a ministering angel sent to guard her in her life in a new world.

"Edith," said she one day, "your mother is looking down from heaven and rejoicing now to know that at last her little girl has escaped from what she called a 'hell upon earth.' I did not think when I tried to grant her request and send you into the Gentile world that you would wait and go with me—that we should escape together."

Edith turned to hide her face from the speaker, but did not reply. As soon as the latter gained strength she spoke again:

"I wonder sometimes where I am, but have felt too weak to ask or to care as long as I knew Mayon and I were safe in the Gentile world and you were with us; but now, Edith, tell me how we came here, where we are, and whose house this is? Who are the kind people who have taken us in?"

"We are in one of the pleasantest of places, and Mrs. Martin is the lady of the house. She is very kind, and glad to know you are improving."

"Have I been very sick, Edith?"

"Yes, very; but you have had excellent medical skill, and we have tried to give you the best of care. Now, can you not rest before you talk any more? Your physician says you must be kept very quiet till you grow stronger. Try to be patient, and when you can talk more I will tell you all about it."

She was obliged to rest, but she did not feel satisfied with the meagre information she received. The next day she said to Edith:

"Sometimes, when I think it all over, I wish I had not taken this step. I am glad for your sake and Mayon's, but I can never be happy away from my husband. I never could be happy with him, I know now, but I know, as I think of it, that he loves me, and I can realize now what pain it cost him to bring this trouble upon me. He did not wish to do it, but was forced into it by his religion. It was not Henry's fault, but the fault of Mormonism. I keep thinking of his assurances that he could not be happy without me, and see, as I did not then, how sad he was, and I think I should have pitied rather than blame him. If he really was grieved to have me leave him, it was cruel for me to do so, and I have done worse than he, for I deserted him for my own sake, and he was true in heart to me, though compelled to an act of unfaithfulness by the Church. Sometimes I think I will leave Mayon with you and go back to him if he would take me back. Do you ever hear from him, Edith?"

"Yes, I have heard of him several times."

"And I suppose he brought his wife to our home?"

"Yes, he brought her there after the marriage."

"Yes, but not till after the carriage I had ordered had taken us away. Is he living happily with her now, do you think, Edith, or do you think he would be glad to have me come back?"

"I know he wants you to come back, dear Mrs. Northfield, and he is not living with her at all now."

"Not living with her! Why not? Where is she?"

"He did not love her, nor she him, and she wished to go away, and so she went and is with her friends."

"And Henry, and Forest, and Nell are living alone. Edith, I hate that wife. I cannot help it; but not so much as I should if she loved him. O, do you think I could possibly go back to him? He has been so kind to me through it all, and some time I believe he will be converted back to the Gentile belief. But, Edith, you do not tell me all I wish to know. You do not answer my questions fully. Tell me the whole now; I am strong enough to hear it."

"If you knew that you could go back to your husband to-day, would you be glad to go?"

"I would, I think, if I could leave Mayon and you here. I would rather be separated from her sooner than I expected, if I could leave her in your care, than to take her back. I would rather leave her than to continue this separation from my husband; but if Mayon had to go back with me I should hesitate. But tell me all about our leaving the Mormon world, and where we are; or, Edith," she exclaimed excitedly, as a new suspicion flashed into her mind, "have we not left it at all? Where are we?"

"My dear friend, try to be calm and I will tell you all. We are still in Salt Lake City. You have not had your reason until now for many months, and here was a quieter, better place for you, and so we brought you here."

"Edith, I know where I am now. I am where your mother once told me I should be—in the insane asylum! I did not believe it then, but she said it would be so, for I was the wife of a Mormon. O, Edith! You and Mayon are still victims of this cursed religion. Your mother told me she would take me to her room when I came here. Is this the room that was hers?"

"Yes, and in your delirium you were constantly calling her to come and take you to her room, so the kind matron gave this room to you."

"Why does not my husband come to see me if, as you say, he wants me back again?"

"He does come every day; but since your reason returned we thought it not safe for him to see and excite you. He came this morning and brought these flowers, and you should have seen how happy he looked when I told him you were stronger. You have for the past few weeks been very sick with a fever, and we have all been hoping that when it left you your reason would return, as it has."

"Tell me, now, why you are with me, and something about the other wife. I would not let Henry tell me anything about her."

"I am with you because I am in a certain sense the cause of your trouble."

"You the cause of my trouble!"

"Yes, my dear, dear friend, can you bear to hear something that will shock you, for I must tell you?"

"Yes, tell me! What have you been hiding from me so long?"

"I am your husband's wife!"

"You—Edith—my husband's wife! The woman I hate! No, no!"

And Edith feared that reason had again fled as Marion pressed her hands to her brow and her eyes again glowed with the wildness of past days.

"I love you, Edith, but I hate my husband's wife! God forgive me for it! You and she cannot be the same! It cannot be that you are so far from being safe in the Gentile world as to have become a Mormon's wife! And my husband's wife! Edith, how you have made me love you in these few days and now you tell me you are the wife I gave to my husband on that terrible day! Am I again insane or is it true that you have told me? I cannot bear to believe it, Edith, for I love you, and how can I ever love my husband's other wife? O, Edith! how could you do it?"

"Let me tell you how, and I am sure you will feel better and calmer about it than you do now. It is a long story, but I think it will interest you.

"My mother's instructions and influence in favor of the Gentiles never lost their effect upon me. I shall remember to my dying day the repugnance with which I regarded polygamy, as I realized that it had blighted my mother's life and made her the wretched woman she was. She taught me to know the many wrongs which Mormonism brought on my sex, and though too young to fully comprehend her, I have grown up looking upon matrimony in Mormonism as the greatest trouble that could come upon me. But since my father, whom I never could regard with any feeling but aversion for his cruelty to my mother—since he took me to one of his homes, I have expected that sooner or later I should be forced into marriage, as all Mormon girls are. It is a little strange that I have been permitted to wait so long, but it was not without persecution. My father has had several offers of marriage for me, dating back to my fifteenth year. All of them I persistently refused to consider, and thus made him very angry. On two occasions he has treated me very cruelly in consequence of my rebellion against his wishes, but of his wife Carrie I will say that she has acted the part of a mother to my brother and me, and has always been very kind to us. She never urged me to marry; and I always felt that I was welcome by her to a home, and indeed, I believe she dreaded losing me, for my father neglected her almost entirely, although providing the means for her support. I felt that my father wished me off his hands, and at last I fell sick, as you remember. You may not know that my foster-mother sent for a young Gentile physician to attend me, and concerning him I have a secret to tell you. He was the first Gentile person I had ever become acquainted with, and as I grew able to converse I used to ask him all about the Gentile faith and life, and

Carrie would join in the conversation. I learned a great deal from them both that made me long to escape from Mormonism. At last my physician ceased to visit me professionally but he frequently called in a friendly manner, and I began to look for his visits with a great deal of pleasure. My father knew of my sickness, but he knew very little of the particulars. It was Carrie to whom I owed my care. But at last he became aware that I was receiving visits from a Gentile, and he very rudely ordered him never to speak to me again. He then forced me to write a letter, which he indited,[24] requesting my friend never to call upon me again, as it would only be a source of trouble to me. I did not realize at the time how great an outrage this was upon me, for I did not know that my friendship for my Gentile friend was anything more than friendship. As weeks passed, however, I realized that he was dearer to me than any other friend on earth, and my separation from him was very hard to bear. I do not know whether my love was returned or not, but I have some reason to think it was. I should blush to tell all this to any one but you, but I owe you an unreserved statement of all that influenced me to marry Elder Northfield, and this was one thing that led to it. Well, my father was so angry at me and at Carrie for entertaining a Gentile that he declared I should marry the next opportunity. He threatened me with violence if I refused, and so it was not long before I was persecuted by the attentions of a young man whom I detested. I dared not resent his advances, however, for fear of my father, and was obliged to submit to his vehement lovemaking, till at last my father came to me, saying he had had another offer for me, and a much better one, and I was at liberty to choose between the two. So I met Elder Northfield, and in a respectful, gentlemanly way, without any professions of love, he asked me to become his wife. I asked time to consider, and at last consented. Now, I will tell you why I accepted his offer. At first I was shocked at the thought of being the one selected to cause the kind friend of my mother and my childhood the trouble I knew this would cause, and I tried to persuade him for your sake to abandon his purpose of marrying again; but though he expressed his grief at the necessity of paining you again, yet he assured me that it was his duty to marry, and the question was not whether he should take a wife or not, but who that wife should be. If I would not accept his offer, he should seek another; but he told me that he preferred me to any one else, for the reason that he thought it would give his wife less sorrow, as she was fond of me. He frankly told me that you had his whole heart, and it was only as a matter of duty that he sought another wife; but, apologizing for making me such an offer, he said he would assure me that all my wants should be carefully provided for and he would promise always to be a kind husband if not a devoted one.

"This was just the offer I wanted, if I must be married to a Mormon, for I could never love one and could never endure that one should love me, and it seemed like a way of escape from my tormentor. I was in a terrible situation. I felt that my father had cruelly doomed me to a life of misery, and all there was left for me was to choose not the least of two evils, but the least dreadful side of one great evil. I reasoned that if I became your husband's wife, you surely would never be neglected for me, and if I robbed you of your sole claim to him, I should never rob you of his affections, as some other woman might do. If I became his wife, you surely would never receive the hatred and insults second wives sometimes inflict upon the first, for I loved you too well to wish to cause you any trouble. I felt that I might be able to compensate in part for the affliction by devoting myself to you and yours, in any way possible. I was almost sure that by marrying your husband I could save you from worse trouble. With all these considerations, and the fact that I was forced to choose between two, how could I have done otherwise?"

"You could not. Poor Edith! I am glad now that you did so, but I pity you."

"I asked him if anything had been said between you on the subject, and he said there had not. He did not wish to speak of it till it was all settled, to avoid distressing you sooner than need be. I did not agree with him on that point, and wished him to consult with you, or allow me to do so, as I could not bear to enter your home without your permission. But I conceded that point, and at last the day was set for our marriage. I was then one of the most miserable of human beings. My lifelong fear was about to become a reality. My mother's worst apprehensions for me were about to be realized, and I was on the point of entering into polygamy. I would have tried to escape from the Territory, if I had believed that possible, but I did not. Elder Northfield attempted to tell you who he was to marry, the day before the ceremony, and you would not let him. At that ceremony I believe you were scarcely more wretched than the bride, and the bridegroom was anything but a happy one, I am sure, though he had the comfort of thinking he was doing his duty to console him. We had not even that delusion to stay our fainting hearts. Altogether, I believe there were never three more wretched people entering into a marriage contract than we were. It seems that you were so nearly beside yourself that you did not know whose hand you placed in your husband's. When you fell in a faint, I rejoiced to see how anxiously your husband cared for you, and almost forgot my presence. I tell you this to comfort you, and show you how devoted he still is to you. You recovered from your faint soon, but your reason had gone, and you were raving with delirium. We cared for you at your home as long as we could, but at last were obliged to bring you here. A few weeks ago you were prostrated with this fever, and then the physician said your reason might come back to you as the fever left, if you survived. Now, dear friend, we can thank God for allowing the fever to attack you. After all I have told you, can you forgive me for putting myself in this place?"

"Forgive! It is I that should ask you to forgive me for reproaching you. There is nothing to forgive on your part, but, O, so much to thank you for. You have acted the truest, best of friends, and you shall be like a younger sister to me. Edith, I will do what I can to make your life a happy one. O, if I had only known all this before, how much suffering might have been spared me!"

The bitterness of the trial was gone now, and Marion knew that again the weight of her burden was lifted. She now felt that she had done her husband great injustice, and she longed for his coming, that she might assure him of her sorrow and love for him. But he was nearer than she thought. Edith was called out, and returned saying Elder Northfield was at the door and waiting to see his wife, if she was able to bear the interview. Marion signalled for him to come in, and Edith left her, feeling that her presence would be an intrusion.

Too sacred for pen to describe was the meeting between husband and wife, and the scene must be left for the imagination to paint.

From this time Mrs. Northfield rapidly gained in strength, and it was not long before she was able to be removed to her home. Then there was great rejoicing in that reunited family. Even Nell had missed her motherly care, and was very happy at her return. She had been quite lonely without Mayon, who had begged so hard to go with her mother, that she could not be denied.

Edith felt some misgivings now at entering this home a polygamic wife; but she soon settled into her place as assistant to her friend and sister-wife in the domestic cares, and in the care of the children. She kept herself secluded, as much as possible, from their husband, avoiding him almost exclusively. Her evenings she spent in her own room, or with the children, never joining Marion when her husband was present. Marion protested against this, but Edith expressed her desire that it should be so, for, although she respected her husband, yet his society revived unpleasant thoughts, and was a source of irritation to her. She wished to live more as a helper in the family and companion to Marion, than as a wife. She was treated with the utmost kindness by the whole family, and in no respect could Mrs. Northfield look upon her as usurping her rights. Still, had she really been what she seemed—a sister, or merely a dear friend—there would not be the fact for her to realize that she was living in polygamy, that her husband had another wife.

There were yet obstacles in the way of her happiness, and one unknown to any but herself. Mayon was growing older, and unconsciously nearing the destiny foreordained for her. The prospect of the building of the Great Pacific Railway[25] seemed to open the way for the carrying out of Mrs. Northfield's plan. A most formidable undertaking it seemed for Mayon to attempt such a terrible journey as would be necessary with the facilities for travelling existing then. How her object could be accomplished with personal safety to Mayon, and with security from discovery and pursuit from her father and the Church authorities, was a question the mother had been unable to solve. But she believed a way would be opened before the time came. Therefore the news of a railway to be constructed from ocean to ocean, just at that time, seemed to her like help sent from Heaven.

Here was to be provided a way of escape for her darling, safe from the perils of the emigrant life, and sure to succeed in bearing her away from pursuers or enemies. This scheme of Marion's was a heavy burden on her conscience and a weight on her spirits, as she realized that it was deceit and treachery towards her husband. She felt that it was wronging him, to rob him of his daughter just as she bloomed into womanhood, and that in sending her away from her father's religion and people, she was assuming more than her right in their child. She sometimes entertained the thought of confessing to him her scheme for Mayon's future, and trusting to his kindness and affection to allow their child to decide for herself, and she felt sure he would decide wisely. But she knew his unwavering faith, that in Mormonism only lay the salvation of himself and family, and she feared that duty—a terrible word to her—would lead him, against the dictations of his own heart, to use influences or commands which could not be resisted. She dared not confide in him for fear of his terrible religion—a religion which could force a fair young girl into a wretched bondage, and destroy or outrage every womanly instinct of her soul.

Mrs. Northfield could not run that risk. Better, a thousand times better, wrong her husband, than wrong her daughter to the extent of blighting her whole life! Better bring down his anger and indignation, and even the malignity of the Church, upon her own head, than allow Mormonism to bring upon Mayon what it had brought upon her mother. So the mother carried the burden of her secret year after year.

Chapter 11

Many hundred miles from the scenes portrayed by the preceding pages, in a house furnished with every luxury and comfort its inmates desired, sat an elderly lady reading stories to two little children, sitting at her feet, and eagerly listening to the words as they fell from her lips. At one side of the room, near a window, a girl, who had outgrown such childish stories, sat poring over a book of her own, all oblivious of everything else. The lady had a calm, sweet expression, and her eyes had not lost their youthful brilliancy, though her hair was silvery gray. The little girl at the window suddenly tossed her sunny curls from her face, threw down her book, and her blue eyes sparkled, as she exclaimed:

"There come mamma and Harry! I'll meet them first, Dot and Daisy."

The stories were unheeded now, and the two little ones scampered away down to the gate, with their sister Lillian, who good-naturedly fell behind and allowed them to win the race.

The mother was the perfect picture of health, beauty, and joy, as she received the hearty welcome of her little ones. Harry, who had previously trudged along demurely by her side, caught the infection of the race, and instituted another, for his own benefit, calling on his mother to catch them. One and all they merrily brought up at the door, where the elderly lady stood watching them, with a smile of satisfaction.

"Well, aunt Wells, have these babies been good?" asked the

young mother as she caught up the little twins, who went by
the names of Dot and Daisy, and hugged them to her heart.

"Very good, Elsie. And now what letters have you?"

"I have scarcely looked at them, but I will now. O, aunt
Wells! Here is—I do believe this is Marion's handwriting. At
last she has written again. My sister is alive after all! I thank
God!"

Marion had not written to her sister for years. Since the re-
ceipt of Elsie's letter, which had so wrung her heart, coming
just when her happiness had received its first crushing blow, she
had wished to keep her in ignorance of her misery and humiliation. She had nothing but sorrow to write, and she could not
bear to write it. Thoughts of her sister and longing to hear from
her had, however, after a time, almost persuaded her to write,
but the dreaded ordeal was put off from time to time or forgotten in her family troubles and cares. So the years had passed,
and Elsie feared Marion was dead. She did not cease to write
to Marion for a time, but receiving no answer, at last gave up
in despair of ever hearing from her again. Elsie, or Mrs. Bernard, whom she had now become, hurriedly opened the letter
and read aloud:

MY OWN DEAR SISTER:

Can you forgive the long silence that I have kept these
years towards you? Your letter congratulating me upon my
husband's faithfulness, and the needlessness of your fears
for me, came when I was plunged in the deepest of
darkness by what you then—and I always—supposed
impossible, and I have since had not much but sorrow to
write of and could not bear that you and aunt Wells
should know of my trouble and humiliation. And now that
I have taken up this task, dear sister, do not, I beg, blame

me too much for the selfishness that kept me silent when
it only pained me to speak and prompts me now to write
to you when I want your help. I must tell you all that has
passed in my life since I last wrote you.

Then followed a narrative of the events already known to the
reader, written in a way to shield her husband from blame as
much as possible. Toward the close was the following appeal
to her sister:

Elsie, judge by the maternal love that doubtless exists in
your own heart by this time what I must feel at the
thought of my Mayon growing up amid such
surroundings, and with a prospect of such a life before her
as mine has been. I know your deep love for me has not
died, dear sister, and will it prompt you to help me save my
little girl from such sorrow as I have known? I have reared
her so far with the prospect continually before me of
parting with her when she is grown to womanhood, with
the determination, cost what it may, of sending her forth
into the Gentile world at last. You are the only one to
whom I have confided my plan. I would not dare let any
person here know of my determination. Mayon herself
does not dream that my assiduity in teaching and training
her is due partly to my wish to prepare her for a new and
untried life. She is the pride of my life, the joy of my heart,
and my home will be desolate when she leaves it;
nevertheless I shall be glad. You have repeatedly written
deploring our separation, Elsie, and wishing I might come
back to you and aunt Wells. Although I cannot come, may
I send my child to you? She will need a shelter, a friend
and protector. Will you receive and love her as I know you
would me? Inasmuch as you do this kindness unto her you

do it unto me. I think she need not be dependent on you long for support, for I am trying to rear her with strength of body and mind to make her own way in the world as you and I did. Her father has means to defray all her expenses, but I am not sure that I can appropriate one dollar to support her in the Gentile world, although he would deny her nothing for her happiness did it not conflict with his ideas of duty. I tremble when I think of the storm that I shall raise in his bosom by this long premeditated act of treason to him. I grieve that I must do him this wrong, but there is no help for it. A worse result might come from an abandonment of my purpose than all my husband's anger or grief. And he has his heart's desire in our son's belief in the religion, for I grieve to say Forest is growing up an earnest Mormon. Now, I trust to your love, kindness, and generosity, not to deny me. I know you will open your heart and home to my child. I do not know your husband's circumstances, but suppose them to be such that he will not feel the burden, and I trust the love he may have for little ones of his own may prompt his heart towards kindness and pity for mine. I remember dear aunt Wells with affection, and suppose she is with you now. Ask her if she will in the future bestow the love and care upon my child that she offered me. Tell her I have life-long regrets that I did not heed her warning, and at least make an effort to save myself from the fate she too truly predicted would be mine. And now, dear sister, do not pity me or blame my husband too much, for with the exception of a few months he has been as true and affectionate towards me through all my trouble as he was when you knew him in my bridal days. It is not he that has caused so much wretchedness to enter into my life, but the doctrines of Mormonism through his belief in it. He is a victim and a slave to false teaching and fanaticism, and I have faith that the time will come when he will throw off his shackles and stand forth free from the delusions that influence him now. Then he will forgive his wife's deceit in this matter, and we will live in the Gentile world again. Dear Elsie, I believe I shall again be with you before I die. Now, may I look forward with a definite hope of a home for Mayon with you when the few remaining years that I may still keep her are passed? May I have the consolation of knowing that when she leaves me she will go to one who will be like a mother to her? If you say 'yes,' as I feel sure you will, the thought of our coming separation will lose half its bitterness.

There was not much more in the letter, and as Mrs. Bernard folded it she exclaimed:

"Poor, dear Marion! O, that she might come too! How gladly will we receive her child. Do you not say so, aunt Wells?"

"Yes, my dear, with all my heart, but you have Walter to consult."

"I know well what he will say, aunt. He will say—"

A voice behind her interrupted her and finished the sentence.

"Extend to the child the warmest welcome, and give her the happiest life that human efforts can secure her."

"My noble Walter! I knew you would say that. But where have you been to hear it all?"

"Just behind my wife's chair. As you did not observe my entrance, I raised my finger as a warning to aunt and the children to be quiet, and thus I have heard the whole of your poor sister's story. How a man, made in the image of God, and endowed with the natural gifts and graces that man evidently possesses, can become such a slave to superstition, stoop to such wickedness in the name of religion, is beyond my comprehension."

"We will write directly to Marion," said aunt Wells, "and I will ask the privilege of adopting Mayon as my special charge and giving her every advantage in the way of education that she may need."

"Would you rob us entirely of the pleasure of providing for her?" asked Walter Bernard.

"You have four little ones of your own, and I should esteem it a privilege to give to this little Marion what I expected to give her mother."

"Be it so, then, aunt," said her nephew, and a message, long and loving, was despatched to a waiting one in Utah, which filled her heart with thanksgivings.

As Mayon grew older she did not need to be told of the saddening effects of polygamy on the Utah wives. She realized what was the cause of her mother's past insanity and depressed spirits, and had heard from her lips the story of Nell's mother without, however, being told of the indifference and neglect that her father exercised towards her own mother. She could not tell her daughter this part of her sad experience for fear she would turn against her father, for whom her affection was never very strong. As Mayon realized the difference between Mormonism and Gentileism she became more and more dissatisfied and regretful that her life was cast in with that people. She knew occasionally of some Mormon apostatizing, and never without a wish that it might have been her father. Every item of information with regard to Gentile life she eagerly devoured, and her mind was constantly exercised with a desire to live in the Gentile world. This was as her mother wished. But the thought had not entered the girl's mind that she might go out into the world, unless a change came over her father, and thus change their prospects as a family. For this change Mayon hoped. Too much of a child she yet was to look forward with apprehensions to her own matrimonial prospects, and if she thought of them at all, it was with a purpose never to marry, but always to remain with her mother. But as she observed and realized more of what was passing around her she became more thoughtful on the subject. A conversation with her brother and sister tended to awaken her fears somewhat for her own future. She and Nell were sitting alone one day, busily sewing, when Forest entered. He had now become almost a man, a very attractive young person, and a great assistant— thanks to his mother's instructions in mathematics—to his father in business.

"Well, girls," said he, "have you heard the latest news?"

"What news, Forest?" the girls asked in a breath.

"Alice Clark is to be married to-morrow to John Andross."

"Not Sarah Andross' father!" exclaimed Nell.

"The same," said Forest.

"Forest, you do not mean it! Alice Clark is not old enough. She is scarcely two years older than we are," said Mayon.

"Can't help it. It's a fact."

"It is a shame for that young girl to marry a man old enough to be her father. Indeed his daughter Sarah is older than Alice. Alice to become a fourth wife! I know it was not her wish. Did the elders counsel her till they made her consent, or did her father bring it about?"

"A little of both, I guess."

"I know it could not be Alice's wish, and I believe she had no more thought of marrying so young than Nell and I have."

"Well, they said she cried and made some fuss, but, like a good girl, concluded to be obedient."

"Poor Alice!" said Mayon.

"Poor Alice, indeed, Mayon!" said Nell. "I don't see why you should make such a fuss over the affair. You know that she will not be nearly as poor when she is John Andross' wife as she is now. Her father is very poor, and can hardly support his family, and Mr. Andross has plenty of money; and as his other wives are all quite oldish, Alice will get everything she wants. I have no doubt he will make a great pet of her."

"Well said, sister Nell," said Forest. "Besides, are you not aware that it will be much more to her advancement and honor in the Celestial kingdom to have married an elderly man than a young man? 'Better trust to an old man's head than a young man's heart,' they say."

"Better trust neither, if that head or heart belong to a Mormon," said Mayon, spiritedly. "Nell says Alice will be her husband's pet. So she may till he wishes for another pet, then he will break her heart if she loves him, as even our father has almost broken mamma's heart."

"Your mother has nothing to complain of," said Nell, who felt this thrust on her mother's account, whose story she had heard from her own relatives in childhood. "She selfishly kept our father almost entirely to herself. If I do not speak of my poor mamma, you certainly need not speak of yours."

"Come, come, children," said their brother with a fatherly air, "don't quarrel. Why can't you live in peace? I'll wager my new hat, Nell, that Mayon will put her trust both in the head and heart of some good Mormon before she is three years older."

"Never!" exclaimed Mayon, with flashing eyes.

"Calm yourself, my little volcano," said Forest; "you certainly would frighten any lover away with such a temper as that."

"I tell you, I never will be a Mormon's wife. I never shall marry. I think all the women here are miserable, and unless papa apostatizes, and we go into the Gentile world, I shall never marry."

"Girls and women here do not have the privilege of doing as

they please in everything, whatever they may do in the Gentile world you are so fond of. Mayon, mamma is spoiling you for Mormon life, and you are a disgrace to your religion."

"It is not my religion. I do not believe in Mormonism. I hate it and all its doctrines. God never blesses such a faith as this."

"But, according to the Bible, he did bless it in the persons of Abraham, Jacob, etc. Mayon, look about you and see how many girls have arrived at the age of twenty without marrying."

Mayon could scarcely think of one, and was silent.

"If you are so blind as not to see that all girls marry here, and that counsel and commands of elders and parents are to be obeyed, others are not so blind."

"Do you mean to intimate that I shall be forced into marriage, either by the elders or by my own father?"

"I mean to say that I believe he will think it his duty to do what will be for your highest good. And though he, of course, would never exactly compel you to marry, yet he will expect to be obeyed in the matter. But, Mayon, do not take it to heart so. You are too young now to think much about such things, and I did wrong to trouble you with the doctrines. I forgot that it was a forbidden subject between us. I do wish, though, that you and mother could agree with the rest of us on these points. 'A house divided against itself cannot stand,' you know, the proverb says. Now let us sign a treaty of peace, and all go out for a walk."

"No, Forest," said Mayon, sadly. "You and Nell may go, but I want to talk with mamma."

"Then, good-by, little girl. Never mind what I have said."

But Mayon was excited now, and no effort of her brother could calm her. She sought her mother and said:

"Mamma, does any woman escape living in polygamy? *Must* every girl here marry sooner or later?"

"Almost every one does marry, my child."

"Then, must my fate be like yours, and must I live to be as

wretched as most of the women here appear to be? Is there no way of escape for me?"

"Yes, my child, there is a way for you to escape the ordinary Mormon woman's lot. But what has set you to thinking of this?"

"Forest has been talking to me. He said he forgot it was a forbidden subject between us. I never thought much about my own future till now; and now he has told me of Alice Clark being about to marry an elderly man with three wives, against her own will, and I feel frightened. Will father always believe as he does now, I wonder, and remain here? I would rather die than become the wife of a Mormon."

"You never shall be the wife of a Mormon, my dear. Do not fear."

"Can you prevent it, mamma, if the authorities should counsel me, as they did poor Alice, and if my father should consider it his duty to command me to marry? Can you save me?"

"Yes, my child; all your life I have looked forward to just such a time to come as you speak of, and I have provided you a way of escape."

"Tell me what you mean."

"Mayon, my child, you say you had rather die than marry a Mormon. It will not cost you your life to save yourself, but it will cost you your separation from a mother who almost idolizes you. The only one way for me to save you from a life like mine is to send you away from here. Your aunt Elsie will receive you, and our aunt Wells has asked the privilege of giving you an education."

"What, mother!" exclaimed Mayon in an agony of excitement. "Do you mean to send me away from you? Must I leave my darling mother? Is that the only way to save me from polygamy?"

"Yes, my poor child. It has saddened my life for years to

know that in the future was in store for me and for you this separation. But I determined it from the very beginning of your life, and I thank God that a way has been opened to help me in the fulfilling of my plan."

"Mother, I cannot leave you! Come with me! mother, come with me!"

"And leave your father, Mayon? He never has intentionally wronged me in any manner. He has never brought trouble upon me except as it came in consequence of the performance of what he believed his duty. It is not your father who is to blame for all my misery but the faith that he believes in. Do not cherish one hard thought towards him, Mayon, for his belief has saddened his life also, though he still clings to it. Could I desert him now? No, Mayon, it is wronging him enough to send his daughter secretly away, as I shall have to do some day. I could not rob him of both wife and child."

"Will he need you more than I shall? He will still have Edith. Perhaps they would love each other if you left them." Mayon's words unconsciously brought a pang of jealousy to Marion's heart—the first she had ever felt for Edith—and they had an effect contrary to Mayon's design.

"No, Mayon, there can never be any love between them. Edith was as much opposed to marriage as my Mayon is; but she was forced to marry some one, so she accepted your father."

"Poor Edith! I shall love her more than ever, now I know that," said Mayon. "But, mother, let me tell my father all about my feelings, and plead with him to leave the Mormons for our sakes, and he can still be a Mormon, although in the Gentile world. Then we shall not have to be separated."

"You must never mention it to him, my child. Believe that I know best. No human being this side your aunt Elsie's, except you, knows what I have in my mind, and no one must know, or you cannot escape. Those who apostatize and flee from here are if possible overtaken and brought back, and there have been times when to be openly an apostate was to peril one's life. I do not fear danger for you if our plan is not suspected, for I hope the railway will be completed long before the time of your journey."

"Mother, this is dreadful! I would almost rather stay with you, and risk the consequences. Do you believe my father would wish me to marry against my will?"

"I cannot tell, Mayon. I never believed he would ever take another wife, but he has taken two. There is no sacrifice he would not make for his religion, so I do not feel safe from anything while he believes in Mormonism."

"But, mother, if I leave you, you may come to me some time."

"Yes, I hope to, my child. I hope that some time your father may be undeceived, and we may again be united in the Gentile world."

"O, mother, mother, I cannot leave you!"

And Mayon, with her head in her mother's lap, as in her more childish days, gave herself up to the most passionate of sobbing and weeping.

Marion, after a time, though her own heart ached with sorrow and pity for her child, succeeded in calming her, and then she talked to her long and confidentially of their relation to Elsie and her family. She told her much of Edith's sad story beginning with Edith's mother.

What Mayon had learned that day changed her. She became more thoughtful, and seemed older by a year, and the prospect of a coming separation bound her more closely to her mother, and the latter was pained to notice that notwithstanding her efforts to lessen in no degree Mayon's regard for her father, yet she seemed to shrink from him and avoid his society.

This did not altogether escape the father's observation, though he was far from suspecting the cause. But Nell made up in her attentions what was lacking in Mayon, and she installed herself the favorite with him, as she had been in her infancy.

Two years passed without any great change in the household. The mother had gained a look of more sadness, which, however, was relieved at times by an expression of happy content, when her face had a far-away look, that Mayon could readily interpret. She knew her mother was seeing in anticipation her child safe and happy with the friends of her own youth, and was herself happy in the thought.

Edith had not ceased to appear in the light of a ministering angel to the different members of the family, and Mayon particularly was drawn towards her more strongly than ever, through her sympathy. She was still as a dear sister to Marion, and the latter was surprised at times as she realized that she was living in love and peace with another wife—something she had thought utterly impossible. But she also realized that this harmonious state of things was entirely due to the peculiar attitude Edith held towards herself and husband. She blessed Edith, and felt that there could be no nobler conduct than hers; at the same time she pitied her for the blight that had fallen on her so young, and robbed her of all life's natural joys. She endeavored in every possible way to make up for this loss, and repay her for the months of weary watching and care which she had received from her.

So Edith was not without many sources of comfort, Mayon's society proving not the least, as she was gradually becoming more womanly and companionable. Nell had not outgrown her childish shortcomings, but had become more expert in hiding them, till her father had come to believe that she was as sweet in disposition as Mayon, and certainly more winning. Mayon was never winning to him, and it was not his fault that he did not love her as much as he did Nell, for she avoided him almost as entirely as Edith did. But when his whole family was assembled and visitors were present, he could look with pride upon Mayon, as he could not upon Nell, for it was Mayon who entertained them with music, and Mayon who could converse most intelligently, if occasion required. Elder Northfield wished Nell might add to her winsomness the culture and intelligence Mayon possessed, and that Mayon would give him the love and confidence his other daughter bestowed upon him.

Forest had inherited his father's eloquence in public speaking, and was about to be ordained an elder, and sent to the small villages and towns in the Territory as local missionary.

Elder Northfield was still prospering in business, and apparently his family was a happy one. Forest and Nell, however, were the only really happy ones. Polygamy had clouded the happiness of the others, even the husband and father, for when his dear ones had suffered he had suffered too. But his conscience was clear, and he had much pride in his children, especially in his son.

From time to time emigrant parties from all parts of the Union and from across the ocean arrived in the city. Among them there were many young girls who had left father and mother, brother and sister, for their religion's sake—wives and mothers who forsook even their husbands and little ones to gather to Zion. There were men who counted their religion more dear than wives and children and left them all behind. There were parts of families and whole families, from the gray-headed man to the child too young to lisp its mother's name. For this was a religion that bade men sever the strongest ties of nature and outrage the purest of domestic affections.

Strenuous efforts had of late been made to gather in converts from all parts of the world, and especially from the United States. Elders and missionaries had been sent out in all directions. The most winning, attractive and persuasive men were selected for these missions; also those most talented and intelligent. They were now reaping the fruit of their labors. Although but few were the converts each elder secured, yet their aggregate was a most goodly number. Enlightened New England furnished a small band, for talent, perseverance and persuasiveness will win their way anywhere, even though they can work only on the credulity, excitability and emotional sensibilities of their victims.

Among the band of New England emigrants which arrived in Salt Lake City about this time was a young girl named Flora Winchester. It came about that in the providing of temporary homes for the newly-arrived converts Elder Northfield agreed to receive one into his family, and accordingly this one was sent to him. His family were, of course, prepared to receive an emigrant into their home, but they were not prepared for the sweetness and intelligence that came to them in the person of Flora. She was an attractive, educated girl, but she had an air of sadness and homesickness, although firm in her faith in the new religion. She was so quiet, so sober and undemonstrative, that Nell voted her a bore, and made little attempt to make a companion of her, but Mayon took her to her own heart and the two girls became firm friends. Mayon pitied her for her apparent loneliness, and was interested in her because she came as a representative of that world which she was some time to enter. She kept Flora talking by the hour of the Gentile people and their institutions, and felt that she had thus gleaned much worldly wisdom. But of Flora's personal friends and circumstances she was very reticent. Mayon often wondered why she would not speak of her home, her family and friends, but she would not ask about them, for Flora evidently did not wish to speak of them.

Mayon was not the only friend Flora made among the young people of the house. Forest began to pay her many little kind attentions in the hope of cheering and lifting the veil of sadness that seemed to hang over her. She received any kindnesses from them in a pretty, grateful way, that won their hearts, but she nevertheless seemed very unhappy. Mayon and her mother had many a confidential talk concerning the new-comer, and they were sad to think that such a promising young girl should be deluded into believing in such a religion, and that she had been influenced in all probability to leave home and friends for her faith. They longed to try to undeceive her and persuade her to return to her friends. But they dared not say much to her against the religion for fear of the elders, who kept a strict watch over their emigrant converts till they were firmly established in Zion. One day, as Flora returned from a ride with Forest, who had taken her to see the country, she rushed into Mayon's room, which she shared with her, and without removing her wrappings flung herself into a chair and burst into tears. They were the first Mayon had seen her shed, and now very much touched, she placed her arm lovingly about Flora and said:

"Dear Flora, what is your trouble? Why are you so sad? Do not tell me unless you wish, but I would so like to comfort you if I might."

"I want to see my mother. I want my father to look kindly on me once more. I do miss Jessie and the boys so much. I am homesick here, Mayon, in spite of all your kindness, and now what your brother has said to me makes me feel that I have no right to stay here longer."

"What has he said, Flora?"

"He says—he says—he asked me to marry him. I did not think of such a thing, and do not love him, though he has been very kind to me, and you all have, and I feel very grateful for it all; but I could not give him the answer he wished. How could I marry a man I do not love?"

Poor girl! She had yet to learn that Mormon women were expected to do what she felt she could not.

"No, Flora, you could not, of course, and I am sorry Forest asked you. I should grieve to see you become my brother's wife."

"Why?"

"Because he is a Mormon, and you know mother and I, though Mormons by name, do not believe in the religion; and, Flora, I wish for your sake you never had, but had remained with your father and mother. You cannot tell how I regret that I was not born in the Gentile world—how I long to go there away from this false religion and these deluded and deluding people."

"Forest has told me that you and your mother are not in the faith, and that it is a great trial to his father and to him."

"Yes, I suppose it is. Mother was once a firm believer in Mormonism as you are, but when she learned that polygamy was one of the doctrines it destroyed her faith in the whole, and poor mother has had enough sad experience to destroy her faith. O, Flora, how could you have been persuaded to leave your home and join this Church?"

"I will tell you all about it, Mayon. I have not felt like speaking of my family before, and I presume you have wondered at it; but now I will tell you how it all came about, as near as I can, though I hardly know myself. Elder North and Elder Burnside came to our village and appointed a meeting. No one knew they were Mormons, and a good many people gathered to hear them preach, among them my brother Carlos and myself. They were very eloquent and adhered at first to doctrines not particularly strange or new, and they had held several meetings before the people discovered that they were Mormons. When they did make the discovery, however, almost all left the meetings; but I had become very much interested, and felt that I had perhaps, like others, been prejudiced against the Mormons, and

I resolved to continue to attend and learn for myself whether their doctrine was from God or not. My brother would not take me after that, and I was forced to go alone, which I did, till my father forbade my attending the meetings again. I disobeyed him once or twice, however, and then it seems that the youngest elder—Elder Burnside—learned that I had been forbidden to attend the meetings, and he called upon me in my father's absence. He asked me to meet him at his boarding-place and he would explain to me all I wished to know. I met him several times, and at last became a believer in the faith."

"Flora, how could you believe in polygamy?"

"I did not fully, but he assured me that it would all appear right to me if I held on to my faith. I felt that at last I had been given a clean heart, and entered God's Church. I felt quite happy. Then both elders urged me to leave my home and emigrate with a party they were forming to Zion. I could not make up my mind to that for a great while, for I dearly loved my friends; but when I realized that 'Whoso loveth father or mother, brother or sister, more than Me, is not worthy of Me,' I decided to give up everything for my religion, and I informed Elder Burnside that I would be ready to start with the company. My family did not know what had been going on, I had been so secret about it, and it came like a thunderbolt on them when I told them that I was going to leave them in a few days. My mother wept and pleaded with me; my brothers and sister said I should not leave them, and my father kindly tried to reason and persuade me, till he found how useless it was, for I had made up my mind to brave all this storm, which I knew would come. At last my father gave way to anger, and he told me if I left his house as a Mormon convert I should never enter it again. He said he would never own for a daughter one who could so demean herself as to become a Mormon. This angered me, and notwithstanding my mother's entreaties, I immediately took with me a few articles of clothing and went to the house of another convert and there remained till we left for Utah, which was in two or three days. The next day my mother came to see me, and I never shall forget our agony as we bade each other farewell. She tried with all her might to persuade me to remain, but I would not. She then said: 'Remember, Flora, that notwithstanding your father's anger, your mother will always love you, and if you ever wish to come back, as I fear you will, mother's heart and home will always be open to you.' She had come against the commands of my father, who had forbidden any member of his family coming to me, so I did not see my brothers and sister again. I felt that I had given up all for the Lord, and expected to be very happy, but somehow I am not. I long for my home and friends, and sometimes wonder if I have not been foolishly deceived, and if you and your mother are not right."

"Flora, believe that we are right, and go back to your mother. She will be made so happy, and your father will forgive you and take you back when he sees how penitent you are."

"I cannot do that. Mayon, you do not know the scorn and derision that would be heaped upon me were I to return. And my pride will not let me go back and plead with my father after he has said I never should enter his house again. If he kept his word, what would become of me? Mother and Jessie and the boys I know would welcome me back, but even with them I could hardly hold up my head, and much less could I acknowledge to my father my error, or bear the scorn of my former friends. It was considered by them all a great disgrace to become a Mormon. As a penitent Mormon among them I never could live. No, Mayon, I cannot go back now."

Then Mayon determined, even at the risk of increasing Flora's trouble, to inform her of the sadness of woman's lot there, and to impress upon her mind a horror of polygamy, hoping that her fear might actuate her to return to the Gentile world. She longed to tell her of her intentions with regard to her own future and persuade Flora to go with her to New England, but this she dared not do as long as Flora was in any sense a Mormon. Flora listened with a failing heart to Mayon's description of the lives of the women of Utah, but she was not persuaded to abandon her purpose of remaining, now that she had entered the Church and arrived in the city. She said it was of no use; she could not go back now; it was impossible, and she must make the best of it. Mayon was very sad as she confided to her mother her attempt to right the wrong done to Flora and its utter failure. Flora became more gloomy than before, and Forest avoided her, not from any ill feeling, but his heart was sore with disappointment, and her society now was only painful to him.

But Flora's face at length brightened in a manner unsuspected by her friends. Elder Burnside, who did not arrive with the company, but remained by the way to preach, had now returned to the city, and he called upon Flora. As Mayon and her mother saw the girl's face light up, and a flush of joy come to her cheek on greeting the elder, they read the secret of her conversation and attributed her unwillingness to leave Mormonism partly to her unwillingness to leave its young champion. Mrs. Northfield knew too well the influence of the Mormon elder over the one upon whom he bestows his love, and she felt that Flora's case was hopeless. Elder Burnside's visits were often repeated, and the whole family were now sensible that a change had come over her. She was no longer the quiet, sad girl they had known, but was cheerful and even gay at times. Elder Northfield was, however, the only one in the house who rejoiced at this change, knowing, as they did, its cause. Marion, Edith, and Mayon felt that it was but a sealing of her doom as a Mormon woman, and Forest could only look upon Elder Burnside as a rival in his efforts to win Flora for his wife. It galled him to see that this man's affection made her happy, while his advances had only seemed to increase her sadness. Nell became more sociably inclined now towards Flora, but the latter would only confide in Mayon, whom she loved devotedly, although she would not be influenced by her in the matter of the greatest importance.

"Mayon," she said one day, "I told you my story, but I did not tell you quite the whole. I could not then. But now all is decided, I will tell you. I am going to marry Elder Burnside."

"O, Flora! I have known it ever since he came, but I wish, so strongly, that it was not so. I fear you will in time be miserable. Are you not afraid to trust your happiness in the hands of a man who believes in polygamy?"

"No, for I think he will do nothing that is not right, and I shall try and trust God for the rest. I cannot, however, think much about the future, I am so happy in the present."

Not many days passed before Flora became the wife of Elder Burnside—a beautiful, blushing, happy bride. But, ah! How changed she was ere many years rolled by!

Chapter 12

Since the completion of the railway, Edith, all unknown to any one, had harbored thoughts of leaving the Mormon world and attempting to seek a support for herself among the Gentiles. She felt now as some other women felt—that escape was not so utterly impossible for them as it had been hitherto.

At last she resolved to speak to Marion about the matter, knowing she would not betray her. Marion was very much surprised, but she felt that the hand of Providence was guiding all things for the best. She then told her of her determination with regard to Mayon—of the home that was ready and waiting for her child, and doubtless welcome to her also, as it would have been to her mother. She had corresponded regularly, though not frequently, with Elsie, and the kind offer of aunt Wells was open for her acceptance at any time.

"Now, Edith," said she, "though I shall sadly miss you, and shall feel doubly bereft if deprived of you and Mayon at once, yet if you might go with Mayon as her protector on her long journey—if you might find for yourself the happiness you deserve in the Gentile world—I shall be content."

"I will gladly go with Mayon, and care for her even as her mother would. I do hope for a less sad life than I have known here, but I never expect to find happiness. My father struck a death-blow to all happiness for me years ago."

Then Marion knew that the wound in Edith's heart had never healed. No word had been spoken in all these years; but though Edith could be silent, she could not forget.

"O, the cruelty of this so-called religion!" said Marion, "to blast, if not in one way in another, the happiness of every woman coming under its influence. Why does God allow his creatures to work such wrong? Why will not the Government, instead of making now and then a weak effort to abolish polygamy, passing laws which they do not take means to enforce—why does it not make a mighty effort to free us—slaves that we are—as it did to free the poor negro slave from his bondage?"

"I have thought of that and have felt almost like doubting God's mercy in allowing this evil to continue, and when I see sweet young girls like Flora Winchester, not growing up in it, but coming into it from enlightened New England, I can but wonder at the power for evil it has in the land. That poor child, now so happy, will know, as all others do in time, the wretchedness of a woman's life here. I sometimes pray God to spare her if it be possible."

"Poor Flora! It was not love for her religion alone that brought her here. She has too much sense for that, but Elder Burnside won her heart, as well as her faith in his teachings. She is blind, and when her eyes are opened it will be too late."

Now, these women had another interest in common to bind their hearts more closely. They resolved that when the time came that Mayon must fly for refuge to her aunt's home Edith should go also. Edith's heart was lifted up with hope at thought of freedom from a polygamic life, and Marion, though really regretting the loss of such a friend as Edith, felt that she should again rejoice in being the only wife of her husband. Mayon was glad to know that when she was obliged to leave her mother one familiar and dear face might still be by her side to lighten the grief of the separation. She was now in stature almost a woman. A close companionship with her mother all her life, and a keen realization of the sorrows that surrounded and affected her, had made her very womanly.

Her face had the repose of maturity, and her manners the grace of womanly dignity. Her mother realized that her efforts to fit her for a change in her life had probably been the means of hastening that change. For a young lady of Mayon's attractions, her age, and her position in life to remain long in Salt Lake City without suitors she knew was impossible. So she regretted that Mayon had arrived at the age when she might fear other eyes would covet her treasure—other hands seek to pluck the flower she had so tenderly reared.

Mayon seemed fully two years older than Nell, who was but a few months younger. Nell was slight in form and childish in the extreme, but she did not wish, as Mayon did, to be regarded as a child, but was flattered very much by attentions from older people.

"Why," exclaimed Mayon one day, "was I not made small instead of Nell? She fairly longs to be a grown lady and to be considered one, while I envy her her childish appearance. She puts on a woman's dress, which gives her the look of an over-dressed doll, and I make myself ridiculous by clinging to a girl's manner of dress, while I am several inches taller than Nell. But, mother, why should we fear so much? Perhaps no one will ever want me for a wife, and then, mother dear, I can stay with you always."

As the mother lovingly caressed the glossy hair, and looked into those large eyes full of a beautiful intelligence, noticed the sweet mouth and rosy cheeks of her daughter, she felt that her beauty was fatal to such hopes. That alone would ensure her bondage to Mormonism if she was not saved from it.

But neither the mother nor daughter suspected how soon the former's fears were to be realized. Forest was an agreeable young man, fond of company, and some of his young friends visited him at his home frequently, spending the evening with the family in the parlor. Edith always excluded herself from these family gatherings, unless Elder Northfield was absent, except by special request that she would be present. But no other member was missing, and Mayon and Nell were valuable assistants to Forest in the entertaining of his friends. Nell was attractive for her liveliness, Mayon for her music and intelligence. There was one young man—a recently made partner in their father's business—who came oftenest. He was intelligent, and probably a better man could not be found among the Mormons than he. From spending many evenings there he began to call during the day, when at liberty to do so without neglecting his business, and as Mayon and Nell usually entertained him, it became evident that one or both attracted him thither. But the mother breathed more freely when she observed that as Mayon gradually withdrew herself and left Nell to entertain their caller alone he came no less frequently. He asked for Mayon, but was apparently not disappointed in the least at her non-appearance, and his visits, and even walks and drives with Nell, appeared to be very enjoyable to them both. Nell was delighted with her admirer, and her little head and heart were quite full of thoughts of him. With these existing circumstances, what wonder that Mrs. Northfield received with consternation the announcement from her husband that Edward Ellis had asked him for the hand of his daughter Mayon in marriage.

"Our Mayon!" exclaimed the distressed mother. "Why she is nothing but a child. How can you think of such a thing?"

"I know she is a child in years, but she is very womanly in her ways, and as this will be a fine settlement for her, and a better man than Ellis cannot be found, I am anxious that she shall accept this offer if she can be persuaded into it."

"But we supposed Nell was the one he was seeking, if either. Both are too young, however, to think of matrimony. Why has he spent so much time with Nell if he wished for Mayon?"

"He accepted her company because deprived of Mayon's, and he has learned a great deal about Mayon from Nell's prattle.[26] I knew he was not trying to win Nell, but he has had his eye on Mayon for a long time."

"But Mayon has no idea of anything of the kind, and I think it would only be repugnant to her, and Nell is entirely carried away with him, and not without some reason. I think he has done wrong in allowing her to be deceived so. Why cannot a change be made and Ellis be persuaded in favor of Nell instead of Mayon?"

"Because, unfortunately, Nell is not the one he wants. Why could I not have married Elsie instead of Marion? Because I did not love Elsie, and I did love Marion."

"But, Henry, it is not right to urge the acceptance of this offer upon Mayon if she is opposed to it. If it was for Nell there would be no obstacle, for she is more than half in love with Ellis already."

"I do not wish to crowd or hurry matters. If Mayon wishes the marriage postponed, I shall not object to a year or two of time for her, but I am determined that she shall not slight this offer, notwithstanding her youth, and I wish the matter to be settled immediately. I have almost given Ellis a promise of Mayon, and he will take it very hard if he is disappointed, so I do not wish him to be refused. I have left her affairs almost entirely to you, Marion, in the past, and have never interfered with your wishes concerning her, but in this matter I feel that I have a father's right and a father's duty to perform, and hope that you will use your efforts to secure my wishes. I count on your help if Mayon proves obstinate, for it is only her own best good that I seek, and although she may at first feel opposed, no doubt she will soon listen to reason and offer no serious objection."

"But Mayon is not so ordinary a person that she may not

have plenty of good offers of marriage if she does not accept this."

"No; but she cannot have a better one, and 'A bird in the hand is worth two in the bush.'"

Mrs. Northfield could say no more. Her heart was full. She felt that in this matter as in other matters that affected her vital interests "duty" was to decide against her. "Duty," that stern tyrant of her life, was to wrest from her possession her dearest treasure, or offer it up a sacrifice on the altar of Mormonism. Her husband rose to leave the room, saying:

"Now, Marion, shall I speak to Mayon about this or will you? I hope ere long to see her the wife of Edward Ellis," and turning the speaker beheld Mayon, who had entered the room unnoticed by her father in time to hear his last remark. She stood riveted to the spot in terror. Her large eyes dilated till they were immense, and all the roses were gone from her cheek. Her father was frightened at her appearance and hastened towards her, but she avoided his approach and glided to her mother's side. She kneeled by her in agony, and without a word buried her face in her outspread hands. The father felt that his presence was unwelcome then and he considerately left them alone.

"O, mother, I did not think it would come so soon!"

"Hush, my darling! Be very guarded in what you say. Perhaps I can save you yet a little longer."

"Do, mother, if you can. How can I leave you now?"

Mrs. Northfield told her husband that Mayon wished to put off her decision for a while and in the meantime requested that she might not see Ellis. Elder Northfield said he should expect Mayon to be able to decide in a few weeks at most, and that he trusted she would decide wisely. And thus Mayon's days of life with her mother were numbered. Nell now became quite forlorn as her supposed lover deserted her, and she was really to be pitied. But when she learned that Mayon was considering the question of marriage with him her young heart was filled with jealous indignation.

"Mayon," she said as she stamped her little foot, "you were all the time playing a game to win. You knew he liked you and meant to increase his desire for his prey by keeping it just out of his reach. I now see what your modest retirement in my favor meant. It meant treachery to me. No doubt you laughed in your sleeve at thought of the dupe he was making of me. But you are welcome to him. Such a deceitful man as he is cannot be much of a prize, and I am glad that it is you who have won him instead of me."

"I have not won Edward Ellis. I do not wish to marry him. If I do it will only be in obedience to my father. If you can win him for yourself, Nell, that I may go free in peace, you will do me the greatest favor you ever did. I do not wish to marry for a long time."

Nell was rather surprised, but faltered out:

"O, it is too late now. It does very well to say so when all possibility of such a thing is past."

"I did not know or suspect it till father told us of his proposal for me. I supposed he was given his heart's desire in having your society. Now, Nell, do not torment yourself or me any more, but make yourself attractive and win the prize."

"I don't think I could now, and don't know as I care to try," said Nell, petulantly.

Edward Ellis did not feel like trusting fully to Mayon's decision, uninfluenced by higher authorities, although her father was quite determined that he should have her. But he went to Brigham Young and stated the case, and Brigham, as ever, was ready to help on the good work.

He had known something of the Gentile element in Elder Northfield's family, and was of the opinion that the sooner an unbelieving daughter was settled with a Mormon husband, the better.

He therefore interested himself in Ellis' case, and promised to call upon the girl. He did so, and as Mayon went to the door to answer his summons, she experienced, to a degree, the same horror that her father's words had caused. He noticed her fear, and in a pleasant, fatherly manner strove to talk with her in such a way as to put her at her ease, but that was impossible, and soon she politely attempted to excuse herself, saying she would call the other ladies of the house. But he stopped her and said she was the one he had called to see. Then he referred to her matrimonial prospects, and congratulated her upon the honor which had been conferred upon her, trying to draw her into conversation on the subject.

But Mayon could scarcely speak, so great was her agitation. He gave her what was considered much good advice, and she could only falter out that she thought she was too young, and wished to wait till she was older. He then asked her how old she was, and though Mayon felt that she could not stoop to answer him, yet she was too frightened to refuse.

"O, nonsense," said he, " you are quite old enough; besides, you look much older than you are. Now I hope you will be a good girl, and make no trouble about this affair. I counsel you, for your own best good in this world and in the world to come, to accept Edward Ellis as your husband, and do not delay your decision, my girl."

And with an attempt at a friendly conversation, the great head of the Church left the subject, having done this duty in the fear of the Lord (!)

It was not till now that Mrs. Northfield became aware of the ordeal her child was undergoing alone, or she would have come to her relief. Now she entered, and as Brigham Young requested to see the whole family then present, Edith and Nell were called and presented to the President. He tried to make himself very agreeable, and manifested some curiosity with regard to Edith, as it had been rumored that she was ill-treated by her husband and his first wife. He impudently asked her, in the presence of them all, if such was the case, and though her eyes shone with anger at his insult, she felt obliged to answer him.

She told him that no human being could be treated with more kindness than she received. She feared he would suggest to Elder Northfield that he take her out more, and that she could not bear.

He then playfully pinched Nell's cheeks and pulled her hair, saying:

"This little girl will before many years be contemplating matrimony as her older sister now is."

"I am as old as Mayon now, into a few months," said Nell, feeling hurt at being called a little girl.

"Indeed!"

"Yes," said Mrs. Northfield, "Mayon is but little older, though she does not look like it."

"Well, well; Nell, we hope you will soon have the good fortune to receive as good an offer as your sister has."

"O, I do not care for that," said she.

"What do you care for? Riding? If so, put on your hat and shawl, and take a turn with me."

Nell instantly obeyed, feeling very much elated with the honor of riding with Brigham Young. It almost compensated for losing the attentions of Edward Ellis.

"That man's insults are unbearable!" exclaimed Edith. "I hope I may never meet him again. Poor Mayon, to have to endure a *tête-à-tête* with him."

"I thought I should faint," said Mayon. "O, do you think I

shall ever have to be tormented with his presence again! I believe I could even part with you sooner, mother, easier than I could bear to meet him again."

"You shall not meet him again, my child; I will guard against it."

The next evening her father sought Mayon, and talked a long time to her in a persuasive way, referring to the prospect of her marriage. His words, though kindly spoken, gave her a secret assurance that all opposition on her part would be vain; though she had suggested to her mother the thought that if she utterly refused, her father would not force her into the marriage.

She could hardly control herself till she was at liberty to seek her mother. She was almost frantic with excitement, and almost beside herself with the constant torture she was being subjected to.

Her mother feared that in the excitement of her terror she would unguardedly betray her secret, and she decided with Edith that the sooner she was sent away the better. She feared for the condition of Mayon's mind if her torture was continued, and decided that a final separation from herself would not injure her as this constant harassing on the subject of marriage. Mayon and she both knew that that must come, and perhaps the sooner the better for them both, as matters now stood.

Mayon consented, like a poor, frightened child, to any means for her safety, and seeing her half-wild condition, Mrs. Northfield thanked God that even through her own past trouble He had raised up a friend for her child in this her hour of need; for Mayon was incapable of caring for herself, so great was her mental excitement; but her mother knew she could trust to Edith's clear head and loving heart to shield her child from all harm on the journey.

This had come so suddenly, that neither of the three could fully realize what had happened and what was before them, and there was little time to indulge in mourning, for there was much that the loving mother must do for her child, and many preparations Edith wished to make for her own entrance into a strange land. A letter was dispatched to Elsie, to inform her of the arrival she must immediately expect.

Suspicion must not be roused, and so the preparations for the departure had to be made very secretly. Once let Nell become aware of what was going on, and Mayon was lost, for Nell was perfectly in sympathy with her father and brother.

At last came the morning of the day previous to the one on which the fugitives were to take their flight. With Mrs. Northfield they were assembled in Edith's room, sadly talking of their coming separation, and speaking of the journey they were to undertake on the morrow.

"Hark! " said Mayon, in a whisper, "I think I hear footsteps."

All listened, but in vain, and her mother said:

"It was only one of your nervous fears, Mayon. No one can be near us here."

For Edith's room was in a retired part of the house, where it was seldom any one went except her.

They resumed their conversation, and again Mayon's strained ear caught a sound.

"Mother, there is some one listening at the door. It is Nell's light footstep that I hear. O, what shall we do if Nell has heard what we have been saying!"

They watched the street from Edith's window, which commanded a view of it, and soon Nell's figure was seen speeding in the direction of her father's business.

Their hearts sank and their hopes failed them, but the mother's love quickened her faculties, and she exclaimed:

"Never fear, my dears; I will save you in spite of them all! I will, God helping me, defy every Mormon in the land but my darling shall escape!"

Her impassioned words revived the courage of Edith and
Mayon, and she continued:

"You must not wait till to-morrow; it may be too late. In
three hours a train leaves here, and you must go on that train.
Get yourselves ready instantly for a start somewhere away from
the house. How can we tell but that in a few moments your
father will be here, brought by the news Nell has given him, to
put an end to it all. Probably he will wait till his return at night,
but I dare not risk a moment's delay. Mayon, go to your room
and dress quickly for your journey, and leave me to think what
to do. O, God, help me! God help me now!"

Edith proceeded quickly to dress, while Mrs. Northfield
went on as though thinking aloud:

"No, there is no hiding place I dare try; no one I dare trust
to ask for help. What shall I do? O, where can I hide them?
Edith, it will never do for you and Mayon to take the train
here; it will be watched. Henry or Forest will be there, if Nell
has turned traitor and told them, as we think. You must walk
to the next station, for I dare not procure a carriage. You can
get there in three hours. Mayon is strong and a good walker,
and can do it comfortably; but you, Edith, can you walk so far
in three hours?"

"Yes, for I shall be walking towards freedom from this bondage. I shall be helping my dear friend, who has been so kind
to me and my mother years ago. Those thoughts will give me
strength."

"You have not a moment to lose, and I will now go and hasten Mayon."

As Mayon proceeded to dress, the hot tears filled her eyes,
almost blinding her, and everything she touched was wet with
tears. She was sadly in need of help. They made all the haste
that desperation could give to their movements, and then the
mother left Mayon, to procure the money that was to pay the

expenses of their journey. This sum was one which she had been hoarding for years for this very purpose, and which she had accumulated, little by little, by an economical saving from her own expenses, unknown and unnoticed by her husband. She had within a few days materially added to it, by the sale of her watch and other jewelry, so that now there was enough, and more than enough, to meet the wants of the refugees till other provision was made for them. She now hastened to Edith, and placed in her hands the well-filled purse. They could take no clothing with them, and must give themselves the appearance of being out for a walk merely. Mrs. Northfield was to send their trunks after them.

"And Edith," said she, "you must travel as fast as possible. Do not stop over one train anywhere on the journey, for you may be pursued. I think Henry will not go so far as that, but I do not know what his anger may lead him to. I am certain that he will be very angry for once, and not without cause. I dread his wrath."

"My poor sister," said Edith, "how will you bear it all, added to your sorrow of losing Mayon? O, it seems cruel to leave you to endure the blame alone!"

"I am so used to trouble, Edith, that I can bear this, though my husband's anger and my separation from my daughter will be new troubles; but do not fear for me. I shall be content when I hear that you and Mayon are safe in New York."

Mayon looked about her room that was so dear to her, where were many little reminders of Flora's ingenuity in the execution of Gentile ideas of little ornaments, and then she thought of Flora's grief and homesickness at her separation from her mother, and felt that she too was leaving her native land and all that was dear to her. Why could not she have changed places with Flora and each remained in the home so dear to her? She longed to see her friend once more before she was forever separated from her, but her mother recalled her thoughts to her own affairs, and with her she descended to the parlor, where Edith stood waiting, all equipped for a start.

Words cannot paint, pen cannot portray—the agonies of that last farewell, as mother and daughter were locked in one final embrace.

"Mother," said Mayon, as the former at last released Mayon's hold on her, "I cannot leave you. I would rather stay and suffer the consequences, mother; let me stay with you!"

Mrs. Northfield felt faint, but she motioned them to go. They turned towards the door, and looking back, Edith saw the agonized mother's face grow white as marble. She dared not leave her thus, but started back to her. Mayon then darted to her mother again, and with the most passionate grief covered her face with tears and kisses.

"Now, my dear ones, go," said she faintly, and they obeyed.

After they had gone, many minutes passed unconsciously to Mrs. Northfield. But nature restored her from her fainting fit, and soon Nell entered with a conscious, guilty look.

"Where is Mayon?" she asked.

"Gone with Edith for a walk," was the answer.

"When will they come back?" asked Nell suspiciously.

"I cannot tell. They have only just gone out."

Again hatred came into her heart for this girl, who she knew was seeking to defeat all her hopes and plans. She hated her and feared her. She now continued to keep Nell occupied, and with her, fearing that through her a discovery would he made of Edith's and Mayon's premature flight. As the hour passed, however, when she knew the train would leave the adjoining station, whither they had gone, she trusted they were safely on board and speeding away from all that had made her life so sad. She now, with a sigh of relief, relaxed her efforts to absorb Nell's attention and breathed more freely. She now had leisure to think of her own situation and to dread her husband's return at night. But Forest came without him.

"Where is your father, Forest?" she asked.

"He had some unexpected business to attend to and took the twelve o'clock train, saying he would be back early tomorrow morning."

That mother's heart then sank within her. He would be upon the train with his wife and daughter, and would see them as they stepped into the car at that little unfrequented station. He would bring them back and their lives would be ruined after all her hopes, plans and efforts. During the evening, while locked in her room, she heard Forest and Nell calling to her, and she knew they had missed Mayon and Edith and were seeking them. But she could not answer them. That night was a sleepless one to Mrs. Northfield. At the coming of dawn she expected to see her husband returning with the dear ones she had sent away; but dawn came, and with it her husband, but he came alone. Now her heart gave a great bound for joy. He had no affectionate greeting for her this morning, but looked very stern. She trembled as she met him.

"Marion," said he, " please call Edith and Mayon. I wish to see them this morning before I go to my business."

"They are not here, Henry."

"Not here! What do you mean? You have not accomplished your wicked scheme already, have you? Where are they?"

"They are on their way to New York, Henry. My dear husband, I beg you will forgive me for doing you this wrong, but I was obliged to do it."

"Obliged to do it! Marion, do not try to excuse your conduct in that way! Why have you sent our daughter away from me in this way? Was she not mine as well as yours? What right had you to rob me of my wife, even though I do not care for her? Marion, I tell you you have gone too far!"

Her husband's eyes now glowed with anger, and Marion was roused to resentment. Her fear was quite gone. Her trembling ceased, and she boldly pleaded her cause.

"I sent Mayon away to save her from a wretched life like mine. I repeat, I was obliged to do it. Could I, knowing the curse, the misery, the anguish that would surely come upon her if she accepted the fate you have prepared for her—could I be justified in making no effort to save her from a life that would be worse than death? Does God give a mother her children and not hold her responsible for what they become in future years? If you saw a man in certain danger of death and reached out no hand to save him, you would be guilty of murder. If I see my child approaching what is worse than death and calmly and unconcernedly allow her fate to overwhelm her, am I not guilty? That is why I was obliged to do this. My Mayon I long ago resolved should never be offered up a living sacrifice, as I have been, to the shrine of Mormonism. I have looked for this day to come for years; but it came at last sooner than I expected. But I was ready for it, and I do not regret what I have done. I only regret that it *must* be done, and that I have in a certain sense acted the part of a traitor to you, but better that than a lifetime of misery for Mayon."

"You speak of a union with Edward Ellis as a lifetime of misery. What reason can you give for that impression?"

"The reason that every woman is miserable in polygamy, and this man would in time enter into it, no doubt—every Mormon does. Henry, even though I have had a husband kind as any Mormon husband could be and live up to his religion, have I not suffered a lifetime of misery? Have I not been robbed of my reason, and almost of my life, by the terrible workings of Mormonism? Tell me, Henry, if you do not believe I have suffered enough to make me fear to expose my beloved daughter to trials like mine?"

"Yes, Marion, I admit that you have taken your life very hard, notwithstanding that I have tried to lighten the burden that all Mormon women must bear; but that does not alter the fact that you have acted very wrongly in sending Mayon and Edith away. Although you do not see it in that light, you have sent them out of God's Church, where alone can be found eternal salvation for their souls. You have basely deceived one who has always trusted in you, and never willingly wronged you. Marion, I did not think this of you. You have twice in your life determined to desert me, and now you have caused my wife and daughter to do me that wrong. And yet, Marion, you have accused me of not loving you. Have I ever given you the cause for such an accusation that you have given me?"

Henry Northfield when angry could give utterance to the most cruel sayings, and in a calm manner that made every word cut the deeper. Marion felt the pain that no words of his had ever inflicted before on her already aching heart. But for Mayon's sake she could bear them. No mere words of his could bring her back again.

"Henry," she said, "you have no right to refer to my actions of those times. You know that I was goaded almost to madness by my trouble, or I never should have thought of leaving you."

"Well, Marion, what is done is done, and I shall not at present try to undo your work, for Ellis would not now accept a wife who had run away from him, and a wife and daughter who prove what Edith and Mayon have proved themselves to be are not worth pursuing. Mayon never seemed to love me much, though I have had a father's affection for her, and now she has proved that she has no regard for me. I have not deserved this. I have tried to be a kind father, and even in this matter have acted only for her best good, if she could have been allowed to see it so."

Thus he left her in anger—something that, amid all her troubles, had never occurred before. This came upon her already desolate heart, and it seemed that her burden was greater than she could bear. Could Mayon have looked into her mother's heart, and read the woe and suffering that was borne for her sake, she would have wished to return and suffer with her, rather than that her mother should suffer alone. Years had passed since Mrs. Northfield had been called upon to bear such deep sorrow as now. Her husband continued his cold, injured manner, and Forest and Nell avoided her as though she had been guilty of some great crime.

The Sabbath came, and as Elder Northfield took his Sunday garments from their place, a little piece of folded paper met his eye, as it protruded from one of his pockets. He mechanically unfolded it, and it proved to be a letter from his daughter Mayon. It was as follows:

DEAR FATHER:

Please do not think I do not love you to thus flee away from you. I see that you are determined I shall marry Edward Ellis, even against my wishes. It seems to me, father, that I would rather die than marry a Mormon, or a man I do not love. Polygamy, even with a kind husband as you have been, has made my mother's life miserable, and can you blame me for wishing to escape such wretchedness in my own life? You cannot realize the misery of being forced into a marriage that is repugnant to one's feelings. I know you would not wish it if you did. I know, dear father, that you seek what you think is for my good, and, believe me, I do not leave you without regret. But, father, put yourself in my place. Imagine that you had the faith I have, instead of the Mormon belief. Try to feel as I do, that what you are seeking for me would be a wretched fate, and then you will freely forgive me, I know, for trying to save myself. Please, father, think lovingly of Mayon, if you can, and forgive her. But O, whatever you may think of me and feel towards me, I beg of you, do not be angry with poor mother. Her heart is ready to break with her sorrow at parting with me, and angry words from you would be cruel. She has only done what she thought was her duty; and though it seems a wrong to you, have not you followed your convictions of duty, even though it brought greater sorrow on mother than this act of hers can possibly bring on you? You were pained to grieve her, and she is very unhappy to think of being obliged to deceive you, and send me away from you. But mother believed you did not willingly afflict her in acting as your conscience dictated, and she forgave you; and how many times she has told me, lest I feel hard towards you, 'It is not your father, Mayon, who has done this, but his religion through his faith in it.' Cannot you forgive as mother has, and believe that in wronging you she only followed the dictates of her own conscience, as you have done, and should not be blamed? When you think it all over, I am sure you will not wound mother's already aching heart with one unkind word, but will pity her for her loneliness when I am gone, and will try to make up to her for my loss. Do not blame mother for Edith's flight. They tell me she never has been happy in Mormonism since she realized its misery, when a little girl, and she spoke to mother about leaving before she knew that I was some time to go away from here. Mother told her then, and it was arranged that we should go together. Once more, dear father, I ask you to be forgiving and kind towards mother and—

YOUR DAUGHTER, MAYON.

Nobly had Mayon pleaded for her mother in her calmness, as Mrs. Northfield in her excitement could not plead for herself. Kind deeds were not all on the mother's side, and Mayon had now performed one office of love which went far towards repaying the great debt she owed.

Elder Northfield read this letter, and his eyes were opened to the cruelty and injustice of his manner to his wife. Mayon's pleading and expressions of affection touched his heart, and he sought his wife and turned her grief to joy by begging her forgiveness for his unkindness. Although he still believed she had acted very wrongly, yet, as Mayon had suggested, she had forgiven what she considered wrong in him, and he should be no less magnanimous now towards her. Therefore pleasant relations were again established between them.

Chapter 13

Had Edith and Mayon succeeded in reaching their destination in time for the train, they would have undoubtedly been forced to accompany the husband and father back into Mormonism. But a kind and merciful Providence, often working in mysterious ways, ordered it otherwise. They had proceeded nearly half the distance when Edith, in her fast walking, stepped on a rolling stone and fell, spraining her ankle. She tried to hobble on, but it soon became impossible for her to walk. Here was a new trouble, and an insurmountable one. Edith urged Mayon to go on and leave her, for there was no time to be lost; and if she could not board that train, it might be too late, for there was no other till the next day.

"But what will you do, Edith, if I leave you?"

"I will wait here by the roadside till some farmer comes along to take pity on me, and take me either to the station or back to the city. Then I will follow you on the next train, if possible; and if not, it will not matter much if only you are safe. Take the purse and hurry on, Mayon."

"Never! I will not desert you! As you cannot walk, I will stay with you."

Mayon had regained her self-possession now that she felt she had started towards liberty, and acted as the leading one of the two, since Edith was almost helpless from her pain.

They sat down to rest and consider the situation. They were in a part of the highway enclosed by fields and forests, and not a house or human being was to be seen save one little hut in the distance. Mayon spied it and said:

"I will tell you what we will do. I will help you to walk to that hut, and if it is uninhabited, as I hope, we will secrete ourselves there till morning, when I hope you will be able to go on. If not, or if we are overtaken before morning, I will go back to my mother, whom I almost feel that I am a coward to leave—whom I had almost rather not leave, even if I must be a Mormon's wife. We will go back, and I will marry Edward Ellis and submit to my fate. Why should I seek a happier life than my mother had? Why should I deserve it?"

Mayon concluded to go first and examine the hut. She came back and reported it empty. Then, with her help, Edith succeeded in walking the intervening distance, and there they hid themselves for the night. The weather was not warm, and they suffered some from cold, though more from their fears. No sleep came to their eyes; but when morning dawned Edith was able to walk with difficulty to the station, and their hearts were filled with thankfulness that at last they were speeding towards the Gentile world. Later, when Edith learned how they had been delivered from capture, she blessed God for the accident and pain she had been allowed to suffer, and believed more firmly in God's mercy, which she had felt inclined to doubt.

"Lillian," said Elsie Bernard to her daughter, "here is a letter from your aunt Marion. Poor Marion!"

"What does it say, mamma, about Mayon?"

"It says we may expect her immediately, for she will start for New York in a few days."

"What! So soon? It can't be those Mormons have driven Mayon from her home already, by wanting her to marry before she is grown up!"

"But it is so, my dear. My sister writes that they are all in great distress, caused by her father's determination that Mayon shall marry his partner. She is secretly planning to send her to us, and what is more, the other wife Edith is coming with her."

"O I am so glad that I shall soon have Mayon here with me; but, mamma, did you ever hear of anything so ridiculous as a girl travelling in a friendly manner with the polygamic wife of her father? But aunt Wells will be glad, will she not, for she is the daughter of her lost Lillian's governess, of whom she was once so fond?"

"Yes, Lillian, and we will all be glad that one more soul will escape from Mormonism, and will give her a cordial welcome for her own sake as well as for aunt Wells'. But let me see the date of this letter. Why, it must have been delayed! Lillian, they should be here by this time. Every train must be watched, for they are strangers in a strange land, and will not know how to find us."

So some member of the family was at the depot, and watched the passengers of every train that might bring them. But two days passed and Lillian began to be impatient, when she and aunt Wells returned, and as the carriage door was opened Edith and Mayon stepped out.

"Mamma!" exclaimed Lillian, "come and greet Mayon and Miss Parker" (for Edith decided to assume her former name—the name she considered her only lawful one). "We only knew them by Miss Parker, whom aunt Wells declared was her dear Frances. And she could hardly be persuaded that it was not her old friend instead of her friend's daughter."

The fugitives could ask for no more of love and welcome than they here received. Lillian and Harry were overjoyed, and their mother, as she warmly embraced her sister's daughter, was blinded by tears of emotion.

"O, my child," she said, "would that my dear sister might have come, too. But where are the golden curls and blue eyes that Marion's daughter should have? You are like your father, Mayon."

Mayon answered, "Yes, I am like my father. You should see Forest: he has mother's golden hair and blue eyes. He is very handsome."

Elsie's heart went out towards Mayon with almost a mother's love, and aunt Wells was almost jealous of her affection for her.

When Walter Bernard returned from business, with all the sincerity of his noble heart he welcomed the fugitives to his home, saying to Mayon:

"We have regarded you as one of our family for years, you know, and feel now that our absent member has come home. Lillian's happiness will now be complete, I believe, and our friend Edith has always belonged to aunt Wells' family, and as she and her friends belong to us, you see we are now to be a very happy reunited family."

As Edith and Mayon sought their rest, the one sharing aunt Wells' room, and the other appropriated by her cousin Lillian, there were two thankful hearts giving praise to the all-wise Father, who had brought them safely to this haven of rest. Sad were the thoughts of dear ones left behind, but nothing could make them very unhappy in the bosom of such a loving family, and though Mayon's pillow was wet with tears, as she thought of a dear mother far away, yet they were not altogether tears of sorrow.

The family life they had now come into, with its perfect love and affectionate spirit, its absence of all jealousy, lack of confidence, family jarring, and, above all, sad faces, was a delightful study to these young Mormon women, who were themselves inclined to sadness, and who were unaccustomed to seeing happy women, young or old.

Elsie, with her exuberant spirits, smiling face, and playful manner, even at her age, formed such a contrast to her sister,

once as fair and gay as she, that they could only look at her
with wonder, even though they had been prepared for change
in every way in Gentile life.

Aunt Wells, too, though she had passed through life's sorrows and was nearing the grave, had a look of calm, sweet content that surprised them.

They realized then the beauty of these family relations as
they could not from the teachings of a mother. Each had been
carefully taught in childhood all her mother was capable of
teaching of Gentile life, but even from those teachings no cor-
rect idea could be formed. Now they were in the world and of
the world. Though their mothers had longed in vain for this
blessing, the daughters were now enjoying it.

Edith gradually lost her quiet sadness, while Mayon, in the
warm influence of Lillian's sunny, merry temperament, changed
rapidly from a quiet girl, thoughtful beyond her years, to a
sprightliness in voice and manner which greatly added to her
charms. Thoughts of home and mother, however, oft brought
the tears to her eyes and a quiver to her tones. Her first act was
to write a long, loving letter to her mother, which was greed-
ily devoured by the latter in her anxiety to know of her daughter's safe arrival.

The question of Mayon's education was now to be considered. Lillian had entered a girls' school on the banks of the
Hudson a year previous, and was anxious that Mayon should
go there with her when she returned at the close of her present vacation.

Mayon shrank from the publicity of a school, and felt that it
would be a painful ordeal for her to enter one, ignorant, as she
was, of all public institutions, and of the manners and customs
of the people. She had been reared in the greatest of retirement,
never having been in a school, and was consequently very timid
and quite embarrassed with strangers. She believed, however,

that all Gentile girls were kind and lovable. Her little experience of them justified that opinion, and she wished she might have courage to become one of the great number of pupils at Lillian's school. Her anxiety to obtain an education was very strong, and she was by no means ignorant of the knowledge that books could give her, for her mother had taught her well.

Aunt Wells, with her kind, clear good sense, settled the question by saying:

"Mayon's studies should begin not with books or school-life, but she must first learn of our manners, customs, religion, and social life. I say that the coming winter should be devoted to society, pleasure, and sight-seeing in our city. Mayon's first study should be of the geography of her new home. We must make her life as gay and happy as a young girl's life can be in New York City."

"Well said, aunt Wells," said her nephew, who was an important member of that family council. "I am glad you agree with me that the poor girl should not be weighed down with Latin declensions or mathematical problems now, when all her life has been a thoughtful and somewhat sad one. Make her so gay and happy that her voice will ring with laughter as it does now with song."

"If only Lillian was to be at home," sighed aunt Wells, "it would be so much easier for Mayon to mingle in society."

But Lillian's whole course of study could not well be interrupted, and soon Mayon had to part with her cousin, who had assisted so much in rendering her first few days of life in "the world" very happy ones.

Edith would not consent to remain dependent on the bounty of her friends, and insisted on trying to obtain employment; and at last, to content her, they gave her needlework to do, and thus she became the family seamstress.

She was treated, however, as her mother had been by this

same old lady in her younger days, not as a servant, but as a friend and member of the family. She could not be persuaded away from her life-long habit of remaining at home; and though Mayon was constantly going to see every phase of life and entertainment the city afforded, yet it was only when, with an affectionate caress, she said, "Please, dear Edith, come with me this once," that she yielded.

Mayon was fast learning what her friends wished. She became less shy and sensitive in company, with much tact learning to avoid the oddities of manner peculiar to her former life, and to adopt the customs of the people with whom she associated. Always graceful, always beautiful and intelligent, and distinguished as being a Mormon refugee, it was no wonder that she made many friends in a short time. The sights and sounds of the city, its schools, libraries, etc., ceased after a time to be such wonderful objects of interest to her as at first. But attendance at church was always a great delight. Never had she heard the preaching of the Gentile religion, and with Edith she drank in every word that fell from the minister's lips; and though they harmonized with her mother's teachings, yet new light seemed to come to their souls, and they were something like the poor heathen of other lands, receiving with wonder and delight the gospel of Jesus Christ. Whenever they had attended worship in Salt Lake City, they had listened to exhortations to duty, obedience and sacrifice, the glory of suffering for religion's sake, until, had it not been for the teachings of careful mothers, they would have never known that there was anything more cheering, more beautiful than these sterner attributes. They were not told of the love of God the Father to his children, and Christ's sacrifice once for all for the world, was not referred to. Now they were led to realize the beauties of the Gentile religion, and many times Mayon's eager, happy face, sometimes tearful, attracted the attention of her fellow-worshippers as she listened with an absorbing interest, all unconscious of her surroundings. As the service closed it was with difficulty sometimes that she could recall her mind to the practical affairs of life. Edith, too, intensely enjoyed these religious services, and began to experience much of real happiness, which she had said she never expected to enjoy. They faithfully made record of everything of interest in their lives for the comfort of one who had sacrificed so much for her child.

When spring came, Edith began to tire of city life, sights and sounds, and longed for the country. She felt a languor and failing of strength, that caused her to contemplate seeking occupation out of the city. Though loth to part with her, as she was to leave them, her friends thought it wise to grant her request, and seek employment for her with some good family in the country. Dependent she would not be, and they could not persuade her to accept support unearned by herself. Mrs. Bernard found a situation for Edith with a friend of hers some forty miles distant. Her duties were confined to the partial care of two children and assistance in the family sewing. She was very pleasantly situated, and began to recruit in health and strength. Another vacancy was made in the family circle of the Bernards in a few months. During Lillian's long summer vacation she made a new plea for Mayon's companionship in school.

"Mayon," said she, "I know you will be happy there, for you love to study so well and there are so many dear good girls that you cannot feel lonely or timid among them all. You will soon feel perfectly at home, and things will not seem so strange or new as when you first came."

"Yes, Lillian, I dare say I should soon get accustomed to it, and like it very much. I think I should begin to study now, for I wish to fit myself for teaching, and should lose no time."

"As to the teaching, I am sure there is no need of that; but I will go to aunt Wells with my heart's desire, as she seems to assume the right to guide your interests, and she will not refuse if she knows we both wish it strongly."

"I will go with you, Lillian, and will be guided entirely by her wishes; but I now feel as though I would really like to try school life. That will be as great a novelty for me as my experiences the past few months have been, for you know I never entered a school-room till aunt Elsie took me to visit the schools here."

Aunt Wells was inclined to grant the request of her nieces, and it followed that one day two happy young girls bid their friends good-bye and entered D—— Seminary, one as a returned member, the other as a new pupil.

Mayon endured the scrutiny of a room full of school-girls and a corps of teachers quite bravely. As her classes and lessons were assigned to her, she went to work with a will, and soon the embarrassment of her position wore off and she began to make friends with her schoolmates. She felt that zest and enjoyment in school-life that can only be known by one whose education has been conducted hitherto in private. Life to her was a glorious thing now; she was enjoying all the blessings and advantages, all the joys that she had longed for in Gentile life, save one—the companionship of father, mother and brother. Thoughts of longing for them and shades of homesickness troubled her at times, in spite of all her happiness.

Mayon had from her first entrance into the school noticed a slight, frail girl, whose graceful, pleasant ways and tone of voice resembled her old friend, Flora Winchester. Then her features reminded her of Flora, though the resemblance was not strong. She heard one of her schoolmates address her as Jessie, then she learned from Lillian that her name was Jessie Winchester.

"O Lillian!" said she, "can it be that she is poor Flora's sister?"

And then for the first time she told Lillian the story of Flora Winchester. She resolved to seek her and learn for herself. So Lillian asked Jessie Winchester to come to their room during recreation hour. She complied, and thus began a friendship between Jessie and Mayon which was firm and true, and lasting.

"Have you a sister Flora?" asked Mayon.

"Yes, I suppose I have. Why do you ask? Have you ever seen her?"

"I have seen a Flora Winchester from W——, a girl who had a sister Jessie and two brothers. I have seen her, and known her, and loved her. She has shared my home and my room, and was like a sister to me, and is even now dearer than my own half-sister."

"O tell me! where did you see her? It cannot be, then, that she went to Utah if this is true. You are not from Utah, are you?"

"Yes, I came away from Salt Lake City a few months ago."

"Then, where and how is Flora now?"

"She is there yet, and is the wife of Elder Burnside."

"I knew it! I told mother so. I knew that man had bewitched our Flora, or she never would have left us. O dear! She was the light of our home, and we have not been happy at all since she left; and I think father is the most unhappy of us all, though he is still so angry at her that he will not allow her name to be mentioned; and we are all forbidden to write to her, or to receive letters if she should write. But mother and Carlos did write her two or three letters, notwithstanding, though they never received any answer. It was not long after she went away. Do you know whether she ever received the letters?"

"I think she never did," said Mayon.

"Father, I know, loved Flora the best of us all; but he is very stern, if offended, though always kind if we obey him. And I believe he would gladly receive Flora to-day if it were not for his will and pride. I am so glad to see one who can tell me about her, and one who has been kind to her. How I thank you for being a friend to my sister! Little did I think, when I noticed the tall girl, with large, dark eyes and long curls, among the new-comers here, that she was a friend to my sister. This is the first we have heard from her. Now, please, tell me all about Flora, and I will listen."

Then Mayon told the eager, anxious girl all that she knew of her loved sister and how she had vainly tried to persuade her to return to her home. Jessie was affected to tears by Mayon's account of Flora's homesickness, her longing for friends and her marriage. She could not rest till she had gained the consent of Mayon and Lillian to go with her to her home, that her mother might hear from Mayon's own lips Flora's recent history. They lived but a few miles from the school, and Jessie returned to her home every Saturday, there to spend the Sabbath.

"Father must not hear a word," said Jessie; "but mother and the boys will be so glad to see you and hear you talk of her. Mother has been almost crazy about her, wondering what has been her fate. Almost any certainty would be better for her than this suspense. We feared she would marry if she went among the Mormons, unless she repented and came back, and father made it almost impossible for her to do that; besides, she is so proud she could never bear the odium that would attach itself to her. Father feels her becoming a Mormon a disgrace; but if he were not so proud, I know he would be as glad to hear from her as we are. Perhaps in time he will change; but, dear! it is too late even now to get her back, but it is such a comfort to meet one who has been a friend to her. Mayon—may I call you Mayon? I shall always love you for your kindness to my sister."

Then she became interested in Mayon's own history, and they talked till the bell rang for prayers.

The next week Lillian and Mayon went with Jessie to her pleasant but unpretentious home, there to spend the Sabbath. Jessie had written that she would bring friends home with her, but had given no further information. When she presented them to her mother, and explained that Mayon had recently come from Salt Lake City and was a friend to Flora there, and that her home had been Flora's home, then the mother threw her arms round Mayon's neck and wept. As soon as she could calm herself she requested Mayon to tell her all she knew of Flora. Mayon did so, and emotions of love, grief, thankfulness and fear for her daughter, filled her heart as Mayon gave the different phases of Flora's history. The existing fact of her matrimonial alliance checked all feelings of hope for her return. It cast a gloom over all contemplation of her daughter. Poor Flora was doubtless eternally lost to them; but, in spite of the sadness of this conviction, there was comfort in hearing from her and meeting one who had been her friend and confidant.

Carlos Winchester had just finished his collegiate course, and was now pursuing the study of law with an able lawyer in the village. Leonard, who was the youngest of the family, was preparing for college at the village academy. Their father, who was in moderate circumstances, was yet able to give his children the advantages of education, though his business did not yield an income sufficient for the indulgence of many luxuries.

Unknown to the narrator of Flora's history, also to his family, this man was a listener to the last of her story. His return from business was earlier than usual, or he would not have heard Flora's name mentioned, for it had been forbidden, and never was spoken when there was any danger of being heard by him. Though outward obedience was yielded him, yet in private it was not seldom that the mother and her three remaining children referred to the missing fourth. Mr. Winchester paused to listen at the door as his ear caught the name, Flora, spoken in unfamiliar tones. He continued to listen till he had learned much that roused his paternal feelings. He left the house unperceived by his family, and returned at supper time. Then was gathered the entire family: the dignified, though kind father;

the quiet, subdued mother; Carlos, with his tall, lithe figure, brown wavy locks, lofty forehead, and kind, clear gray eyes, so resembling Flora's that Mayon almost gave a start at sight of him; Jessie, whose sweet, graceful ways gave her a strong influence on her brothers; and Leonard, sturdy, merry Leonard, who tried hard to be quiet and dignified, like his father, but in vain, and who often made his home ring with laughter by the exercise of his fun-loving propensities. Lillian and Mayon soon felt quite at ease with their new friends.

Carlos and Leonard were still in ignorance of Mayon's knowledge of Flora or of her former home. Mr. Winchester, after cordially greeting his daughter's friends, soon relapsed into a preoccupied silence, and once, as his wife made some reference to their visitors, he abruptly addressed Mayon as Flora, and immediately recalled the name; and again, on being asked where a certain acquaintance of the family was, he absently answered, "In Utah," then, seeming very much embarrassed, he emerged from his absent-mindedness and forced himself to become sociable, as was his custom with his family.

On the following day the young people were assembled by themselves, and Mayon repeated Flora's story for the benefit of her brothers. They were intensely interested, and there were tears in Carlos' eyes and a tremor in his voice as he grasped Mayon's hand and said, "God bless you for your kindness to my sister," while Leonard fidgeted uneasily in his chair, and at last exploded with, "Hang it! why don't the government put a stop to the whole thing? I would like just to put a bullet through that scoundrel Burnside, who robbed us of our Flora."

Mayon and Lillian were treated with the greatest of attention, and every possible means was employed to add to the pleasure of their short visit. Each seemed to vie with the other in showing grateful kindnesses to Mayon, and when the three returned to school, the warmest, heartiest hand-grasp was that of Mr.

Winchester. Mayon heartily wished she dared speak freely to him of his daughter, but Jessie enjoined her to refrain from such a course. This was only the beginning of an intimate companionship and much time spent in the society of the Winchester family. For Mayon came to them something like a representative of their lost one, and in a certain degree began to fill her place in their hearts. Carlos said she must allow them to regard her as a sister when with them, and, as he had formerly been devoted to his favorite Flora, he now monopolized much of Mayon's time, and delighted in her society; not, however, exhibiting a warmer feeling than that friendly brotherly interest which had been awakened through his affection for his absent sister. Mayon sought to learn from her mother's letters of Flora's present circumstances, and to open through their letters a correspondence between her and her family, but she had removed with her husband to a distant part of the Territory, and moved again, till Mrs. Northfield had lost all trace of her. She at last was told where they were living, and sent several letters to her address, but received no answer; so the efforts to establish a correspondence with her or concerning her were fruitless, and her friends could learn no more of her than what Mayon had told them.

A year passed, and rapidly and profitably to Mayon, whose only sorrow was her separation from her mother. They constantly cheered each other, however, with long letters of unreserved confidence.

Mayon and Lillian, who excelled in scholarship, were among the competitors for prizes, and proved formidable rivals for their classmates. Mayon made good use of her time, and had become a great favorite with teachers and scholars. Even her schoolmates' petty jealousy for the Mormon girl's superiority she warded off by kindly ignoring its existence, and winning the love of all.

Although in Mayon's intercourse with the Winchesters no

attempt now was made to keep secret from Mr. Winchester her former home and life in Mormondom, yet no word had been spoken by him to any one with regard to Flora. But all were glad to observe that he always listened with peculiar interest to anything Mayon had to say of her life in Utah, though he never had asked her one question on the subject. But one day he invited her to ride with him alone, and then he questioned her concerning the doctrines, regulations and marriage relations of the Church. He asked particularly of the latter, and showed much desire to become informed concerning the character of the Mormon men, from Brigham Young down to the most obscure male member of the Church. He sought to learn whether they were, as a rule, kind and humane, or otherwise. Mayon could not give an answer to this question very favorable to the generality of Mormons, but, speaking from her own experience, she had little to say to their discredit. She told him, in the course of their conversation, of a young girl who came to them from the East, deceived into the belief by an elder, and forbidden her father's house in his anger. She spoke in strong terms of the girl's unhappiness and homesickness, of her longing to receive the kind, loving look of her then angry parent, of her sorrow at separation from mother, sister and brothers, and of her own effort to persuade her to give up her false religion and return, a penitent, to her father's house. She repeated the reply the girl had made, saying it was too late, for her father had declared she never should enter his house again; and, though she longed to return to her home, yet it was now impossible, and she would make the best of it.

Her companion was silent at Mayon's conclusion, and when he spoke, his voice was husky, in spite of himself. Mayon hoped she had softened his heart towards his erring daughter, and not without reason. Though still too proud to speak of her, yet the ice in his heart was thawing.

Chapter 14

At the close of Mayon's second year at school Lillian graduated, and with honor, and Mayon knew that when she returned after vacation she must come alone. Therefore graduation day was rather a sad one to her. But Jessie's parents had invited her to spend the summer months at her home, and, as she had never spent much time in the country, she was very glad to accept the invitation. Lillian, and indeed her aunt's whole family, regretted to be deprived of her society, but aunt Wells said: "It is just what she needs. She has become familiar with city life and with school life, and it is time she now enjoyed the delights of the country." So Mayon left the school with Jessie instead of with Lillian as usual. How she enjoyed the pure air, the green fields, the wild flowers and freedom from all the restraints of school discipline or city conventionalities!

Carlos was also taking a vacation from his studies, and as Jessie was busy mornings assisting her mother about her household duties it fell to Carlos' lot to entertain his sister Mayon, as he called her. So together they read Shakespeare, or took long morning drives or walks in the fields and forests with a view to a practical study of botany. But one, at least, was learning in the close companionship of these sunny days, a lesson of a different character. Carlos did not so often call Mayon, sister, as he had done, and, as he offered her many little tokens of esteem, spoke words expressing his high regard for her, he was annoyed to see how composedly she received them, with perfect unembarrassment. They never called a conscious blush to her check or hesitating tremor in her voice. He knew her heart was stirred by no answering emotion to the sentiment he now felt for her. Perfectly unconscious Mayon continued to enjoy his society, and received at his hands the many pleasures the country afforded to one who had never known its attractions. Perhaps a Gentile girl would have seen in his manner more than a brotherly affection, but Mayon did not yet thoroughly understand Gentile life, and anything that seemed strange or peculiar to her in it she attributed to her own ignorance of anything outside Mormonism.

"Jessie," said Carlos one day when alone with his sister, "do you think Mayon ever thinks of me in any way but as a brother or intimate friend?"

"Why, Carlos?" innocently asked Jessie.

"Because," and then Carlos' cheek reddened—"Jessie, I will tell you a secret. I am tired of being her brother: I—I—I wish to be regarded in a different relation. You understand, Jessie. I love Mayon with my whole soul, and I believe she does not suspect it, and cares no more for me than for many another friend. I have tried to give her little hints, but she takes them so exasperatingly cool, and returns my affection in such a wise, sisterly manner, without the slightest shade of embarrassment, that sometimes I get desperate and have to bite my lips to keep them from saying certain things. I think she would be shocked and very sorry, and would go away from here, and then—Jessie—how lonely we should be!"

"Dear Carlos, I did not think matters were so serious as that. Do not be so hopeless. Even if no such thought has entered Mayon's head there is plenty of time yet for that result, and at least you have the comfort of knowing she is fond of you. Carlos, nothing would suit me better than that you should make

Mayon really what she seems, my sister; and father and mother I am sure would be very much pleased. Remember, 'Faint heart,' etc., Carlos."

"Yes, sister, I will, but I will control my tongue till Mayon's happy summer draws to a close, at least, unless she gives me more reason for hope." Thus saying Carlos left her, but alas for the frailty of human resolutions!

Not a week had passed when one day as he and Mayon had seated themselves on a mossy bed, by the side of a little fairy stream in a valley thickly wooded with pine, and were analyzing specimens of the forest wild flowers, Carlos became so confused as to awkwardly pull the delicate flower to pieces, scattering it upon the ground at his feet, making the most absurd blunders in the use of botanical terms.

"Carlos, Carlos," exclaimed Mayon, "what are you saying and what are you doing? Look at that poor little blossom all torn in pieces. What are you thinking of to destroy it so? You look as though you would like to annihilate the whole floral kingdom."

"Mayon," said he, and he clasped her hand in his, "I will tell you what I am thinking of, if you will hear me. I am thinking of one who came to my home and filled a sister's place in my heart. A dear sister she became too, and I find too dear for my peace of mind, if our present relations toward each other continue. Mayon, I love you with no brother's love. Be a sister to me no longer, but promise to become my wife some time."

"O, Carlos," said Mayon, as she attempted to withdraw her hand, but he held it fast, "I am so sorry. I never dreamed of this. I love you, Carlos, but not in that way. No, I cannot be your wife. I never thought of that. Please do not blame me for letting you say this. How could I know you thought of me in this way? Please, dear brother, forget it all, and let us be the same to each other as before." Mayon's cheeks were rosy enough now with blushes, and her voice had all the tremor in it that Carlos would have been glad to note in past days.

"But, Mayon," said he, "if you have never thought of this, won't you think of it now? You confess that you love me as a brother, and may not time ripen that affection into something stronger? At least, give me some hope, Mayon!"

"I can't, Carlos. O, do try to forget it all and be the same to me as before. You have been such a kind brother to me I feel that it will be hard to lose you, but I am sure if I—if—if I ever marry I must love very differently from this. I should wrong you to give you in return no more affection than I have for you."

"But I could win your love in time I do believe, for, Mayon, I would be so kind to you. I would devote my whole life entirely to you. I will wait, so patiently, if at last you will be mine. Mayon, dearest Mayon, let me ask you again, in a year—two years?"

Mayon became very sad now. It wrung her heart to refuse this passionate plea for her love, and she was tempted to give him hope. But she felt in doing so she would be doing wrong, and at last found courage to utterly refuse him. "O please, Carlos," said she, "please forgive me for wounding you. I wish it might be so, but it is impossible. Please do not blame me for letting you come to this, for I never suspected it. I think I had better go to New York now."

"No, Mayon, I will be man enough not to trouble you further; and since you decide against my suit, we will again be to each other as brother and sister, and we will try, as you say, to forget all this; but, Mayon, in spite of all you say, I shall hope that some time you will change. It is not quite impossible that some time you may know that your sisterly love has changed to a warmer sentiment. I shall comfort myself with that hope. In the meantime we will try to be happy as we have been."

"Shall we go now, Carlos?"

"Yes, Mayon, and we will come again to-morrow and attend more closely to our botanical studies. These poor flowers have been torn to pieces as my hopes have: but see, they are not quite destroyed, neither are my hopes."

They returned to the house, and Mayon spent the afternoon with Jessie as usual. But before her head rested on its pillow she had confided that day's experience to paper for a loving mother's eyes to read, and she felt more tranquil and happy. But though Jessie never referred to the subject she felt sure she knew what had transpired, for she seemed a little sorrowful and thoughtful, though not one whit less kind and affectionate. Carlos, too, did not abate in his zeal for Mayon's happiness, and her heart was touched. As matters stood she was rather glad when the close of her vacation drew near, and she returned to New York for a few days before beginning another school year.

The farewells with these friends and the greetings of her uncle's household were hardly over when Mayon received a short letter dated at Salt Lake City, informing her that her mother's health was failing rapidly, and that if she cared for her as a daughter should, she would return immediately, for her absence was a source of much suffering to her mother. Said the writer: "Mrs. Northfield is not fully aware of her own condition, and therefore has probably refrained from alarming you, or requesting you to return. Trusting that you will act wisely and dutifully, these lines are penned by a friend." The writing was unfamiliar and no name was signed to the letter, but Mayon's heart was filled with fear and grief. "O my poor mother! and I have been away from her so long—more than two years since we parted. It is just like her thoughtfulness, to keep me in ignorance of her suffering that I might not be troubled. But some kind friend has informed me, and instead of going back to school I will go back to my mother, and remain as long as she needs me. Perhaps (with a sigh) I shall remain all my life, but at any rate I have had two beautiful years of life in the world."

Her uncle examined the letter and expressed the fear that it was far from a friendly one, but written with the purpose of decoying Mayon into Mormonism again.

Mayon said: "If it is so, I can come back again."

"But," said her uncle, "would it not be wise to wait till you can write and hear again from your mother?"

"O, I cannot wait, uncle! See, the writer says she is failing rapidly, and if I wait, I may be too late. My poor mother sick, and with her daughter so many hundred miles away! I feel that I was almost cowardly to leave her at all."

"But, Mayon, I feel afraid there is something underhanded about this. Anonymous letters are suspicious. It will only require a few days to settle all doubt."

"But a few days may be too late. The letter says she is rapidly failing, but is not aware of her own condition. That is why she has not written of it to me; she did not know her real condition and did not wish to alarm me. O, uncle, please do not refuse your consent to my immediate return to my mother. Think how I have not seen her for two long years, and what if she should die with no Mayon by her side and I should never see her again!"

"But, my dear, are you not afraid that it will be impossible for you to get away again if you once return?"

"No, I think not, for mother writes that father feels very different now towards me; and even if I never leave Utah again, I must go to my mother. O, uncle Walter, please let me go."

"Well, Mayon, I shall not refuse you, but I am afraid the writer is dealing in foul play."

"No one could do such a cruel thing as that. I think some kind-hearted person has written for mother's sake and mine."

The separation from Mayon's new friends was entirely unlooked for, and as she thought that possibly it might be a separation for life, it was a very sad one to them all. There was not the anguish and agony of fear, however, that made her separation from her mother so terrible, and she was not fleeing like a slave or criminal now, but was in God's free land, and could leave with no fear of molestation. Sad thoughts were hers concerning the giving up of her school life and departure with no final farewell to the Winchesters, but they were only fleeting thoughts, for her heart and head were too full of anxiety for her mother and preparations for her journey.

Mrs. Northfield was sitting quietly and alone in her little parlor one day re-reading Mayon's last letter, written on the day of Carlos' proposal to her. She laid it down and sat, with eyes closed, thinking. From the expression of her face, though there was a look of longing there, her thoughts were evidently not unpleasant. She had the appearance of resting in mind and body. There was a quick, nervous peal at the door-bell. She started, and opening the door, wonderingly faltered,

"Mayon, Mayon, can this be you!"

"Mother! mother!" exclaimed Mayon, and mother and daughter were again locked in each other's arms. Again their tears mingled, though their lips refused to speak.

"You are better, are you not, dear mother?" asked Mayon as soon as she could speak.

"Better! What do you mean, my child?"

"Have you not been ill?"

"On the contrary, my health has been very good of late— better than usual."

"O, I am so glad! I expected to find you sick, perhaps dying. That is why I am here; but I am glad I am here after all. O, mother, the years have been long when I thought of you, but so short for the happiness that has been crowded into them!"

"Thank God for that, my darling; but why did you think I was sick?"

"Some one here has written to me, saying my mother's health was failing rapidly and advising me to immediately return to her. Uncle was right; some one has deceived me; but why should any one do it?"

"O, Mayon, I almost wish you had not come, though my heart has ached with my loneliness, and I am so happy to see the face I feared I should never behold again. But I fear there is something wrong about this—some injury contemplated towards you."

"Can it be that my father had anything to do with it?"

"No, Mayon. I am so happy of late to see a change coming over him, especially in the last few weeks. I think—I do believe that in time he will see the error of his whole life and apostatize. Mayon, I believe better days are coming. Your father has seen so much dishonesty and avarice in Brigham Young and the councillors and apostles, and so much of the sad results of polygamy, that I think his faith is wavering. He does not say much on the subject, but I notice he does not attend the meetings as regularly as he has done, and he is studying the Bible a great deal. Thus, Mayon, what has affected his personal interests has affected his faith somewhat. Some of the most religious men of the church,—men in whom he has always had great faith,—have by their dishonesty been the means of the loss of so much money to him that he was fearful his whole business would be swamped. I have been waiting to see how the affair came out before writing to you about it; but though all were lost, and we became penniless, I could rejoice if it were the means of opening up the way to our freedom from this religion."

"That will be a joyful day if it ever comes," said Mayon; "and, mother, how will father receive me? I have dreaded to meet him, but perhaps if he is so changed he will receive me kindly."

"I think he will, for he has been quite lonely since Nell was married."

Nell had been married a few months previous, and was the third wife of a still quite young man. She was yet his reigning favorite, and still looked with favor on Mormonism with all its institutions. She had yet to learn that she was only the plaything of the hour, to be thrust aside as a child thrusts aside a toy that has given him great delight, for a newer and more attractive one.

Mrs. Northfield's happiness had not been lessened by Nell's departure, for she had never been a source of pleasure to her, but very many times the reverse. Forest was away from the city preaching in some of the smaller settlements, and the house was quite lonely, though Marion did not feel the loneliness as she would but for her happiness at hope of a change in her husband and her pleasure in her daughter's happy life and prospects.

She noticed with joy that a great change had come over Mayon in two years. She was now so happy and buoyant, in contrast to her former depressed manner. Her face had lost its look of fear and dread, and her eyes shone with a new light. Her mind had become stored with knowledge in many departments. The same vigorous health was still hers, and her mother felt that two years of absence had but added so much of beauty, cultivation and goodness to her child.

They talked of Edith, who was still in the country earning her own livelihood, of Elsie and her family, of Nell, and of Flora and her friends. There was so much to he said of the occurrences of two years that hours fled unheeded by them both. At last the father's footstep was heard in the hall.

"O, let me hide, mother, till you have told him I am here," said Mayon, and she started to leave the room; but as she opened the door at one side of the room, her father entered at the other.

He stopped short at sight of Mayon, in bewildered astonishment. Mayon turned back to her father and said:

"Father, have you forgiven me?"

"Forgiven you! Yes, my child, I have forgiven you. Have you forgiven me?"

"O, yes, father, with all my heart."

Then he folded Mayon close in his strong arms, and both felt that they were in loving sympathy as they never were before. The mother witnessed their meeting with a heart overflowing with joy. Happiness was at last coming into her life after many years.

"Now, Mayon, how came you here, and why did you attempt to run away from me a second time?"

"I only meant to give mother a chance to tell you I was here before you met me. I confess I did not think you would be so glad to see me."

"But I am, my daughter, very glad indeed. I think I was a little mistaken with regard to my ideas of duty. I think now that each one should be allowed to follow the dictates of his or her own conscience, and I regret that I took it upon myself to decide and determine upon your course, but I thought I was doing what was for the best at the time."

"I do not doubt it, father, and it has resulted, I hope, in no harm."

"But, Mayon, you have not told me why you came back to us so unexpectedly."

Then Mayon gave an account of the letter, and handed it to him to read. As he read he grew serious and his brow darkened.

"I am afraid there is something evil in this," said he. "The leaders were all very much stirred up at your departure, or apostatizing as they call it, and Brigham Young in particular, as he had interested himself enough in your case to call upon you and counsel you. Ellis was very much chagrined and disappointed, but said had he any idea you were so much opposed to his acceptance he would have withdrawn his suit. I received many expostulations for not pursuing you, and there was even talk of attempt among themselves to get you back by some means; but I warned them not to interfere with my affairs, and Ellis did the same (for he is an honorable man), and then they charged me with conniving at your escape. They accused me of being next door to apostasy; but after a time the storm blew over and I have heard nothing on the subject for a long time. But this letter looks as though they had not forgotten it, and were attempting to get you back into Mormonism again."

"But, father, there is no danger that they can keep me here, is there? I can step on the train any time, you know, and go to New York."

"No, they cannot force you to stay. When you wish to return to New York, you shall do so, if I have to go with you to protect you."

Certainly her father had changed, and that wonderfully; and Mayon was quite happy at thought of the possibility of his accompanying her out of Mormonism.

"Marion," said Elder Northfield to his wife, "who can be the author of this letter, and what does it mean?"

"I think," said she, "it is only an attempt to decoy Mayon back again, with the hope that she will remain. You know they fear the influence of apostates in the Gentile world, particularly educated persons. And they may know of the course of study she is pursuing. But there can no harm come from it, for Mayon can never be persuaded to become a Mormon, so let us not give ourselves any uneasiness concerning the letter."

"No, we will not trouble ourselves; but I shall quietly endeavor to discover the rascal who wrote it."

Mayon was now home again—home, even though it was in the midst of the iniquity and superstition of Mormonism. Here all her childhood days had been spent, and here all tender memories of the past centred. Again she was with her dearly beloved mother, and the barrier was broken down between her and her father. For the last years of her life at home she had hidden in her bosom a secret from him—a secret jealously guarded, and from its nature it instigated a feeling of defiance towards him. This was all gone now, and complete confidence was restored between them. Mayon now began to regard her sojourn in the city as a visit, for her mother insisted on her return to her school in a few weeks. The term had now begun, but Mayon had brought her books, and as well as she could, without her teacher, she continued in her studies. She went with her mother to see Nell in her new home, and was received quite cordially. She was established in a fine house, but it was cursed like most houses there with polygamy. One of the first wives entered the room, and was presented to Mrs. Northfield and Mayon. She seemed to be in no very amiable mood, and soon left the room.

"Eliza has the sulks worse than ever to-day," said Nell. "She and Mary are very jealous of me, but that does not trouble me at all. I know they cannot harm me; they have had their day, and ought to be willing that I should have mine now. Are you not tired of Gentile life, and come back to remain now, Mayon?"

"No, Nell, I shall return in a few weeks. I am only making a visit."

"Forest's prophecy does not seem to be fulfilled with regard to your marrying a Mormon—I mean the prophecy he made the day we three quarrelled so about Alice Clark's marriage."

"No, Nell, I am of the same determination that I was then. But, speaking of Alice Clark—how and where is she?"

"O, she is dead. The other wives led her a wretched life, and during a quarrel between them Alice fell down the stairs, and died soon after from her injuries. She had not the faculty for getting along with them, as I do with my husband's wives. I have no trouble."

Mayon felt a lack of sisterly love for Nell, as she conversed with her, and they did not remain long, but went to the home of Carrie—Elder Parker's now deserted wife.

She had taken a smaller house and had to nearly support herself. Francis, Edith's brother, had now a wife and two children. Edith had left for him, at the time of her flight, an affectionate letter, urging him to discard Mormonism, and be guided by the teachings of their mother, and follow her into the Gentile world. She enclosed a farewell letter to Carrie, who had been like a mother to her. Francis was a Mormon, more through the force of circumstances than from heartfelt faith in its teachings. Polygamy he looked upon with disfavor, and had no intention of practising it. He was well situated pecuniarily, and did not contemplate entering the Gentile world, though his mother's early teachings and sufferings had made too deep an impression upon his mind to give him any religious zeal. Carrie never had any children, and was a lonely and sad woman, though Francis did not neglect her, but with his wife and children were her devoted friends. Elder Parker was again on a mission to England, but it made little difference to Carrie where he was. There had always been a bond of sympathy between Marion and Carrie since they emigrated in each other's company. Marion had gone out more since Edith and Mayon left her, and a firmer friendship was established between them. Mayon promised to visit Carrie again, and they returned home.

Mayon felt that, though she had entered her cage again—the

cage of Mormonism—yet she was not secured in it, and was free to take her flight at any moment. So she breathed freely, and the days passed very happily, although the sorrows of polygamy touched her with a new sympathy: for she had been in the world and enjoyed its happy domestic relations, and the contrast only brought before her mind more vividly the miseries of her native land. One day, after she had been very thoughtful on this subject, she said:

"Mother, you know the Gentiles are sending missionaries to foreign countries to enlighten and convert the heathen ill-treated women. I have often wondered why they never think of sending missionaries to convert the poor women here, for many believe that polygamy is right, and those who do not are so forced to submission and ignorance that they do not think escape possible. Now, what is needed is that enlightened women go quietly among the women here and tell them of the love of Jesus, show them the right religion, and persuade them to leave Mormonism; and there should be a society to aid them with funds to leave.[27] Why does the nation send such generous supplies for the heathen in the old world, and let the heathen in their midst continue in their ignorance and debasement?"

"I do not wonder you ask, Mayon, for if ever missionary work was needed, it is here; but a missionary would perhaps meet with worse persecution here than in many so-called heathen countries, for here an attack upon the religion is an attack upon the government. Brigham Young's tyrannical rule is accomplished only through his influence on his subjects' religious sensibilities. Otherwise this bondage would be impossible in free America."

"Mother, let me tell you what I have been thinking of. I want to try to help some poor souls out of this bondage. Why can I not, in a limited sense, become such a missionary, and try to persuade some of the young girls here to renounce Mormonism?"

"It would be a noble work, my dear, but a dangerous one. Our family has called down so much indignation from the Church that I dare not risk the enterprise."

"But I would work very cautiously and secretly, and, mother, ought I not to try to give something to others, when so much has been given to me?"

"If I dared, Mayon, I would bid you God-speed, and hope for some good accomplished."

"You know, mother, that even if the authorities became aware of it and attempted to trouble me, I would only have to leave for New York. I ran away once; I can again, if need be. All I should fear would be the anger of Brigham Young and the rest against you and father, if I should be so fortunate as to make any apostates."

"You need not fear for us, Mayon, and I have half a mind to bid you begin your missionary work, if you will promise to be very discreet and cautious."

"Then, mother, I will go to-day and find some of the girls I used to know, and try to open the way to the accomplishing of my purpose."

So Mayon began a work which, though at first unknown, unsuspected even by those she strove to influence, at last led to the deliverance of a few fair young women from the lives of sorrow their mothers had lived. As no opposition was made, and apparently no notice taken of her quiet talks with the women, of Gentile life and religion, without any reference to her object of accomplishing their apostasy, she began to feel confident that she would be undisturbed.

There was a Gentile by the name of Demming, who had recently come into the city and opened a store. He made himself acquainted with, and agreeable to Mr. Northfield, and the latter invited him to his house, thinking Mayon would enjoy his society, particularly as he was from New York City. Demming gladly accepted the invitation, and he proved a very agreeable acquaintance. He was a fine singer, and Mr. Northfield and his wife enjoyed their songs and their conversation concerning the Gentile world as much as they did. He became a frequent visitor, but, though Mayon could not tell why, she began to tire of him, and it seemed to her that there was a lack of frankness and honesty in his character. His eyes would drop as they met her clear gaze, and she felt that he was not quite to be trusted.

Chapter 15

Thus matters stood, when Mayon received a most unexpected visit. Her mother called her one day to meet a friend in the parlor. She entered the room and beheld a girl apparently about her own age, clad in a rather shabby dress and bonnet. Her face was very thin and sad. Her large gray eyes were sunken and her hands extremely emaciated, and trembling violently. Mayon stood regarding her for a second, trying to recollect where she had seen those features before. The slender girl stretched her arms toward Mayon, saying: "Mayon! Mayon! don't you know me?"

"Flora, can this be you?" exclaimed Mayon. Flora would have fallen to the floor, but Mayon caught her, and with her strength it was an easy task to lift the light form of her friend and carry her to the sofa. She had fainted, and now Mrs. Northfield entered, and together they soon succeeded in restoring her. Then followed exclamations of love, surprise and joy, not unmingled with pity at Flora's feeble condition.

"Why have you never written to us, my dear?" asked Mrs. Northfield.

"I could not. I was prevented, and if I could, I had nothing but misery to write. O, Mayon! would to God I had listened to your pleading and gone back to my father. I received a letter from you, Mrs. Northfield, saying Mayon had seen my family, and containing messages from my mother and from Jessie and the boys. I read your letter, and began to read their messages when my husband entered and snatched the letter away from me, reading it, and then tearing it in pieces before my eyes. He also destroyed a letter I received a year ago from my father. That, however, I had not opened, but was passionately kissing the superscription, which I knew to be my father's writing. I knew that he had forgiven me, and wished to take me back, and was so happy when suddenly it was seized from me and thrown into the fire. I attempted to rescue it and in doing so burned my hand terribly."

"O, Flora, my poor, dear Flora!"

"Now, Mayon, I found out that you were here, and have walked all the way from L—— to meet you and hear from my mother and the rest. I am so glad you have found them. Now tell me all about them."

And Mayon told Flora all she wished to know about her father, mother, sister and brothers, not omitting her talk with Mr. Winchester concerning Mormonism, which both agreed was the cause of his writing to his daughter immediately after. Flora seemed overjoyed at hearing from them all again, and then Mayon asked her to tell them of her life since she left the city.

She sighed, and said: "There is not a great deal to tell. "We went first to M——, and there my husband left me to hold some meetings in a town a few miles away. He at first wrote to me frequently, but, after a time, I heard from him very seldom. Finally he came home and said he was going to take another wife. It seems that one of his converts, as I had done, had fallen in love with him, and, as he returned her sentiment, they were to be married. Mayon, thank God you never can know what I suffered, for you are free—free as I once was; but you, Mrs. Northfield, know something about it, though you do not know what it is to suffer from the cruelty of a husband as I did. All his love seemed gone from me, and at sight of my tears he would become very angry and say the most cruel things. When

I begged him to be kind to me and love me again, he turned from me rudely and told me not to be silly. I then thought and spoke of leaving him and going to my mother, and asking her to take me in and let me die with her, for I did not think I should live long, my health was so poor. Then he raved at me again, and told me that there had been one Mormon runaway girl, and bade me not to dare try to follow my friend's example, for he would surely thwart my plans, and I knew he would. Soon after that my father's letter came, and probably no one but he knew what its contents were. My husband threatened me if I attempted to write to my friends, and said he should take means to prevent any letters from passing through the mails. I think he was afraid to have me leave and go where I might expose his cruelty. We soon moved from M—— to A——, and then he brought his wife there. How I hated them both, and I think they hated me too! It seemed to me that I should go insane. My baby was born soon after that."

"Your baby, Flora! have you a baby?"

"No, not now. She is dead," and Flora could not go on for the tears choked her so. "In a few months my husband went away preaching again, and he took his new wife with him. I was glad of this, and now I had my little Jessie to love, and to love me; but my husband left me but a little money, promising to send me some when I needed it. He did not send it, however, and baby and I suffered from hunger and cold. Then Jessie fell sick with fever, and though I wrote to her father for help, yet without the assistance of my neighbors, who learned how I was situated, I fear we should have starved. But though Jessie did not actually starve to death, she was killed by the want and cold her father's neglect caused us. I could not weep or mourn when my darling baby lay cold and stiff in my arms. I felt that God had mercifully taken her away from her suffering. The day after she died the undertaker came with a beautiful casket and a quantity of the loveliest flowers. I thought there had been some mistake, but the man was positive that this was the place to which a gentleman had ordered him to bring them. I tried to learn who my benefactor was, but could learn nothing. After my child was buried I was sick, and a strange woman came and nursed me well, and a physician attended me faithfully. I tried to find who had employed them, but they would only tell me some one who knew of my need had provided for me. At last I became able to be about my house again, and as my physician made his last call upon me he put some money into my hands, saying it was from my unknown friend, and he hoped it would supply all my wants till my husband returned. I can only wonder who my friend was, but God knows, and He will reward him. I could worship him if I could find him. My husband and his wife came soon after that, and he seemed surprised and sorry, I think, to find our baby was dead, and he was not quite so unkind to me. A few weeks ago we moved to L——, only four miles from here, and it was from listening, a few days ago, to a conversation between him and some elder from the city, who had come out to see him, that I learned you were here. And I came, not only to hear from my friends, but to tell you, Mayon, of the plot that is working, as they think to their satisfaction, to keep you in Mormonism."

Mayon gave a frightened start, but Flora said:

"Never fear, however; I have found it out in time to save you."

"What do you mean, Flora?" said Mrs. Northfield, excitedly.

"First, Mayon," said Flora, "tell me truly, are you going to marry Mr. Demming?"

"Marry Mr. Demming! No, never!"

"I am so glad of that, for he is not a Gentile, as he represents himself to be. He became a Mormon a few years ago, and is now acting the part of an impostor to you. The elders are seeking to ruin you by bringing about a marriage with this man, and when your fate becomes irrevocably fixed, he is to throw off his Gentile cloak and you are to find yourself the wife of a Mormon. O, Mayon, it is too horrible to be true, yet it is true. And I heard them congratulating themselves that you had fallen into their net; was delighted with the young Gentile merchant, and there was no doubt that you would marry him soon. I learned that even his store was stocked by the church funds to give him influence with you and your parents. It was a scheme of their own, from the writing of the anonymous letter to this day, and they thought it was working admirably. They said, 'Even Northfield himself does not suspect the trick, and soon our fair apostate will be withdrawn from the Gentile world for life.' O how my blood ran cold as I heard their diabolical plans and feared you had fallen into their snare and given your heart to this man!"

"Thank God she did not," said Mrs. Northfield. "We have regarded young Demming as a very pleasant acquaintance, however, particularly as he was a Gentile, but they are mistaken in supposing there is any entanglement with Mayon."

"Then the plot would have failed at last, but I feared it would not."

"Darling Flora, how I thank you! Had it been as you feared, you would have saved me from a fate worse than death."

"Yes, much worse than death," answered Flora; "you *think* so, I *know* so."

"And, Flora, if you will consent, you shall be saved from it, too. When I go East again, you must go with me; and O, how happy your father's whole family would be!"

"No, Mayon, it will not make them happy to have me come back such as I am now, and I could not bear to go. Thoughts of my wasted, ruined life would torment me more there than here. I do not think I shall live very long, and I had rather remain here the little while I do live, and be buried by the side of my little Jessie. I think my return home would give rise to such sadness there that they would never be the same again. I have made them wretched enough, and do not deserve to be taken to their home in my last few miserable days. I will patiently remain here now till death comes, and then I shall find rest. I think God will forgive my errors, and mercifully give me peace and perhaps happiness at last."

No effort of Mayon or her mother could persuade Flora to abandon her purpose, and so at last they talked of other things, principally of affairs at the East. Toward night they procured a carriage and drove Flora to her home, or as near there as she dared have them seen, for she did not wish her husband to learn where she had been.

And this was the wreck of that once happy, lovely girl! This was one of Mormonism's victims, and still that curse is allowed to blight our country, and the young, the fair, the innocent are sacrificed to its superstitious ordinances.

Mr. Northfield regretted that he had not been at home to meet Flora, for he was much attached to her, and very indignant when he learned that Elder Burnside had proved to be so inhuman. That knowledge, however, was one more addition to the tide of influences which were carrying him slowly but surely towards a renunciation of his life-long faith. Still more was he influenced and angered by the discovery of the base deception that had been practiced upon him and his daughter. He had tried in vain to ascertain the source of the letter to Mayon, but at last the mystery was solved. But a life-long faith—a faith which had become a part of himself—was not to be easily uprooted. A gigantic tree may become unsound; it may be shaken to its roots; it may sway and totter in the wind; but it takes a mighty power to uproot it entirely. So a faith established and strengthened with the growth of many years—almost a lifetime of years—was not to totter and fall at inferior attacks. The attitude of the Northfield family towards young Demming was materially changed now, and though they judged it best not to make their discovery known, both for Mayon's safety and for Flora's, yet when Demming again called he met with a cool reception, and soon his visits ceased. Mr. Northfield feared that if the Mormons knew of the failure and discovery of their scheme, they would attempt some other form of intrigue, and Mayon, for safety, would be obliged to shorten her stay there. He also feared that by some means Flora would become implicated, and that the result would be fresh trouble for her. It soon became evident, however, to the conspirators and the principal actor in the plot—who had become very much interested personally by this time—that their scheme was a failure, and they were very much enraged.

Mayon's missionary work had progressed and increased, and now bid fair to bear fruit, for she had persuaded several women, mostly young, to contemplate privately leaving the Mormons, in her company. They were necessarily from the few families where money for travelling expenses could be obtained by stealth or the sale of valuables. They trusted that they should be able to find employment in the Gentile world, and Mayon hoped that her uncle in New York would be able to assist them in that direction. The authorities of the Church, of course, were not aware of the extent of Mayon's influence over some of their women, but they were not so ignorant and unmindful of her doings as she supposed. She would not have been allowed to continue her visits and talks against Mormonism and in favor of Gentilism, had it not been for the security they felt that her days of liberty would be few. "Let her work," they said, "she can do no harm, for she is surely failing into the net we have prepared for her, and will soon find herself a devoted Mormon woman by virtue of necessity, instead of the Gentile seducer of our women that she now is." Elder Northfield was deceived as well as his daughter, for he was known to be quite in sympathy with her now, and they were fearing he would apostatize. Forest, they felt, was their stronghold in that family, for he was still as devoted as ever in proclaiming his faith about the Territory, but he was ignorant of what was transpiring at his home. After it was known that Demming had failed to accomplish his purpose, Mayon's enemies no longer looked with unconcern and leniency upon her missionary labors. A stir was now made, and one of the apostles went to many houses where Mayon had been known to visit, and commanded the women not to allow her to enter their homes again. Then one of the women whom Mayon had persuaded to renounce Mormonism was seized with a panic of fear; and, conscience-stricken, because of her infidelity to her religion, she exposed the scheme, and thus all were thwarted in their plans to escape, though several were permanently converted to Gentilism, and in after years apostatized.

Brigham Young himself visited Mr. Northfield at his place of business and angrily accused him of apostasy, saying, "If you do not keep your daughter at home, I will not be answerable for her safety. All good Mormons are rightly very indignant at her attempt to make our women turn traitor to their friends and their religion, as she has done. The public feeling is that no punishment could be too great for her. It is enough that she apostatizes herself, but as to going further, Northfield, I warn you to put a stop to it. *If you do not put a stop to it, someone else will.*"

After this warning there seemed but one course to be pursued, and Mrs. Northfield said to Mayon:

"Mayon, your father and I agree that the sooner you leave us for New York the better, as we consider it unsafe for you to remain here, the hatred of the Mormons is so intense."

"But, mother, you do not fear that any personal harm will come to me, if I now remain quietly at home, do you?"

"My child, a religion that would excite men to the deeds committed by the Mormons, is not to be trusted; and if lives were once openly taken in a religious zeal against the Gentiles, what would they not do now, if they dared? I have never told you of the 'Death Society,' 'Avenging Angels,' or 'Band of Danites,' as they were called,[28] which the old Mormon women have told me used to exist here in full force, and even now exists in secret, but the Mormons dare not now be so bold in their persecution of the Gentiles."

"Tell me about them now, mother!" and Mayon's eyes dilated with horror.

Her mother related what she knew of the horrors of the past, when a band of men—tried, true and trusty Mormons—was formed for the purpose of exterminating apostates or Gentiles who were found to be opposing God's Church. To apostatize then, during that reign of terror, was to have the throat cut from ear to ear, or to suffer some other ignominious death, for God's chosen people were to cut off any who opposed his cause. They were led by the hand of God in inspiration, and though murder in the Church was a terrible crime, yet the killing of the Gentile was no murder. The whole earth, with its cattle upon the thousand hills, was the Lord's, and therefore belonged to his people, and they hesitated not in appropriating their property, even though the wicked Gentiles claimed it as their own. Polygamy was established, and a massive temple built in what were then their headquarters, farther east, and the reviving of the old Jewish sacrifices was even contemplated.[29] Thus she showed Mayon that the most terrible crimes of all descriptions had been the dark results of Mormonism's teachings.

Mayon was now almost trembling with terror, and she agreed with her mother that it was best for her to depart immediately.

"But, mother," she said, "isn't it a pity that that woman should prove a traitor and expose us all? Now none of them can escape at present, and perhaps never. O, mother, you cannot tell how disappointed I am that my efforts, which seemed so successful and gave me so much pleasure, have proven a complete failure! I did so long that they, and particularly Annie Huchins and Josie Parks, might get away from here, for they are both very unhappy. And, mother, I must leave you so soon! But it will not be so hard as our other parting was, for then I thought I should never see you again. Now I think you will come to me, and perhaps before many years. O, how we should thank God that light is slowly, but surely, creeping into father's mind! I never loved my father as I do now, and I believe he will miss me very much."

While Mrs. Northfield was necessarily absent from her home a few moments that evening, and before Mr. Northfield had returned, Mayon sat thinking of Annie and Josie, in whose welfare she was especially interested. They were both very dissatisfied with Mormonism, and being naturally refined and intelligent girls, though not educated, they longed to escape into the Gentile world. Annie was persecuted, as Mayon had been, on the matrimonial question and Josie, whose own mother was dead, was treated very cruelly by her father's wives. Mayon had influenced them to determine to escape with her, and now, that she knew how disappointed they must be, she longed to comfort them, and give them her address and urge them to write to her, if ever she could be of service to them in any subsequent attempt they might make to escape. So she resolved, in spite of her fears, to disguise herself by wearing her mother's cloak and a thick veil, and visit them once more before she left the city. A few moments later Mrs. Northfield returned, and was a little disappointed to find Mayon was not at home. She supposed, however, that she had gone to a neighbor's house, and would soon return. But as time passed she became uneasy, and, by the time Mr. Northfield entered the house, was quite alarmed. Without stopping for supper he immediately set out to find Mayon, saying:

"She was very imprudent to go out in the evening unattended. Why did you allow her to do so?"

"I did not allow her. She went without my knowledge, and during my absence from the house. O, I hope no harm will come to her."

"Do not be alarmed, Marion; I will bring her back with me, if I have to search the city over for her."

But before he returned Mrs. Northfield was in the greatest suspense, and her fears were doubled. After an hour, however, she heard steps approaching, but they were irregular and slow. She hastened to open the door, and, sure enough, Mr. Northfield had brought Mayon back with him, and almost literally carried her, for she was scarcely able to walk. She looked frightened and very pale, and her mother exclaimed:

"O, Mayon, what has happened? Henry, what does it all mean?"

"I do not know myself," said he; "but get something to revive and stimulate her, and we will try to learn what is the matter."

While Mrs. Northfield proceeded to obey his directions, her husband removed Mayon's cloak, and saw that her dress-sleeve was stained with blood. He could hardly suppress a cry of horror, but was relieved to find that her arm was only slightly grazed, apparently by a pistol ball. Her forehead, too, was badly bruised and swollen. She was soon recovered from her half-fainting condition, and her father said:

"Now, Marion, I will tell you all I know of this affair, and I hope Mayon is now able to tell the rest. I searched for her among the neighbors, and then it occurred to me that she might have been so rash as to have attempted to see some of her converts again, and I had not proceeded far in the direction I thought she would take, when I met a woman almost staggering along on the sidewalk. Something about her seemed familiar to me, and I stopped and watched her after we had met and she had passed on. I turned and followed her, and she seemed terribly afraid of me; and when at last I spoke to her, she screamed, but was soon calm when she realized who it was that was pursuing. Her thick veil blinded her so that she could not recognize me in the darkness. I brought her home as fast as I could, and checked all her attempts to speak, for she had scarcely strength to walk. Now, Mayon, can you tell me how you came to be in this condition?"

"Yes," said Mayon; "I went to see Josie and Annie once more. I did not feel afraid to do so with the disguise I adopted, and as I was hurrying home, going on Elm Street, which you know is an unfrequented one, I ran against a rope, stretched across the street, about a foot from the ground. I fell, and immediately heard a laughing, hooting and rough talking at my expense, behind the fence, only a few feet from me. I rose and found my head was badly hurt, but I commenced to run. I had not proceeded far, however, when I saw a flash of light, heard a pistol report, and felt my arm tingling with pain; but I continued to hurry on as best I could, expecting to be killed if I could not reach home soon. I heard the ruffians swearing, as if in great rage, but I hastened on, as well as I could, with weakness from pain and fright, and when father spoke to me I was so excited that I did not recognize his voice at first, and thought the men had pursued me. I never was so thankful, I think, as I was when I realized that it was he. Now you have the whole story, and what does it mean?"

"It means, my dear," said her father, "that the Mormons, as a body, are enraged and excited because you have stirred up rebellion among the women, and a few of the villanous men, who are everywhere to be found, have allowed their passions to excite them to an attack upon you. I shudder to think what might have occurred, but if those criminals can be found, they shall be brought to justice."

"But Mayon is not safe a day longer here," said her mother.

"No," replied her father, "and if these wounds prove to be no more serious in the morning than I hope, she had best leave on the early train. I will go with you, Mayon, as far as Cheyenne, for your protection."

But before morning Mr. Northfield was visited with a severe attack of a disease from which he often suffered, and he was unable to leave his bed. He thought best, however, for Mayon to proceed as she had intended, though she must journey alone. He did not believe the respectable Mormons would wish any violence done her, and thought the attack on the previous night was an outburst of the indignation of ruffians, or the resentment of those who might feel personally injured by her. He thought Annie Huchins' lover, who was a man of rather low character, might be among the latter class. That any attempt whatever would be made in daylight, or by the body of Mormons at any time, to do personal violence to his daughter, he did not think possible. So with regret, rather than fear, he bade her good-bye, and she left them again. Again she was fleeing from her persecutors, but not as before from her father, as the greatest of them. Her parting with her mother was cheered by a whispered hope of meeting again, and that in the Gentile world.

Before the train had borne Mayon out of the Territory, she felt that she was watched by two men, who entered the same car in which she seated herself at Salt Lake City. She changed cars twice on the train, and was much annoyed to find that they soon followed her in her changes. At last she resolved to stop over a train at one of the prominent stations, hoping thus to rid herself of her disagreeable travelling companions. She did so, and was really alarmed to find that the two men had also stopped, and again, as she resumed her journey, were seated near her. She was now quite nervous and frightened, but tried to calm her fears, and attribute them to her fright of the previous night. The men were strangers to her, and she did not like their looks. They were also quite profane, and indulged freely in oaths and tobacco. At last, after two days of weary travelling, tormented by fear, while waiting in a depot in one of the large towns on the route, these men came to her, and one of them said:

"Miss, I am authorized to arrest you, and you will oblige us by offering no resistance, for it will be entirely useless, and only make a scene, which you can just as well avoid. You will go with us quietly to the police station, and after trial, if you are proved not guilty, you can continue on your journey."

"You must not arrest me. You are making some mistake. I have violated no law, and cannot be held for trial."

But they were already putting handcuffs on her wrists.

Then she burst into a violent fit of anger and excitement, attracted the attention of the people about her, declaring her innocence and that these men were committing an outrage upon her, and then said, turning to some gentlemen who were looking at her with half-pitying, half-curious faces: "Gentlemen, I am an escaped Mormon girl. I have been in New York two years, and was decoyed back again to Salt Lake City by Mormons, who hoped by a plot of theirs to keep me there. Their plot failed, and their anger on that account, and because of my influence among the women against Mormonism, nearly resulted in my death the night before I left. These men boarded the train at Salt Lake City at the time I did, and they have followed and shadowed me all the way, and now pretend to arrest me for trial. I appeal to you, gentlemen, for help."

"Gentlemen," said one of the men who had hand-cuffed Mayon, "I shall be obliged, I see, to tell my version of the story though for her sake I wished to be quiet about it. This unfortunate young lady is insane, and on one point principally: she imagines what she has been telling you is true, and has told every one the same story for two years. She never was in Salt Lake City or New York City, and knows no more of Mormon life than what she has learned from books. She is the daughter of a merchant in B——, and escaped recently from the insane asylum back here a few miles at N——. The wound on her head was occasioned by her beating it against the walls of her room. We are officers, and it is our disagreeable duty to take her back to the asylum."

Mayon's plea had enlisted the sympathy of the people standing about and excited their indignation, till the gentlemen were ready to interfere for her protection. But this explanation of affairs was believed, apparently, as Mayon beheld with horror. She became terribly excited now and tried to convince her audience that she was telling the truth, and that she was sane. But her words had a contrary effect, and her eyes gleamed, as the people thought, with insanity, and indeed they were wild with terror. Her frenzy at the treatment she received was easily mistaken for insanity, and the ladies turned away, saying: "Poor creature, I hope she will recover. She is so beautiful and naturally intelligent!" and the gentlemen remarking: "Well, there's no doubt she is insane, judging from her appearance. I pity her, though."

Mayon saw how useless all appeals for assistance were, and submitted in despair to being placed in a carriage and driven mile after mile over roads, which she attempted to recollect in case she succeeded in escaping and wished to go over the road again. It was dark when they stopped before a large brick building, and Mayon was lifted from the carriage. Again she became desperate and tried to spring back into the carriage, hoping to be able to start the horses before her captors could prevent and thus escape. But she was rudely caught by the arm, and her wound hurt so badly that she screamed. She was forced inside the building, and really had the appearance at the time of being a raving maniac. She heard such expressions as the following from the attendants and other patients: "Poor thing!" "How very crazy she is!" "What a beautiful girl to be brought here!" "We shall have to resort to discipline, I fear, with her." When Mayon was at last locked in her room alone she realized that in her agony she had acted in perfect accordance with her captors' wishes, and had corroborated their statements of her insanity by acting like an insane person. She resolved now to be very calm and to convince the attendants by her manner that she was sane, and tell them her whole story. But the villains were prepared for that, and had instructed the officers of the peculiar phase of her insanity, and they in turn had informed the attendants, so when she told the kind lady in charge her story, she said: "Well, my dear, if that is so, we will make it all right in a few days," and Mayon knew that she was not believed. She then laid her case before the superintendent, asking him to write to her father's address in Salt Lake City for proof of her statements. He promised to do so to quiet her, and Mayon believed he would, but he did not. This was only one case among hundreds, where patients had friends in certain places, and he believed or acted upon the belief that her father was just as visionary a person as these friends usually were.

Thus two days passed, the longest, most wretched days of Mayon's life, but she hoped for release as soon as the superintendent could write to her father and hear from him. He would come to her she knew, if able, and perhaps in case of his inability to come her mother would fly to her relief. No one else in Salt Lake City could be trusted to come. O what would her father's and mother's feelings be when they learned that her enemies had placed her in a lunatic asylum! At the close of the second day of her imprisonment the attendant turned the keys of her door and admitted a visitor, and Mayon recognized one of the gentlemen who listened to her plea for help at the time of her capture. The sight of his kind, intelligent face inspired her with hope. Said he:

"My young friend, I have come all the way from —— for the purpose of learning whether the story you told there is true, and, if so, to assist you if possible to escape. Although your appearance that day warranted the belief that you were insane, yet I half believed your story, and could not get your distressed look from my mind. Your face haunted me all night long in my dreams and in my waking hours, and I became more and more convinced that there was some foul play about the affair, especially as the more I thought of it I did not like the appearance of the men who claimed to be officers. I told my wife about you, my fears, and half determination to look into the matter, and she would not rest till I set out for this place. When I inquired of the officers here about the escaped lunatic that had just been returned, they did not know to whom I referred. Then I discovered through them that you had never been here before, and that strengthened my belief in the rascality of those men. Now tell me anything that may lead to a further solution of this matter, and what you wish me to do to help you out of this place."

Then Mayon told him all, and he was perfectly convinced of her sanity, and went to the superintendent and demanded that she should be released. The superintendent blandly replied that that was impossible. If he released every patient who succeeded in procuring a friend to demand his or her release, every maniac in the institution might soon be at large and the country be endangered by their liberty. He could not release a patient without the most positive proof that he was right in so doing.

Why should he take the word of one man against two others, and the appearance of the girl besides? "for," said he, "the girl was certainly one of the most raving of insane persons I ever saw when brought here."

"So she was when I saw her captured," said Mayon's new friend, "and what innocent, right-minded girl would not have been under the circumstances? Would you, sir, if attacked by rough-looking men, hand-cuffed, and told you were insane, and were to be taken to an insane asylum—would you quietly and calmly submit, or would you make resistance and struggle for freedom? Would you be unmoved and calm under such circumstances, or would your blood boil, your anger rise, and, in your indignation, would you not give vent to your excitement, and would not your eyes gleam with something which might be taken for insanity? If you as a man were thus treated, what would be your sensations? But still farther: imagine yourself a young, unprotected female, with no power to resist, and obliged to submit—would such a person be likely to be very calm, think you? Why, man, it was enough to make the girl insane, and take care, sir, that you do not do it."

"No doubt your arguments appear very deep to you, sir, but fortunately I am more familiar with insane people than you are, and shall take the liberty to judge for myself as to this case, and nothing but the most positive proof that this girl's story is true will ensure her release. Procure me that proof, sir, and I will release her. Not till then."

The gentleman went to Mayon and told her how matters stood, and that she would be obliged to remain a few days, till he could correspond with her friends both in Salt Lake City and New York. Meantime he would go to his home and at the earliest possible hour return with proof to insure her freedom. Mayon gave him the address of her father and also her uncle, and it was not without a flood of tears that she parted with

him, for she feared some further plot at the hands of her enemies before he should be able to secure her release. Therefore
with his departure much of her hopefulness departed also. She
looked upon him as her protector and saviour, and her gratitude towards him knew no bounds. A few weary days of life
in a lunatic asylum passed, and Mayon began to think she was
to thoroughly know Gentile institutions of every nature. The
scenes in that insane asylum were among those most vividly
impressed upon her mind in after years. She felt that the misery
there and the frightful sights and sounds of the maniacs would
drive her crazy if she must endure it long; but her friend did
not desert her; her enemies did not give her further trouble; and
at last as evidence, of a quantity and quality beyond a doubt,
of her sanity and truthfulness were produced, the bland superintendent gave orders that Mayon Northfield he released, and
with her friend she once more breathed the free air of heaven,
and her heart was filled with joy as she realized that again she
had escaped from Mormonism's toils. She, however, felt that
she should not be free from fear till safe in her aunt's home
at New York. She expressed this thought, and her friend said:

"I shall accompany you to New York, and see you safe under
Walter Bernard's roof before I leave. I have corresponded with
him, and also with your father. Here is a letter from the latter."

Mayon read it. It was in answer to one written by him, and
it expressed grief at Mayon's affliction, gratitude for her deliverance, and regrets that he could not come himself to her relief. "I am sick," wrote he: "hardly able to pen these words. Tell
my daughter that I have had a very severe attack, but am now
improving. I have no one I can send to her relief, for I am a
Mormon, and have scarcely a Gentile friend in the world, and
a Mormon I cannot trust. If you will allow me to become still
more indebted to you, and will yourself accompany Mayon to
New York, and place her under her uncle's protection, I will

gladly defray every pecuniary expense it may occasion you; or if that is out of the question, will you send some one whom you know you can trust to act as her escort? Either way, I will enclose a check which will go far towards expenses, if not sufficient. Sick, and friendless in the Gentile world at least, I appeal to your noble heart to continue the care over my daughter, which I am unable to give her, and, if money can reward you, you shall have that; if not, God will reward you for nobly helping your fellow-beings in distress."

Chapter 16

At D—— Seminary one room, at least, was in the most perfect order. Bouquets, in spite of the season, ornamented its little table, and filled it with sweetness. Jessie, with eager, expectant look, was attired in one of her most attractive costumes, and her slender hands and feet could not be made to keep quiet, as she excitedly rocked to and fro in her chair, looking involuntarily from her window down the long, wide carriage way leading to the building. For Mayon was coming back to school to-day, and was to share Jessie's room, now that Lillian was gone, and Jessie was prepared to give her the heartiest welcome ever given by one school-girl to another. At last her eyes were rewarded for their diligence by the sight of a carriage coming up the avenue; and, flying down to the door, she received Mayon with open arms. After leading her to what was henceforth to be their room, Jessie exclaimed:

"Little did I think, Mayon, that when you left us all at home, it would be weeks, instead of days, before I saw you again. What a terrible thing that conspiracy was! and O, Mayon, you can't tell how I hate and fear the Mormons, since we received your letter telling us about Flora. That poor, poor girl! Perhaps she will listen to reason now, and come back to us. Has she received the letter we wrote her?"

"I do not know that she has received any letter from you of late; but I should not know if she had."

"But it was directed to your mother, with the request that she would forward it privately to Flora, and that thus her brutal husband would not destroy it. It should have reached your mother, I think, before you came away."

"But, Jessie, I have been a great while on the way. I stopped a week on the route."

"Where, and why did you stop?"

"I will tell you soon; but first please tell me who wrote the letter you speak of—did your father have a part in it?"

"Yes, and that is what I was going to tell you of. It makes such a change now in our home. Your letter completely broke down father's sternness, and actually the tears rolled down his cheeks, as he read of poor Flora's suffering and determination to remain away; and mother put her arms around his neck, and of course she cried and we all cried, from father down to Leonard, who walked up and down the room, trying to wipe away the tears unobserved by us, and interrupting father continually by saying, 'I wish I could kill every Mormon! How I would like to set up Burnside for a target to shoot at! Father, let me go to Utah and get Flora. I'll bring her, if I have to shoot every man there!' and other similar expressions. The ice was now broken between father and the rest of us, as it seems it was already between him and Flora, and we wrote a genuine family letter, father beginning it, and so on till Leonard finished it up with bad writing and blots, and the fiercest epithets against the Mormons. We hoped that letter would reach Flora, for father assured her that, if she would only come back to us and forgive all his past unkindnesses, she should be received with warm hearts and loving hands, and she would make us once more a happy family, as we were when she was with us. I do hope she will come now; but, Mayon, tell about your stopping on the way. Where did you stop?"

"I stopped at an insane asylum."

"An insane asylum!"

"Yes."

"What do you mean? Why did you stop at an insane asylum and stay a week?"

"Because, Jessie, my Mormon enemies saw fit to place me there, and had it not been for a friend, that I shall always believe God raised up for me, I might have been there now—yes, I might have spent my life there, for aught I know. Mormon animosity would have been equal to that, I do believe."

Then Mayon related the whole of her history, that had transpired since she had written to Jessie. Though it required hours for the accomplishment of all that must be told on both sides, at last they were able to fix their attention upon the present, and studies, teachers and school matters in general were discussed. Mayon had been able to pursue some of her studies while at her mother's, but was, in many respects, of course, behind her class. She now resolved, if permitted, to continue with her class, and by extra study make up for what was lost. This, by hard work, she succeeded in doing. Meanwhile Flora had received the letter from her parents, brothers and sisters, and answered it, sending her letter through the same medium, through whom their letter came to her. She expressed much love and gratitude for them all, but firmly and gently declined to return to her home, as she had declined to yield to Mayon's plea.

Mr. Northfield recovered from his sickness after many days, and then set about the task of bringing about the arrest of Mayon's assailants and her captors. He went to the officers of the city, but found there was little ambition towards the enforcement of the law; and though they promised to try to find and arrest the criminals, and apparently made some effort in that direction, yet it was evident even to Mr. Northfield that there was little heart in their efforts.

No one was arrested, and after a while all effort in that direction ceased. But all this was another strong cause of Mr.

Northfield's increasing dissatisfaction with Mormonism. But yet his business was here, his home was here, his life-long associations were here.

Forest now came home, expecting to find Mayon, and saying he came home for the purpose of meeting her. He was quite disappointed at finding she had gone, and was ignorant of all she had suffered, and also of the cause. He was inclined to look upon her missionary labors as a great outrage against the Church, and felt that the blame of her subsequent troubles should fall largely upon her own head. Forest was a model Mormon, as his father had labored to make him. Now, however, at listening to his views of Mayon's experience, he did not feel so well satisfied with the success he had achieved, in rearing his son in his own religion.

Towards the close of Mayon's last year of school-life, one of her classmates, named Mary Carson, was taken suddenly and seriously ill. She was a girl whom no one liked, on account of her churlish disposition, and consequently no one was ready to sacrifice for her what might have been sacrificed for a more worthy schoolmate. Mayon learned of her illness, and immediately went to her room, and, as Jessie was at home on that day, she remained with Mary almost constantly for twenty-four hours. The school authorities procured the sick girl a nurse as soon as possible, but at first, except for Mayon, she would have been much alone. Mayon read to her, bathed her burning brow, and, kindly ignoring her irritability and fault-finding, ministered to her comfort in every way she could. After a day or two the physician decided that the disease was a case of a very malignant fever, and that no person but the nurse should enter the room for fear of contagion. At this announcement a panic ensued, and the nurse immediately left the premises, the pupils prepared to leave the school, and some even did so on the spur of the excitement. For the welfare and also the safety of the school, it was decided that the patient should be removed to a house in a retired part of the town. But who could be obtained to go with her and nurse her? So great was the fear of this disease that it began to appear that the poor girl would be left without care. Mayon saw how matters stood, and with a serious but determined face she said to Jessie:

"Jessie, I will tell you who will take care of Mary Carson. I will."

"You! O, no! Mayon. Remember the danger. Don't go."

"Jessie," said Mayon, rather sternly, "put yourself in that girl's place. Imagine you are many hundred miles from home, as she is, very sick and with no one to care for you—and can you say one word to deter me from going with her?"

"Mayon, you are right, and I will go, too, and help you take care of this poor girl. If anything dreadful comes, we shall have the satisfaction of knowing we have done right."

"No, Jessie, you must not go with me. There is no need that two should be exposed to the danger; and, as I have already been with her a great deal, there can be no further exposure for me, and so I will go with her. I will tell Dr. Saxon to-day that I have found a nurse for him to take with poor Mary."

Then came days of weary watching beside a sick-bed, and the severest tax upon Mayon's bodily strength, for her patient needed continual care, and there was no rest for her. A boy was procured to remain in the house and wait upon its occupants, and also to bring Mayon's meals to her, which Dr. Saxon arranged should be prepared at a neighboring house. Aside from him Mayon was alone with the suffering girl, who was at times wild with delirium, and in moments of reason was unceasing in her demands upon Mayon's strength. And yet Mayon was not alone, for the tender-hearted physician, who was but a few years Mayon's senior, gave all the time he could to this patient, and often bade her go and rest while he remained by the sick-bed. From this common sympathy for their patient there arose a sympathy between their hearts that Mayon little suspected at first. Dr. Saxon's visits began to seem to her like oases in a desert. She looked for his coming with what she thought was an eagerness for Mary's welfare; but why was it that, after her ear had been strained to catch the sound of his coming, his firm, quick step at last caused her heart to beat violently, and her hand became too unsteady to carry the medicine or nourishment to her patient's lips? Why did she now become embarrassed and confused when he took her hand for a cheering greeting or parting grasp, when once she had, with all the dignity and grace of her nature, received and returned these friendly civilities?

Dr. Saxon's eyes, so like Mayon's own, had looked into hers with too much tenderness for her composure. His manner spoke to her of more than friendly regard, and his noble qualities inspired her with a feeling of worship, which no man had ever awakened in her before. She was mortified at her inability to disguise her feelings, and tried with all her might to regain her former composure, but her effort resulted in complete failure. She feared she had given her heart unsought, and looked forward to the end of her self-imposed task, as a relief from her embarrassing position. The end came sooner than she expected, and together they watched the afflicted girl as she struggled in the agonies of death. This was the first death-bed scene Mayon ever witnessed, and when she realized that her patient was beyond the reach of all earthly joy or pain, she kneeled beside the bed, and, with face buried in her hands, gave vent to her grief and terror in a passionate flood of tears, for she had grown to love this poor girl, who had so little affection shown her in the school. Dr. Saxon bent over Mayon, with his dark locks, his curling beard and tender, pitying expression, and gently stroked her bowed head till she grew quiet and arose. Then there was a sound of wheels at the gate, and friends of the stricken girl had come, as they thought, to her relief; but they had come too late. A stronger, mightier Power than theirs had wrested Mary from the suffering and pain of life, and they could only mourn and weep, and tenderly care for their dead.

Mayon remained secluded at the house where kind hands had prepared her meals until time had passed and a blessed assurance was hers that she had not sacrificed her own life or health in the performance of what seemed her duty. Dr. Saxon did not neglect her now, but closely watched her, to check, at the appearance of the first symptom, the fever which he feared would prostrate her. But careful habits, a free use of disinfectants, and a strong constitution, with hope and cheer, and, it should be said, an overruling Providence, prevented the attack of the disease, and soon Mayon, recruited by her few days of rest, was again in school, striving with all her might to graduate satisfactorily to herself, teachers and friends. During her self-imposed task, Mayon's friends in New York were ignorant of her procedure till towards the last. Then Dr. Saxon took it upon himself to inform them. They were quite alarmed, and were about sending a nurse from the city to take her place, when news reached them that her patient was dead. She was far dearer to them for the sacrifice she had made, although they would have prevented it had they known in time. Mayon now saw little of Dr. Saxon, save as she saw him in her dreams and her recollections of her days of exile beside Mary's sick-bed. She wondered often if he had quite forgotten her.

Graduation day came at last. Mayon's uncle and aunt, with aunt Wells and Lillian, were there, and she had met and greeted them; and as she and Jessie looked over the hall, Jessie saw, among the throng gathered there, her parents and brothers.

"Look, Mayon," she said, "there are father and mother and the boys, after all. I thought they had not come."

Mayon saw them, but she had also seen another, whose face she had missed of late, even though most earnestly devoting her mind to study. Dr. Saxon, with his tall, manly form, and handsome, intelligent face, was one to be singled out in a crowd. But it was not his striking physique that interested Mayon in him to such an extent that she almost forgot the presence of others. Neither was it the bouquet which he held, composed entirely of white lilies and half-opened rose-buds, although this did not escape her attention. Her heart beat a little more rapidly as she wondered who would receive that bouquet. She watched it and its owner, who retained it until at last her turn came to deliver the valedictory, for it had been given to her, and among her floral gifts was the one of lilies and roses. The prizes were now given, and after all which had been offered were awarded, the principal said:

"Ladies and gentlemen: I have still another prize to give this year, one entirely unexpected, and unoffered. Miss Mayon Northfield was one of the promising competitors for the prizes in Latin, notwithstanding her interruption in study in the early part of the year. Again she has been interrupted in the pursuance of her studies in an unusual manner. She left her school, which she dearly loved, and secluded herself by the sick-bed, and what proved to be the death-bed of one of our number, at the imminent risk of health and even life. She was the only person to be found who dared make this sacrifice. A merciful Providence has spared her from all harm from the danger, and she has been able, by the greatest of diligence, to graduate with honor to-day. But the Latin prize slipped from her grasp and was won by another. The prize for heroism which the faculty have decided to award cannot be competed for by any member of the school. I am authorized to present Miss Mayon Northfield with this medal of gold, as a well-earned prize for heroism. Miss Northfield, please come forward."

All eyes were now fixed on Mayon. Poor, frightened, delighted and embarrassed Mayon! She did not move. Again the principal, in reassuring tones, said:

"Will Miss Northfield please come forward?"

Then Mayon rose, and, blushing and hardly knowing what she did, she went forward, and the medal was hung about her neck by a fine, golden chain. Everybody was surprised—everybody was delighted—for the friends of the pupils had learned of the noble conduct of the Mormon girl, and a murmur of applause began and increased, till the sounds were drowned by the music which the orchestra struck up.

Later, as Mayon and Jessie were examining the flowers presented to them respectively, Mayon found a dainty card nearly hidden in a basket of flowers, which was almost a counterpart of one given Jessie. It contained only these words: "For my dear sister Mayon."

"Carlos gave me this, Jessie," said she, "dear Carlos! I have scarcely seen him for a year."

Then, on examining her bouquet, she found a little slip of paper, buried among the lilies, with these words: "A tribute to one who is like the lily in its purity and the rose in its bloom."

Mayon read the words and shyly glanced at Jessie, who had been too busy with her own gifts to notice Mayon's discovery. She did not show this paper to Jessie, but thrust it into her pocket like a guilty person. Why she wished to hide it she could not tell, but she felt that it was meant for her alone, and it seemed to her that at sight of it all eyes would penetrate her secret.

But Jessie read her secret without the aid of these words, in Mayon's face and manner as she examined her treasure. "Mayon," she exclaimed, involuntarily, "Dr. Saxon is your lover! I know it is so. Your face betrays you."

"No, Jessie," said Mayon, now regaining her composure: "you

are mistaken. Dr. Saxon is a very good friend to me, but he has never given me any reason to warrant your assertion."

"Then he will! O, Mayon, I did so hope that at last you might become my sister. Carlos is so fond of you, and always will be, I know."

There was no time to say more, for there were friends to greet, farewells to say, and but little time in the hurry and bustle of leaving school for private conversation. Mayon's school-life had been very happy, and her departure from the place so dear to her was a sad one, but Jessie was to accompany her to New York, and later to the sea-shore with her uncle's family; thus the ending of her school-days was robbed of half its sadness.

Mayon and Jessie had not been many days at Mr. Bernard's in New York, when at dinner one day her uncle said: "Mayon, I met your friend. Dr. Saxon, and learned from him that he has secured a substitute, and is off duty for a few weeks, for the purpose of attending a course of lectures here in the city on surgery, and also to give himself a little rest which he much needed. His only home is at a hotel, and he has no friends here. I invited him to visit us as freely as his pursuits would allow, and assured him he would always be welcomed by my family. So I hope we shall see him here frequently."

Jessie watched Mayon with jealous eye, for her brother Carlos' sake, and was annoyed to see her face crimson either with embarrassment or pleasure. Mayon was saved the necessity of a direct reply, for all became much interested in their prospective acquaintance, and conversation was very brisk. So it came about that Dr. Saxon was again much thrown into Mayon's society, and again his presence had the same influence over her as in that sick-chamber miles away. And when the house in the city was closed and its inmates occupied a cottage on a rocky part of the shore, Dr. Saxon followed them there. It soon became evident to all eyes that Mayon was the magnet that attracted him. Lillian and Jessie complained that he deprived them of Mayon's company much too often. Jessie was really quite disappointed at prospect of Mayon's future. But Mayon herself was perfectly unconscious of their feelings on the subject, for into her life there had come something of more absorbing interest than consideration for these friends.

These were delightful days to Mayon. Life on the sea-shore, in itself, was something new to her, and the picturesque scenery, the water, the sea-breeze, the boats and bathing, were fresh delights. Little excursions, in small parties, were daily made to some point of interest; beaches were searched for shells, islands explored; and short sailing trips taken. In short, Mayon's first visit to the sea-shore gave her perfect happiness.

One day she had stolen away from the others and climbed down the steep rock that jutted out into the water near the cottage, and seating herself in a cleft in the rock, with book in hand, settled herself to read, where the music of the splashing waves just below her, and the occasional sound of the oars and the voices of the oarsmen of passing boats, were all that disturbed the quiet of the place. She did not open her book, however, but unconsciously began singing softly a song of the sea. Soon she saw a boat approaching her, rowed by Dr. Saxon, who was its only occupant.

"Mayon," said he, "will you come down and get into my boat? The day is lovely, and the tide just right for a visit to Shell Island. Let us row there and explore it in advance of the others."

Mayon complied with his request, and just as they began to speed away from the shore a shrill, childish voice screamed: "Mayon, Mayon, we want to go too. Do come back and take Daisy and me," and looking back there stood the little twin brother and sister, their arms extended beseechingly towards the boat.

Dr. Saxon turned his boat in the direction of the children, then said: "Mayon, the boat is too light to take them too." Then he shouted: "Dot, I will take you and Daisy out when I return; won't that do?"

But they turned disappointedly away. Dr. Saxon watched them, regretfully, out of sight, but sympathy for their little woes was soon forgotten. "Mayon," said he, when well away from shore, "sing me the song you were softly singing on the rock."

Mayon did so, and many more followed, in some of which he accompanied her. An hour passed rapidly, and then Mayon inquired if they were nearing the island. It was nowhere in sight. The sea was very still, the waves gently rocking the light boat in their bed, the sun reflecting its beautiful rays in the water. The air was fine, though the day was calm and still, and all nature seemed at once grand, serene and beautiful. At length Dr. Saxon observed a cloud in the horizon, and watched it a little anxiously, pulling swiftly in the direction of the island. But the cloud grew rapidly in size, and soon had spread over the whole sky, completely obscuring the sun from sight. It grew very dark, and Dr. Saxon pulled the slight oars with strong arms and the boat glided swiftly over the waves. Silently they sat looking at each other and the approaching storm. Peals of thunder rent the air. The sharp flash of lightning terrified Mayon for the first time in her life. A strong gale of wind tossed the little boat to and fro, and the oars were almost powerless to guide it. Large drops of rain began to fall. The air had suddenly changed, and the chill of night, which was coming on, added to the cool wind and the rain, caused Mayon to shiver with cold. Darker and darker it grew. Fiercer the waves dashed and tossed their frail craft. Louder was the crash of thunder and the rain seemed to fall in torrents, and, by Dr. Saxon's direction, Mayon commenced to bail out the water that fell into the boat as fast as she could. Each felt that they were working for dear life. The island was now just discernible in the distance, and with the cheering sight of land ahead the strong arms that plied the oars increased the speed of the boat, till suddenly there was a sharp snap, and one oar was broken, just below the oar-locks. In the sudden whirl that this gave the boat it was nearly upset, and Dr. Saxon looked with agony at the white, calm face of his companion, fearing she would immediately disappear beneath the waves. But the boat righted, and was now carried by the wind and waves directly away from the island, for one oar and a broken piece were powerless to resist the mighty currents of wind and water.

There was no course now but for them to drift with the tide and watch and wait. Dr. Saxon laid aside the remnants of his oars and relieved Mayon of her task. At last the rain lessened and finally ceased to fall, but the strong wind and high waves were carrying them far from home and friends. There was no doubt they were drifting far out to sea, in the darkness of night, with no eye to pity, no arm to save.

The billows increased in size, as they were carried farther and farther from shore, and the end of it all seemed only a question of time. Scarcely a word had been spoken till now, for while there was any effort to be made for life there was no time to talk, but now all efforts to save themselves were useless. There was utterly nothing they could do. They could only accept their fate whatever it might be. Dr. Saxon now drew Mayon to him, and wrapping around her an old blanket, which had been stowed away in the bow of the boat, and of which some parts were dry, he put his arms firmly around her, and held her closely to himself, that her drenched and dulled form might be warmed by contact with his own body. Mayon realized that it was no time for prudish scruples, and she was perishing from cold; therefore she unhesitatingly accepted the only relief that could be given her.

"Mayon," said her companion, "do you realize our condition?"

"Yes," said Mayon: "I believe that we must perish soon."

"Mayon, dearest Mayon, do you forgive me for being the cause of this? I would give my life to be able to place you safely on land. Why did I venture out in this frail boat! O, Mayon, can you forgive me?"

"There is nothing to forgive. You did not think of this result. Please do not blame yourself," answered Mayon.

At his words of endearment, which filled her with happiness, even with death staring her in the face, Mayon's heart beat so heavily that her companion, as he held her closely to himself, felt its wild palpitation, and he said: "Mayon, since my eyes first looked into yours, I have loved you and longed to call you mine. Although I have felt I had no right to speak, yet now our hours are numbered, and you can never be mine in life, yet we can die together; and will you not give yourself to me, and be mine till death comes—mine now—mine in death—and mine in eternity? Will you give yourself to me, Mayon, tell me!" and convulsively the arms tightened their grasp, and Mayon whispered: "Yes."

"And if God in his mercy should interpose in our behalf, of which I have no hope, if, Mayon, by any possibility, we are saved, will you be mine in life, Mayon, too? I did not mean to ask you yet. Perhaps I have no right, but I love you, Mayon. Will you be mine, if we are saved?"

Mayon's answer was to slip her hand in his, and thus in the darkness of night, with the angry billows ready to swallow them in their fierce grasp, with the thought that every large wave they saw approaching might prove to be their death shroud—thus these two were betrothed. Half the sting of death was removed, as they felt that though in all probability they must die, yet they would die together. In his own arms Dr. Saxon now held his treasure, which had become priceless to him in the days of her unselfish devotion to another, and even death could not wrest her from him. The words, "till death doth part," would never be used to bind them in marriage, and they had no force, for death could not part them.

Mayon thought of her mother and all her dear ones, and in the solemn hour that followed it seemed to each that his or her lifetime was lived over again. Calmly and peacefully these two—one in heart—waited for death. But suddenly a glimmer of light was seen in the distance. A corresponding glimmer of hope came into their hearts, and departed as suddenly as the light departed. Again the light was seen. This time it was visible for a longer period, and at intervals it appeared and disappeared, till at last it was constantly shining away in the distance, and Dr. Saxon exclaimed:

"Mayon, I believe we are saved!" Then releasing her from his grasp, he shouted with all his might for help. He did not hear any reply, but at intervals continued his cry, and, at last, a faint shout was heard in the distance, and ere long a cry of joy escaped their lips, as a large, strong boat rode safely through the billows, and they knew that they were saved.

As Dr. Saxon and Mayon did not return at nightfall, their friends became alarmed, especially on the coming up of the shower, and several boats, rowed by skilful men, put out to sea in the direction Dot and Daisy said the little boat had taken. Anxiously waited the friends on shore. Mrs. Bernard and Lillian and Jessie could only watch and listen and pray God to speed and guide the boats for their friends' deliverance. And as the night wore on, and they saw the lights of the returning boats, they flew to the water's edge; and when at last the boat reached the wharf, and Mayon was once more in their arms, they wept for joy. Mayon was ill a few days, in consequence of her exposure and excitement, and unable to leave her bed, but immediately on her recovery they all returned to New York.

Dr. Saxon's relation to Mayon was now known to her friends. All were pleased save, perhaps, Jessie; but she bravely tried to conquer her disappointment, and, to her credit, be it said, that her congratulations to Mayon were no less sincere and heartfelt than those of the others. But it was a sad task she set herself to write the news to Carlos, and very tenderly and considerately she tried to perform it. Dr. Saxon's days of respite from labor were now over, and he returned to his professional duties.

Chapter 17

All this time, though Edith had been urgently invited to join
the Bernards at their cottage by the sea, yet she remained with
her country friends, and led a peaceful, happy life, forming a
strong affection for the family and especially her little charges. She had long ago procured, according to Mormon practice,
a divorce from Mr. Northfield, although she did not consider
herself his lawful wife. But she wished the connection to be
severed in the eyes of her Mormon friends. She steadfastly refused a maintenance at her so-called husband's hands, which
he kindly offered her, and heartily wished her to accept. She always respected him, and was extremely grateful for his consideration, but kindly and firmly declined to be dependent upon
him. As the summer days were waning she had allowed her
thoughts to carry her back to the days of her childhood, and
she lived over in imagination the scenes of her life in Mormonism. Those days were dark, but not all dark. There was a time
when something of the love and hope that came into other
girls' lives was hers also. There once was one who came to her
bringing with him joy and teaching her, though perhaps unconsciously, to hope for a life with him in the Gentile world.
And on one evening, while alone in her chamber, she fell to
wondering where her Gentile friend might be, and whether he
had entirely forgotten the poor, sick Mormon girl, who drank
in so eagerly the knowledge she was thirsting for. Did he ever
bestow one thought on her now? He had faithfully fulfilled the
request her father had forced her to make that he would never

see her again. Edith longed to know whether he received this letter with any degree of pain, and if a brighter life might have been hers had her father not thus cruelly treated her.

While she was sadly pondering on her life, letters were brought up to her, and opening one from Mayon, who never forgot or ceased to love Edith, with whom she constantly corresponded, she read the announcement of her engagement to Dr. Will Saxon. Dr. Saxon's name had before been mentioned in Mayon's letters; but though Edith thought of the Dr. Saxon who was her friend of Salt Lake City, yet the whole name never before had been mentioned to her, and she did not suppose for a moment that the two were identical. Now, however, at the information, evidently written with so much happiness, Edith almost gasped for breath. Was it the Dr. Will Saxon that she had loved so long ago, and now realized that she still loved? Could it be that Mayon was to marry her Gentile friend of old? O, why had she been so foolish as to remember him with such feelings? But it might not be the same—she would read on and perhaps learn. When, however, Mayon spoke of his having spent some months in Salt Lake City in the beginning of his medical career, all Edith's little hope was gone. She then realized for the first time how strong a hold this man had gained on her affections, and how she had cherished, through all these years, secret thoughts of him. Somehow she felt that a blank had come into her life now. Something she hardly knew existed had been taken from her, and Mayon's happiness was the cause of Edith's silent, unknown heartache. Doubtless he had never cared for her as she had for him, and now she felt a secret shame that she had been so easily won, and resolved to conquer her foolish sentiment, which had been so long-lived. No one should ever suspect, by her word or manner, that it ever existed. Within her own heart it must be crucified and buried, and Edith went on with her quiet, useful life, and no one knew the cause of her increased quietness and gentleness, and the approach to the sadness of her first days in the Gentile world.

But Dr. Will Saxon had cared for Edith, and in all the efforts which he had made in those days to shake off his affection for her, which by her letter she evidently did not return, he had failed. He had been deceived in her, and from her own words it was evident she never wished to meet him again. He, at times, almost resolved to disregard her request and boldly seek to win her and save her from the Mormon life which she so hated. But no; he had been deceived, and he would obey her request and would not add to the sorrows of her unhappy life by forcing his presence upon her. He would forget her in the absorption of his professional interests. He returned to his eastern home and plunged with all his strength of mind and heart into his profession. And though Edith had no rival in his heart, yet by the power of will and determination, in time he had nearly forced himself to forget her. Mayon's attractions at last won his heart, and she was installed in the place once devoted to Edith. Mayon had told him of her friend Edith, but never mentioned her girlhood name, and in turn he had told her of a Mormon girl he had known and loved by that name. Neither, however, suspected the truth, for it did not occur to Dr. Saxon that Mayon's father would take a wife almost as young as Mayon, and it was in complete ignorance of the pain she was giving to Edith that Mayon confidingly told her of her joys and hopes.

Mayon had requested that her marriage might be deferred for a time, with the hope that her father and mother would leave the Mormons and come to the East before that event took place. She earnestly wished her father might be the one to give her away, and that her mother should be present when the daughter whom she had loved so well and for whom she had sacrificed so much took this step.

Dr. Saxon agreed to Mayon's request, and they were now separated. Jessie had also returned to her home, and Mayon was not a little lonely. Dr. Saxon's duties would not allow him to visit his promised wife often, and she could only solace herself with the letters for which he always could find time, even in the greatest demand upon his professional skill.

With great difficulty he succeeded in getting release from his practice for a day or two, that he might visit his friends with whom he had made his home. These friends had consisted of an uncle named James Saxon, and wife, and a maiden aunt, Julia, sister to James. The uncle was now dead, and, as he left no children, the elderly people naturally leaned upon their nephew, and bestowed upon him their affection. His uncle had educated him for his profession, and treated him in every way like a son. In one respect, however, the young man always felt that injustice was done him. Although assured that he was James Saxon's nephew, he never could learn from either of the three one word further on the subject of his relation to them, or anything concerning his parents or birth. He felt that it was his right to know about these matters, and harbored many bitter thoughts against those who defrauded him of the knowledge. Whether of honorable or dishonorable birth he knew not, but strongly feared the latter, as they so persistently refused to inform him on the subject. Once, in private conversation, his uncle said, when he had arrived at a certain age, he would tell him all he wished to know; but before that time came, James Saxon had died, and his wife and sister refused to give to Will the information which now, more than ever, he felt it was his right to receive. He harbored much bitterness towards them on this account, though, except for that, there was a great degree of affection and confidence between them.

Since he had known Mayon and loved her, he was more anxious than ever to learn about his birth and parents, and determined that his lips should be sealed to her till he had gained this knowledge. If he found that he was of honorable descent, and could offer her a stainless name, then he would ask her to be his. If not, he would go many miles away and try to forget her, for he would not ask Mayon to stoop to marry a man who could not bear his father's name. Therefore he had refrained from saying one word to her which might compromise him in her eyes, if the worst was true. But this had not deceived her, for he could not disguise from Mayon his affection for her. At last, with the prospect of an immediate death before them, there could be no reason why his tongue should keep silence longer, at least she might be his in death, and he yielded to the great longing of his heart, and Mayon became his. Now that they were saved, however, he was very much troubled that he had allowed himself to speak prematurely, and resolved again to vehemently demand of his aunts a knowledge of his birth, and with this end in view he set out for the only home he had ever known.

One day Mayon returned from a ride with Lillian and her aunt, her cheeks aglow with health, her eyes sparkling with the pleasure of her drive. On entering, to her surprise and joy, she found Dr. Saxon; but though his greeting was all she could wish, there was such a look of sadness and grief in his face, and so much misery in his tones, that she was instantly alarmed, and inquired the cause.

"I can scarcely tell you, Mayon," said he. "My own loved one, can you bear trouble, greater perhaps than you ever knew, and can you pity and forgive me, who has brought it to you?"

"O, yes," said Mayon, her heart sinking with fear; "but how can you have brought trouble upon me? Is it my mother—my father? Tell me quickly. I can bear it."

Her face was blanched with dread, her eyes distended with fear, but her lips were set with a firm determination to endure with fortitude the blow she knew was about to fall upon her. Dr. Saxon seized Mayon's hands passionately, and, looking into her face with unutterable pain, he said:

"Mayon, we can never marry. I have found out what I have all my life longed to know, and the result must be our separation. Perhaps not quite that, but you can never be my wife, for, Mayon, do not be too much shocked when I tell you that you are my sister! I can never be your husband, for I am your brother. Your father is my father, too."

Mayon exclaimed, with horror, "No, no, no! that cannot be! What are you saying?" and she pressed her hands to her temples, and wildly walked the room. "My father your father, too! Will, that is impossible. Are you insane?"

"No, Mayon, I am only too sane. It is too true. I never knew what my parentage was till now. I never meant to ask you to be my wife till I knew, and not then unless I could offer you an honorable name; but on that terrible night, when death was seemingly about to obliterate all inequalities between us in station or birth, I yielded to the temptation of the hour, and thus I have terribly wronged the one I loved as I never loved human being before. But, thank God, there is no disgrace attached to my birth. You cannot be my wife, but you need not blush to call me brother." And the young man, in spite of his grief, drew himself proudly up with a new sense of his manliness.

"But, Will," said Mayon in a subdued, plaintive tone, as she scarcely realized the situation, "how can it be? I do not understand it. Tell me, please, and why have they kept you ignorant?"

"Yes, why have they? I could almost curse them for it," said he, fiercely. "I will try to tell you the whole, Mayon. I have learned most of this from my aunt and my uncle's wife, but have corresponded with your father—my father—and thus corroborated the truth of their statements. It seems that when Henry Northfield, then a very young man, first embraced Mormonism in England, he secretly married a girl named Saxon, whose friends were very much opposed to him on account of his religion, and who hated all Mormons. He was immediately ordained elder, and sent to a distant part of England to preach. He parted with grief from his young bride, regarding it his duty to leave all for the religion he had espoused. They corresponded secretly, however, for nearly a year—he constantly hoping his superior in the church would allow him to return to his home and wife; but obedience to them was his first object, and he proved too successful a missionary to be recalled from his labors. When nearly a year had passed, the friends of his wife informed him that she had died at the birth of her child, telling them of the circumstances of her marriage, and producing proof and sending loving messages to her absent husband. The letter was written in a way to mislead him and give him to understand that the child was also dead.

He never spoke to any one of this marriage, for his wife had bound him by a promise never to disclose it till she gave her consent. She never could release him now from his promise, therefore he was forever silent, notwithstanding that she herself had confessed it to her friends. His wife was already buried when her friends wrote of her death, and it was two years before he left his missionary work and visited her grave and her friends to learn all he could of her last days. His little son was secreted from him by the friends of the child's mother, for the reason that they knew he would be brought up a Mormon if his father discovered and took possession of him, and they were too much attached to him to willingly part with him. Therefore they kept the father in ignorance of his son's existence, and soon sailed with him to America. Not long after this Henry Northfield met and married your mother, keeping secret even from her his former marriage. That poor young wife, who died while her husband was many miles away, was my mother, and

I am the child who has been defrauded of my name, my father and my wife. Notwithstanding that my father was a Mormon, and that I would in all probability become one also, yet I think they (believing, however, that they were acting for the best) committed a great wrong. If they had informed me on my entering manhood, they would have been more pardonable, and all this mischief would have been prevented. I only learned since I left you, by demanding of them that they should tell me, and telling them of my engagement to Mayon Northfield. Then in horror, as they learned whose daughter you were, they told me the whole story. I wrote to your father to discover positively if he were my father too, and his answer leaves no room for doubt. So, Mayon, all our hopes are blasted, and we have now only to love each other as brother and sister. But there is some comfort, at least to me, in the thought that the discovery I have always desired to make need not alienate us from each other. Though the strongest human tie can never bind us, yet we are bound together by a strong natural tie, and my darling Mayon is my sister, if never my wife. Dear sister, do you forgive me for bringing all this trouble on you—for winning your heart and hand before I had a right to do so?"

"O, Will, do not say forgive—forgive is not the word; say pity, for you deserve nothing but pity for it all. God will help us to bear it, and in time we shall forget our disappointment in our brotherly and sisterly love. There is much to comfort us, Will, in the knowledge that we are closely related, and our affection can continue as strong as ever. Will, it might have been worse—indeed, much worse. Let us try to feel that God orders all things for the best."

"You are a blessed girl, Mayon, and I will try with all a brother's power to make you happy, to atone for the trouble I have brought upon you. Here is the letter your father—our father—wrote me. Shall we read it together?"

They did so. The writer expressed surprise and joy at the knowledge of his son's existence, and described his indignation at first at knowing the deceit that had been practiced upon him, but finally expressing gratitude that it had been so, for otherwise his firstborn might, like his second son, have been a staunch Mormon, and although a Mormon himself in name, yet he regretted that Forest was what he was, and felt that God had overruled Will's destiny for the best. He felt that the relatives of Dr. Saxon, however, had acted very wrongly in keeping him in ignorance of his history, and deeply regretted and blamed them for the continued deception which had caused such grief to his son, and must cause the same to his daughter when she learned of it.

"Poor Mayon!" he wrote, "I hope she will not take it too hard. She seemed so happy, as in her letters to her mother and me she told us of you. God bless you both, my children, and grant that you may find much of the happiness as brother and sister that you expected as husband and wife."

Letters to Mayon from both parents were enclosed for her to read directly on making the discovery. She perused them, and at last her many emotions found relief in tears. Dr. Saxon wept with her, and from that hour they began to live what seemed to them a new life, and a purer, stronger love than theirs never existed between brother and sister.

In a few days Dr. Saxon returned to his duties, for life to him was no holiday; and Mayon, subdued and saddened by the change in her life, was yet not made miserable by its strange results, for Will was still hers to love and trust and care for with a sister's right. The discovery was kept a secret from the world for a time, Dr. Saxon retaining the name he had always borne, and Mr. Northfield and his wife did not choose to inform Forest of the existence of a half-brother till they could see him face to face. This they expected soon to do, for Forest was soon to come home for a time; but the Mormon authorities ruled it otherwise. They desired to keep him away from the influence of his father, who was little less than an apostate, for they could ill afford to lose so useful a member of their church as Forest Northfield. He was informed that he was appointed on a mission East, and was instructed to proceed immediately to New England and secure all the converts possible and gather them into Zion.

With the same missionary zeal, and the same spirit of obedience to the church, that his father had exercised in his younger days, Forest went to New England, and there he found he had a thorny path to tread, for Mormonism was so obnoxious to the people that he met with great persecution. In some towns he found it impossible to preach to the people, for he could not procure a place of any description in which to hold his meetings. In others he dared not remain on account of the indignation of the people against him. Indeed he felt that he was suffering many and severe persecutions for the Gospel's sake; but yet he persevered, having faith that God would bless him and his labors. In some towns he was enabled to preach the doctrine of the Latter-day Saints, for a few would go to hear a Mormon preach as ever from motives of curiosity, and though sneered and hissed at, and pointed out with derision, yet as he went from place to place he went with the encouragement that now and then a convert was made, a few were being added to the church through his instrumentality.

When Mayon learned of her brother's mission East she became very much troubled, and feared that some poor girls would be ensnared into Mormonism and thus their lives be forever blighted as Flora Winchester's had been. She resolved to do what she could to counteract her brother's influence, and by means of her mother's letters, and by diligent writing to different places where she supposed her brother to be she was enabled to follow him in most of his movements. She found out the address of a few of his converts, and wrote to them stating that she was the sister of the preacher who had persuaded them into the Mormon belief, and setting forth the horrors of Mormon life, as she well knew how. The result was that scarcely one adhered to the new faith, and when Forest discovered that his sister was undoing the work he had suffered so much to accomplish, his wrath was terrible. He wrote to Mayon the most angry, cruel letter a brother ever penned to a sister. Although Mayon was very much grieved, she was not surprised. She had anticipated the consequences before she began the work, for she well knew Forest's devotion to his religion would outweigh all regard for herself. He resolved to go far from any of the towns in which he had labored, and acquaint no person with his destination, hoping that thus she would be unable to trace him. Accordingly he journeyed many miles north, and without allowing the people at first to suspect his religion, he began lecturing in a very careful manner.

It happened that the place in which he established himself was one of those old retired towns among the mountains of northern New England, and the home of Dr. Will Saxon and his aunts. Dr. Saxon had been called home on account of the severe sickness of his aunt Julia, and as she continued very ill he was obliged to remain with her. Forest had been pleased with the size of his audiences in the place, for there was little but the religious service, the sewing circle and local literary society, to call the people out ordinarily, and a lecturer was seldom seen among them. Therefore his meetings were an object of not a little interest. He had fed his hearers on the "milk of the word," as the Mormons called the more unobjectionable doctrines of their religion, and they had received it with little opposition; but on the introduction of the "strong meat," or more radical parts of their belief, they began to recoil with disgust. But Forest was too much accustomed to the disapprobation of the body of the people to be easily discouraged, and was preparing for a mighty effort for success, when he was taken suddenly ill, and Dr. Saxon was called.

Dr. Saxon experienced strange sensations when he learned that his half-brother was in the place lecturing on Mormonism, but he had not met him, for he had been too closely confined by attendance upon his aunt. Now, however, as he entered the room and saw the white face surmounted by an intelligent forehead and a mass of curly light brown hair, met the glance of those handsome light blue eyes and realized that it was the face of his brother lying on the pillow, it was with no small effort that he controlled himself. He longed to give that delicate hand a brother's grasp, and with a brother's influence win that man from error. But no one knew that he took more than ordinary interest in his patient. He advised his removal from the hotel to a quieter place, and Forest was received into one of the most happy and refined families in New England. Each member, in spite of the abhorrence to his religion, vied with the other in ministering to his relief, for they were touched with sympathy for his sufferings, and strove to make him as comfortable as it was possible for him to be. He was very ill for a few days, and then began to recover.

Now he had ample time to observe the domestic relation of Gentile life, the first he had ever seen. As he lay upon his couch or was wheeled about in an easy-chair by the father, mother or children, two or three of whom were nearly grown to womanhood and manhood, little by little there came over him a sense of the great difference between the Gentile homes and the Mormon homes: between the appearances of this mother and his own mother, whose life had been robbed of its happiness by Mormonism's stern decrees. He witnessed the perfect confidence and sympathy that existed between husband and wife, the affectionate agreement of the young brothers and sisters, and realized, as he thought of Mayon—as he thought of all that had passed in former years between his parents—that in his father's family there had not existed any approach to this domestic happiness. He taxed his mind to recall something similar in the Mormon world, but in vain. Never had he seen there a family so happy in its domestic relation as his father's, and that but poorly compared with this.

Dr. Saxon was now able to devote much time to his patient, and soon began to be regarded by him as a friend and welcome visitor. He gradually and gently led the conversation upon religious topics, and skilfully aroused Forest's curiosity concerning the Gentile faith and Gentile institutions of all kinds. Forest was soon able to join the family at the morning devotions, and as the word of God was read, and a simple, earnest prayer offered; as he heard the family together study the lesson for the Sabbath-school, he longed to know more of the religion of their life—more of the faith that made this family so happy.

Dr. Saxon rejoiced as he realized the influence that was working on his patient, and he spent many hours trying to persuade him that his own religion was a false one, and providing him with all the books he was able to read. At length, one day, when he had nearly recovered sufficiently to pursue his lectures, Dr. Saxon entered, and Forest exclaimed:

"Saxon, I have made up my mind that I have been a fool all my life, and that my father has been a fool before me. My father has been gradually learning to see his life-long mistakes for many months, but I—I have been as blind as ever, even through all the Mormon wickedness that has disgusted my father. I lay awake all last night, Saxon, trying to cling to my old religion, but I have this morning flung it to the winds, and now realize with shame and sorrow that I have been the dupe of wicked and ignorant men. I have been a useful tool in their hands, and would have been still more useful to them had it not been for the interference of that noble sister of mine. Saxon, you cannot tell how I hate and despise myself for the letter I wrote her. Poor Mayon! she has had troubles enough in her young life, without my adding to them. I thank God now that she wrote those letters and undid the work I labored so hard to do."

He had told Dr. Saxon of Mayon's interference in his work, and in turn Saxon had told him of his acquaintance with Mayon, withholding all that had transpired of the greatest interest between them, however, as he saw that Forest was ignorant that any engagement had existed. His parents were about to write to him the news from Mayon, when they received Dr. Saxon's letter, and therefore suppressed the whole. Forest thought he had eluded Mayon's vigilance in coming here, but he had not, for his physician had written every few days informing her of the condition of their brother, both physically and mentally. She had forgotten her grief in the joyful news that Forest was being led to see the error of his belief. At first, on learning of his illness, she wished to come to him, but Dr. Saxon advised her not to do so, for he had every care he could need, and was not in a kindly enough mood towards her to be benefited in the least by her presence. But now, when Forest had announced in this positive manner his conviction, Dr. Saxon felt like leaping for joy for Mayon's sake; and still more when Forest said:

"I have written to Mayon to-day, asking her to come and see me. Do you suppose she will come?"

"I have no doubt of it, my friend."

"And when I tell her that henceforth I am a Gentile and forever renounce Mormonism, how her large, dark eyes will shine for joy! Do you know, Saxon, that your eyes are precisely like Mayon's, your hair is like hers, and somehow you look so like her that you have continually brought her before my mind; and when I was very weak and sick, I sometimes thought it was Mayon that came in and took my hand and spoke to me. Yes, you are very like Mayon. Perhaps that is why I have become so fond of you. I remember well how, when we were children, I used to terrify the child by explaining the most frightful of our doctrines; and now, that everything looks so different to me, I do not wonder that she was terrified. I do not wonder that she tried to counteract the effects of her brother's teachings, or sought to win the poor Mormon girls away from their unhappy life. O, it is bitter to think I have wasted so much of my time; but poor father must feel that his life has been wasted! I mean to go home as soon as I am able and persuade him to leave them all."

Two days later there was a happy meeting in Forest's room, as Mayon there met with her two brothers. Never before had Forest and Mayon been in such sympathy with each other.

"Mayon," said Forest, "Dr. Saxon has proved the truest, best friend I ever knew. He has been the means of freeing me from the bondage of a false religion, showed me the beauties of the Gentile life by bringing me into this family, and if he were my brother, I could not love him more."

"Forest, let me tell you something hitherto a secret between us. I *am* your brother!"

Forest looked at him in amazement, then at Mayon, as if trying to read from her face what the speaker meant.

"My brother! Saxon, what do you mean?" and Dr. Saxon then gave Forest the whole of his recently learned history.

At the close Forest grasped him by the hand and said: "God bless you, my brother Will! and I thank him that you are my brother, for you might never have been the means of making me what I am, if it had not been so."

In a few days Forest started for Salt Lake City, Mayon returned to New York, and her brother Will accompanied her, for he was again to spend a few months in the city in pursuance of his surgical studies, and Mayon's friends insisted on his making his home with them.

Chapter 18

After a few weeks Mayon received a letter from Jessie, containing an urgent request for a visit from her. As she had spent but very little time with them for a year, she accepted the invitation, and soon old scenes were revisited, old friendships renewed, and old intimacies continued. Mayon's engagement with Dr. Saxon and its peculiar termination were known to these friends, and in their hearts was a tender feeling towards her for the singular trial she had passed through. Jessie did not harbor one exultant or hopeful thought for Carlos, but was a nearer and dearer friend, if possible, to Mayon than ever. Carlos was not at home now. He had been admitted to the bar and had begun to practice, bidding fair to become a successful lawyer. Mayon missed him very much, and after a time found that she was thinking of him, and their walks, drives and talks, a great deal. The place scarcely seemed the same without him, and she was constantly looking forward to the time when he was expected home for a few days.

At last the day of his arrival came, and the whistle of the train that was to bring him had been heard in the distance. But it did not reach the station. A shrill whistle to down brakes, a sudden crash, and cars and passengers were mingled in one broken mass. The fortunates who escaped were quickly at work, and among the forms that were borne on shutters to the surrounding houses the body of Carlos was taken to his home, and when Mayon saw his face, apparently cold in death, she fainted, and was carried in and laid on Jessie's bed. Kind friends soon restored her, and when they told her that Carlos had only fainted from loss of blood, and that though very weak, yet his injuries were confined to a severe flesh wound and some bruises, from which he would soon recover, Mayon could not speak, but burying her face in her pillow she gave vent to her emotion in tears.

It was not long before she was again walking with Carlos in the green fields and beside the little streams that abounded in the vicinity, for it was summer, and one day he led her to the same mossy bank where two years before he had asked her to become his wife. Then, he was confused, embarrassed and absent-minded, and she was perfectly composed and unconscious of his emotion. Now, as he asked her again to be seated, where he had ruthlessly destroyed the flowers they had gathered, and as he referred to that day so well-remembered by them both, Mayon's eyes could not look into his; her cheeks were like the rose and her voice trembled.

"Mayon," said her companion, "two years ago you told me you never could love me only as a brother and friend. I replied that I should hope you would change. I did hope for a year; then when Jessie wrote me from the sea-shore that you had given the love to another that I had craved, that hope died within me, and through all the changes of your life and mine it never revived till since I met you here. Jessie told me of the grief you could not conceal as I was brought home apparently dead, and it made me too happy. It gave me hope that after all the desire of my heart might be granted. I have watched you since then and fancied I detected something stronger than a sister's love for me. Was it only fancy? Mayon, I do not wish to pain you as I did two years ago, but I must ask you again to be mine. Mayon, do you love me now well enough to become my wife?"

Returning in the twilight, as Carlos and Mayon neared the house, Jessie came to meet them. Carlos seized her around the waist, and, kissing her impulsively, said: "Little sister, it is all right now. Mayon is mine!"

"O, Mayon!" exclaimed Jessie, "I am so glad. I always thought Carlos deserved this reward. Now I have my heart's desire, for you are to be really and truly my sister."

One year before, Mayon had thought no one but Will Saxon could ever have the love of her heart, without him her life would be a blank, and when the blow fell that separated them—in a sense—she looked upon her future as a lonely one to be unshared by any nearer relation than those given her by the ties of nature; but a year had taught her to regard the lover as her brother,—the brother as a lover, and Mayon was happier than she had thought it possible for her ever to be. She now felt that it would be a delicate task to communicate to Will what had occurred, but unreservedly confided everything to him in the letter she sent him. His answer contained the following words:

I am heartily glad, dear sister, that such happiness has come into your life, and that he who has so nobly earned the prize he has patiently waited for and at last won, and who deserved it so richly, at last has his reward. It is as it should be. I feel humbled when I think of my failure to act as my conscience directed, and the consequence which was a sad entanglement for us. He is worthy of the first place in your heart. And for you, Mayon, could I have known one year ago that another would soon make you as happy as I had made you, notwithstanding the pangs of jealousy I might have suffered, I would have rejoiced as I now rejoice. May God bless my sister and make her life a very happy one.

Later Mayon received another letter from Will, from which we quote the following:

I have strange news to tell you, Mayon—to me very happy news, and I hope it will be the same to you for my sake, and for the sake of one who has had a joyless life. Your friend, Edith, came here a few days ago, not knowing of my presence, and we met in your uncle's parlor. Notwithstanding the changes years have effected in both, we recognized each other, for, Mayon, she is the same Edith I knew in Salt Lake City, and whom I told you requested me by letter never to see her again. That letter she was forced to write by her father, and through all these years she has remembered me in spite of her efforts to forget me. I believed she did not love me, and that helped me to trample out all my affection for her; but, Mayon, I am sure it will not grieve you when I tell you that at sight of her face, and with the conviction that I had been mistaken in my estimate of her, my old love for her returned, and this day she has promised to become my wife. Her father succeeded in blighting her happiness for years, but, thank God, not forever, for my whole life shall be devoted to her, and, if it is in my power to accomplish it, she shall make up for her years of sorrow by years of double happiness. Poor Edith! but she is mine now! Why did I never suspect the Edith you told me of was the one I had known and loved? I never thought of her being a young person: and think, Mayon, of the strangeness of the fact that I am to marry my father's wife! I bless him that he was always so kind to her, and am devoutly thankful that though the greatest of kindness existed between them yet there was no love. Little did I think, Mayon, when I received the news of your engagement, that I should have a similar story to tell so soon.

Enclosed was a missive from Edith, of which we give a part.

MY DEAR MAYON:

Will has written the news to you, so I will only add a few words for myself. I can scarcely believe that it is all true—that I am, at last, after my sorrowful life to know what happiness is—perfect happiness. You little suspected the pain that your letter gave me, telling of your engagement to one I had loved since my girlhood days, and I determined then that you or no one should ever suspect it. But, Mayon, believe that on learning of the discovery which must separate you from him, I did not harbor any but feelings of sympathy for you, and were it not that you have learned to give another the love you once had for Will, I should fear to pain you as your letter once pained me. But I know now, dear Mayon, that you can rejoice in my joy, as I do in yours. O, how God has seemed to guide everything for our good, since the day we set out, two frightened fugitives, from our bondage, and the night we spent together in that lonely little hut by the roadside, fearing our enemies would discover us! Surely, "God works in a mysterious way his wonders to perform."

As Mrs. Northfield, away in her home in Utah, was preparing to go out riding, she heard what seemed a familiar step at her door; it was boldly thrown open, and to her surprise and delight, her son entered, and with all the fondness of his boyhood days he clasped his mother in his arms.

"Forest! my son! my son!" she exclaimed, "can this be you! I supposed you were many hundred miles from here. Why have you come back so soon? Have you been recalled?"

"Yes, mother. I have been recalled, but not by Mormon authority. My own conscience recalled me, and how I have longed to arrive and see you! The train seemed to move at a snail's pace, I was so impatient to get here. Mother, I am a Mormon no longer. I went to New England to convert others. I come home converted myself. Behold your apostate son!"

"O, my son, thank God!—at last he has heard my prayers. It seems too good to be true. As I begin to tread the down-hill side of life, new blessings are being bestowed on me. There is yet to be a happy ending to my checkered life. Forest, it has of late been almost my only grief to know that my son was so strong in the Mormon faith; that he in all probability would, in time, cause the misery his father has unwillingly caused; and, worst of all, that he has been using all his influence, all the talent God has given him, to bring those of Gentile faith into the church. I have feared he would be the cause of some other lovely girl being led to suffer, as Flora has suffered. How, Forest, was this change in your faith brought about?"

"Through the instrumentality of my half-brother. Dr. Saxon, mother: for when I was taken sick, he was the means of my being removed to the home of one of the best families on earth, and their influence and his, combined with what I learned there of Gentile religion and Gentile domestic life, opened my eyes at last to the truth; and O, how I regret now that I have not been brought up in my mother's religion, instead of my father's! I almost envy Mayon, for she can never have to regret, as I do, years of ignorance and superstition. Her life has so far been so well spent, and she has been as earnest for the right as I have been in the wrong. O, why did my father ever come to believe this religion! It seems to me, if I had known the Gentile religion, Mormonism could never have deceived me."

"But, my son, when he and I embraced it we knew nothing about the doctrine of polygamy and other horrible doctrines; but, when once firmly established, it was impossible for your father to give it all up, and little by little he embraced the whole."

"What a strange discovery it is about Will! I knew nothing of it till he told me, or of his engagement to Mayon."

"We were just on the point of writing to you of the engagement, when we learned how it terminated, and then waited to see you; but you did not come home, as we expected, and therefore you have been left to find it out in this way. But tell me more of your sickness, and of Mayon and Will, and of the people who cared for you."

So they talked a long time, and Forest inquired for his father and for Flora, whose husband had been sick some months.

"Poor Flora is in deep trouble. I was just going to ride out and see her. Burnside is growing rapidly worse, and probably cannot live long. Flora nurses him as faithfully as though he had been a kind husband, and the poor girl is nearly worn out herself. She has a frightful cough that it makes me shiver to hear. I have tried to help her all I could, but he only wants Flora near him; and though I believe he is more humane towards her than when well, yet he is too selfish to realize that she can ever be tired or need rest. In short, she is wearing her life out for the man who has made her so miserable."

"The wretch!" exclaimed Forest. "How could a man treat that sweet girl in the way he has done?"

"It is not the man, my son, who is first to be blamed. It is Mormonism that has made him what he is."

"Yes, mother, I can see now that what you say is true."

"There is something mysterious in the way Flora is provided with funds, for they became very poor and were really in want. I did not know it, for Flora would have been too proud to tell me or your father, or we would have been glad to relieve them; but some one must have found out her condition, for, as in the days of her infant's sickness and death, her physician, at regular intervals, gives her a sum of money, and, try as hard as she will, Flora can learn no more."

Mr. Northfield now returned to his home, and his surprise at meeting his son was only equalled by his astonishment and pleasure at learning of the change in his faith. Mr. Northfield was hardly considered a Mormon now, and though making no active opposition to the church, yet its officers hated him thoroughly. He dared not attack their religion while living among them, but his business kept him there, and he felt that he had nowhere else to go, although Walter Bernard had extended a cordial invitation to him to come to his home, and an offer of assistance in business, and Mayon had written repeatedly, asking him to leave the Mormons and come to New York. Mrs. Northfield did not urge him away from what had been their almost life-long home, though she wished for the time to come when they should leave it. She longed once more to live in the Gentile world and to meet her sister, and again have her loved daughter near her. But she felt that she could afford to be patient, for the time was surely coming, and, at least, her husband's eyes were opened, and he was no more a victim to the fanatical delusions of Mormonism. He now rejoiced that the effect of his teachings on his son were counteracted by the influences that had lately been exerted over him so effectually.

"My son," said he, when he had heard the story of Forest's conversion, "I thank God that, though I shall have to repent to my dying day the instruction I was only too successful in giving you, yet I shall not have to know that my teachings have made you what I am—a worse than useless man in the world."

"Father, you are not that, and with your business talent you can become far from a useless man in the East. Why not leave this city and go to New York, and, with Mayon and Will, we can be so happy all together? I was so impressed with the happiness of the family life I saw and enjoyed among the Gentiles, that I long for the same happiness for my father's family; and now that we are united at last, I see no reason why we may not be as happy a family as there is on this earth."

"True, my son," said his father, "and I wish for your mother's sake to leave this place, and have been trying to see my way clear to do so; but it is impossible to dispose of my business here without sacrificing almost everything. I fear I shall be obliged to go into the Gentile world a poor man; and at my age, and after laboring as I have to accumulate something, such a prospect is anything but cheering. But, Marion," said he, turning to his wife, "no matter what the sacrifice is, I am determined that another summer shall find me forever departed from this city. The longing of your lifetime shall be granted, and my dear wife shall yet enjoy the closing years of her life, and may they atone in some measure for the many years of sadness that my superstition and fanaticism have caused her."

Mrs. Northfield's eyes were dimmed with tears, and her emotion kept her speechless; but her husband knew by the look of gratitude and joy in her face that she was made happy by his declaration, and he was satisfied.

On his dying bed lay one of Mormonism's champions. His last hour had come. His frail and awe-stricken wife wiped the death dew from his brow. Another wife sat weeping in a corner; but this one—this feeble, tottering young woman—though she shed no tears, tried to soften the terrors of death for one who had tried so little to soften the terrors of life for her. The dying eyes opened and fixed on the frail form by his side, the lips parted and whispered the words:

"Flora, you have been kind to me, but I have not been kind to you."

That was all. In a moment more he was beyond the reach of all human pity or care. Forest and his mother had been with Flora constantly of late, and Forest had insisted that Flora leave her husband in his care and obtain some rest, which she persistently refused to do. Now she herself required the tenderest care. The necessity for exertion being over, her strength failed her, and one wife followed the husband to his grave, while the other lay prostrated. Mrs. Northfield remained with Flora, and after the lapse of many days she was able to be removed to the home of the former. This was her first home in Mormondom, and again its shelter, its kindness and its loving care were hers. Mr. Northfield was arranging to close out his business and remove to New York with his family, and Flora now yielded to the entreaties of her parents and was to accompany them. But her wasted form and sunken eyes, her flushed cheek and her lagging footsteps, plainly told that her friends could not keep her long, and the journey was again and again deferred that she might gain strength to endure it. Finally her physician pronounced her able to travel, and then Forest told his parents that Flora was to go to New York as his wife.

"If her life is nearly spent," said he, " I shall have a husband's right to try to make her last days happy ones. If not, as I must hope, then by a lifetime of devotion to her I will strive to make her forget the wretched years of her life in Mormonism."

Flora had once refused the offer of Forest's hand, but in the following years, when she drank deep of sorrow's bitter cup, that hand, though unseen, unknown, was extending aid to her and relieving the only one of her troubles that it had power to relieve. The heart which she unconsciously won, only to thrust aside, retained its tenderness, and prompted its possessor to noble deeds for which he could never hope to be rewarded, and at last Flora discovered who had been her secret benefactor.

At the home of the Bernards all was life, joy and bustle, for the house contained not only the Bernard family, with aunt Wells, Mayon and Edith, but Mr. Winchester with his wife, sons and daughter Jessie, and Dr. Saxon, as he was still called. But the capacity of the Bernard hospitality was not exhausted, for more guests were eagerly looked for, and when at last two carriages arrived and from one stepped Mr. Northfield and his wife, quickly followed by Forest, who tenderly lifted Flora from the carriage and carried her into the house, placing her in her father's arms—when from the other alighted Edith's brother, Francis, with his wife and two little ones, whom he seemed to forget for the time in his happiness at meeting his sister—then followed a scene which words would be inadequate to portray. Mayon was embraced by her father and mother, and the sisters, who had parted in such grief in that same city when they were young and fair, now met after a quarter of a century had passed, and each felt that years, cares and nearer relations had not lessened in any degree the affection they then had for each other. Mr. Northfield could not speak for his emotion, as the son he had never seen approached him with outstretched hand and the one word, "Father!"

It was a thrilling moment when that father and son beheld each other for the first time. Mr. Northfield was then warmly greeted by Mrs. Bernard, the Elsie whose clear eyes and sound arguments, in years long past he had sought to avoid. While his father was speaking with her, Will stepped back and gently drew Edith with him to his father. Then the first shade of embarrassment was felt as Will said: "Here is my bride that is to be."

And Mr. Northfield greeted his former wife, soon to become his son's wife, saying: "God bless you both, my children."

There was a mother weeping for joy that her long-lost daughter was returned to her, though such a wreck of her former self; father, brothers and sister, unconscious of the presence of the others, in their joy that their treasure was restored to them, and it seemed Forest's right to her possession was almost disputed, but he was watching her with jealous eye, fearing the effects of the excitement.

There were "God bless you's" from the father of Flora to the Northfields for their care of her, and from Mr. Northfield to aunt Wells and the Bernards, who had done so much for his daughter, and from Edith's brother to Will, who had made his sister at last so happy. There was a warm greeting between Mrs. Northfield and Edith, between Carlos and Mayon's parents, Will and his stepmother, and between those who had been heretofore strangers to each other. Jessie, Lillian and Mayon were like birds darting here and there in the general commotion. Leonard and Harry could scarcely refrain from giving three cheers, and little Dot and Daisy, without comprehending the cause of so much emotion, glided about here and there, putting up their rosy lips to be kissed promiscuously. When the greetings were over and some degree of calmness had been restored, Walter Bernard said:

"Friends, should we not thank God for this happy meeting, which is so like a heaven upon earth!"

All assented, and as he rendered praise to an all-wise Father for the guiding of His hand, and the bringing about of such happy results by mysterious and unlooked-for circumstances, all hearts went up to God in thanksgiving.

A few days later aunt Wells, with her aged dignity and snow-white hair, occupies the warmest corner of that parlor and one of the easiest chairs, and her kind glance wanders about from face to face, and finally rests alternately upon her nieces, Marion and Elsie; the latter yet blooming and fresh though past life's meridian; the former, though her face is lined with sorrow, and her head is plentifully decked with silver threads among the gold by her years of sadness, yet her eyes beam with no less happy light than those of her sister, as they are now united after so many years of separation.

In another easy-chair, which is surrounded by Mr. Winchester, his wife, and Leonard, sits, or rather reclines, Flora— Flora Northfield now, and behind her stands the tall form of her young husband, watching her with all the fondness and solicitude of his affection. Mr. Northfield watches this group with a half-sad, half-gratified look, while Mr. Bernard, with Daisy in his arms and Harry and Dot at his side, is the picture of satisfaction as he surveys the little gathering under his roof.

A rustling is heard, and now all who have been missing from this group enter. The man of God rises, a solemn hush pervades the room, while he reads the marriage service and Mr. Northfield bestows his daughter Mayon upon Carlos Winchester, and Francis Parker gives his sister Edith to Dr. Will Saxon, while Lillian and Jessie officiate as bridesmaids.

Would that a veil might be drawn here; but this otherwise happy ending must be marred by one more scene, for sunny skies and paths strewn with flowers are not for all. In some troubled lives peace and happiness only come by crossing the dark river and passing through the pearly portals of heavenly gates; or when life is almost over to gild at last, by a ray of light, a sad past.

In a darkened room, on a snowy couch, lay a feeble, wasted form, scarcely less white than the couch on which she rested. Around her were gathered father, mother, brothers and sister. By her side, with her emaciated hand clasped in his, sat the strong young man, who only a few short months before clasped that hand in the marriage-service, his manly breast now heaving with sobs. He was not ashamed of his weakness, though for his loved one's sake he strove to repress his emotion.

"Forest," said the dying wife, as her eyes, full of love and peace, rested on him, "do not grieve so. Only a little while and we shall meet again."

"My darling, I cannot have it so! I hoped the change of climate might restore you, with all the care I would give you, and with the happiness of being again at your home. I did not believe you would surely leave me so soon. My poor, poor wife!"

"O, no: not poor wife. Poor Forest! you should rather say. As for me, I am only too content—too happy in being allowed to die at home. It would be too much to ask that I should be permitted to live. Never was a person made happier than you have made me for the past few months—you and father and mother and the rest. Heaven cannot be sweeter, more lovely, more beautiful than home has been and is to me. Angels cannot be more lovable than you have all been, nor heavenly music more enchanting than the songs you have sung to me. I am going to find my little Jessie. O, it is not hard to die—it is harder to live. You, Forest, and you, father and mother, and the rest of you, are to be pitied—not I—for I know you will miss your Flora more than she deserves to be missed. But try not to mourn for me. Do not be sad, but rejoice that I am so happy at last."

The friends all knew that Flora could scarcely breathe the day out, and their hearts were torn with anguish, as they realized that they were so soon again to be robbed of their treasure, and this time she would never come back to them. She breathed fainter after the exertion of speaking, but after a time she spoke again, this time to Mayon and Carlos, beckoning them to her side. As they bent over her she wound one arm about the neck of each, and said: "Mayon, I am so glad you took my place here long ago—try to fill it more than ever when I am gone: won't you?" She then called Jessie to her; then Leonard, giving them each a fare-well caress and parting word, striving to check their tears. Then she bid her father good-bye with the greatest of tenderness, for his heart was nearly broken with sorrow and remorse. Her mother clasped her child to her breast, but did not shed one tear or make one moan.

As the sun was slowly sinking. Flora asked Forest to hold her where she could once more see its brightness, and look at the hills and fields where she used to wander in childhood with her brothers and sister. Forest held her in his strong arms, and at last she said: "We shall all meet again there. Forest, dear Forest, good-bye!" and as the sun went down in all its brightness, so did this life go out in all the bright loveliness of youth,—one sacrifice on the Mormon altar.

The end.

Notes

1. The formal name for the Mormon Church is the Church of Jesus Christ of Latter-day Saints. The name denotes Jesus Christ as the head of the church. The term *saints* refers to the entire church body, rather than selected individuals, as in the Roman Catholic tradition. *Latter-day* distinguishes this church from the body of its members who were contemporary with Jesus.
2. Contrary to Bartlett's assertion, the Mormon Church was a pioneering force in education in the frontier West. As they moved west, Mormons established schools in Ohio, Missouri, and Utah. Church doctrine encourages members to gain knowledge, both doctrinal as well as "a knowledge of history, and of countries, and of kingdoms, of laws of God and man, and all this for the salvation of Zion" (Doctrine and Covenants 93:56). Over the course of church history, as well as in the present, some conservative church leaders have expressed a fear that too much secular learning can lead to apostasy.
3. A title for a Mormon man who holds the priesthood, often but not always a missionary.
4. As a collective noun *Zion* refers to followers of God who are "pure of heart," and links them to the church of Christ's era. The term also names the place where these followers live.
5. A moment marked by the restoration of doctrinal truth. Joseph Smith claimed that he was to lead a new dispensation in which God's one true church would be restored and its original practices—including polygamy—resumed.
6. Mormons believe in an afterlife in which immortal souls will live in one of three realms. The most righteous saints will inherit a place in the celestial kingdom, the most glorious of these realms.

7. Ordination is the rite through which the priesthood is conferred upon a worthy man.

8. Joseph Smith claimed that God commanded him to practice plural marriage, a dictum he followed beginning in 1831. In 1843 he informed church members of this doctrine, which was then canonized as section 132 of the Mormon scripture titled Doctrine and Covenants.

9. In the nineteenth century, Mormons, who considered themselves to be regathered Israelites, referred to non-Mormons as Gentiles.

10. The Perpetual Emigrating Fund was established in 1849 to assist impoverished new converts in emigrating to Salt Lake City. Members of the church donated to the fund, and those who received its assistance were expected to repay the money, which was then loaned to others.

11. A building used for religious ceremonies in the years before the Salt Lake temple was completed.

12. In the LDS church, the president is advised by a group of twelve apostles as was Jesus.

13. A large meeting hall, the first building to be completed on what is today known as Temple Square in Salt Lake City.

14. There is, of course, no one "Gentile religion." Here Bartlett uses the phrase as a shorthand term to refer to any and all Protestant denominations.

15. In 1852 the Utah Territorial legislature passed the most liberal divorce law in the nation. Church courts granted divorce degrees from polygamous marriages, for federal and territorial governments did not recognize polygamy.

16. A herbal compound, the active ingredient of which is opium. This highly addictive drug was used to treat a variety of illnesses in the nineteenth century.

17. In nineteenth-century law, children were the property of the husband; the mother held no custodial authority, even in cases of divorce.

18. To reject church doctrine and withdraw oneself from church membership.

19. One of God's curses on Egypt. See Exodus 10:21–2.

20. Widely used in everyday discourse in the nineteenth century, juggernaut refers to the temple car used to transport idols during Ratha-Yatra, the Hindu chariot festival. Because many accidents occurred in which worshipers were run over, the term has come to be associated with unstoppable force.

21. The Bible and three additional books of scripture, including the Book of Mormon, comprise the canon of the Mormon Church.

22. This passage is directly quoted from Joseph Smith's revelation on plural marriage. See Doctrine and Covenants 132.

23. As part of the plural marriage ceremony, the first wife signals her consent to the arrangement by placing the hand of the new wife into that of her husband.

24. To write or compose.

25. The Central Pacific and Union Railways joined their tracks at Promontory Summit, Utah, on 10 May 1869.

26. Empty chatter; gossip.

27. In 1886 a group of antipolygamy activists founded an interdenominational group, the Industrial Christian Home Association. The group opened an Industrial Christian Home, funded by the federal government, in Salt Lake City in 1889. The Home welcomed "women who renounce polygamy and their children of tender age" (qtd. in Pascoe 27).

28. Marion's reference to "lives . . . openly taken" likely is a reference to the so-called Mormon War of 1838 between the Mormons and non-Mormon settlers in Missouri. After being harassed for several years, Mormons formed militias to defend their properties. One such group, the Danites, operated outside the officially sanctioned militias. This vigilante group may have persisted in Utah, although credible documentation of their relation to the church is scarce. Tales of Danite atrocities were a staple of dime novel fictions about Mormons, including several written by Edward Wheeler.

29. From 1839–1846 Nauvoo, Illinois, served as the headquarters for the Mormon Church. "Sacrifices" here refers to ceremonies performed in the Nauvoo temple, which were understood to be part of the restoration of practices that had characterized the Old Testament church.

A Law Unto Herself
By Rebecca Harding Davis
Edited and with an introduction by
Alicia Mischa Renfroe

Elder Northfield's Home: or,
Sacrificed on the Mormon Altar
A. Jennie Bartlett
Edited by Nicole Tonkovich

To order or obtain more information on these or other
University of Nebraska Press titles, visit nebraskapress.unl.edu.

www.ingramcontent.com/pod-product-compliance
Lightning Source LLC
Chambersburg PA
CBHW020639030726
47498CB00002B/284